MW01068083

ELMINSTER
ENRAGED

Ed Greenwood

Sage of Shadowdale

Elminster: The Making of a Mage
Elminster in Myth Drannor
The Temptation of Elminster
Elminster in Hell
Elminster's Daughter
The Annotated Eliminster
Elminster Ascending
Elminster Must Die
Bury Elminster Deep
Elminster Enraged

Shandril's Saga

Book I
Spellfire

Book II
Crown of Fire

Book III
Hand of Fire

The Knights of Myth Drannor

Book I
Swords of Eveningstar

Book II
Swords of Dragonfire

Book III
The Sword Never Sleeps

Also by Ed Greenwood

The City of Splendors: A Waterdeep Novel
(with Elaine Cunningham)

The Best of the Realms, Book II
The Stories of Ed Greenwood
Edited by Susan J. Morris

ELMINSTER ENRAGED

Sage of Shadowdale
ELMINSTER ENRAGED

Published by Wizards of the Coast LLC. Hasbro SA, represented by Hasbro Europe, Stockley Park, UB11 1AZ. UK.

PRINTED IN THE U.S.A.

Cover art by: Kekai Kotaki
First Printing: August 2012

9 8 7 6 5 4 3 2 1

ISBN: 978-0-7869-6029-3
ISBN: 978-0-7869-6127-6 (ebook)
62039851000001 EN

Library of Congress Cataloging-in-Publication Data

Greenwood, Ed.
Elminster enraged : sage of Shadowdale / Ed Greenwood.
p. cm.
"Forgotten Realms."
ISBN 978-0-7869-6029-3
1. Elminster (Fictitious character)--Fiction. 2. Wizards--Fiction. I. Title.
PR9199.3.G759E56 2012
813'.54--dc23
2012017359

For customer service, contact:

U.S., Canada, Asia Pacific, & Latin America: Wizards of the Coast LLC, P.O. Box 707, Renton, WA 98057-0707, +1-800-324-6496, www.wizards.com/customerservice

U.K., Eire, & South Africa: Wizards of the Coast LLC, c/o Hasbro UK Ltd., P.O. Box 43, Newport, NP19 4YD, UK, Tel: +08457 12 55 99, Email: wizards@hasbro.co.uk

Europe: Wizards of the Coast p/a Hasbro Belgium NV/SA, Industrialaan 1, 1702 Groot-Bijgaarden, Belgium, Tel: +32.70.233.277, Email: wizards@hasbro.be

Visit our websites at www.wizards.com
www.DungeonsandDragons.com

tantaene animis caelestibus irae?

For Susan Morris
Because dreams are brighter shared.

Welcome to Faerûn, a land of magic and intrigue, brutal violence and divine compassion, where gods have ascended and died, and mighty heroes have risen to fight terrifying monsters. Here, millennia of warfare and conquest have shaped dozens of unique cultures, raised and leveled shining kingdoms and tyrannical empires alike, and left long forgotten, horror-infested ruins in their wake.

A LAND OF MAGIC

When the goddess of magic was murdered, a magical plague of blue fire—the Spellplague—swept across the face of Faerûn, killing some, mutilating many, and imbuing a rare few with amazing supernatural abilities. The Spellplague forever changed the nature of magic itself, and seeded the land with hidden wonders and bloodcurdling monstrosities.

A LAND OF DARKNESS

The threats Faerûn faces are legion. Armies of undead mass in Thay under the brilliant but mad lich king Szass Tam. Treacherous dark elves plot in the Underdark in the service of their cruel and fickle goddess, Lolth. The Abolethic Sovereignty, a terrifying hive of inhuman slave masters, floats above the Sea of Fallen Stars, spreading chaos and destruction. And the Empire of Netheril, armed with magic of unimaginable power, prowls Faerûn in flying fortresses, sowing discord to their own incalculable ends.

A LAND OF HEROES

But Faerûn is not without hope. Heroes have emerged to fight the growing tide of darkness. Battle-scarred rangers bring their notched blades to bear against marauding hordes of orcs. Lowly street rats match wits with demons for the fate of cities. Inscrutable tiefling warlocks unite with fierce elf warriors to rain fire and steel upon monstrous enemies. And valiant servants of merciful gods forever struggle against the darkness.

A LAND OF UNTOLD ADVENTURE

Chapter One

A Darker Fate For Me

He had been falling forever.

Drifting. Sifting. Down, down, trickling through cold, stony darkness in a vague, half-awake state as his ashes worked their separate ways down through earth and rocks and stone dust, into . . . open emptiness amid the chill rock. It was a cavern of the Underdark, part of a network—Elminster knew this from the gentle but ceaseless flow of damp, mineral-scented air drifting from distant elsewheres.

Whole once more—well, as "whole" as a swirling cloud of ashes could be—he turned to face the source of that breeze. He was back in the Underdark, and curiously safer than on all of his previous visits. To travel alone in the Underdark is to be desperate and all too often swiftly doomed, but he was now drifting along bodiless, attractive prey to nothing. He hoped.

He drifted along seeking a body, just as so many stealthy hunters in the deep gloom all around him were no doubt doing. *In the endless dance of death in the dark,* El sang silently to himself, recalling one of his favorites among Storm's ballads. Ah, but she and he had been at this for a long time . . .

Serving Mystra. Our Lady of Mysteries, the goddess of magic. Who had been swept away in the Spellplague, but had returned. "Returned" after a fashion, that is. Lessened, to be sure. Yet She was his beloved tyrant now as before, her commandments were still the map by which Elminster steered his life.

However difficult or nonsensical that life might sometimes seem, without Her his life would have ended long, long ago, though it might have been a much easier, happier life. Still . . . he'd felt lost without her, the past century. Obeying Mystra had become not just habit, but what gave him purpose.

Mystra had ordered Elminster to recruit Cormyr's wizards of war to her service, so he would do that. She'd told him to work with Manshoon, so he'd try to do so. Though the founder of the Zhentarim was as hot as ever to destroy a certain Sage of Shadowdale, El could not—would not—seek to slay Manshoon. No matter how richly the mad fool deserved to be blasted apart . . . or torn asunder and left to perish in slow agony. No matter how much Elminster ached to break him, humble him, and then destroy him forever.

He found himself staring at memories of Manshoon's startled, furious, and pain-wracked face on the various occasions when El had humbled or slain him . . . and as those images rose into his mind in a long and varied flood, his flare of rage faded into satisfaction. He had dealt with the founder of the Zhentarim fittingly before, and likely would again, in time to come.

Now, though, his orders ran along different lines. He and Manshoon were to gather blueflame, and Mystra also wanted her trusted Elminster to train his descendant Amarune Whitewave to succeed him, in time, as her Chosen.

Her young, defiant face came to mind. Spirited, reckless, beautiful. El tried to sigh, his ashes swirling with the effort. His successor; he knew very well what sort of life *that* would mean for Amarune. El wanted very much to guard Rune, to hide her and watch over her very closely, to keep her from even a tiny measure of what he'd suffered . . . but that would be a mistake, likely a fatal error. A coddled Chosen would be weak, easily shattered. Rune was going to have to take what the likes of Manshoon would delight in hurling at her.

Not that Elminster of Shadowdale could protect her properly just now, anyway. Here he was, bodiless again. Easily defeated by the mad, weakened dolt Manshoon had become. The powers of the

Chosen of Mystra were almost all lost to him, his own Art faded far from what it had once been . . . and the Spellplague had shattered and twisted all magecraft. Many spells were now nigh useless, difficult at short range and impossible from afar—and dangerous to a caster's mind, regardless. Every last spell that sought to pry into or control minds, translocate, or detect things was unreliable and fraught with peril, and most of them were beyond Elminster's skills as long as he lacked a body to study and incant and recall magics no longer familiar.

Aye, the shattering of the Weave—of Mystra, who was the Weave—had wrought great change in the Art. Just as the Realms themselves had been transformed, with entire lands fading away and being replaced. Yet not everything had changed. Not down in the Underdark, for instance. Where the usual dangers were still . . . usual.

Elminster drifted, keeping close to the rocky floor to avoid being swept apart if the breeze strengthened. Eerie glows beckoned here and there, the barely visible amethyst hues of rock radiations and the brighter, varicolored radiances of scores of fungi—some edible, some ambulatory and semi-sentient, and all of them dangerous. That standstool was deadly to eat, and this nearer one deadly just to touch, whereas yonder scabrous green-white and brown growths stole body heat from any living creature that ventured too near . . . aye, being bodiless had its advantages. Thank the twisted humors of the gods for such small favors.

Elminster drifted along, shaping his ash motes into a long, undulating line, hoping that if he were spotted—for a man who sought a body to inhabit risked such—he'd be mistaken for an errant strand of cave spiderweb. And down here, such would most likely be alert patrols of drow.

Ah! To think of a foe is to find him, as the saying went. Hastening out of yon side passage, at full speed were sleek black bodies, a score or more, heavily armored. A drow war band, ready for battle but moving with more speed than prudence; warriors fronting spider priestesses. The shapely backs of a few of Lolth's holy worshipers were acrawl with message spiders, and many tame blade spiders scurried alongside the patrol and across the rock ceiling above . . . eight such, nay, ten . . . twelve, other sorts of spiders among them, like an eagerly hurrying pack of war-hounds. *Definitely* a war band.

El had little hope of finding whence they'd come, but wherever they were bound in such a hurry could only be . . . interesting. A battle meant bodies, and a drow or drow foe weakened or mind-mazed might offer the perfect new body for a down-to-ashes old archmage. Not that he'd puzzled over this decision; he was already rushing after the drow as they sped down the passage, faces into the breeze, heading along an obviously familiar route.

He *felt* their destination before he saw it. Those who worked long with the Weave grew used to feeling the ebbs and flows of natural forces, and even with his might gone, El could feel a strange, unsettling pulsing, a repeated echoing, a rippling . . .

Rippling, aye, that was the best word. Wave after wave of . . . weakness, a momentary sucking emptiness succeeded by a surge of energies, then weakness again, rolling over him repeatedly like waves heading for a beach. Ripples that grew stronger as the drow rushed on, headed for the source of the disturbance. It was something that could now be seen ahead, pulsing in time to the ripples he felt. With each sucking, reflections of purple-blue radiance flashed across the rocks, then faded as the next surge of energy came, then flashed again, over and over.

Elminster had seen that particular hue before. That precise shade of glowing purple-blue meant a rift. The drow were rushing to a planar rift, a break where his own world and another had connected by way of a breach uncontrolled and inevitably growing or changing . . . seldom for the better. Hence the feeling of weakness: the very fabric of Faerûn was being tugged or sucked at nearby, somewhere up ahead.

The drow rushed on, forcing El to hurry to keep up. Other drow war bands streamed out of side passages into the widening way ahead, all of them racing toward the rift. The passage rose, curved, then hooked around a great shoulder of rock into a large cavern where several passages converged—and a purple-blue sea was raging.

The rift was like a great giant's eye on its side, opening vertically to flood its purple-blue light across the cave, its pulse a deep, thunderous, inexorable heartbeat.

And out of the dazzling heart of the rift, a nightmare menagerie was pouring out into the cavern and crashing into an outnumbered, battered line of drow who struggled to stop them, weapons flashing. This was the battle the drow war bands were rushing to join.

The beasts from the rift surged into the drow defenders, charging and sometimes rearing above the dark elves. There were hulking, shell-armored monsters with great mandibles and long, barbed stabbing antennae—or what looked like antennae. They were the largest, but were outnumbered by tigerlike cats that savaged the drow with the snapping jaws that darted and lunged at the end of the long, eel-like tentacles that sprouted in profusion from their powerful leonine shoulders. There were stranger rift creatures, too, including pillarlike glistening things that swayed as they fought, spitting long needles with deadly aim, lances that impaled dark elves and plucked them off their booted feet and hurled them away to crash against the cavern walls.

A great bloody fray raged in front of the rift, as the endless flood of monsters struggled over a growing heap of bodies, fallen drow mingled with a wild variety of dead or dying rift beasts. El could see great cages along the far walls of the cavern, barred enclosures rocking under the frenzied attempts of caged monsters to break out.

So this rift had been there long enough for local drow to mount a standing guard over it, and to establish a routine of capturing or slaying the beasts arriving through it. Aye, the creatures in *that* cage were probably intended as steeds, those in yonder distant cage as pack beasts, and the smaller motley heaps of squirming, crowded beasts filling that line of cages were probably intended to become food. If El knew anything at all about drow, they'd be seeking monsters they could use as weapons against Underdark foes, too.

Aye, probably the beasts in *those* cages, the ones almost buried in struggling drow and newly arrived monsters. A creature that looked like a great razor-toothed lamprey, and as large as the oldest sawmill back in Shadowdale, briefly reared up out of the tumult to shed struggling drow into a rain of blood-drenched dark elf body parts . . . and El got a glimpse of shattered, open cages beyond it.

Empty cages. Monsters had gotten free in the midst of the fighting, and were taking savage revenge on their captors.

Not that any drow seemed chastened or frightened in the slightest. The war band El had followed hurled itself into the nearest fighting without hesitation, the spiders racing up rift monster bodies to where they could bite and stab, the dark elf warriors drawing blades and plunging into the slaughter, and the priestesses stopping just shy of the fray to work a flurry of spells.

Ah, but mindless combat is always popular entertainment, El reminded himself wryly—then stopped, gaping in unthinking astonishment. Below him, priestesses gasped and cursed aloud, awed by the same sight.

The vivid purple-blue light of the rift had momentarily darkened, occluded by something gigantic moving through it, crushing smaller beasts in its way as it came, wriggling and humping like a gigantic inchworm. It slid out into the cavern, vast and glistening and blood red, its huge maw gulping a path through struggling dark elves and monsters alike.

Then it reared, towering. It *was* a worm, of a sort El had seen only once before—but that one had been a tortured captive in Avernus, an imprisoned, keeningly insane hulk cruelly enchanted to continually regrow itself as it was endlessly devoured alive by an ever-changing rabble of lesser devils. This one was no captive, and it was aroused and hungry, its great helm-shaped head almost black with rage.

A glaragh, such creatures were called in the Hells. But this one was far bigger than the huge captive he'd seen. It was as long as a Suzail street and as thick around as a three-floor house. It crashed through stalactites as it reared, but was unable to stand on its tail thanks to the low cavern ceiling. Elminster had seen hundreds of oversized worms in his time, from the infamous purple worms to the rockgnawers that ate endless passages out of solid bedrock in the deepest places of the earth, but this one beat them all.

Eight tentacle arms sprouted down the length of the monster worm, each ending in a sucking maw and a retractable bone talon that jutted like a spear when the beast desired but vanished back into hiding the rest of the time—and that meant "glaragh," and only glaragh.

The mighty worm shuddered for a long, swaying moment as it was struck by spell after spell hurled by drow priestesses amid a hail of spears and darts—then crashed down into the midst of the largest knot of drow, crushing many to a bloody pulp. It surged forward, wriggling so as to strike out in as many directions as possible. Its tail lashed out, straightening in a great sweep that slapped foes into spattering meetings with cavern walls, ere it slid forward like an impatient snake to maraud freely among screaming, vainly fleeing priestesses.

Two or three of the larger rift monsters gave challenge as it came at them, roaring or rearing in defiance—and the glaragh tore them apart with glee, dashing the remains aside with its tail as it advanced. It was heading into the passage breeze, El noticed.

What carnage! Not that drow deaths tugged overmuch at his heart at the best of times, but once the glaragh reached the surface, its slayings would likely be human. Nor was this a lone peril. The many invading beasts endlessly pouring through a rift...

Mystra, preserve us all. That prayer, made out of long habit, carried little force now. Yet who else should be prayed to, to close rifts?

El glanced at that purple-blue sundering, yawning wider than ever, the deep drumbeat of its pulsings almost deafening now that the battle clamor had died down to the scattered moans and cries of the dying. Even if he'd had a body and all the spellbooks he could think of at hand, he might not be able to seal it and mend the Realms around it. Not without a Weave he could work with, or the right artifacts of power to expend, blueflame or otherwise.

Perhaps not even then.

Aghast, El looked one last time into the flood of lesser monsters coming through the rift, the stream of beasts quickening once again, flooding out into the cavern to overwhelm the few fleeing drow the glaragh hadn't slain. Then he turned to fly after the great worm, fearing for the future of Faerûn around him more than he'd done in years. He'd been facing a slow, sour decline and his own powerlessness for nigh a century, but *this* . . . A hundred rifts like this one, a thousand . . .

Mystra forfend. Hells, every *god forfend!*

Yet all he could do just now, without a body, was watch as the glaragh slid onward, roving at will, devouring everything it desired, shattering all who stood against it. An eerie whuffling arose from it—the glaragh smelled the drow trails branching off into the side passages.

Abruptly, it shook itself and stopped whuffling, gliding off toward the source of the breeze instead, undulating like a swimming snake as it gathered speed. Off it went into the Underdark, faster and faster.

With a grim line of ashes in pursuit. This was the very thing Mystra wanted him to stop, and right now El couldn't do a hrasted thing about either worm or rift. He had been humbled like most wizards in the Realms; his reputation now far outstripped his power. And when he faced a foe who realized that . . .

"Rorskryn Mreldrake, what do *you* think your fate would be, if you walked into the royal palace of Suzail this evening?"

Mreldrake could just make out two cold eyes staring into his own, out of the dark shadow of the questioner's cowl. Eyes that . . . glowed. Their regard was neither friendly nor comforting. Not in the slightest.

He swallowed, and strove to sound calm, even casual. "Imprisonment and lengthy spell interrogation. I would be regarded as a traitor to the Dragon Throne."

Three cowled heads nodded, ere the centermost spoke again. "I'm glad you're aware of that," came the flat reply. "It buys you our acceptance."

Mreldrake waited, trying to avoid showing his fear.

"Acceptance of your proposal," added the leftmost figure. They sat facing him, their faces hidden in their deep cowls. "We shall feed and house you, and bring to you what we deem prudent of what you request for your spell researches—in return for your complete obedience, your compliance to remain within these walls, and betimes your willingness to take direction from us regarding the nature of your magical work."

"Should you offend against this pact," the last of three murmured softly, "the price will be your life."

"Terms that should be clear and simple enough for even a wizard of war to understand," the centermost cowled mage said coldly.

"*Former* wizard of war," Mreldrake dared to say. He got a silent shrug by way of reply, ere the three cowled figures rose abruptly in a swirl of dark robes and strode for the door.

Something glowed in the air above the vacated center seat. It was a disembodied human eyeball, floating in midair, wreathed in a faint and fading blue radiance.

It stared coldly at Mreldrake. He gazed glumly back, not hiding his sigh.

Across the room a heavy iron door slammed. He heard the rattle of a key in a lock, ere that sound was drowned out by the sharp *klaks* of heavy metal bolts crashing into place. One, two, three bolts.

He was locked in. By wizards greater in Art than he might ever be. One of them—the cold-voiced, tall one who'd sat in the center of the trio—had eyes that glowed more than a man's would. By their pale gleam, he'd seen enough of the dark, dull-skinned, drawn face around them, with its black teeth and tongue, to recognize a shade. He was a captive of fell Netheril—or of renegade Netherese.

Not that he could begin to tell which alternative was worse.

Chapter Two

I Alone Shall Conquer

"Out of clever ruses, Sage of Shadowdale? No more sly spells up your sleeve, Elminster? *Die,* this time! *Die forever!*"

He was shouting wildly, Manshoon knew, babbling along the slippery edge of weeping in his rage, as he hurled spell after spell. Magic to rend, heave up, and scatter the ground into which he'd driven Elminster down.

Powerful magic. At his behest earth and stones flew in all directions, his reckless blasting magics opening up a deep, raw pit in front of the cave.

Down, down, five man-heights and more, and still his spells tore and clawed and dug. He had to make certain Elminster was gone. Shattered, dead—utterly, completely dead.

"Where is his blood?" Manshoon shrieked. "*Where?*"

Fury overwhelmed him, red and yellow mists flooding his mind and blinding him. Through that haze he gasped and snarled out incantation after incantation, until every last battle spell was gone.

Leaving him gasping in his beholder body, somewhere in the wilderlands nigh Shadowdale.

Almost dazedly he worked the magic that would return him to human form. He would fly back to Suzail as a mist, as he, being a vampire, could. Back to the city where, in a cellar, one of his beholders would be shriveling and collapsing, ruined and gone.

Yet if—*if*—he'd truly destroyed Elminster of Shadowdale at last, the loss of one enslaved eye tyrant would be nothing. Nothing at all. A price too small even to think about.

Tentacles, eyestalks, and levitation melted away in a queasy shifting that still felt unsettling, even after thousands of transformations. And Manshoon found himself standing on the lip of his deep delve, silently seething.

Elminster *had* to be dead. No one could have survived that!

Yet he'd seen no body, not one smear of blood . . .

Bah! His magic must have vaporized the old fool, reduced Elminster to dust lost amid all the sand and specks of dirt and rock drift.

For an instant, as something made him calmer, Manshoon felt a slight sense of disorientation, as if gazing upon memories not his own. Then it passed and he promptly forgot the feeling, lost in a new confidence that took hold of him and told him firmly that Elminster was gone for good. Even if the Sage of Shadowdale wasn't destroyed, the right thing for Manshoon to do was to *move on*, to proceed with life as if his hated nemesis was no more.

Elminster *was* destroyed. The original Elminster, that is—for of course the fool would have copied Manshoon's brilliant ploy, and crafted clones of himself. Any archmage would.

"Which means," the founder of the Zhentarim murmured aloud, as he turned slowly all around to make sure no one was watching, and no stricken Elminster was desperately crawling away, "I must now hunt down all the lesser, later Elminsters. To ensure the Old Mage is gone forever, never to return."

He could see no fleeing, cowering, or spying creature—not so much as a songbird. He was alone. Permitting himself a long, slow smile, Manshoon became mist. He circled the edge of the pit where his longtime foe had perished, then soared into the sky, flying in a wider circle and peering down to look for spies from on high.

None. Finally, he allowed himself to gloat.

"You found your doom at last, old goat of Shadowdale—and behold, it was me!" Great wild bellows of laughter rolled out of him then, in a flood of exultation.

Mirth and triumph that died away all too soon in fresh anger as Elminster's remembered taunts came to mind . . . the Old Mage's laughing face, the Sage of Shadowdale defying him and lecturing him and . . . and . . .

Bah! He'd rend them all, every one of those hated laughing faces. And the clones were just a part of the work ahead. Identifying and eliminating all of Elminster's descendants must be part of this, too, for there was a chance—a good chance—the Sage of Shadowdale had hid "echoes" of himself inside them. It's what he himself would do, after all, and Elminster was no better than he was, wherefore *of course* . . .

So his victory this day was a beginning, not an end. It would take years to find and eliminate every clone and all of Elminster's offspring, so he couldn't drop all his other plans to do it. He would not.

He, Manshoon Emperor-to-Be, would proceed with conquering Cormyr—just not declaring himself openly as ruler until he could be certain Elminster was gone. Rather, he'd use various human puppets, putting one after another on the throne to face all the work of ruling and the inevitable assassination attempts, leaving himself free to hunt Elminster, coerce nobles, and gather his own arsenal of blueflame items, too, if they were so important.

Let Mystra, if Mystra truly had returned, treat *him* with respect for once. Favor Manshoon as he deserved to be favored.

After all, if she could rely on Elminster—become *intimate* with Elminster, if the tales could be credited!—her tastes could not be too lofty to encompass Elminster's better.

And if there *was* no Mystra and the mad former queen of Aglarond had merely been raving, deluding herself into thinking Mystra was guiding her, he'd seen enough of what an idiotic young noble could do with blueflame ghosts to know blueflame magic was worth having, regardless.

Yes. Yet he was getting ahead of himself. Return to Suzail first, to his bases there, the shop and home of Sraunter the alchemist and the half-ruined mansion of Larak Dardulkyn. There to sit and take wine and ponder. Decide which of his puppets to awaken, how precisely to proceed in conquering Cormyr, and where to begin seeking Elminster's clones and blueflame items. It would not do to—

Hah! Of course! He'd begin by hunting down Elminster's three companions: Storm Silverhand, Lord Arclath Delcastle, and the dancer Amarune Whitewave. None of them could hide themselves as the Sage of Shadowdale could, with all his magic—and whatever remained of Elminster, be it a clone or offspring, would not be far from them. Or from Storm, at least. So she and the other two would readily lead any seeker to Elminster, time and again. It was simple, really, the moment one stopped to think about it.

Right. Settled. Yet he had his own long-cherished schemes to set in motion first. He'd mind-touch his most recently subverted nobles—Crownrood, Andolphyn, Blacksilver, Loroun, and the rest—into doing this work for him. It was high time to start working in earnest on asserting control over suitable war wizards, too. Using both nobles and Crown mages to isolate the royal family and their few remaining trustworthy and effective courtiers, until they stood alone against those more loyal to *him*—and Manshoon could conquer his kingdom with ease.

Yes. Ah, but it was time at last . . .

"I haven't noticed much eagerness on your part to seek my counsel before," the spiderlike thing told her flatly. "Or even to accord me the minimum respect of addressing me, looking my way, or granting that I exist at all—when the king or Royal Magician aren't present."

"So you *admit* you're no longer Royal Magician of Cormyr?" Glathra snapped.

Vangerdahast sighed. "Attacking, always attacking . . . young lady, d'you know how to do anything else?"

Glathra Barcantle gave the little monster a sour glare. In truth, she was afraid of the infamous Vangerdahast. Not to mention revolted by what he'd become. A blackened human head trailing wisps of hair and beard, balanced atop an unpleasant wrinkled black sack of a body like an untidy collar, sprouting a spidery cluster of gray-black human fingers on which it scuttled along like a confident shore crab. She was looking at something that resembled a heap of human remains salvaged by a priest or wizard after a fiery death, for identification purposes. No longer a man or a "he" . . . no, this was an *it*.

She hated it as much as ever.

"I know how to do all that's necessary to safeguard Cormyr," she snapped, "and I'm doing so right now. Quite capably, despite whatever you may think. Kindly stop evading my question. I ask you again, *thing*: do you admit you are no longer the Royal Magician of the realm?"

"I will always be Royal Magician, so long as I am Vangerdahast," came the swift reply. "Yet I grant that Ganrahast is *also* Royal Magician of Cormyr. You seem unable to accept that state of affairs. Tell me, are all wizards of war so inflexible these days?"

"And if we are?" Glathra spat.

"Then I must needs test every last one of you, dismiss most of you, and begin training and rebuilding until Crown mages are once more fit to serve the realm. I've done it before."

"Oh? And you think we'll just heed and obey, I suppose? Accept your judgment, you who are a monster and not a man, who could be any devil or undead horror that has plundered the memories of Vangerdahast? You who demonstrate such a *flexible* grasp of Cormyr's laws and rules and chains of command? *I think not*."

Snatching two wands from her belt, Glathra shook them in front of the thing on the shelf. "*These* are power! These can blast you back to whatever Hell you came from, if I so choose! These are very like the scores—hundreds—more, wielded by dedicated wizards of war all across this realm! Dodge mine, and you'll be blasted down by wands aimed by the next loyal Crown mage! *These* make me every bit as useful to the Dragon Throne as some scuttling black *thing* from years gone by, who—"

"Made all of those wands, and can master them," Vangerdahast said softly—and sprang off the shelf, right at her face.

With a shriek of rage and terror Glathra triggered both wands, frantically trying to blast the monster before it touched her. Staggering back, she tripped and fell over backward, aghast.

The wands hadn't awakened. She was clutching two sticks of whittled wood that bore no magic at all.

Someone touched her bosom, fingers on her bared flesh. The spider-thing was walking along and up her body on its fingertips . . .

The black, bearded face loomed over her, staring at her nose to nose, eyes afire.

"Lady," it said sternly, "I do not require you to like me, or be my friend—though it *would* be easier. I *do* require you to serve Cormyr, alongside me—or get out of the way. Don't make me have to hurl you aside. Forever."

The fingertips moved past her collarbone, drawing near her throat. Their noses were almost touching.

Vangerdahast gave her a wide, warm smile. "I *can* be charming, you know."

Glathra fainted.

Mreldrake looked around at bare, yellowing walls that were by now all too boringly familiar, and couldn't help but sigh. This was a prison, all right, a cell as secure as any deep dungeon lockhole—and he'd walked right into it. Willingly.

Yes, he himself had kicked aside the last shreds of any doubt as to what sort of fool he was. Yet it was the first trap in which he'd ever been excited to be caught.

Yes, excited. His despair had faded, and most of his bitterness at the narrowing prison his life had become was gone, too.

Swept away in the mounting thrill of the magic he was working. For once, ideas for refining and manipulating the Art flooded into his mind, his thoughts often outracing his scribbling pen. Experiment after experiment was working, or at least shaping the unfolding enchantments well enough to reveal the way onward.

For the first time in his life, he was truly excited at his own magical prowess.

In this litter of notes and runes and scribbled incantations, with these powders and jars and braziers, he was creating magic—*real* magic, far beyond the silly make-yon-chamber pot-glow cantrips of his youth.

Magic that could change kingdoms, change *everything*. Magic that could make its wielder the greatest mass murderer ever . . .

The glaragh was in a hurry. Elminster raced along, his ashes swirling and tumbling in their own wind of haste, just to keep it in sight. Ahead, the passage was rising, and becoming well lit by frequent patches of overhead and high-wall fungi that the great worm ignored in its relentless race onward.

What was the monstrous worm seeking? Or had it been there before, and had a destination?

El tried to shake his head ruefully, though he had no head to shake. Well over a thousand summers, and I still know so little about Faerûn. All my time I've spent fighting, worrying, or manipulating so I need not fight and so a few more folk may live rather than die . . . and failing in my strivings, too often failing . . .

The passage hooked around a corner, and he heard sudden yells. Liquid, fluting voices—drow.

By the time El got to where he could see them, they were all dead, crushed and bloody smears on the rocks, spears and handbows splintered and strewn about.

The glaragh had burst right through a guard post and out into a great cavern beyond. It was headed straight for a dark prow of rock that jutted out into open space like the bow of some gigantic entombed ship of the gods—a wall of stone pierced by many balconies and ramparts, eerie glows of worm lamps and glow fungi showing through hundreds of windows.

A drow citadel, its *arraugra*—the swifter and more elegant dark elf equivalent of what most humans called ballistae—cracking forth a rain of racing lances at the oncoming glaragh.

El dodged one hissing lance instinctively, though a line of ashes really didn't need to avoid anything, and peered at the rushing worm to see its reaction.

Lance after lance thudded home—the thing's hide wasn't all that tough, after all—but the glaragh didn't even seem to notice.

The barrage ended as the drow defenders ran out of loaded and ready *arraugra*. El could see sleek dark bodies dashing around on balconies trying to reload, but the glaragh wasn't waiting. It plunged straight into the midst of a hastily assembling wall of warriors in front of the citadel's nearest gate, and kept right on going.

It swept inside, where it couldn't help but get stuck in the narrow passages and tiny rooms, smooth though their walls undoubtedly were. Dark elf architecture might favor the sweeping curve and the smooth surface, but tight quarters were tight—

The glaragh thrust itself into a very narrow passage, thinning down like a ribbon, then suddenly surged. The rock around it groaned and shattered in countless places, falling away in a thunder of rubble from which the glaragh freed itself with two great sweeps of its tail, and surged on.

There was a *crack* followed by a rumbling fall, and then the same tumult repeated itself. Mined at its heart, the great citadel was falling in.

Much of the stronghold's center—the prow itself—had been hollowed out by the glaragh in less time than it would take Elminster to get out a wand, and the glaragh was stabbing with its head into the open sides of shattered rooms, biting and sucking. Drow fought vainly against the pursuing tentacles thrusting out of the great worm's sides—and were gone.

Whereupon the glaragh fell silent and still.

Then, the moment the echoes of its destruction had finally died and stillness had fallen, the creature suddenly rose again in one great heave. That mighty convulsion preceded a mental onslaught that smote Elminster like a tidal wave, a thunderous silent darkness that broke over his thoughts and almost swept him away, dragging him far closer to the glaragh than he'd ever intended to get.

As it happened, he'd been watching some drow mages hurriedly claw out enchanted scepters to deal with the invader, so he saw the effects of the glaragh's mind attack all too clearly. One moment the dark elves were all frenzied agility, scrambling to undo latches and pluck out wrapped and stored scepters—and the next, they crumpled like so many discarded puppets, emptied of will and wits, toppling like mindless meat to the floor. One even heedlessly impaled himself on his own scepter.

Somehow—he never knew quite how—Elminster tore himself away from the glaragh's pull, free of the dark and hungry mind that sought to lure and feed on his, and got a good look at the face of one fallen drow mage. Eyes blank, mouth open and drooling, everything slack. Mindless meat, to be sure.

Behind him, the glaragh gave another great heave, slicing off the mind pull as if with a falling knife. Then the great worm veered. A lash of its tail swept more rooms down into ruin and gave it space enough to freely turn around and depart.

It glided out into the cavern more slowly than it had charged the citadel, and paused. It seemed to sniff the available passages before choosing one—turning again into the breeze—and plunging on into the Underdark. The jaunty flick of its tail as it left the cavern behind seemed almost . . . satisfied.

Elminster watched it go. He had already decided to stay behind in the citadel. Among so many mindless drow bodies, he might well find a new body for himself. Dark elves were nothing if not supple, and—*Mystra*!

What by all the Nine Flaming Hells?

He had not felt that sudden tingling stealing into him for years, had not thought to ever feel it again. A cool sweetness, the almost sensual rising tide within him that made him purr aloud involuntarily, a soft growling that spat brief silver flames in front of his nose.

The silver fire.

Mystra's divine fire was flowing into him from somewhere nearby, somewhere in the shattered citadel!

Astonished, Elminster forgot all about the glaragh and turned his attention to the ruins around him. The great prow had been split open, its center destroyed. Below him yawned a rubble-filled gulf. The prow had been reduced to two torn, separate walls of rock, with nothing between them but debris and a few sagging walls and pillars that wouldn't stand for long ere they joined the heaped and broken stone below.

He felt invigorated, stronger than ever. Well, of course he would, with this new fire in him—but he had to know who was dying, which Chosen of Mystra was sinking into death and yielding up their divine fire, leaking it out into the Realms around. He *must* know!

And who *dared* to slay a Chosen of Mystra?

Aglow with silver fire, wild with the excitement such energy always brought him, and hungry for more, the swift stream of radiant ashes that was Elminster arrowed down into the ruins.

Who or what was waiting in there that could slay keepers of the divine fire of the goddess of all magic?

Chapter Three

A Citadel Become A Tomb

El plunged into shattered rooms, through arches that leaned and ceilings that sagged, seeking silver fire.

Its flow into him had faded swiftly after that first flood, down to a trickle. Which meant he had to hurry . . .

Broken drow bodies were everywhere, half-buried in rubble, wet ribbons of blood running from under many stone piles.

Less gruesome but more eerie were the last victims of the glaragh, the untouched but mindless bodies draped and sprawled atop the rubble.

El darted past them, racing this way and that, following the fading trail of Mystra's divine fire deeper into what was left of the citadel . . . into the intact rooms on one side of the devastation.

He would be finding death, he knew, the last moments of someone who might well be dear to him. Was this Mystra's will, this timing? The fire her gift to him?

That might be the most comforting way to think of it, aye, but . . .

What if it was a trap? What if he was rushing to his doom? Lured by someone or something eager to slay Chosen, or someone who cared not who came racing, but would smite any unwelcome arrival?

He cared not. He *had* to know who was relinquishing silver fire, had to taste more of it if he could, had to . . . had to . . .

El came at last into a room where grandly robed drow lay slumped in profusion—spider priestesses and mages—around a table where chains held spread-eagled remains that had been butchered beyond recognition. The sacrifice, or victim, had been both a Chosen and a she-elf. He could tell that much.

Grim anger grew in him as he came nearer. The drow had removed organs from her, and cast experimental spells on her, while she lived.

A jar still cradled in the arms of one crumpled and mindless dark elf held a freshly severed human tongue, and . . . were those eyeballs, glistening on a tray across the room?

Aye, staring sightlessly now, forever. Black rage flared, rising until Elminster wanted to snarl, or choke. As ashes, he could do neither; he could only swirl.

This death will be paid for. This I swear.

He looked wildly around for a greater foe, but saw or sensed no one. Only all these cruel, now mindless drow . . .

Dark rage rode him. He was trembling, every ash mote of him. He did not know which was stronger: his grief or his rage.

Mingled with them was shame, as El furiously circled in the air above the sad remnants of a fellow Chosen he could neither name nor aid. Feeling no better than her drow tormentors, he fed on her instead, drinking in the very last of Mystra's fire escaping from her.

Those precious silver flames streamed past a trail of purple and black fire tracing a slow and endless circle in midair above the blood-drenched table; a poorly crafted dark elf spell that had sought to capture the escaping divine essence for drow use. It had failed. El gave it a glance. Such magic could never have contained the silver fire . . .

He shuddered in astonishment as the last of the silver fire flooded into him, plunging him into feeling . . . unsettled. Strange, mildly sickening . . . more expansive, as if he were not alone . . .

Mystra's fire had lingered long enough to drink and drain yon drow flames and several other failing dark elf magics in the room, bringing them into him. Was something now amiss within him? Had—

No, Old Mage, you are as tough and enduring as ever, an amused voice said from the depths of his mind.

"Who—?" Elminster blurted out, staring wildly around as if some magical mirror might spring into being, right in front of him, to show him who'd spoken. None obliged.

It could only be the Chosen on the table, come into him with the last of her silver fire . . . but the voice didn't *feel* familiar.

It was weak, and fading; she'd probably not last long without the Weave to sustain her . . .

Not long, I agree. I've not much time left, Elminster. Use my fire well, and remember me when you do.

"I—" Elminster found his voice rough, and he fought to speak. "I'd find that easier to do if I knew who ye were."

Are, impatient man, still are, *thank you very much!*

That tart mindspeech stung; El winced and bowed his head.

"My apologies, lady, I pray ye. Are still, of course. Ah, are still whom?"

That's better. There was a time when you knew me. Symrustar Auglamyr, once of Cormanthor. We did not part on good terms.

"*Symrustar?* Lady, how . . . how . . ."

How came I here? Taken by the drow long ago, my mind assailed by their spells for years. I fought them and won, again and again, until they despaired of conquering me and decided to destroy me instead, to get at Mystra's might within me. And they managed it. In the end, Our Lady fallen silent, it seems I was not so special, after all.

The voice in Elminster's head fell silent for a moment. When it spoke again, it was laced with amusement.

Or do you mean, how is it that I became a Chosen? And you never knew of me?

"Ah . . . aye. To thy first, I mean. As for the second, Mystra shielded ye from me, of course."

She did. For both our sakes. I love you, man.

"And I ye. I believe ye when ye speak of love—but ye had, ye must admit, an odd way of showing it."

I was torn, and more than torn. I hated you, too. For being a human, El. It was . . . shame to me to desire a human. Until my heart told me otherwise, I was as certain as the rising and setting of the sun and moon that humans were stinking, hairy, brutish savages. A young, reckless, lesser race that deserved no respect and was unworthy of their ever-rising power. A blight upon the Realms that despoiled and ruined without thought or caring, and responded with angry violence when their faults were pointed out to them. You shattered all I knew of the world, all at once, and . . . and I saw what was to come. That seeing would not be easy for any elf, high or low. It was poison to me. You were poison to me.

"I . . . Lady, I was young and foolish and proud, and—and did ye ill."

I tried to do you worse. Even prayed not just to the gods I knew well, but to Mystra, for the means to destroy you.

"Sweet shattered spells . . . ," El whispered, aghast. "Did ye not know—?"

The ties between you and your goddess? I soon learned. The voice in his mind was wry. *Yet never have I known such love, such mercy. Instead of destroying me or playing me false, she gave me kindness and wise counsel. That I spurned. When at last I fell in battle, she came to me as I was flung across the sky, my body rent in fire, and offered me a new life. I said yes. She promised me you would never know while she flourished. I wonder now if she foresaw her fate.*

"I . . . I think Mystra's fall was part of a cycle fated to happen again and again, as the Weave—as all magic of this world—needs renewal. Mystra has returned."

WHAT? I've felt her not!

"She is . . . much changed. Diminished. Needing my service urgently, where before I was but one able-handed servant and messenger among many at her disposal."

And so you'll endure, as I fall into the darkness. Yet I'll have this brief time with you, ere I fade. You always had the hardest road, Lord Aumar. You prince. The voice lost its forlorn and wistful feeling, and turned warmly affectionate. *You right rogue.*

"Lady," Elminster replied, "I . . . I wish matters had been different, between us."

If wishes were armies, Cormanthor would yet stand bright. I had my second chance, El, and made much of it, and long ago moved beyond regret. I found lovers and soulmates and good friends among Mystra's faithful, then peace over what befell when we were both in the City of Song. Mystra often showed me your unfolding exploits, as entertainment for us both. Know that I . . . The voice seemed to choke for a moment, as if suppressing a sob. *That I often cheered for you.*

Symrustar's voice slid back into wry amusement again. *Even when you were . . . wenching.*

Elminster winced. "Mystra never told me . . ."

Mystra never told you a lot *of things. Yet know that she regarded you above all others in her service, gave you the hardest tasks, trusted you more than any other. You were her lion. I . . . I often wondered what your mind would feel like.*

"And now?"

It feels . . . comfortable. Friendlier and kinder than I thought it could be. You are *a bright lion, man.*

El winced again. "I—I bumble along, these days. Trying to do what I'm bidden without doing too much damage to the Realms around me. All too often failing at that, I must tell ye."

Modestly said, Lord Aumar, but just now, I perceive from your thoughts, body snatching is your foremost interest. Hardly a modest pursuit.

"Ouch. Thy tongue still stings with casual ease."

I'm not quite dead yet. So share. This is my last ride, and I want to enjoy it.

"Lady, flying around as a sort of sightseer has its fleeting attractions, but Mystra has laid urgent orders upon me, and much depended upon me before that. To fulfill any of these tasks, I require a body, hands and all. Not some thrall under compulsion I might try from a distance, but the defter, closer control I gain by inhabiting the body, wearing it as my own."

So how did you happen to be so careless as to lose your own body?

El sighed. "A longish tale, lady. Do ye really want me to spend the time to—?"

No. I was . . . needling you. A besetting failure of mine. Forgive me. Explore away. The sooner you're wearing a body, the sooner we can be out of this place. Those last mental words came wrapped in rising fear, revulsion, and a hastily suppressed flare of gruesome memories of grinning drow cutting into her ere the excruciating pain made her faint.

Elminster sent her all the soothing, loving emotion he could muster, which earned him a sharp: *Spare me the romance, Sage of Shadowdale. A little late now for both of us, wouldn't you grant? So get looking!*

"Thy wish, lady," El told the elf in his mind wryly, "is my command."

He drifted forward. But even for swirling ashes, haste among freshly fallen rubble, with pillars and fragments of ceiling often crashing down suddenly, was nigh-impossible. Caution had to govern.

What El had watched the glaragh do suggested mindless bodies would be plentiful if he picked promptly. He could see silent, empty-eyed drow drooling and aimlessly staggering in distant galleries, heedless of peril; were those the best and strongest bodies to choose from, or should he take one that was unmarked but unconscious?

Take the most beautiful she-drow, Symrustar suggested tartly. *Drow males and human men are alike in this: beauty distracts them from instantly seeking to slay. They'd rather have some fun first.*

"Cynical," El muttered, "yet astute."

The one does not preclude the other, man. Even among humans. As for elves, have you so utterly forgotten your days in Cormanthor?

"No," Elminster whispered. "Never."

Gently, El. I did not mean to wound.

"I bear many wounds," he murmured. "The worst healed are those I carry in my mind."

Carefully wrapped in shrouds and hidden away, I see.

Elminster winced again.

In the rubble-heaped cauldron where the prow of stone had been, most of the drow were dead or maimed, half-crushed or missing limbs. El floated into the intact rooms deeper along the surviving side of the citadel where Symrustar had been slain.

This may be the wiser place to search, his newfound guest said approvingly. *Or the most dangerous—the most powerful priestesses had chambers in this direction.*

"The glaragh stole every mind it could reach," El told her. "Unless other drow come before I'm done, I don't expect battle."

Nor did he find any. Staring drow were everywhere, their bodies intact but their minds quite gone, some of them silent and seemingly unaware of him or anything, others slinking away like cowed dogs at any nearby movement.

He floated through room after room, the furnishings growing grander, with ever increasing numbers of poisonous guardian spiders—some curled into tight balls of agony or spasming, quivering insanity, others frozen in awe, thanks to the abrupt disappearance of the drow minds to which they'd been linked.

He found priestesses clad in elaborate high-cowled spider robes, who bore scepters and wands of darkly menacing power. Some were slumped in spots that suggested they'd been guarding locked rooms beyond them—and in one such room Elminster was astonished to find a long table surrounded by mindless, feebly fumbling male drow whose robes, enchanted rings, and wands suggested they were wizards of some sort. Laid out upon the table were spellbooks.

Human spellbooks! Tomes and grimoires and mages' traveling handyspells books, brought down into the Underdark from the World Above, the surface Realms El knew. Dark elves were collapsed over the pages or fallen back in their chairs away from them. These wizards had obviously been studying when the glaragh struck.

El peered at this rune-adorned page and that, feeling the silver fire roiling within him; more, now, than he could comfortably carry. He could hurl it forth at foes, aye. If he did not, it would leak slowly away in his wake . . . or he could make use of it as he'd done a time or two before in his a thousand-some summers. Expend a trifle here and a trifle there, to brand particular spells from these pages before him into his mind for a good long time. Forever, if no silver fire burned them away again. Making them magics he could henceforth cast by silent force of will alone. Only a few, for each one he branded into his sentience stunted and constricted it. He must choose carefully.

After he chose the best body to become his new home. He might need an excess of silver fire to break enchantments on it, or purge poisons or internal ills from it. Yes, he must find a body first.

El coiled around the fallen priestess who'd been guarding the room of the tomes. A tall, sleek drow—or would have been were she not sprawled in her own drool all over the scuttling-spider-crowded stone floor of a citadel passage. Her arms and legs were flung wide, spiders biting them as if avenging years of slights.

Aye, and that was another concern; any of these myriad fist-sized and smaller arachnids might be eyes and ears for the Queen of Spiders. El had no desire to fight scores upon scores of ruthless spider priestesses or the minions they could command, or earn the furious attention of an insane and rapacious goddess best dealt with when a restored and whole Mystra stood at his back.

At last *you reach the obvious conclusion that you must hurry, Elminster.*

"Yes, Mother," El answered Symrustar mockingly. He was rewarded by a mental image of her giving him a witheringly scornful look, her face looming up so suddenly in his mind that he flinched. And promptly felt the warm flare of her satisfaction.

"Not *now*," he told her grimly, and he started to steel himself mentally, steadying and gathering his will. This might be rough . . .

El hovered before the beautiful but alarmingly slack face of the priestess—then plunged down into her open mouth, seeking the nasal passages to drive up to storm and occupy the dark, hopefully empty mind.

He was in! And it was empty; he was falling, plunging into unknown depths, rolling . . .

There followed a few moments of whirling, sickening disorientation, a seemingly longer time of feeling queasily "not right" . . . and then the body was his, moving fingers then legs at his command, rolling over—and up, as lithely as he'd done in his youth on the rooftops of long-vanished Athalantar.

He had a body once more!

"Lady," he asked aloud, the words coming out as a deep squawk at first, ere settling into a softer, higher-pitched echo of his former voice, "are ye still with me?"

Oh *yes, Lord Aumar. You'll not be rid of me* that *easily.*

"Ah, lass, this is in no sense an attempt to be rid of ye—but if taking a body is this easy, it occurs to me that ye could have one, too, with my help, and take back thy fire and live on!"

The reply, from the back of his mind, was slow in coming.

That was cruel, Elminster. I am much too far gone for that. There's not enough of me left to do more than think, and mindspeak. I can't even . . . no. I can't. If you tried to bestow silver fire on me now, even a little, it would rend what is left of me, and snuff me out like the candlestub I've become. I'm . . . I'm almost done. Don't leave me.

"Lady, I've no such intentions, I assure ye! I—"

Always had a glib tongue. Let us speak no more of this, waste no more of the time neither of us has left. The silence of this citadel must have been noticed already. There are—or were—portals to other drow holds somewhere in this place; you may very soon have rather hostile visitors.

"I—aye, ye have the right of it. The spellbooks . . ."

Hurry, man, hurry.

Elminster hurried, clawing through the keys he found on his new body's belt with long, deft, able fingers. This shapely, graceful, and pain-free body was clad in diaphanous robes of a hue he hated, and covered with hrasted spider badges! Impatiently he tore at the cloth.

That's the El I remember. All shes should go bare, yes?

"Lady," he growled aloud—it came out as an angry purr—"ye're *not* helping!"

I will, Elminster, I promise. When I can, as I can. This I swear.

The sudden fiery determination in the voice in his mind almost scorched him.

Touched, El found himself on the verge of tears—larger, oilier tears than any of his human bodies had wept. He sniffled.

Stop that. Spells, remember?

"Yes, dear," he replied mockingly. There was silence for a moment in the back of his mind, then the delicious thrill of a feminine chuckle.

How many Chosen had paid with their lives, down all the long years? Do we mean so little to Mystra?

Hurry.

El rushed to the books, silver fire rising into his mind. He must be careful not to let it leak out of his fingertips and damage spells he might want.

He must be careful, too, to choose those magics wisely. Yet he must hasten.

El growled again.

Aye, that purr *was* a delightful sound . . .

Chapter Four

This Place Is Dangerous Enough

A small, high-flying cloud of mist crossed the great green sward of pastureland, rushing south for the stout walls of soaring-towered Suzail. Never sundered or driven aside, even by the strongest breezes, the mist headed straight for the capital of Cormyr, taking care to stay higher than any Purple Dragon bowman would trust his eye, and to seem mere wild wisps rather than anything manlike in shape.

The half-ruined mansion of Dardulkyn wasn't much of a welcoming familiar hearth. Nevertheless, the mist was heading home.

One day soon, of course, this would all be his: every chase and pasture, every palace and high mansion and hovel.

Yes, soon. The nobles were aching for a chance to take out swords and have at each other—the moment they'd finished butchering every hated courtier and the decadent, far-fallen ruling Obarskyrs. Divided, sick of old ways, and hungry for blood, they would be the toys of Manshoon.

A Manshoon none could gainsay. The Netherese postured and sneered from on high, yet were so weak they must needs skulk to power in Sembia and elsewhere, taking command like thieves where truly mighty mages would boldly declare themselves and blast down all defiance.

The Simbul might have fleetingly recaptured her sanity, but she was so feeble that she had to pretend to speak for a dead goddess, and wanted Manshoon—as well as her tamed lapdog Elminster—to pilfer enchanted baubles for her.

Hah. Manshoon the Mighty had no need of magic items. Manshoon need never trifle with them again. Manshoon—

That thought fled from him and was gone, as the towers of Suzail rushed up to meet him. A quickening sea wind brought the tang of salt, seaweed, and dead fish to him, for this mist could smell without a nose.

One more curious little property of vampirism, Manshoon mused, as he drifted over the city wall. He rose higher as he swept on, not out of any fear of war wizard spells or watchers on the walls, but mindful of the wards of the noble mansions he passed over, that might—carelessly or otherwise—extend high into the skies above their turrets and grand gardens.

His lofty vantage revealed something unusual on a street below. A small procession of grand walkers, the gleam of polished plate armor fore and aft, a man in a tabard in the middle . . . a Crown herald, flanked by what could only be a pair of wizards of war, a trio preceded and followed by two armored Purple Dragons. Big men, in the very best of armor; this must be an important formal call.

Curiosity afire, Manshoon arrowed down, taking care to keep directly over a street where no wards should reach. He should be able to recognize that tabard . . .

Yes. He was spying upon the herald Dark Dragonet, and those were war wizards, all right. Veterans, by their looks, though he recognized neither of them. The escorting Purple Dragons were *huge*, muscled and stern-faced giants. None of the three they were escorting were anywhere close to smiling, either. Well, well. Bad tidings for someone.

Manshoon drifted lower, just as the solemn procession arrived on the doorstep of Ambershields Hall.

Soaring stone, bright-gleaming copper doors as high as two men, sculpted winged lions flanking them on a raised stone porch wide enough for twelve men to stand at ease: the city mansion of the Ambershields noble family. Stiff-necked lovers of tradition who'd resisted his attempts to corrupt them just as they resisted the reforms of King Foril Obarskyr. Strong shoulders supported heads of stone.

Manshoon sank down into the ornate carved stonework surmounting the grand front doors of the Ambershields to eavesdrop. Dolphins and seawolves, sporting with merfolk and men with lances riding what looked like wyverns decorated the door; very warlike and striking, to be sure.

"Nay, my orders are not to enter, but to deliver my message from the threshold," the herald was telling the doorwarden. "Summon him, please."

If the mist could have crooked an eyebrow in surprise and amusement, Manshoon would have done so. Oh, this was better and better.

Nor was the wait long. Staunch upholders of tradition, to be sure.

"Yes?" Lord Ambershields gave the herald the briefest of nods.

Dark Dragonet bowed, then declaimed grandly and formally, "Lord Ambershields is commanded to hear my words, in the name of the king!"

As the noble nodded curtly, the herald swept on. "This same message is being delivered all over the city, right now, to all the heads of noble houses known to be in Suzail. King Foril Obarskyr, who sits the Dragon Throne and hath lawful and absolute dominion over all Cormyr, has taken to heart the misgivings of the foremost families of the land to many of his recent decrees. It is his most royal decision to cancel the Council of Dragons and spend the next season meeting personally with any and all nobles who desire to speak with him, to discuss privately and frankly their ideas for the governance and future of Cormyr, that all notions and wants be given fair and full hearing. The nobility of Cormyr are deeply thanked for attending the council and for their staunch love and caring for the realm, and are asked to return peacefully to their homes and the affairs they laid aside to attend, while a wiser King Foril considers what they have told him thus far, and begins these private meetings."

Lord Ambershields made reply to this with another curt nod. "Tender my thanks, good herald," he said coldly, and he closed the door in Dark Dragonet's face.

The herald shrugged and turned away, waving the Purple Dragons to accompany him. A moment later, the Crown party was hurrying away to make the same proclamation to the next eager audience.

Hovering above the door arch of Ambershields Hall in a pale writhing of mists, Manshoon gloated.

"The Obarskyr grip on the Dragon Throne has become a last, frantic clutch," he murmured to himself. "And it's slipping. My empire will rise soon."

"Glemmeraeve soup," Lady Marantine Delcastle announced with pride, setting the steaming tureen before them.

Catching her son's look, she added sharply, "*Yes,* I made it myself. Not catching the glemmeraeves—netting sea turtles is a bit beyond my skills—but I did all the rest. I *do* snare ground garanth."

Arclath gave her a wide, admiring, and genuine smile.

She held his gaze suspiciously a moment longer, then relaxed into a smile of her own, deftly swept the lid off the tureen in a smooth move to prevent trapped beads of moisture from raining down on the table, and reached for the ladle.

Wanting to hear all about what had been unfolding at court, Arclath's mother had not only invited Storm and Amarune to a late eveningfeast at Delcastle Manor, she'd banished the servants from the room to "keep unwanted ears at a distance," and was serving the meal herself.

Arclath was clearly astonished, but carefully refrained from any comment on how well his imperious she-dragon of a mother did serving duties. Lady Delcastle was the deft and attentive equal of any smoothly gliding maid—and far, far politer than her usual self, to boot. Patient, too. Though she had professed to want to hear all the latest from court, which nobles had been saying and doing what, and all the clack about the future of Cormyr, she hadn't yet pressed her three guests for gossip. She usually pounced on every uttered word, wheedling and threatening with fierce enthusiasm and without pause, as if in great haste to wrest forth the next juicy revelation.

Seeing her smile grow increasingly strained, Arclath took pity on her. Her maid act was *perfect*, but who knew when all this forbearing would be too much, and she might explode?

"I'm sure the herald's visit was a surprise, Mother," he said politely, pouring more wine for everyone before she could. "You'll be wanting to hear something of what we've seen and heard, out and about in the city, yes?"

"Indeed," Lady Delcastle said gratefully. "I'm . . . less than patient in my desires to know whatever gossip may have reached your ears as to which nobles are obeying and supporting the king, which factions are crying open defiance, who's posturing, and in what ways? Has the king made warning examples of anyone, yet? Has any jack or lass been sent to a very public bad end? I—"

She abruptly clamped her mouth shut, shook her head fiercely, and relaxed into another smile. "Forgive me; I was starting to babble." She shot her son a look, and added dryly, "Yes, dear, I *was* about to erupt. Your mounting fear was all too apparent."

"Your glemmeraeve," Storm murmured, spoon in hand, "is *marvelous*."

"Thank you," Marantine Delcastle said in genuine pleasure, taking up her own spoon. "You like the hint of mustard?"

"Mustard and . . . daeradorn wine, in the snails . . . well simmered before you added in the garanth gravy," Storm said slowly, savoring the last of a spoonful. "Beautifully done."

"Best soup I've ever had," Amarune echoed softly. "I wish I could cook like this."

Lady Delcastle beamed. "You shall, Rune, you shall. I sport in my kitchens all too rarely these days, I'll admit, but—" She interrupted herself with a slice of her hand through the air like an executioner's axe. "Later. Gossip first!"

Storm almost managed to quell a snort of amusement, which made Arclath say hastily, "Well, Mother—not that this will come as fresh news—the realm *is* still astir. The wiser and more loyal lords, such as Spurbright and Wyvernspur, are soothing and calming in all directions—and trying to get the most flame-tempered lords out of Suzail and back to their country keeps before more trouble erupts. While the likes of Lady Harvendur and Lady Dawningdown are working their usual verbal poison, spreading malicious rumors and setting as many lords and ladies at each other's throats as they can. The entire city garrison of Purple Dragons is patrolling the streets in endless overlapping shifts—"

"In crowds, not patrols," Storm murmured.

"In crowds, yes, to keep nobles' bodyguards from fighting with each other. If a punch is thrown in a tavern, the Dragons flood in even before the shouting begins. The Crown is trying to keep trouble firmly sheathed."

"Amid an ever-increasing flood of noble complaints about the high-handed misuse of the soldiery against loyal and innocent citizens, I suspect," Lady Delcastle said dryly.

"Indeed. Some legitimate complaints, too."

"Oh? Such as?"

"Well, for one, the Crown's inability to ah, 'eliminate or at least curb' increasingly bold outlaw bands raiding in the northeastern reaches of the realm."

"The usual orcs and lawless blades, north of Hullack? Taking advantage of all the shouting and the lords all gathered in Suzail for the council?"

"Some of that, but there *have* been some bolder raids than usual. Broadshield's Beasts, for one, have been going right into towns, and not just by night, to—"

He broke off as Storm tensed beside him, and his mother's face changed. Following her gaze, Arclath cast a swift glance back over his shoulder.

Unannounced and unescorted by servants, three silent visitors walked into the room, anonymous in long, dark nightcloaks. Their hoods were up, hiding their faces, and their hands—and any short weapons they might be holding—were unseen inside flared, long-hanging sleeves.

"Purple Dragon forfend!" Lady Delcastle burst out, more astonished than afraid. "We are invaded!"

She twisted a ring on her left hand, which obediently began to glow, ere springing to her feet to thunder, "Halt! Halt and reveal yourselves!"

Arclath was already out of his chair, his sword sliding out.

"Stay your steel," the shortest, burliest—and nearest—of the three dark-robed guests snapped at him, "in the presence of the king!"

Arclath knew that voice, even before its owner threw back her cowl: Wizard of War Lady Glathra Barcantle. The other two unhooded themselves more slowly, revealing themselves as Royal Magician Ganrahast, and . . . King Foril Obarskyr, the Dragon of Cormyr.

Arclath bowed deeply to the king, and Amarune hastily bobbed to her feet to thrust back her chair and give herself space to kneel. Storm kept her seat but smiled and nodded a friendly wordless greeting to the aging monarch—and Marantine Delcastle went right on giving him her best glare.

Ignoring the wand in Glathra's hand that rose to aim right at her, the matriarch of Delcastle Manor spat, "Is there a *reason* for this unwarranted, unwanted invasion of my home? Has Cormyr fallen so far that we no longer ask admittance, sending heralds ahead to request the *honor* of a meeting? Is the realm at war? Or have you just utterly forgotten due courtesy and the rights of citizens—those same rights you daily trumpet and hurl in every highborn face?"

"Mother," Arclath murmured.

Lady Delcastle rounded on him. "Don't 'mother' me, whelp! I bore and raised you, and expect your loyal support! I—"

"Merely desired to point out," Arclath interrupted her smoothly, "that you've asked His Majesty enough questions and that you owe him a breath or two to provide answers before you bury him under the next part of your tirade. As a man, I know when I'm reaching my limits of queries—and my mind is far less burdened than that of our Dragon."

"That's for certain," his mother replied with tart triumph. "Coherent thoughts all too seldom—"

"Cormyr is not at war," King Foril put in gently, his voice bringing instant silence. He added a wry smile. "Yet."

He took a step forward. "I apologize unreservedly for the invasion of your home and, ah, family peace, Marantine. I'd not have done this were matters not grave. I appeal to your love of Cormyr to give us of your patience, and I assure you that none of your people have been harmed in our intrusion. Is your friend and colleague Elminster here?"

"What?" Lady Delcastle asked, at the same moment as Arclath and Amarune both replied, "No."

"Why do you seek him?" Storm asked calmly.

"And why *here*?" Arclath asked sharply, earning his mother's approval. She nodded vigorously at his question, still favoring her unexpected guests with a stern frown. "Has Elminster been seen at Delcastle Manor?"

"No, no," Ganrahast said in a soothing voice. "We, ah, traced Lord Delcastle to this place."

"*How*?" Amarune snapped with sudden fire, surprising everyone. "Are you keeping watch over Arclath?"

"Ah, no, no," Ganrahast replied hastily, with all the uneasy smoothness of a temple priest unused to blunt challenges, "we merely hoped to find Lady Storm"—he favored Storm with a bow—"and Lord Elminster in his company."

"Evade not the question," Lady Delcastle snapped. "You traced my son magically, I take it? How, exactly? This high house and most others have wards to prevent such pryings, wards that I assure you will be renewed and redoubled on the morrow, but I *demand* to know by what means, as well as by what right, you presume to—"

"The means," Glathra said flatly, "are a state secret."

In the suddenly silent wake of her words, she realized everyone in the room was regarding her with a sour expression. Even Ganrahast.

"I'm permitted to say more?" she asked him, dubiously. "Is this wise?"

The Royal Magician sighed. "Tell them," he murmured, waving to her like a grand orator presenting a learned speaker.

Glathra sighed in clear exasperation and misgiving, then said to those seated around the table, "The name Vangerdahast will not be unknown to you. His continued existence to the present day should also come as no surprise to present company. Well, when Lord Delcastle here was recently assisting the mage Elminster to make use of the body of Wizard of War Appledown, Vangerdahast cast . . . a little something on Arclath. He didn't tell us this until now, whereupon we made immediate use of it."

"To find your way here. Does this trace persist?"

"You'll have to ask Vangerdahast, but he gave us to understand that our use of it ended it," Glathra replied reluctantly.

The snort Lady Marantine Delcastle emitted then was loud and impressive. "As if anyone can trust *anything* that old terror says," she told the ceiling. "I recall a night when he told me he'd respect me deeply in the morn—"

"Not *now*, Lady Delcastle," Glathra said hastily. "Please, not now."

King Foril's widening smile was a little sad. "We hastened here to confer with you, Lord Delcastle, hoping to find Lady Storm and Lord Elminster, too. We do *not* want strife between the Dragon Throne and Elminster, whom we judge could slay or harm many war wizards, given that the Crown and court are at present so beset by rebellious nobles and lurking enemies of the realm in Sembia and elsewhere—but his thefts of magic items in Cormyr *must* end."

"Foril," Lady Delcastle asked with a faint smile, "have you learned the habit of stern royal decrees at last? 'Tis a bit late, mind, but—"

"I have, Marantine," the Dragon of Cormyr said gently, his quiet voice again bringing silence. "Yet pray distract the converse not.

I have tarried too long, and in so doing plunged us into urgency. Lady Storm—I address the Marchioness Immerdusk now, as her monarch—where can we find Elminster?"

Storm met the king's gaze directly. "I know not. Both his fate and current whereabouts are unknown to me. He thrust all three of us back here to Cormyr in some haste. Yet rest assured he has no more need to take any magic from anyone, save for a few, very particular things. None of which, so far as I know, are to be found any longer within the Forest Kingdom, let alone the grasp of the Dragon Throne."

"Blueflame items?" Glathra snapped, as if interrogating a less than cooperative prisoner.

"Blueflame items," Storm confirmed.

"How can we trust you?" Glathra asked bluntly. "Forgive me, Lady Immerdusk, but you Chosen—you Harpers, for that matter—are known to say anything to get your own way, and we have no way of proving your words true."

Storm gave her a wry smile. "Rather like courtiers, or wizards of war, or nobles, aren't we?"

"There! That's *just* what I was speaking of! You turn me aside with a snide—"

"Lady Glathra," the king of Cormyr said firmly, "enough." He gave her both a quelling look and a raised reproving finger to still any protest, then he turned back to Storm.

Who said gently, "I should remind everyone I've known Elminster for a very long time, and serve the same Divine One he does. Forgive me, Glathra. Hear me, look into my eyes, and judge my honesty as I tell you: Elminster serves the goddess Mystra, as I do, before all other loyalties, even over his love of Cormyr—but he has been watching over Cormyr, in one way and another, for centuries. Longer than every king or queen, each Royal Magician and battle commander, every last highknight and gallant Purple Dragon veteran, Elminster has worked against Cormyr's foes, so this land could survive to settle its own scores, find its own way, and forge its own destiny."

"Forgive *me,* Lady Immerdusk," Glathra replied. "I think you sincere, and don't wish to give offense, but I must point out that pretty speeches are just that. You attest to Elminster's nobility of purpose, but we have most lately seen him as a thief, who repeatedly and very rudely defies rightful authority—and just now, we see him not at all. You tell us of his long service to the realm, but right now he could be anywhere, doing anything!"

"And courtiers deem we *nobles* 'rude,'" Arclath told the ceiling.

Storm put a quelling hand on his arm, and told Glathra, "Indeed he could be. Yet I've spoken with him on many recent occasions, spending more time with him than any other person alive, and can tell you that Elminster very much wants to work with the wizards of war—behind the scenes, that is, neither threatening the independence of the Dragon Throne nor awakening fears among your nobility that yet another sinister wizard seeks to make them dance to his desires. He'll contact you when he can. Service to Mystra governs him now, and has hold of him."

"I accept that," King Foril announced. "Let us have no more dispute as to the truth of what Lady Storm has told us. We can trust that Elminster is done with taking Cormyr's enchanted items, and would be our ally. Good." He nodded to Ganrahast and Glathra as if giving them a silent command, started to turn away . . . and then turned around again to give Storm a level look. "And you? Can we count on your loyalty?"

Storm regarded him calmly. "I am Mystra's servant first, and a Harper second, but serving and defending Cormyr has been one of my dearest strivings for some centuries now. Ask Alusair or Vangey, and you'll hear those words affirmed. I'll help Cormyr in any way I can, that Mystra forbids not."

"You speak of the Lost Goddess as though she yet lives," Ganrahast observed thoughtfully.

"Yes," Storm replied challengingly, "I do. Doubt not my sincerity nor sanity, Royal Magician. To do so would be a mistake."

Glathra shook her head. "Does anyone here suppose, just suppose, that you can be induced to tell us a little of what's been going *on,* this last tenday or so? Your running around the palace day and night, to the haunted wing and the royal crypt and seemingly every last broom closet we possess; the Sage of Shadowdale jauntily stealing all of our royal treasures that bear the slightest enchantments; that parade of you and the rest striding into the palace to use the Dalestride Portal . . . all of that?"

Storm smiled. "How much time can you spare? There's a lot to tell . . ."

Chapter Five

Deadly Good Breeding

"Dear tart," Mirt growled wittily, in his best imitation of an alluring purr, "have a tart."

The longer-limbed of the two beautiful and uninhibited ladies he'd hired for the evening gave him an impish smile and opened her mouth to receive the honey tart Mirt was offering her. The Lord of Waterdeep obligingly stuffed it in.

Then he sank back, a little light-headed. The scent of the mulled wine that filled their shared tub was getting up his nose, and beginning to slosh around in his head. Stars and sea storms, but he could get used to this!

"None for me, lord?" his other companion—aye, Lhareene, *that* was her name—pouted in his ear, the laughter lacing her voice reassuring him that she was jesting.

"*Plenty* for you, m'dear," Mirt replied, turning to kiss her. There was already a tart in Lhareene's mouth, and a strong thrust of her tongue shared it with him.

The Lord of Waterdeep found himself grinning through the inevitable shower of crumbs. Lhareene deftly glided up his chest, gently submerging him in wine until it started to soften the tart and sail it down his throat.

The taller pleasure lass—Arelle, aye, he *must* get back into the habit of remembering names, truly—reached past him to pluck some of the spiced and nut-studded sugared fruits from among the tarts on the floating platter. Mirt watched her consume them with as much hungry wanton abandon as if they'd been her lovers, and chuckled as he sank down under the wine and then surged up again, in a location and manner that evoked an explosion of mirth and a flurry of smooth limbs brushing against him.

He was really enjoying it in Suzail.

Free of the role of well-known target he'd grown all too used to in the City of Splendors, for one thing. Suzail wasn't half as large or wealthy or *raw* as his beloved Deep, but it offered plenty of excitement and danger, ready pleasures-for-hire such as those he was enjoying right now, and . . . well, he'd been thrust right into the heart of important doings, in a realm where things were *happening*. All in all, he was more alive, and having more fun, than he'd been for many a year.

"Lord," Arelle murmured, sliding over his wine-slick chest, "will you take . . . more?" She scooped up a handful of sugared, cinnamon-tinged icing and held it out to him.

"After I take care of this icing?" he jested, and her eyes danced.

"Of course."

Not wanting to be left out of things, Lhareene wormed her way up his other arm . . . "Aye," Mirt decided contentedly, aloud but telling himself more than either of his tubmates, "I'll stay here a while longer, I will."

Stay, rather than making the long, bone-jolting wagon or saddle trek to Waterdeep. Seeing as magic seemed to have become far less reliable, with fewer mages abroad who could casually teleport an aging Lord of Waterdeep across half Faerûn for any sort of affordable fee with much of a chance at all he'd arrive at his intended destination alive and . . . unaltered.

Elminster preened.

The tall, slender mirror was undamaged, the bedchamber around it untouched by the ravages of the glaragh. It was an odd, curlicued and dagged crescentiform shape, its "glass" a sheen-smooth sheet of polished mica that had been enspelled into a single gleaming sheet of black that reflected what stood before it.

Right now, that was Elminster in his newfound body. He turned it this way and that, setting his long, lithe legs to strike pose after hip-foremost pose.

This young body looked as good as it felt. Strong, supple, shapely—if a bit sharp-featured, both about the face and below—and attractive, oh yes, by Mystra and Sharess both . . .

He turned and watched himself—heh, *her*self, now—move, in the mirror.

"Hungry goddesses, aye," he murmured, turning again to thrust his behind at his reflection, augmenting it with an impudent flash of his tongue. "I might even fancy myself. Not that many men would dare pursue such a fancy far, given the reputation drow ah, enjoy . . ."

Oh, have done, *old goat. I was never* this *bad, even at my youngest and most ardent! We're in a hurry, remember? Portals? Spider-kissing priestesses? Perhaps a bored glaragh coming back?*

"Lady," El protested, "spare me a moment, at least. D'ye know how long I've been in pain, dragging around an aging carcass that failed me a mite more and a mite more with each passing day?"

Elminster, I do. Yet think on this: you'll have that aging to do all over again, dragging yourself around the Realms for another thousand years, or if not that, still long after I'm no more than a memory. A fading memory . . .

"Ye'll *not* be forgotten, lady," El said swiftly. "This I *swear*."

He struck another pose. "Now enjoy this with me! Regard the sleek line of flank, hip, thigh, and calf! I've never had *that* before!"

Not for lack of trying—if half I've heard about you is true, Symrustar said tartly. *And you sound like a butcher deciding where to land his cleaver!*

Elminster made a rude sound, waved one long-fingered hand in a less than polite gesture, and glided into another pose with fluid grace.

Ah, but it was good to have a body that obeyed his will again—without stiffenings and stabs of pain and ever-present aches!

El squatted deep and then sprang high, again and again, in a series of frog hops across the room, just because he could, ere joyously doing a cartwheel through the door into an antechamber that seemed to be half wardrobe and half armory.

He swept up out of it to the tinkling accompaniment of delighted laughter in his mind. Symrustar evidently approved.

Now to cover his oh-so-velvet and shapely newfound hide . . .

He cared not if this body strode the Realms unclad in any of the various diaphanous drapery robes—hideously hued in dunglike, glistening mauves and yellows, wherever they weren't black or sluggish-blood russet—he'd seen on most unarmored fallen she-drow around the riven citadel, but he did fancy some of the black drow armor. The lesser leather sort, rather than the fluted, pointed glass stuff. And knives, aye, he'd have himself some of those. There were wicked-sharp little obsidian daggers everywhere, their black blades upswept and beautifully balanced for throwing—and he'd always loved a good throwing knife.

Why, he'd taken down a magelord with a knife in the eye once, about twelve centuries back, and then there'd been that little duel in Cormanthor. Not to mention slicing a finger off that Zulkiir to ruin the spell the Thayan had been so proud of, and—

Is all this rolling around in past glories going to take long? In the depths of his mind, Symrustar sounded decidedly waspish. *"Long" isn't something I can spare much of, any more . . .*

"Sorry," El grunted, and he started to search. Hurriedly.

Despite that haste, it took him quite a while to find armor that fit properly—local dark elf fashion was skintight, which made finding the right garments rather important—but clouts and undercorsets and daggers in clip-on sheaths were plentiful. Good clouts had many uses, so El took an armful. Then he strapped daggers all over his body, not forgetting to fasten two sideways beneath his small, sleek breasts and a trio down inside the front of the corset to serve as extra armor.

"Not what a dark elf of good breeding might do," El murmured, "but I fear I'll never be that. Corrupt and fallen human, me." He twirled, just to feel such a spin done without pain, and laughed aloud as a thought struck him. "I'll be able to wear some of those splendid thigh-high boots! I've got the legs for it at last!"

Trying on the wrong boots can be painful, he discovered, but he was soon shod in comfortably fitting, soft lizardskin boots of a shining ebony hue. The mirror, at least, very much liked the look of them.

Deep in his mind, Symrustar snorted. Loudly.

Now a proper sword—the drow blades on hand all had wicked curves rather than a long, straight reach, but with this supple body he could dance in and out against a foe, rather than leaning and reaching as had slowly become his habit down the years, as his own aging body had gone gaunt and stiff. And he would need a staff.

Then he'd need two grapnel-ended climbing cords of the sort drow patrols hereabouts always carried; they could be tied around the trim waist he now had, riding on the largest hips he'd *ever* possessed. Then a shoulder sack, and food and drink—especially drink—to make that sack bulge to the last notches on its straps.

Hurry, man. You're worse than an elf maiden primping for her first revel!

"Oh, I doubt that, lass," El muttered, rushing along passages in search of kitchens or pantries to ransack. "I very much doubt that."

He found both almost immediately by literally stumbling into a small dining chamber dominated by an oval table heaped with slumped, mindless drow. The food under them was almost all crushed or spilled, but archways at the back of the room led into similar feasting rooms clustered around a central kitchen—a kitchen connected to larder after larder.

Dodging collapsed or wandering drow who had no minds left to notice a boldly wayward priestess in warriors' armor clambering among them, El ransacked the citadel's food stores at will. The good wine was all in fluted, fragile, utterly impractical bottles and decanters, but the soldiers' swill was in double-thickness skin belt pouches, and there was cheese, thin hard-smoked pack lizard steaks, and plentiful vallart, the dark, chewy crescentiform wayfarers' bread favored by many near-surface drow.

He took all he could stow, along with a battered metal mug a cook had been using as a measuring cup and a wickedly sharp little carving knife as long as one of his newly gained little fingers, thrust everything into two shoulder sacks that rode one atop the other like ungainly bulging bladders, one of them half-full of someone's huge, rock-dust-soiled, dark old cloak, and departed the ruined citadel, heading the way the glaragh had: with his face into that faint breeze that blew along the passage.

That Underdark wind just might be coming from the Realms Above, the lands he knew, and provided the only firm direction point in this endless subterranean labyrinth. Symrustar was right—

Of course.

Aye, and thank ye. Symrustar was right: he did not want to tarry overlong, and be caught there when more drow arrived and saw what had happened to their mighty fortress.

No, he wanted to be back in the surface lands, as swiftly as he could get there without blundering into death for his new body, or great delays. Not that he could call to mind any ways up that should be nearby.

He recalled the places he wanted to avoid, all right. Haunted Ooltul, with its phaerimm and beholders, and the patrols of giants that ranged out from Maerimydra. Yet if he stayed too distant from those perils, he risked walking right into the drow hunting bands that would become ever more numerous and frequent, the closer he got to Cormyr—and the drow city of Sschindylryn.

There were ways that rose—if they'd survived the initial tumult of the Spellplague, and the century or so since—up into caverns in the Stonelands, and some in the Storm Horns, too . . .

The Thunder Peaks routes might be best, if the dragons and dracoliches that laired in their uppermost caverns were gone, asleep, or preoccupied. Hah; *if.* Those ways would bring him to the surface on the easternmost border of Cormyr, where the Purple Dragon outposts were few and scattered. He had spells enough that he should be able to evade the notice of Cormyr's soldiery and easily reach the heart of the realm, where he could begin to follow Mystra's commands. Which he recalled precisely: "By any means you deem best—becoming their head or turning their leaders to my service—recruit Cormyr's wizards of war. They must become the ready allies, helping hands, and spies for all my Chosen."

If he conducted himself properly, El could do that without instantly coming to Manshoon's attention. Oh, that malevolently twisted one would notice him soon enough, and would need dealing with sooner or later . . . but for now, if El could manage matters thus, let it be later. He'd seen too many men and women—and Fair Folk, too—fall into the folly of fighting a favorite rival, spending their lives seeking to thwart and eradicate a foe; ere long, that striving became all their lives held and accomplished.

And you haven't taken that very same fall? Symrustar's voice rang through his mind in challenge. *Don't tell me you're such a fool that you can't see that!*

El sighed. "I see it all too clearly, lady. I've spent century after century being slapped across the face by such an obvious conclusion, after all."

And so?

"And so, Elminster of Shadowdale has more important work to do than to hold hard to any one foe or task. Since I began to avenge my family by bringing down the magelords, and in doing so learned my gift for the Art, I learned I could be more than a skulking slayer, and that Divine Mystra desired my service. Since then, I have *always* had more important work to do."

When we first met, I was drifting, seeing no fitting cause or reward, only corruption and decadence and a slow decline for my family and my city. That was part of my fascination with you: you had many things ahead of you; I could feel *it.*

El grinned. "All too often," he told that inner voice, "I felt it, too. Usually the lash of a spell, but sometimes the kiss of a blade."

All right, clevermouth. So, the Thunder Peaks?

"The Thunder Peaks," he confirmed. Those routes appealed for another reason, too. They crossed and crisscrossed, and ultimately came to the surface in a dozen different caverns or more. There was always a good chance not all of those caves would be blocked, occupied, or guarded.

Aye, he'd seek them, to arrive in the borderlands of Cormyr and there, far from Suzail and the watchful eyes of Manshoon, or for that matter Vangerdahast or Glathra, seek to join the war wizards under another name. Either in this new body, explaining it away as the result of a magical mishap—a lost spell duel, perhaps—or in another one, if a human body somehow became available. Then he'd take the slower but better road, making friends among them so as to rise in respect and usefulness, and spread his influence that way.

You make it all sound so easy. I hope it proves to be.

"So do I," El murmured, as he went cautiously on down the passage, well aware of the perils facing any lone creature on the move in the Underdark.

Surprisingly, he felt not the slightest foreboding, and his earlier rage had vanished. Now, he was almost merry; happier and more carefree than he'd felt in a long time.

Why so?

My, Symrustar was swift.

He grinned, and found himself saying, "Well, I'm back at work, serving Mystra—and that striving is what my life holds to, and accomplishes."

He walked along humming silently to himself, utterly contented.

Though he'd been lonely and longing for someone—anyone—to visit, to speak with him, to just to say his name, Rorskryn Mreldrake was less than happy now that it had happened. He was scared.

Just one cowled man had entered Mreldrake's prison, though he'd glimpsed—been shown—a man-high roiling darkness through the briefly half-open door that warned him his visitor was not alone.

It was one of the hooded wizards. He'd brought a sack heavy with cloth bags and small, fragile clay jars—no glass, nothing metal that could be used to cut or pierce—and set it down with the words: "The magical needs you so *calmly* requested."

Mreldrake had flushed at that, remembering his own angry shouts through the locked and bolted door. He'd lacked this and that—and any measure of patience, too.

Yet any mage as excited as he was over his work would be impatient to get on with it. For the first time in his life, he was creating something useful and important. Something more than a mere clever variant of a spell crafted by someone else, centuries ago. Something . . . new. Something his captors were interested in, which confirmed his suspicion that they were magically spying on him.

His visitor leaned back against the wall, folded his arms across his chest—his hands were male, and human, and looked strong but not young—and announced, "Time for a little demonstration, Mreldrake. Show us what you've accomplished thus far."

Mreldrake found himself sweating. "It . . . it's not much."

His visitor sighed. "I do, as it happens, possess some nodding familiarity with magical experimentation and creation. I understand matters can proceed slowly, and achievements may be small. Nevertheless, I am interested in what *little* you may have accomplished. Impress me."

"I . . . yes, of course." Mreldrake went to his notes, wiped his forehead on one sleeve, drew in a deep breath, and blurted out, "Well, you know I'm seeking to make air hard, like the well-known wall of force, but to have a keen cutting edge. Eventually giving me an invisible blade that can strike from afar, but I do mean eventually, and—"

"Words I can hear anywhere," the cowled man said softly. "Show me."

Mreldrake nodded wildly, gabbled assent, and peered at his notes again. Then he pointed across the room to where he'd set up his threads, pulled from the hem of his robes and secured to the top and bottom of an open-frame chair back with drops of wax from the candle lanterns.

"Observe," he gasped. "I—" He threw up his hands and abandoned all explanations, to stammer out an incantation as he carefully touched the things his captor had brought, one after another: down feathers from a she-duck, the shard of glass, the flake of metal from a sword blade that had drawn blood in battle, a human hair, and a drop of elf blood. He folded his touching finger into his palm as he sliced the air with the edge of his other hand, as if swinging a sword at the distant threads.

One of them obligingly parted, the severed ends dancing in the wake of the unseen force that had sundered them.

Mreldrake watched them, breathing hard. He was determined to make himself—a living, whole Rorskryn Mreldrake—part of this magic, somehow, so his captors couldn't simply dispose of him once he perfected the spell. Yet now, before he'd achieved that, he *had* to keep his intent to do so secret from them. Or they'd destroy him instantly, and find some other hapless mage to do this work for them.

That thought brought him right back to what had so puzzled him in the first place. He *wasn't* much of a wizard. They must see that. So why did they want Rorskryn Mreldrake?

"I—I can't . . . the magic fades swiftly with distance from the components, and I haven't yet begun to try to extend its reach." He panted, aware that he was drenched in sweat. He had provided the hair, and so was personally linked to the magic; would the man leaning against the wall suspect that he was deliberately trying to bind himself to the spell?

Whatever his captor knew or suspected, the man seemed pleased. "You've certainly been busy, Mreldrake. Keep at it, and *try* not to dissolve in fear at our every visit. We know more about your thinking than you'd no doubt like—and any fool can guess more of your schemes than what we can be certain of."

As Mreldrake froze, chilled by those drawled words, the cowled man strolled to the door, adding over his shoulder, "Let us know if you feel the need for a break in this work. We'll fill it by discussing with you details of the wizards of war, and daily life in the royal palace of Suzail."

"W-w-why?" Mreldrake dared to ask.

The cowled man stopped, turned unhurriedly to face his captive before tendering an elaborate shrug, and replied softly, "As wizards mightier than either of us have said before, it's always nice to learn new things."

Chapter Six

Danger For Hire

Lurth's Trading was not a shop in which Suzail's haughtier highnoses cared to be seen.

"Squalid" was a fair description of its dingy, dusty interior, a dark labyrinth heaped with stolen, broken, and well-worn wares of all sorts, from rusty saws and cleavers to rags that had been fine gowns thirty summers ago. Trade was brisk, because "used sundry" needs always outstrip ready coin, but few patrons ventured beyond the front of the shop, where the lantern-wielding proprietor and his two scarred and leering young fetchhands met anyone who stepped through the front door.

Very few visitors ventured through the door adjacent to the front entrance of Lurth's mercantile palace, let alone mounted the steep flight of dark and narrow stairs to reach the upper rooms of the building: the offices of Thurbrand and Arley, Wendra of the Willing Whips, and Splendors of the Shining Sea Importations.

Perhaps this was because the building was located in the poorer, rougher western part of Suzail. Or perhaps this was because Thurbrand had been dead for more than the decade that Arley had been a guest of the Crown dungeons, or because Wendra was older than many grandmothers and looked it, besides being less willing to taste her own lashes than she'd once been. Yet again, it might have had something to do with the fact that the Splendors had flourished importing illicit physics and powders that were now easily obtained at scores of Suzailan shops, and had since been reduced to selling daring scanty garments to men too embarrassed to purchase them in shops women might enter.

Wherefore business wasn't, to be blunt, too good, and a new sign was tacked to the Splendors door at the back of the upstairs passage, informing interested Suzail that a sideroom of the Splendors now housed a new establishment. That new sign told the world crisply: "Danger For Hire."

Judging by the looks of the two down-at-heel men lounging with their boots up on their desks, in lopsided chairs that threatened to collapse utterly and deposit them on their worn, sagging rented floor, the sign told the truth.

The more handsome of the two surviving partners in this crisp new business firm rejoiced in the name of Drounan "Doombringer" Harbrand. He was a tall man who always wore black from head to toe, and sported an eye patch that might have seemed more menacing if he hadn't long ago fallen into the habit of switching it from one eye to the other. Harband had just returned from an interview with a new client that had—at her insistence, discretion be damned—been conducted in more savory surroundings. Upon his return, in some triumph, he had tossed her payment for the deal they'd struck onto the vacant table between the desks, where it landed with a satisfyingly weighty crash.

That feeling of exultation had ebbed as he'd begun to tell his business partner the particulars of the arrangement, and they now stared rather grimly at the heavy sack of gold coins.

That partner was shorter and uglier than Harbrand, and far less elegant in appearance. Even if his nose hadn't been broken many times into a wreck of vaguely vertical shapelessness, the many crisscrossing scars that adorned his arms, head, torso, and knuckles told the world all too clearly that he was a brawler. A less than successful one, at that. But Andarphisk "Fists" Hawkspike did not appreciate such judgments, and most folk didn't dare to dispense them in his presence, given the more than a dozen daggers sheathed all over his rotting, greasy, much-patched leathers.

"Hrast it!" he snarled, spitting at the floor with enough accuracy to hit it, "I *knew* there'd be a tail-sting in this! There always is, with nobles!"

Harbrand sighed gloomily. "At least it's work. I've grown more than a bit tired of eating rats and table scraps thrown out kitchen doors."

Their client was Lady Dawningdown, the vicious matriarch of a minor, disgraced noble family of Suzail. She had offered them far too much gold to refuse, to do a "certain task" for her—plus the tail-sting Hawkspike had been expecting: the threat that they'd be hunted down and slain if they turned down her offer, now that she'd confided in them.

"Remember that," Harbrand added grimly. "Old Skullgrin sat there, flanked by four men who had loaded and ready crossbows trained on me. That fired poisoned bolts, she just happened to mention. If she's so determined no one learn of our hiring—well, if we succeed in our task, her bullyblades'll hunt us down and slay us, for that very same reason."

"Huh. Why don't she just send *them* to do it, and save her gold and our necks?"

"Because she has foes she fears, too, and doesn't want to risk being left unguarded while they make the trip," Harbrand explained patiently. "S'what *I'd* do."

His partner gave him a dark look, and spat on the floor again.

Their task seemed simple enough. They were to journey to the remote prison stronghold of Castle Irlingstar in the Thunder Peaks on the eastern border of Cormyr. Not the prison every Cormyrean knew about, the walled Sharren-cauldron of Wheloon, but a small castle few had heard of, where King Foril Obarskyr sent his *special* prisoners—such as traitor nobles too dangerous to put with murderers and thugs they could buy the loyalties of, and agents of Sembia and Westgate and other hostile near neighbors who'd use more public imprisonings as a pretext for war or royal assassinations or the like.

They were to free Lady Dawningdown's son and heir from Irlingstar, and get him safely over the border into Sembia. Officially, fire-tempered young Jeresson Dawningdown had been cast into Irlingstar for murdering a man, and ordering a hiresword to slay two more he'd quarreled with over cards, slayings that had been swiftly accomplished. However, all Cormyr knew Jeresson "the Rager" had really been confined in Irlingstar because he'd joined a cabal of young nobles plotting with Sembian sponsors to murder the entire royal family and put a Sembian on the throne of the Forest Kingdom.

Jeresson was to be delivered safely to Bowshotgard, a hunting lodge in forested northern Sembia, where Danger For Hire would receive the rest of their gold.

"And a handy waiting grave, I'll warrant," Hawkspike grunted gloomily.

He watched Harbrand get up and thrust the sack of coins into their usual hidey-hole in the side of the privy chute, and he spat on the floor again.

"Nobles," he growled. "I *hate* working for nobles. Trouble, always trouble."

Harbrand flashed a mirthless smile. "Goes with the gold. Coin, always coin. That's what *makes* them noble."

"Oh? Not birth? Not good breeding?"

Harbrand snorted. "Have you ever noticed any hint or shred of good breeding on the part of the nobles of this land?"

He let silence fall, then snorted again. "Thought not."

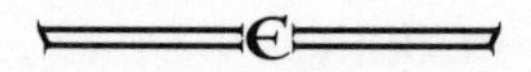

"What puzzles us most," Ganrahast said slowly, "is this 'Lady of Ghosts' who pursued all of you through the Dalestride Portal. Just who—hrast it, *what*—was she?"

Storm grimaced. "A mistake shared by Elminster and Manshoon. Her name is, or was, Cymmarra. Long ago, she was Manshoon's lover and apprentice—as were her mother and two older sisters.

Eventually, tiring of those three and wanting to be rid of them, the Lord of the Zhentarim sent them to kill Elminster. They failed, of course. Cymmarra alone he held back from that mission, but forced her to watch the deaths of her kin. Wild with grief and rage, she attacked Manshoon. He bested her easily with his spells, manacling her with magic, and forced himself upon her one last time—as he sought to slay her with a dagger thrust. You saw that blade, thrusting out of her, as she strode through the palace."

"Elminster's mistake was protecting her but not defending her," Ganrahast guessed.

Storm nodded soberly. "Manshoon couldn't kill her, and didn't—then—know why. She escaped, and for centuries hid from him in various guises, building her skills in the Art, awaiting the right time to take revenge on both El and Manshoon. She thought it had arrived." Storm shrugged. "She was almost correct."

"Almost," Glathra echoed bitterly, shaking her head. "Is Elminster's life one long succession of such cruelties and misjudgments?"

Storm gave her a calm look that was somehow more a challenge than any glare could have been. "Yes. As are the lives of Manshoon, and Vangerdahast, and any wizard who seeks to rule, or dominate, or defend a throne. As you may yet live long enough to have to admit, Glathra Barcantle."

Glathra flashed a glare. "I need no lessons—"

Catching the stern eyes of her king, she stopped in mid-snap, and asked more gently, "So are we rid of your meddlings at court and among our nobles, now? Or have you still unfinished work here in Cormyr?"

Storm's smile was friendly. "We do, so you're not rid of us yet. Forgive me, Foril, but Mystra commands us in this. She sees the wizards of war as vital to a bright future for all the Realms. Wherefore the corrupt among them—and in the ranks of your courtiers, too—must be uncovered and scoured out. *Without* causing *too* much of an uproar amid all the nobles seeking power, who will of course sense weakness and division, and rush to exploit it."

Instead of uproar and anger among the three guests, there was a silent exchange of meaningful glances.

"Good," the king said heavily, lifting a hand to forestall anything Ganrahast or Glathra might have said. "Not a moment too soon. Let that scouring begin."

He looked at Arclath. "With Lord Elminster and Lady Storm serving a higher authority than the Dragon Throne, I find myself still in need of a champion whose loyalty is to me. A personal agent, an untitled hand of my royal will who's no highknight, and who stands alone. Arclath Delcastle, will you—"

"I will," Arclath said flatly. "I'll be your agent, Majesty."

"The work will be dangerous," the king warned.

"That is my expectation," Arclath replied, in identically grave tones. That earned him a genuine royal smile.

Amarune caught the king's eye. "You are *not* keeping me out of this," she announced firmly. "Where Arclath goes, I go."

King Foril smiled again. "Of course. I was, as it happens, intending to hire you into my service, to be Lord Delcastle's Crown liaison. At, ah, four hundred lions a month?"

Amarune blinked in astonishment. Across the table, Lady Marantine hid a smile rather unsuccessfully, but beside the king, Glathra frowned, stirred as if to say something, caught another swift royal look—and kept silent.

Rune found herself swallowing, her mouth suddenly dry. She bowed her head. "Majesty, I accept. I hope you're not—we're *both* not—making a mistake, but I will take your service. Gladly."

"Good," the king replied firmly, parting his nightcloak. Unclasping a massive money belt from around his waist, he set it on the table, and gave the Royal Magician a glance.

Wordlessly Ganrahast divested himself of no less than seven such belts, one after another. As they clanked down in front of Amarune, the king told her, "Fifty lions per belt; your first month's pay. Can you start work immediately?"

"Y-yes, Your Majesty," the overwhelmed tavern dancer managed to reply.

"Good. Go straight to bed and get a proper sleep. By highsun tomorrow, I need you both well on the way to Castle Irlingstar, on our eastern border. Our worst problem just now, it seems, is there. Sembia—or someone reaching out of Sembia—has decided to take advantage of the current tumult among the nobility to take over that fortress and free the worst malcontents imprisoned there to work treason against Cormyr. I need that attempt stopped. I'm reinforcing the wizards of war there, too, but find myself in need of loyal, capable hands inside that keep that *aren't* attached to a Crown mage all nobles mistrust and are guarded against on sight."

Arclath frowned. "Hmm. I *know* some of the nobles you've—ahem, that have decided to dwell there. There may be deaths."

"Yes," the king agreed, meeting his gaze directly. "Unfortunate, but these things happen when a young noble newly sent to Irlingstar due to the displeasure of the Crown rubs up against old rivals and other hotheads, in a confined and remote keep."

"Ah," Arclath replied gravely. "I see."

The Dragon of Cormyr reached within his nightcloak again, and set two tiny metal flasks on the table in front of Arclath and Amarune. "Sovereign remedy. Effective against most known poisons. Given what some nobles are said to dip their daggers in, you may, I fear, have need of it."

"Foril," Lady Delcastle spoke up, sounding less than pleased, "it seems to me you intend to stain House Delcastle's good name. We'll suffer the disgrace of a public accusation of treason against my son and heir. No, more than accusation—confinement. And as a traitor to the Crown. This annoys me."

King Foril bowed to her. "Lady, I'm afraid this will be so. Pray accept my apologies. I might point out that given the current mood in Cormyr, the esteem of the Delcastles in the eyes of the populace—the nobility and those who aspire to nobility, at least—will undoubtedly rise. Moreover, I promise to apologize publicly and profusely, later, for the mistaken injustice I enacted upon your son, when I was led astray by the lying testimony of false nobles. I'll make amends by giving him a Crown office, too—title, salary, a coach and riding horses; the usual."

"Spoken royal promises," Lady Marantine said crisply, "are worth the proclamations they're not written on."

The king grinned like a young lad enjoying himself hugely, and turned to Ganrahast. The stone-faced Royal Magician reached under his nightcloak and produced a scroll, which he unrolled with a flourish to display to those at the table.

It was an already-written, signed, and sealed royal proclamation, outlining all that the king had just promised.

Amarune looked at the large, uncrumpled parchment, and then at Ganrahast's chest, and shook her head. "How did you *carry* all that?"

"Magic," he assured her solemnly. "It's all done by magic."

The drow who was now Elminster stopped thinking of how she might train young Rune—and the difficulties that would undoubtedly attend her appearing to Amarune Whitewave in the body of a dark elf, albeit a beautiful female drow—and stepped to one side, sinking down among the stalagmites and rubble nigh the tunnel wall.

I heard it, too, Symrustar said. *A weapon being readied.*

El nodded silently. Thanks to El's very recent work with silver fire and the spellbooks in the ruined drow citadel, ironguard was one of the spells she could now call on at will, without incantation, gesture, or components. She now did so. But it afforded no protection at all against enchanted darts or other weapons, or against poison. If need be she could use the silver fire—of which she still had a leaking overabundance, thanks to what the drow of the citadel had done to Symrustar, but she did not want to spend it in such a manner if she could avoid it.

She heard another tiny sound, the most fleeting of *clinks*. Metal, touching stone or other metal as it was moved; probably a blade being stealthily drawn, in another spot from the first noise that had alerted her. So more than one steel-armed foe awaited, just ahead. Drow, most likely, given the largely successful stealth, but they could be dwarves or gnomes or even humans. Now, which of those foes would show the most patience?

El had been making good time along a tunnel deserted in the wake of the glaragh, and had walked far from the riven citadel, moving faster than any wary pursuer not using wings or scuttling along the passage ceiling. She'd kept close watch on the ceiling, both before and behind, and seen nothing more than occasional small bats, beetles, and spiders. The glaragh had evidently devoured or frightened away anything larger and more intelligent.

Yet she'd passed through several caverns where the great worm could have taken a different route. She'd kept following the breeze, because the tunnel, though far from straight, was tending onward in the general direction she desired to head. The glaragh might not have taken this particular tunnel, this far. Fair fortune, even for the most favored of Tymora, only lasted so long . . . and the luck of Elminster of Shadowdale, it seemed, had now turned.

Her ears caught the faintest of hisses, sibilants of words she couldn't quite make out. Someone whispering in Undercommon into the ear of someone else; someone with a high-pitched, light, soft speaking voice. Drow, or she was a real arachnomancer.

Not that this new body would protect her in the slightest. Priestesses of Lolth were not loved at the best of times, and if caught alone were likely to be . . .

You have *been caught alone, El,* Symrustar reminded her tartly. *So, now?*

Now, of course, it was spell hurling time.

For an archmage with mustered spells ready, this would have been a mere moment's concern. For a prepared and unharmed Chosen of Mystra, with Mystra and the Weave to call upon at will, even less of a challenge. But for what was left of this particular Chosen, right now . . .

El backed away around a buttress of joined stone pillars—fused stalactites and stalagmites—surrounded by a small forest of lesser stone fangs, and sank down again.

Was that movement, across the tunnel?

Aye, someone seeking to steal forward and flank her. Over there, too, a flash of movement—not forward or back, but a raised hand flicking fingers in intricate patterns. The silent sign language used by drow. Letting a tight smile cross her face, El cast a long, careful spell that would shape stone, on the fissured roof of the tunnel ahead, directly above where most of those waiting to pounce on her were probably waiting. If a worker-of-Art forced stone into a shape that was anchored insufficiently—a large inverted mushroom, say—then sought to rapidly flatten it out . . .

With a sharp *crack* and roar, a lot of stone ceiling plummeted down, to crash amid shouts and shrieks, shatter, and hurl shards in all directions.

El spared no time watching or gloating. She was already snatching out knives and turning to face—

Her stealthy outflanker. The dark elf sprang up over rubble along the far wall and raced toward her, firing a handbow as he came.

El's first flung knife met the bow's dart in midair, sending both missiles skittering wildly aside. El's second snarled across a bracer on the charging drow's raised forearm. And El's third found one of the drow warrior's eyes, and made the last moments of his charge collapse from a hard sprint into a wavering, dying stagger.

El danced back down the tunnel, turning to face the area where she'd brought the ceiling down. More drow warriors rushed her from there, some bleeding from jagged cuts made by flying shards of stone. Males, every one, a scarred and ragtag bunch clad in all mismatched manner of salvaged, patched, and no doubt stolen armor. Outcasts, seven strong—no, there were nine or more. None of whom would revere or obey a lone priestess, no matter how tall and menacing she seemed.

A scrape of sword on stone behind El made her spin around and leap for the tunnel wall at the same time.

Five more drow males were coming at her from behind, grinning unpleasantly.

Surrounded, greatly outnumbered, and—

Doomed?

"Symrustar," El told her gently, "ye're not helping.'

Drow rushed in from all sides.

Chapter Seven

Murder In Irlingstar

Royal Magicians and the senior courtiers they most trusted have been many things down the long years of Obarskyr rule over the Forest Kingdom, but one thing they were not—often—was fools.

Wherefore it had long been the practice in Cormyr to order matters such that one official or soldier watched over another, as part of daily duty. So it was that in Castle Irlingstar, Lord Constable Gelnur Farland was warden of Irlingstar's prisoners, commander of those who guarded them and responsible for that guarding, but did not have command of the keep itself. Above Farland was the seneschal of Irlingstar, Marthin Avathnar, who gave direction to the lord constable and was in charge of the physical upkeep of the castle, but in truth had the most essential task of being a watchdog over any lord constable who might get too friendly with such urbane and wealthy noble prisoners.

Avathnar was a pompous little man, short and stout but proud of his appearance when he strode around Irlingstar in his brightly polished silvered armor. Yet he was neither dull-witted nor lax in his diligence, and had reported three lord constables in his time, all of whom had promptly been reassigned and one of whom had soon met with an unfortunate "accident" that many suspected hadn't been accidental at all. Word of that had reached him, Avathnar knew, as a gentle reminder not to stray from the path of diligent loyalty.

He hadn't the slightest intention of doing so. Cormyr was the fairest land in all the Realms, not to mention the best place to dwell in any hopes of enjoying a retirement to a modest country estate with a decent cellar of wine, boar and rothé enough to eat roasts every night if one wasn't sick of them, and a fair young wife to wait upon one's needs—even if one was short and unsteady and afflicted with bunions.

If Lord Constable Farland loved him not, too bad, and what a proud badge that dislike was, betokening his own proper fulfillment of his duties. A beloved seneschal was a lax seneschal, or even a seneschal happily and frequently bribed. And he would never be either the one or the other, by the Dragon on the Throne, oh, no, not Marthin Avath—

Someone interrupted his thoughts, just then.

Forever.

Someone reached out from a dark, yawning doorway just behind the strutting seneschal—where a door should not have stood open, a lapse Avathnar really should have noticed, though securing interior doors was more properly a constabulary duty—and briskly plucked the seneschal's grandly plumed helm off his head. That headgear had always been a trifle too large for Avathnar, and came off easily—straight up, into midair. The same someone then stabbed a fireplace poker with brutal force, log-spike first, into the back of the seneschal's exposed and balding head, crushing Avathnar's overlarge skull like a raw egg.

There was just enough time, as the little man swayed onward but hadn't yet toppled, to drop the helm back into place. A bare instant before Marthin Avathnar *smacked* down on his face like a large and fresh flounder being slapped down on a kitchen beating board to be flensed into mush for a fish sauce.

The wielder of the poker melted silently away, and a tomblike silence descended on the passage. It lasted for some time before the sound of distant boots arose, strolling in the right—or wrong, depending on one's viewpoint—direction.

Marthin Avathnar had been a coldly polite, precise man. It was his duty to be so, but it was a duty that suited him and one he did all too well. Wherefore no one in Castle Irlingstar liked him. Not even his personal staff. As for the noble prisoners confined at Irlingstar, they didn't like any of their captors much. So it was hardly to be expected two of them would grieve when they came upon Avathnar's body. In fact, had a guard not been right behind that first pair of nobles, and hastened upon catching a glimpse of an armored form sprawled on the flagstones, they'd have swiftly plundered the dead man for weapons or keys. As it was, the two nobles merely bent to make sure the gleaming-armored seneschal of Irlingstar was dead, smirked when they saw he was, then went to lean against the nearest wall to fold their arms and enjoy the spreading tumult among their captors.

"I'm left quite desolate by this," one noble murmured merrily.

"Oh?" another drawled. "Myself, I grieve deeply."

"Desolated, are you? I was desolated once . . ." A third sneered, joining them.

"Go from this place," the guard snapped at them. "All of you."

None of the prisoners moved.

"*Move,*" the guard added. "Get you gone. *Now.*"

"Or?" A noble asked tauntingly, eyebrows rising in exaggerated fear.

"Or I'll regard you as murderers, and execute you forthwith," the guard said firmly, half-drawing his sword. "*Before* you can get word to your families or anyone else."

Scowling, the three nobles pushed themselves off from the wall as slowly as they dared, dispensing rude gestures and insults, and retreated. Not far.

Glowering at them and keeping one hand near the hilt of his ready sword, the guard unlocked a door and struck the alarm gong waiting in the closet behind it. Then he went to stand over the body, giving it a glare for good measure.

This was going to be bad.

It was bad already, and if his years of service had taught him anything at all, things were going to get worse at Irlingstar before they got better.

Much worse.

The little eyeball floated just out of reach, just as it always did, its silent stare mocking him.

Mreldrake tried not to look at it, but he could feel the weight of its regard every instant, as he struggled to wield his new magic with ease and precision and not the wild, sweating messes his last few castings had been.

It was *hard,* hrast it all! Holding empty air together in a sharp, slicing edge of hardened force, an edge gathered around his own awareness, so he could "see" out of it at a distance and through solid walls and other barriers he couldn't truly see through or around. That edge could cleave stone, with enough firm will behind it.

Far more strength of will than Rorskryn Mreldrake seemed to have, even when fiercely determined or desperate. Whenever he dragged his wavering edge of force into a wall or floor, the spell broke, leaving him reeling and clutching his aching head, half-blinded by a sudden flood of tears and momentarily at a loss to recall where he was or what he'd been trying to do.

Right now, in a bare room very similar to the one he was trapped in, on the far side of what until a short time ago he'd thought was a solid wall, a chicken was roaming freely. Pecking, strutting, even fluttering . . . as his will-driven edge of force pursued it, seeking to decapitate it.

It had seemed such a simple command: "Behead yon fowl."

His view of the room wavered again, and with a curse he fought to focus the air once more into a sharp, clear edge. And . . . succeeded. He was drenched in sweat, tiring fast, and this *hrasted* chicken seemed to want to *fly!*

It fluttered its wings again, bounding into the air and squawking loudly. Across the room it scurried, flapping this way and that as it went, and bobbing up and down, too. Almost as if it were taunting him, just like the watching eyeball.

Die, you stupid bird, *die*!

Savagely Mreldrake bore down with his will, sweeping his invisible blade of force up and after the chicken.

Which obligingly landed, folded its wings, blinked, and started to peck.

It bobbed up, took a few steps, looked around—and bobbed again, a scant instant before Mreldrake's blade swept through the spot where its neck had been.

"Nooo, you tluining little harrucker!" he spat, his mind-view of the room next door wavering again as his blade started to thicken, wobble, and slide toward collapse.

"No! Not this time!"

In a sharp surge of rage he narrowed the blade again and turned it, not caring if he crushed the fowl or starved it of breath by sucking every last whit of air in that room into his killing blade. This chicken was *doomed*!

Thinner and sharper than ever, the blade swept down. The chicken bobbed down to peck, took two slow steps forward without straightening up, then suddenly reared up to blink, look around, blink again, and look satisfied.

Which was when he *finally* reached it—and took off its head with the ease of a rushing wind, without it so much as uttering a peep. The bloody head landed with a wet plop behind him as his sharp awareness rushed on, and the room around him turned over and over, wavering . . . and was gone.

Exhausted, Mreldrake sagged down, stinging sweat running into his eyes, seeing his own prison chamber once more. The secret door he'd not known about before today, the one that connected his room to the one he'd just beheaded the chicken in, swung slowly open by itself to reveal the tiny, headless feathered bundle swaying amid much blood.

"Well, now," came the voice of one of his captors out of the empty air above him. "Progress we can all be proud of."

Yes, those words held distinct mockery.

"Rorskryn Mreldrake, you've earned your supper. Well done."

Too breathless to answer, Mreldrake lay with his eyes closed, already knowing what the voice would say next.

"And it's very fresh. Killed moments ago, in fact. Chicken!"

"Did you see the way Lady Glathra was *looking* at us?" Amarune murmured. "I was hard put not to shiver. *She* doesn't want us working for throne and king, to be sure. I think she'd be happiest if neither of us lived through this night."

Arclath smiled. "You think it was an accident Ganrahast told her he needed to meet with her urgently and immediately, as they left? Or that the king seems to have left more than a dozen guards behind, to spend the night standing around outside our walls?"

Rune frowned. "You think she'd *dare—?*"

The heir of House Delcastle shrugged. " 'Twouldn't be the first time a wizard of war—or a high-ranking courtier—decided to 'help' the hand of Tymora. Or even the most likely unfolding of events, either. I doubt Glathra's that bold, myself, but the prepared warrior is the less dismayed warrior, as they say."

He paused at a particular door and knocked softly at it. It promptly opened, and an elderly servant stepped out of the room beyond it to bow deeply to Amarune and hand her a lit lantern.

"All ready, lord," he murmured to Arclath, and he hastened off down the passage without another word.

Lord Delcastle ushered his lady love through the open door. "My mother chose this room for you because the door has stout bolts, here and here, so you can keep all Cormyr at bay, the night through. The window's too small for most men to get through, and overlooks a *long* fall into the courtyard—where some of our men are always standing guard. Oh, and there's *no* secret passage."

They traded grins, ere Arclath added, "Above you is only roof, and beneath you the ceiling of the back feasting hall—a good twelve man-heights above its floor. We've only two ladders tall enough to reach it, and we could scarcely fail to notice anyone trying to sneak in here with a ladder *that* long . . ."

"But if she tries anything at all," Amarune murmured, "she'll use magic, not the swords of Purple Dragons storming your house, surely?"

Arclath shrugged. "We have wards. If they aren't strong enough, well, I guess that'll be that." He grinned. "You really think one angry Crown mage will go to all that trouble to punish the notorious Silent Shadow?"

Rune did not smile back at him. "Arclath," she whispered, "I wasn't thinking about me. My worry is for you."

The lord constable of Irlingstar stared down the passage, over the body of the fallen seneschal, at all the Purple Dragons he'd summoned. Every waking guard in the castle was here except for the on-duty door guards, the stair wardens, and of course the mages. They were all his to command.

The faces staring back at him were grim. The guards of Castle Irlingstar were upset, of course. They'd been more angry than fearful at first, but that had changed when they'd discovered the kitchen staff slaughtered, and much of the food in the castle pantries taken or deliberately tainted. They had been less than gentle while shoving the prisoners back into their cells and locking them in—and the lord constable had agreed wholeheartedly with that rough treatment. Sneering murderers.

"Dumped chamber pots into the open ale keg, they did," one Dragon snapped indignantly, "and emptied their bladders all over the puddings."

"The spitted birds? The sausages?"

"Gone," was the bleak reply.

Lord Constable Farland wasted no effort on curses. He merely pointed at two men and commanded, "Stand guard over the kitchens. They're not to be left unattended for as long as it takes you to blink, from now on. Choose two more to relieve you when you grow tired."

Then he pointed at four more Dragons. "Search everything. The flues of every last chimney, all the spices in the pantry; the lot. Set aside everything that's been spoiled or even *possibly* poisoned, and make very sure the chimneys haven't been blocked and no little traps left waiting for anyone trying to use kitchens or larders. When done, one of you—you, Illowhond—report to me. In my office, where I'll be conferring with both senior constables."

Farland looked slowly around at all of the gathered guards, his face as calm and expressionless as he knew how to make it, and said curtly, "There will be goading. Pay careful attention to anything any prisoner might let slip, but keep a close rein over yourselves. I expect you to remain the professional veterans you all are. Return to your stations and duties."

Collecting Traelshun and Delloak with stares and a jerk of his head, he turned on his heel and started the long trudge back to his office, not bothering to look down again at what was left of Seneschal Avathnar.

This was one more headache he didn't need, but there was something fitting, even satisfying, when the gods saw to it that vain, thickheaded men reaped the rewards of their own stupidity. Now, if the gods could just see to it that Cormyr held a few more Traelshuns and Delloaks, and a lot less of the likes of Avathnars . . .

Not that he expected them to. The gods had a long, long list of things to see to, and some of them had been waiting for centuries.

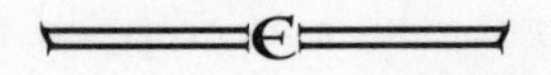

Sixteen left.

Elminster nodded; she was panting too hard to answer Symrustar aloud. This new body was as agile and deft as it was lovely, and she'd managed to find a small stretch of level, smooth rock underfoot, hard against of the tunnel walls, but sorely outnumbered was . . . sorely outnumbered.

It had grown to more than thirty against one when the fray had begun, and at least one of those outcast drow males was a wizard who'd been casting spellstop after spellstop at El, while taking care to keep well out of reach behind the rest as they'd closed in, stabbing and hacking.

The ironguard was all that had kept her alive in those first frantic moments. The profanely shouted desire of some of El's attackers to "Leave enough of her to enjoy!" had helped her kill a few as they'd hesitated to be really brutal to her torso, though most of her armor had been so viciously and repeatedly hacked that it flapped and dangled, protecting her against nothing.

Just once, they'd gained sense enough to all rush her together, trying not to slay but rather to catch hold of her arms and legs and bear her down onto the rocks, to hold her helpless by sheer weight of numbers and cruel strength. So someone could stab her or slice open her throat, and make an end of her. At last they'd taken her down. Spread-eagled and struggling vainly, El had seared those holding her closest with the tiniest outrush of silver fire, a deadly momentary spitting she hoped no one would recognize for what it was.

In an instant, those who'd tasted it most deeply were far too dead to bear witness to anything. Giving off wisps of smoke and the hearty smell of cooked flesh, they sagged and fell away, leaving the less injured to hiss curses and scramble clear as fast as they knew how. Leaving their lone quarry to struggle to her feet and face them, breathless and bleeding freely from the bites of enspelled blades the ironguard could only lessen. El stood alone, the cooked dead slumped around her in a blackened and smoking ring, watching the surviving drow draw back to mutter together.

Their mage was hissing something at them, probably about how he could work a spell to see that most of their bolts got through whatever defenses a lone spider priestess could manage, if they held back and all fired their handbows at her at once. El didn't wait for them to ready such a volley, but ran at the nearest drow, swinging her hooked sword in a vicious slash. The dark elf parried it easily, deflecting her blade aside with a triumphant sneer—whereupon she brought it swinging around to bite into the handbow hooked to his belt, ruining it, before she sprang back and ran on.

The next drow had seen what she'd done, and turned to shield his bow from her with his body. She took advantage of that to rush past and around him in a tight circle, until in his turning to keep facing her he overbalanced. She promptly made the same slashing attack, but this time the parry sent her blade up through his throat.

By then, all the drow were converging on El. She fled back to her open fighting ground with the blades of the fastest outcasts slicing at her backside. More of her leathers fell away as she sprang across a drift of tangled and blackened drow bodies, spun around, and ducked low in a lunge that spitted one pursuing dark elf who was too close and moving too fast to stop himself in time.

He went down noisily and messily, taking El's sword with him, and she sprang back again to give herself space and time enough to snatch up some swords from the fallen before the sixteen surviving outcasts reached her.

She had a scepter that could blast down one drow at a time, if it behaved like all the other scepters of the same design she'd seen in the past, but she needed time enough to use it on one obliging target after another. The bite of just one sword would make it explode—and her ironguard would help this shapely body not at all against *that*.

Gnaw-worms as long as a drow arm wriggled down the tunnel walls, drawn by the smell of spilled blood and cooked death. The wizard's spellstops hung in the air around El like unpleasant smells, clinging to her. They would hamper rather than truly stop spells, but just one of them would slow magics too much to keep her alive in a sword fight—and the dung pile had cast six of them, hrast him.

The drow were wary of her now, and moving slowly to ring her, keeping their blades ready and their eyes on her.

"I don't *like* fighting," Elminster murmured aloud, to no one in particular. "I'd rather be left alone, to spend my days messing around with the Art. Trying new things, creating, feeling the flows . . ."

Inside his head, Symrustar nodded wordless agreement and approval, as together they recalled magic unleashed, beautiful glows rushing out into the night . . .

The drow were coming.

El backed to the wall before the sixteen could encircle her, yielding most of the flat stone floor so as to have solid rock at her back. All they had to do was come at her four at once, one to each side and two in front of her, and not let her draw one of them into another's way . . . and she couldn't hope to parry them all.

Of the spells she'd just burned into her mind, she was using the ironguard, and could see an immediate use for the guardian blades, the timetheft, and the—oh, but *hey*, now! If she . . . aye . . .

Yes, Symrustar agreed.

She mustn't forewarn them. Cast the whirlblade storm in careful silence and then hold it in abeyance, waiting until they were all emboldened enough to draw near. Aye, go down fighting, and let them think they'd slain her. There, 'twas done . . .

And here they came.

Chapter Eight

Rousing The Dragon

The drow advanced on El from all sides, their eyes baleful. They moved in slowly, readying their handbows.

Hrast. She crouched, the swords she'd snatched from their fallen fellows held ready, the blades turned sideways to serve as tiny shields. Yet she'd have to be falcon-fast, and have the very luck of all the gods, to deflect a fired dart before it struck her.

The silver fire could burn away poison, but oh, did it hurt. Her eyes and throat, she must protect above all else—

They all loosed at once, many darts singing in at her.

El flung herself aside, along the rock wall, slashing the air in front of her face with both blades in a wild crisscross flurry that sent three darts or more clanging aside.

A dart smote her forearm hard and stuck there, where her armor had been hacked away. Another ripped into her left breast, and a third hit hard high on the inside of her right thigh.

The drow charged, flinging their handbows down and running hard. Most of the darts had missed her, but a warm burning spreading swiftly through her told El the three that had struck her bore poison of some sort, probably spider venom. If it was handspider or stinglash, it would slow her and eat away at her, numbing and eventually paralyzing her. She had to end this swiftly.

El rushed to meet the closest drow, cut at his face, then ducked aside to slash at the next nearest. Then she spun and raced for the wall, trying to get back to the spot she'd chosen to make her stand. They came after her like wolves.

When she pretended to stumble, then fall, they pounced. Only to watch her roll, spin around on her shoulders, and kick up at them. She boosted one rushing drow over her and sent another staggering aside, then rolled after him and viciously sliced his ankles out from under him.

He toppled, shrieking, and El sprang up, slashed out his throat, and danced forward to meet the next wave of charging drow: four dark elves in motley armor, one lurching along on a leg that had been wounded long ago. Beyond his bobbing shoulder she briefly caught sight of gnaw-worms wriggling among the rocks, seeking the dead, and the drow wizard spending a spell on another arrival: a roaming wild spider he might think she'd summoned. Eerie fire burst into being around the arachnid, making it convulse—and then El was too busy fighting four drow at once to see more.

Two used small knives to stab at her, wielding their swords only to fend her off. Those knives glowed, which meant they knew she was protected against unenchanted steel. The other two drow bore no glowing weapons, so El paid attention only to their arms and movements, to keep them from knocking her down, ignoring the blades that passed through her like smoke. That let her slip behind one, so a knife meant to gut her slammed hilt-deep into his belly instead.

El elbowed that groaningly wounded drow into the warrior behind him, and sprinted away from them all to fence for a moment with yet another outcast, who gave ground, his face tight in alarm as he defended himself, seeking only to parry.

She spun away from him and ran, heading again for the spot she'd chosen for her stand, the smooth rock that was lower than its surroundings. This time she made it.

Spinning around again to face her foes and gulping in deep breaths, fighting to get her wind back, she watched them come for her again.

In a tight pack this time, angry and wary at how many of their fellows had fallen, the wizard crouching low behind them.

"That won't save him," El murmured aloud, slow anger beginning to stir in her. She had her breath back now; let them come . . .

Sound the warhorns, Symrustar murmured in her head, sounding amused. *The* real *bloodletting begins.*

There were fourteen coming for her now. The fifteenth was down among the rocks behind them, rocking and groaning as he clutched his deeply stabbed belly. The boldest gnaw-worms were already converging on him.

Time for a little goading. El gave the advancing drow a sneer, waved the three darts still hanging from her where she'd left them—to let her blood spill more slowly than if she'd plucked them out—like a grand hostess showing off treasures, then struck a hand-on-hip pose and beckoned her foes mockingly.

One drow promptly shouted a war cry. He and four others rushed El, the rest following more slowly.

Good. Now for the ruse. She met them with both blades, seeking to slay rather than defend herself, feigning agony when two drow swords slashed through her. One blade left behind the fresh fire of more spider venom, but neither did her any other harm—as she spitted one warrior hilt-deep on her sword ere letting go of it, and slashed open the face of another.

They all went down together in a heap, one drow dying and another blinded by his spurting blood and oblivious to everything except the agony of holding his face together with both hands. El cut his throat in the same slash that drove her blade into the neck of the drow beside him, who was busily scrabbling to pick up the blade he'd dropped in his fall.

That left two drow alive and unharmed. One was already stabbing her repeatedly, his unenchanted blade doing no harm but his weight and the knuckles of his stabbing hand driving the wind out of her repeatedly and bruisingly. The other was crouching behind the enthusiastic stabber and reaching around to grab at her scepters, trying to snatch them and hurl them away before daring to get closer. El sliced some of his fingers off, then drove her sword up through herself—she felt nothing but a momentary shivering chill—to meet the pumping sword hand of the drow trying to stab her.

He shrieked and fell aside, clutching at his sliced-open hand—and El rolled and reached in an awkward crawling lunge across sharp rocks that slid her sword into the throat of the scepter-grabber. As he convulsed, she rolled back again to deal with the stabber.

The rest of the dark elves advanced slowly, still about seven or so strides away. Good. El threw back her head as she hewed down the stabbing drow and screamed in false agony, her voice loud, raw, and shrill.

Then she slumped, down in her hollow with drow bodies all around, lying as if dead—save for the stealthy hand beneath her that slid a scepter from her belt and awakened it. She lay still, waiting, her mouth slack and open. Smarting from half a dozen wounds and the numbing fire of the venom, El watched through slitted eyes as the drow gathered cautiously above her.

Would they come closer to gloat? Or stab down at her face and breast and throat, to make sure?

They did both—and as the first dark sword tips thrust down, El let loose the whirlblade storm.

It was a vicious magic, not all that different from the blade barriers war priests of old were wont to wield, and as its shards of steel started to flash and whirl above her, and drow blood started to spray, El called up swift silver fire to spin a momentary shield over herself. As it closed over her, she flung the awakened scepter up into the storm of conjured steel, an instant before cowering under her silver fire.

A moment later, the world just above exploded with a roar.

The blast was impressive, shaking her like dice in a gambling cup despite the shielding fire. She heard and smelled drow bodies spattering wetly over rocks all around . . . and when her shield faded and she rolled cautiously over to look up, drow gore dripped down into her face from the tunnel ceiling high above.

She rolled into a crouch, to peer around cautiously. Not a foe remained. Wizard and all, the outcast drow band was no more.

Dead, every last one of them. And all because they hated and feared magic. Or those who misused it against them, like their own priestesses. *No one* should hate or fear magic.

Ah, El, that *would require the Realms to be free of all who use magic to be tyrants over others.*

El sighed aloud. Symrustar was right. And how often had he been one of those tyrants, those misusers?

Memories she was not proud of rose in a swift, dark procession . . .

Wisely, Symrustar kept silent. Rather grimly, El tugged the darts out of herself, then healed her wounds and purged the venom in an agonizing burst of silver fire.

When her helpless gasping and staggering faded, she stumbled on down the tunnel. She was little better than naked now, her leather armor in tattered ruin, and still alone.

Now, now! You do *have me,* Symrustar reminded her. *Nicely done, by the way.*

El nodded wearily. She'd made far too much noise and loosed too much magic to tarry; all that tumult would soon bring more formidable Underdark prowlers—or a strong drow patrol, ready for spell-hurling trouble. By then, it would be only prudent to be far away. Up in the sun-drenched Realms Above, for instance.

Limping a little, and rubbing at aches here and bruises there, El trudged along.

This beautiful new dark elf body of yours, Symrustar chided her, *you're not taking very good care of it.*

Elminster's reply was calm, lengthy, and very colorful. It might have made some Moonsea sailors blush, if any of them had been down in the Underdark Shallows to hear it.

Alorglauvenemaus slept more soundly and more often, these days, than in its younger years. It was well and truly ancient now, and knew from its studies and from wyrms it had met—and in some such moots, slain—that these deepening slumbers were the norm for older dragons.

Not that it experienced many interruptions. No visitors reached this cavern beneath a volcano-like hollow hill, in the heart of a fetid swamp filling a narrow cleft between the stony shoulders of adjacent mountains in the Thunder Peaks. No intruder had ever reached its lair, though orcs had splashed into the swamp once, very briefly. Not good eating, but there'd been a lot of them . . .

It curled its long tongue, trying to remember that taste.

Yes, it so happened that Alorglauvenemaus was awake now—so it was awake a moment later, when an explosive unleashing of magic shuddered through the solid rock beneath its hoard. A blast had befallen several levels beneath its lair.

The ancient black dragon lifted its head in alarm. That had been more than a spell. There was a certain smell . . .

Alorglauvenemaus thrust its dark horned head down the great cleft at one end of its cavern, the opening to the descending chain of caverns that served it as a toilet, a spittoon, and betimes a vomitorium—for armor causes gut ructions, no matter how steaming-strong one's digestive acids—and sniffed, loud and long.

Aye. It *was*. The scent was faint, yet unmistakable, and Alorglauvenemaus had smelled it before. Silver fire, the raw stuff of the Weave, had been unleashed down there.

Which was puzzling, even alarming, given that the Weave had fallen, and its bright goddess with it, some sleeps ago.

The ancient black dragon frowned, shook its head slowly, and let out a deep, cavern-shaking growl that announced to the reverberating cavern walls that it was not pleased to encounter that particular scent. That smell meant trouble.

Yet Alorglauvenemaus knew how to deal with trouble. It drew back its head and spat, letting out a great hissing breath of sickly green acid, a burst that struck foam from the rocks it touched as it bounced and boiled down the long chute of caverns.

As it went, that green, swiftly graying flow hissed and spat and spewed forth many momentary little whirl devils of glowing spume, stuff of the rocks it was eating into; rocks that were already pitted and worn smooth by previous acid spewings.

Three caverns down, the last fading tongue of the acid flowed around a heap of rocks, washing away some of the shoulder of stone they stood on. Almost wearily the heap slumped over the edge, starting to roll and tumble. And awakening a gathering roar as it went on down. In the end, much lower down, it had faded into a small rockslide, but it spilled out of a side cleft in the tunnel almost to Elminster's feet.

El stopped to let the last stones of the rattling little avalanche roll to their various stops right in front of her boots, rock back and forth, then settle. The faint breeze came down into the Underdark by the same route the rocks had taken.

And it was bearing a sharp, fresh reek. She'd smelled this particular acrid stink before.

Black dragon acid. Spewed by a large elder wyrm.

Elminster sighed. A fell and mighty dragon in her way. Of *course*.

She went into the cleft and started to pick her way very cautiously upward. The acid was still fresh; she'd have to be careful indeed if she wanted her boots to last for most of the way up, or longer.

The climb looked long and unpleasant, featuring not just acid, but dragon dung. Sighing out a silent curse—why hadn't Manshoon just obeyed Mystra for once? Or why hadn't the Lady of All Mysteries dealt with him, or freed her *trustworthy* El to deal with him?—Elminster found her first sheltering corner of rock, picked her way to it, then looked for the next one.

More offerings from either end of the black dragon could come raging down at her at any time. Which meant prudence must be paramount. Ah, scale the rocks just *there*, so as to pick her way over yonder, and so on . . .

Unnoticed by the Sage of Shadowdale's newfound dark elf body, there was the faintest of stealthy movements by the edge of the cleft.

Even an alert and staring Elminster could have seen no more than a shadow, just for an instant, as someone—or something—melted silently against the jagged cavern wall, well above the smooth, worn path of long ago acid flows.

The lone drow priestess ascending cautiously out of the Underdark had a very patient pursuer.

Lord Constable Farland looked across the table and found a certain grim measure of comfort in the faces staring back at him. He trusted these two men.

Sometimes he wished he could trust anyone else in all the Realms, but thus far, he'd found only these two. His senior constables. Tall, scarred, taciturn Anglur Traelshun, almost a head taller than grim, stocky, cynical Bradraer Delloak. Thank the gods the two were firm friends, because they were both capable men, and would have made deadly enemies for each other, had they been so inclined.

It was hrasted isolated at Irlingstar, perched on a knife-edged stone ridge running west out of Irlingmount, one of the Orondstars. Just "Oronds," most called them; a cluster of uncharacteristically knife-edged peaks in the Thunder Peaks range, just a little northwest of halfway between the Realm of Wailing Fog and Thunderholme. Only one road reached the castle, and save for striding deep into the Stonelands—not the act of a sane man—it wasn't possible to stay in Cormyr and yet get so far from the rest of the Forest Kingdom.

Which was why the Crown's most secure prison was there, and not inside the walls of Sharran-infested Wheloon. The nobles in the cells at Irlingstar could birth no end of trouble if they were closer to other Cormyreans—folk in need of coins and susceptible to whispered threats, promises, and sly dealings.

"You're no more mages than I am," Farland said wearily, "but have you found *any* sign that the wards have been breached?"

They both shook their heads, wasting no words. They never did.

More than century ago, the infamous Royal Magician Vangerdahast had cast the first wards at Castle Irlingstar. With stark and strong magical barriers renewed annually ever since, this normally invisible dome of magic hampered most spells within Irlingstar, preventing translocation and scrying into and out of the fortress. Although the Spellplague had clawed at Irlingstar's wards, they had survived, and remained crucial in preventing wizards hired by noble families from breaching the castle's security at will.

"Right," Farland said grimly. "You know what you have to do." He got up, ending the meeting. The two senior constables made for the door.

Traelshun would rouse the few guards who'd been off-shift and asleep when Avathnar had been murdered, and Delloak was off to the gatehouse to order the wagon drivers to depart immediately, taking their wagons to Immerford to fetch fresh food. He was to ride ahead of them, to be Farland's messenger to the nearest king's lord—Lord Lothan Durncaskyn at Immerkeep—to report the murder and request war wizard reinforcements, for the inevitably difficult investigation. Mind-reaming, now that it so often left both interrogator and suspect drool-witted, was a thing of the past. Solving crimes was once more a process of threatening, peering, and cajoling—and given Irlingstar's current roster of resentful, sneering, sophisticated, and very *capable* noblemen—the castle's handful of weary duty war wizards were going to need all the help they could get. The sooner they got started . . .

Farland descended the back stair that would take him to the mages' room. Well, they'd have to wait some days, as it was. Immerford, still growing visibly with every passing summer, was one of the newest settlements in Cormyr, centered on the ford where the East Way crossed the Immerflow. But the countryside betwixt here and where Lord Durncaskyn sat in his bright new castle of Immerkeep was hard country indeed, deep swamp wherever it wasn't knife-sharp rock ridges cloaked by thick, dark, wolf-roamed forests. There wasn't a fenced clearing between Immerford and Irlingstar, farm or ranch, because Cormyreans weren't fools enough to try farming or steading there.

Durncaskyn wasn't going to be pleased at Delloak's report, but then Durncaskyn never was. Dragon in the sky, Irlingstar's five duty wizards of war were probably going to be irked, too, but he could do nothing about that.

To say nothing of Irlingstar's own all-too-superior mages, who'd be scared and therefore even harder to deal with than usual . . .

Farland reached the bottom of the stair, stepped through the archway, turned right—and stopped.

A long, wet tongue of fresh blood ran out into the passage right in front of him.

It was coming from under the door of the ready room into which the bedchambers of the war wizards all opened.

"Saer mages?" he called sharply.

The ominous silence continued unbroken.

Swallowing a curse, the lord constable of Irlingstar drew his sword and flung open the door, taking care to keep his feet out of the blood.

Even before it swung wide, he knew what he was going to find.

Chapter Nine

Lord Durncaskyn Is Unhappy

On his best days, the king's Lord Lothan Durncaskyn of Immerford was a difficult man, gruff and cynical. On his worst days, he was as irritable and sharp-tongued as an aging, surly, and sarcastic retired Purple Dragon veteran whose many ill-healed wounds made him limp and ache during his every waking moment might be expected to be.

This was turning into one of those worst days. Lord Durncaskyn was *not* happy.

The messenger from Irlingstar had just departed. A constable of the rare, utterly trustworthy sort; Durncaskyn had believed his every word. Wherefore Immerford below his high windows was afire with the unpleasant news that the kitchen staff at the prison castle—Immerfolk, every one of them—had been murdered. Foul murders that cried out for justice. So of course, the gods having the twisted senses of mirth they did, Durncaskyn couldn't render the aid he was obligated to—Hells, that he *ached* to.

Just when their presence had been demanded to see into these killings at Irlingstar, his best wizards of war were busy elsewhere. Off north, looking into reports of lawless men raiding caravans along the Moonsea Ride—brigands who must be lairing somewhere in the headwaters of the Immer, which made them Durncaskyn's problem. He only had the one competent team, six tested mages led by the capable and well-respected Brannon

Lucksar. The junior team, three jack-dancing idiots led by that utter fool Vandur, were . . .

Durncaskyn's lip curled. He couldn't call to mind a word bad enough for them. "Bumblers" was too polite and harmless, by far. "Realm-wrecking disasters" groped closer, but—

The unexpected knocking on his office door that erupted then was a sudden thunder of blows. By the sharpness of those sounds, the din was almost certainly being made by metal-shod canes . . . three or more of them.

Durncaskyn cast his gaze at the ceiling and waved his hands in an exasperated "What *next?*" flourish, but of course the gods failed to answer. This was shaping into a "worst" day, indeed.

"It's unlocked," he called. "Enter!"

The door was flung open, and the owners of those loudly peremptory canes crowded into the room. Seven good burghers of Immerford, men he knew well, to his cost. One glance told Durncaskyn their mood: furious because they were frightened and just bristling for a fight.

The king's lord of Immerford kept from rolling his eyes only with firm effort. Gods, if they'd only sent their wives, instead . . .

"Well?" the boldest—Harklur, the vintner, as usual—snapped, "What're you doing here?"

Durncaskyn quelled an inner sigh and gave the wine merchant a polite smile. As always, the same script. Dutifully, he said the words expected of him.

"This is, as it happens, my office," he explained gently. "'Tis where I'm *expected* to be, much of my working time. So delegations of honored citizens such as yourselves know where to find me."

"I *mean,*" Harklur snarled, "*why* are you still just *sitting* here, when honest Immerfolk—defenseless wives and daughters!—have been *murdered* in their beds by *foul* young lordlings bent on rape and pillage and . . . and bloodshed?" As he wound down, the vintner's faltering words were bolstered by nods and supportive murmurs from the other six pillars of Immerford.

"King and court expect me to remain at my post," Durncaskyn replied, "particularly in times of crisis. Which this most undoubtedly is, considering that *before* Constable Delloak brought me the terrible news from Irlingstar, I had three other major troubles to deal with, one of which you gentlesirs are all well aware of."

"Never mind that!" Harklur snapped, only to be drowned out by two of his fellow burghers, both bursting out at once.

"My daughter's best friend is dead, and I want to know just *what*—"

"Who's keeping the peace up in Irlingstar, anyhail, and what's to stop these foul murderers from just sweeping down *our* way, hey? I *demand* to know—"

My, but they were truly upset. Not one of them had bitten on his bait, and asked the details of those two troubles he'd told them they didn't know about. Right, then; 'twas "treat with deserved respect" time.

Durncaskyn stood up, planting both hands on his littered desk—and then grandly swept his papers aside in both directions to whirl to the floor.

"Gentlesirs," he barked, "I'm *glad* you came to see me. Your concern heartens me, as it would any true servant of Cormyr. *Please* come around my side of the desk, and behold this map with me."

There were wordless murmurs of excitement and mollification as the burghers hastened to crowd around. Harklur and Mrauksoun still looked angry, but the rest were bright-eyed. Worked every time.

"Here we are in Immerford," Durncaskyn told them, pointing but taking care not to plant his finger on it. They'd want to peer close, trying to pick out their own homes on those intricately drawn streets. "Right in the center of it all."

He moved his pointing hand. "There's Castle Irlingstar, hard by the frontier. Very difficult country between us, you'll see. A determined man or a small band might struggle through, but if an army tried, we have a tenday's warning, or even more."

His hand moved again. "Now, over here, somewhere in these marshes, is an outlaw band that's been butchering honest merchants on caravans traveling the East Way, and plundering their goods. The same caravans that bring trade to *you*, gentlesirs, that make it possible for all Immerfolk to feed themselves, to continue to live here and not become drudges in Sembia or dockhands in Suzail. We've been trying to quell word of just how many murders and robberies they've managed, because to foster rumor will be to harm Immerford's future—*your* prosperity—far more than anything they've done, or are likely to do. We're hunting them right now."

He moved his pointing finger back to Immerford. "I've another little matter, right here at home. Someone who's impersonating honest citizens long enough to inspect their outgoing shipments in the Longhand and Eskurlaede warehouses—just long enough to remove one or two smallish but valuable items, every time. *Your* shipments, gentlesirs, and your reputations and demands for repayment. I have to hunt down and stop that someone, before matters get much worse."

His finger moved south along the East Way, to Hullack Forest. "And then there's the little matter of the Owl Lord."

"The *what?*"

"That's what we want to know," Durncaskyn replied smoothly. "A sorcerer, wizard, or perhaps warlock of power, who dwells in the Hullack and casts spells on folk traveling along the road nearby—especially if they camp for the night here, here, or *here*. He enspells them and worms one or two secrets out of them—magic they know the whereabouts of, or where their wealth is hidden or invested—something he can profit from. Soon thereafter, hired thieves exploit what he's learned. We've only caught one, thus far, and he only knew he was working for a man in an owlhead mask and dark robes, who called himself the Owl Lord. I need to stop this danger before one of *you* becomes his next victim. 'Tis my duty, saers, to learn of such perils and to deal with them. At any time, dozens—scores—of Crown agents and informants, as well as vigilant upstanding citizens such as yourselves, are hastening here to report to me, so I can act. Just as you have done, here and now. So you see, saers, I *have* to be here."

There was a moment of silence, wherein most of the burghers nodded, but Ergol Mrauksoun broke it. The hawk-nosed, energetic moneylender and landlord was still angry but controlling himself with visible effort. "I—we—Lord Durncaskyn, we are not mere dogs barking in the streets of Immerford! We are busy men, men with concerns that crowd us just as these crowd you, and—but—we've reached a point that—that—hrast it, this *cannot* go on, and we agreed to come here today to tell you so!"

"Yes," Harklur interrupted, "to make it very clear—"

Mrauksoun glared his fellow burgher down, and seized the verbal podium again. "For us, these murders are *it*, my lord! We cannot accept things continuing like this! We demand you inform the king—not several score of faceless courtiers who can all safely forget they heard you, and do the same nothing they've been doing for years, but King Foril himself—that we are sick unto choking of ever-higher taxes without much to show for it save increasingly heavy-handed border patrols who almost daily stop and search any Immerman or maid departing town for smuggled goods, ever-higher local prices for . . . for *everything*, long waits for, well, anything at all—"

"Including Crown permissions!" put in raw-voiced Helmur Faerrad, Immerford's jeweler and fine pastry maker.

Mrauksoun nodded. "*Including* Crown permissions—that have to come from Arabel or Suzail. We're also increasingly dismayed at, shall we say, *inadequate* local protection provided for us by the Crown. These troubles you've just shown us are matters we knew little or nothing about! I'm speaking of the outlaws who've afflicted us for years. Why, Broadshield's Beasts have been taking our sheep and goats for more seasons than I can call to mind, now, and growing ever bolder as the Dragons and all the king's spies seem unable to even find or identify them, to say nothing of *stopping* them! Why, they're even snatching oxen, now! *Oxen*, out of drovers' sheds and stables! What we—what all Immerford—wants to know is: what are you going to do about it?"

Before Durncaskyn could make any reply at all, the shortest of the burghers, the gnome wheelwright Askalan Larcloaks, pushed through the taller humans and growled, "Lord Durncaskyn, listen ye well: Our continued loyalty to King Foril Obarskyr turns on this. On *just* how well you and yer Crown officers handle the investigation of these killings at Irlingstar—*including* how you and yours treat Immerfolk as they investigate. Not just the cooks and kitchen maids and porters were from here, mind! There are good—and popular—Immerfolk shut up in that castle! The young Lords Cornyn Risingbroke and Yarland Amflame were locked away there for no more than saying a few foolish things about the Crown, and trying to forge trade alliances in Sembia without bothering to tell some nosy palace clerks what they were up to!"

Durncaskyn nodded, his teeth set. Gods, but his wounds were aching hard and deep! "I recall the lords well, goodsirs, and desire their speedy return to full freedom and to Immerford. I only hope the openly rebellious comments that got them incarcerated were errors of youth and not firm beliefs on their part—for like any loyal officer of the Crown, I must uphold the law, and trust in the law to serve all, equally."

There were some audible snorts from the burghers. They knew as well as he did that those of high birth or station, or having much coin, received better treatment under the law than outlanders, or the poor, or peasants with few friends. Everyone in Immerford had heard of younglings forced to join the Dragons after falling into debt or being caught at some minor crime, and over the last thirty summers or so public regard for the soldiery had slowly shifted from "our trusted protectors" to something closer to "the devils on our doorsteps we know, and must endure."

Durncaskyn watched their faces, and he knew what they wanted to hear, what he must say.

"Goodsirs, you have my personal promise, solemn and made before the gods as well as all of you, that I will do everything in my power—*everything*—to see that the murderer or murderers are revealed, that all that drove or enticed them to do as they did is made plain, and that they are fittingly punished. Wizards of war will be called in, I'll demand whatever aid seems necessary from the palace, and these foul killings won't be forgotten, treated lightly, or excused because of who the slayer or slayers may be. This I *swear*."

They nodded and murmured again, sounding a trifle friendlier. This was language they understood, plain speech that they trusted. Durncaskyn held out his hands to them, empty and palm up, like a beseeching beggar.

"I need you to have patience, to trust in me—and in return, I promise to entrust you, when all the investigating is done and the time is right, with all we learned, to tell you everything. I'll invite you back here to this office, and tell all."

"Well, now," Halston the cooper spoke up, "that's as fair speech as I've heard in many a day. Something I can shake on without hesitation."

And he reached out a long arm to clasp Durncaskyn's hand firmly, starting a rush to do so. The king's lord moved out from behind his desk to reach every burgher, and by slow and continuous steps forward succeeded in starting them back toward the office door.

They drifted out, talking excitedly among themselves about the good lads Risingbroke and Amflame, dastardly Owl Lords, and those right thieving bastards the Beasts. Durncaskyn moved with them, clapping backs and making promises, but keeping his gaze and manner firm until they were well and truly down the stairs.

Turning back to his office again, he permitted himself the luxury of a prolonged and heartfelt rolling of the eyes that would have made all of his sisters giggle, and rather despairingly decided to send the dregs of his local duty team of war wizards to Irlingstar. Better atrocious investigators than no investigators at all.

As he sat back down at his desk and surveyed the map gloomily, his field of view showing him that there was no one lingering who might overhear, he muttered under his breath, "They're the *last* three stlarning mages I'd willingly send *anywhere*—except into exile, to plague someone *else*. And every last one of the Gods Above help us all, I'm sending them into the thick of a prison where a murderer's on the loose." He brightened a trifle. "Perhaps they'll provide him with some fresh victims."

Then his gaze strayed to the papers littering the floor, and he fell into gloom again. "Huh. And if they do, it'll mean *more* paperwork."

"Of *course*, my lord," Immaero Sraunter purred. "I have just the thing."

Lord Danthalus Blacksilver reddened a little, concluding that this alchemist would have to be silenced, and soon. Before the man's loose tongue spread dark rumors across the city of a certain *inadequacy*—gods, the man's false delicacy was revolting!—on the part of dashing Lord Blacksilver. He couldn't have his good name—

The alchemist leaned over the counter, putting his throat within tempting reach of Blacksilver's little nail-cleaning knife, and murmured conspiratorially, "You must be an utter *lion*, milord. All the other lords your age who maintain residences in Suzail came to me years ago. Not that I ever name any names, you understand. Or I'd have all the young ladies crowding in here trying to buy extra dosages, and that would be dangerous for lords less able and fit than yourself."

Blacksilver relaxed, trying not to make his sigh of relief too gustily obvious. Something slender and cool touched his palm. He closed his fingers around it and stared down at it before the alchemist had quite straightened and drifted away. It was a tiny vial of pale blue, translucent liquid.

"Just four drops, into any trifling amount—or large quaff—of milk or water," Sraunter murmured. "*Not* wine or stronger drink."

Blacksilver closed his fingers around the vial, smiled, and plucked forth the purse that held just his "handyspending" gold coins.

A lion among lions, rumor promised.

This little foray had been worth it, after all.

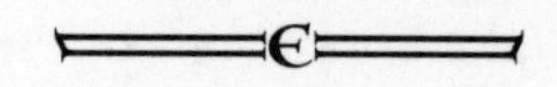

"See?" Arclath said cheerfully. "Both still alive, not so much as a spell-sent 'Boo!' to disturb our slumbers . . ."

Amarune gave him a sour look and rattled the stout chains coming from the manacles that had just been locked around their wrists. "And these are *nothing*, I suppose?"

"Merely part of the clever deception we Crown agents are working. Four hundred lions a month, remember?"

Rune sighed. "I wish I could be as jaunty about it all as you are. How do you manage it, dear? Is it part of being brought up noble, or being well on the way to becoming an idiot?"

"Both those things," the heir of House Delcastle agreed merrily, "*and* being not far off madwits helps, too. That's probably how Elminster's done it, all these centuries."

His Rune winced. "Old many-times-grandsire El . . . I wonder where he is now?"

As the shop bell tinkled its soft chime in the wake of the departing Lord Blacksilver, Manshoon permitted himself a satisfied smile.

After all, Sraunter would have smiled on his own at that moment, if Manshoon hadn't been riding his mind. Another profitable sale, of something so simple yet so desired. Not that he cared a whit for the weight of Sraunter's purse. No, he was satisfied because it had gone so well. He really *was* schooling himself to patience and subtlety in manipulating his subverted nobles. Andolphyn, Loroun, and now Blacksilver. That left just Crownrood, of the important ones.

As "everyone" knew, most of the nobility opposed the Crown and tried all manner of minor seditious and treasonous ploys and gestures. Thus, nobles doing so under his coercion were unlikely to arouse suspicions of anyone being involved in those little ploys but the nobles themselves. Whereas if he took to meddling with the minds of courtiers, such tamperings were far more likely to be noticed by wizards of war.

The solution, to a patient man, was to slowly prune the ranks of those Crown mages, using justifiably enraged or drunken nobles to do so. He'd already subverted a handy collection of expendable lords, but it occurred to Manshoon that *another* handy collection of younger, demonstrably Crown-hostile nobles already existed: those relatively few captives kept in isolated cells beneath High Horn, where Purple Dragons and wizards of war were numerous, alert, and close by. And then there were the inmates of an entire prison keep out on the remote eastern border of the realm, where Dragons were few and Crown mages even fewer: Castle Irlingstar.

Well, now . . .

It was slow and sometimes hard work, this climb. Always avoiding the temptation, even for an instant, to use the rock that had been smoothed by the dragon's spewings into an easy trail. In places it was a slick chute, aye, but more often the smooth-melted rock had been left a mere shell of itself, pierced by many tiny holes above hidden cavities, so a firm boot could crush it down into a bootprint that was unlikely to slip. Yet that would undoubtedly make noise, and there *was* a dragon waiting up above.

El was hoping to find a side cavern that would let her avoid the wyrm. If not, she had magic enough to get past a dragon . . . if she handled matters *just* right.

Aye, there was always that "if." Hrast it, there was never just the easy way, never a time to relax. Right now, it was best to remain wary, and move very carefully, never—

There was a sudden change in the breeze from above, then an echoing, hissing roar. El shrank back into the cavern-wall cleft she was in and braced herself, thrusting knees and elbows against the rock. Even before the acrid stink hit her, the green flood close in its wake, she knew what had happened.

The dragon had breathed acid again.

Chapter Ten

High Time For Screaming And Cursing

Elminster shut her stinging eyes and tried not to breathe as a fine mist of acid drifted past. The main hissing flood, gurgling like a rushing stream, was already on and down, heading for the Underdark below.

The wyrm had probably been listening for small noises that would tell it a creature was climbing toward it, and had concluded, despite the care El had taken, that such an unwanted visitor was indeed ascending its lair's back door. Or perhaps the dragon had arranged some sort of alarm—even a spider or some other tiny cave inhabitant, as a spy—to warn against all intrusions from the Underdark. After all, Elminster certainly would, if she'd been a dragon lairing in a cave connected directly to the vast drow-infested underworld.

Down the chain of caverns the acid flowed, striking rocks into bubbling spume and drifting caustic mists, tumbling and hissing past El in her cleft. Some way below her, something screamed, shrill and sudden and very briefly, a cry that was cut off in an ugly choking.

El dared to lean out of her cleft enough to peer down, and only just caught sight of a dark, dwindling mass being swept along in the fading green glow. Dragon acid was as swift and ruthless as the wyrms that spewed it.

A dark elf? Someone or something that sounded as if it could sing and talk when it wasn't death screaming, that—strike that, *who*—had been following her up from that tunnel where she'd fought the outcast drow. Possibly it had been one of them, a lurking outcast she'd never seen.

Hrast it, too much death followed her, clung to her like a rotting cloak! Even when she fought no one, and hurled not a spell, folk died around her, as if the gods had cursed her to be Walking Death. Why?

She'd been sick of it centuries ago, yet it went on and on, showing no signs of slackening. She was so sick of it now.

But she doubted very much if how she felt would make one whit of difference. The violent deaths were going to keep happening around her. Let them *not* include his Rune, or her Arclath, hrast it.

Mystra forfend, Symrustar commented quietly.

"Aye," El whispered, softly enough that her words should carry no distance at all. "Mystra forfend, indeed."

She let silence fall, and waited a long time before daring to leave the cleft and climb on. When she did, she took great care to keep as quiet as she could, no matter how slow her progress.

After all, that brief scream from her ill-fated follower had been loud. Somewhere ahead and above, an alerted black dragon was waiting.

The lord constable of Irlingstar peered around the ready room. It did not take him long.

Despite his experience of monster scourings and battles with border raiders, Farland's stomach heaved. He fought down his urge to spew, then worked his way around the blood to look into every bedchamber.

They were spartan rooms, and none of the mages had brought much to the castle to clutter them with. They had small, simple wardrobes, customarily left open against the ever-present damp, and all of them stood open. No one was hiding in any place he couldn't see, because there was just nowhere to hide. A guard ward glowed faintly around a stack of shared spellbooks on a bedside table, preventing opportunistic thefts by prisoners—or anyone else.

The youngest of Irlingstar's duty war wizards lay dead, sprawled in the middle of the ready room, headless and handless. Those severed bits of him were nowhere to be seen.

There was no trace of the other four Crown mages at all. Except for the blood.

The lone corpse was spread-eagled in a great pool of gore that filled the center of the room. It was a well-built chamber, its flagstones covered with a thin slurry of rough-pour that sloped ever so slightly away from the walls, to gather any wetness in the center of the room. Only that had enabled him to skirt the blood, for there was so much of it that the body lay in a still-slick pool that had to be two fingerwidths deep at its heart, or more.

No man could have *that* much blood in him; most of it must have belonged to the missing mages.

There were no bloody talon or claw prints, no fallen mage knives or signs of any struggle—and no runes chalked anywhere. No smells of spellwork, those odd scorched scents all Dragons who worked with war wizards got used to. The only reek was from the blood . . . and the bowels of the corpse.

Nevertheless, Lord Constable Farland gripped his sword tightly, and glared all around constantly, as he made his way back out into the passage.

Avathnar had been bad. This was worse.

And he *knew*—knew as surely as his name was Gelnur Farland, and all of this mess was on his platter, his to clear up—that it wasn't over yet, not by a long bowshot.

"Tluin," he whispered, into the gloom around him. "Naed, hrast, and farruking *tluin*."

Curses weren't going to help in the slightest, so he repeated them all several times, as defiantly as if he'd been a young boy.

Sometimes, when the world was falling apart all around you, until you thought of something better, cursing was all you could really do.

"The mountains," Amarune said softly, "are a lot *higher* than I'd thought they'd be."

Arclath nodded, but before he could say anything the nearest Dragon told her, "Most folk we bring along this road say that. If yon peaks weren't so tall, they'd not be the wall that keeps out Sembia."

"Save, of course, for its gold," Arclath murmured, causing two Dragons to lean in sharply, to try to hear.

They'd been riding the Orondstars Road, winding along the western flanks of the Thunder Peaks, for much of a day. Irlingstar couldn't be far off now.

Rune and Arclath rode in manacles, under a heavy guard of veteran Purple Dragons riding in a tight group around them. The plate-armored, heavily armed Dragons obviously had orders to try to overhear everything a prisoner said.

To better fool everyone in the prison castle, none of their escort knew the young lord and untitled lass in chains were secret Crown agents rather than real prisoners. Officially, they were both "under the displeasure of the Crown," which was polite court speech for "imprisoned thanks to being caught at something not quite bad enough for death or exile—or not proven well enough, yet, for you to receive the death or exile you've earned."

Their escorts had been told that Lord Arclath Delcastle had spoken and plotted treason against the Crown with the commoner Amarune Whitewave. Who had now been revealed to the guards and shortly to the inhabitants of Irlingstar as both an agent of an "outland power" plotting against the realm, and the bastard offspring of no less than four noble families—and so, for the security of Cormyr, best locked up. The identities of those four high houses and of the outland power were officially "mysterious," and Rune had been warned to keep them so.

She recalled that warning, now, as Arclath gave her a glance that concealed a reassuring grin very well. All that held his mirth was a wayward twinkle in one of his eyes. Meeting it, she widened her own eyes rather than winking, by way of reply, well aware of the steady stares of the surrounding Purple Dragons. And recalled the last time she'd received that hidden grin from him . . .

Amarune had been more excited than she could ever remember being.

She'd been beaming at everyone. After the king and the two wizards of war had departed the feasting room in Delcastle Manor, and Lady Marantine serenely began fetching out the sugar tarts that she'd somehow neglected to offer her unexpected court guests. Rune almost starting singing. Her heart was that high and soaring.

Even with the money belts hard and heavy in her hands, she could scarcely believe what had just happened.

"The king wanted my service—the king!"

As Lady Delcastle served Rune a dainty little plate of tarts, her little frown gave way to a rather grandmotherly smile.

"I don't mean to be unkind, dear," the noblewoman had said gently, "but the ranks of the loyal are rather thin, just now. When a ship is foundering, any bailing bucket will do."

"Fornrar? Dagnan? Leave those quivers here. All but the prisoners will be in heavy armor, and I don't want you wasting dread arrows. That poison's *expensive*."

"We *heard* your orders, Broadshield," Dagnan replied sullenly. He was lowering the quiver from his shoulder very slowly.

"I know you did. I also know *you*," their leader replied. "Put 'em down."

He stayed to watch until the heavy quivers—twenty-one longfeather shafts weigh far more than most folk suspect—were down and hidden, wrapped in cloaks and with a goodly covering of the dead leaves that carpet every forest floor raked over them. Fornrar peered up to get a good look at the surrounding trees so as to be able to find the cached shafts later, then set off without a word, up and over the brow of the wooded hill, past the cluster of boulders where they'd hidden the axes.

That had been done under Broadshield's orders, too. Otherwise, too many of the lads were apt to get overenthusiastic and start swinging axes at horses—and the dragon, who liked its prey whole and able to flee, to give it sport, wouldn't like that.

Broadshield took care to keep his Beasts afraid of the great black wyrm. It reminded them of the perils of disloyalty toward their leader, the notorious Broadshield—the only one of them who'd befriended Alorglauvenemaus.

After all, some of these lads hadn't been part of his band the last time the dragon had swooped down and devoured the three Beasts who'd been bold enough to disagree with their leader about anything.

"Remember," Broadshield told Dagnan, as they followed after Fornrar. "We want the prisoners unharmed, not wearing arrows. The Delcastles will have our hides if we harm their heir."

Dagnan grunted reluctant assent, spat on a long-fallen log, and asked sidelong, "They know about this, then?"

"No. Nor will they, until both prisoners are safe in the lodge in Sembia. They're always happier to pay the ransom when they know their loved ones are out of Cormyr, and no appeal to Foril is going to result in any daring rescue."

Dagnan nodded. "I wonder," he said slowly, "if King Foril regards us as . . . useful."

Beside him, Broadshield smiled in satisfaction. "Ah," he said. "You begin to see."

Rune found it hard to keep from laughing aloud. The expressions adorning the faces of every Dragon she glanced at were hilarious to behold.

"The Orondstars Road," Arclath told her airily, playing the proud and effete dandy to the hilt, "began as a mining and settlement road in the latter days of the reign of King Duar Obarskyr. It departs the Thunder Way—forgive the repetition in the local nomenclature, but imagination is always in short supply among officialdom, and once they seize upon a halfway grand or decent name, in this case 'Thunder,' they simply *cannot* resist doing it to death—in Thunderstone, hard by the bridge over the Thunderflow, and winds its way north, clinging as closely to the westernmost Thunder Peaks as it can. The Orondstars themselves—just "Oronds" to most locals—are a stand of smallish mountains that resemble nothing so much as a handful of knife-edged serving platters, sunk half-deep in the ground, still more or less in the stack they started out in. Which is to say, they all stand parallel to each other, and are much thinner and sharper than your average mountain. The *rest* of the Thunder Peaks, for example."

"Ohhh," Rune answered him, playing an impressed and empty-headed young lass to the hilt. If the faces of their escort were anything to go by, the Dragons had swallowed this unsubtle act of hers almost a day ago.

The road ahead was rising, a thin wild forest cloaking the mountainsides on their right—the Thunder Peaks—and a thick, tangled wood looming on their left, on land Rune could see became several higher knife-edged ridges, ahead. Winding this way and that like a snake, the road climbed on, out of sight, into the trees.

"The Oronds, now . . . ," Arclath continued brightly, seeming not to see several Dragons rolling their eyes. "We've not *quite* reached them yet, and we're headed for the next to last Orond, the northwesternmost one. It's called Irlingmount, and Castle Irlingstar—the 'star' bit derives from archaic local dialect, and means 'of' or 'pertaining to' or something of the sort—perches atop a western arm of Irlingmount. The Orondstars—there's that 'star,' again, you'll note—stand just a tad northwest of halfway between the Realm of Wailing Fog and the flourishing settlement of Thunderholme. I'm sure they'll have maps we can consult in the castle, but until we get there—"

The Dragon riding at Arclath's shoulder looked like he was going to explode, and he was clutching a mace that looked quite capable of dashing out any Delcastle brains that came within reach, so Rune interrupted hastily, "What's this 'Realm of Wailing Fog,' anyhail? I keep hearing it mentioned, but no one ever says anything about it! It sounds as if it's—"

"Something that's *not* to be talked about, by any of us or either of you," the oldest Dragon said gruffly, in a voice so firm and raw that it was almost a roar. "Now keep talk to a minimum, prisoners! This is none too safe a road, what with brigands lurking along it—*this* is where the notorious Broadshield's Beasts roam, mind—and dragons lairing hereabouts. We'd rather *not* have a pitched battle on our hands, if it's all the same to you!"

"Ho-*ho*!" Arclath exclaimed in delight, "a pitched battle! Did you hear that, Rune? They're going to lay on a pitched battle for us! I've waited *years* to see a—"

Something—no, a *lot* of somethings—suddenly *hummed* out of the air in front of them, bringing the air all around to a brief thrumming everyone could feel as well as hear.

Then the cause of the thrumming reached them, and Dragons started to reel in their saddles or be smashed right out of them, as arrow after arrow crashed onto them, shivered into splinters against the soldier's heavy armor, or speeding on past.

Arclath swung his horse in front of Rune's to try to shield her, at the same time as the Dragon riding beside her caught hold of her mount's bridle, to try to drag it toward the side of the road. The result was a confusing tangle of plunging, bucking horses, neighing amid all the arrows.

"A hail of arrows!" Arclath shouted in delighted tones. "A veritable *hail* of arrows! Is this part of the usual castle defenses, or are you trying to make us feel especially welcome by laying on a special salute? Or—"

The Dragon beside him finally lost patience and swung his mace, but Rune had already kicked Arclath's mount in the ribs, and it bolted forward just in time. The mace struck nothing, and the force of its untrammeled swing sent its wielder toppling from his saddle.

"*Ride*!" a Dragon bellowed, behind them. "Ride hard! On, past this!"

All around, the warriors of the king spurred their horses and ducked low in their saddles. Rune did the same, Arclath reached over to try to shield her, and their horses galloped with the rest. They went hard around a bend, to fully face the wooded hillock all the arrows had come from, a little hill that the road curved right around. Then their racing horses reared and shied back.

Someone had freshly felled half a dozen trees across the road, great pines and shadowtops. These forest giants lay with their great boughs more or less intact, forming a barrier of tangled branches and leaves as high as a big cottage and as long as the palace stables back in Suzail. The uppermost branches of the felled trees had crashed down amid the standing trees on the far side of the road. No horse that couldn't fly would be getting past the wall of fallen wood.

Another arrow whipped out of the trees and took a Purple Dragon out of his saddle by the throat, his head lolling at a sickening angle even before he crashed down into the road.

Then came another arrow, slicing past a Crown soldier's shoulder close enough to make armor shriek.

"Back!" a Dragon shouted. "Back, back around the bend—and ride *hard*!"

In the neighing, kicking confusion, Amarune flung both her arms around her horse's neck just to stay mounted, her saddle bouncing bruisingly beneath her. All around her, Dragons tried to wrestle their horses around, draw swords, and clap their visors down or their helms on their heads, all at once. A few of them managed it. She saw others take arrows through their bare heads or through the open fronts of their helms—and then with plunging hooves everywhere she was slipping, *slipping* . . .

Arclath's strong arm caught Rune and hauled back upright, then slammed her low onto the shoulders of her surging mount. They were headed back the way they'd come at a hard gallop. Ahead she could see men leaping out of the forest, some of them sprinting across the road trailing ropes that were soon pulled taut, a flimsy barrier she was bearing down on.

Around her, Dragons were cursing in bitter, snarling earnest; "Farruking Broadshield's *Beasts*!" seemed to be a popular phrase.

Their attackers—foresters who'd stolen bits and pieces of armor to wear, by the looks of them—were out in the road now, running everywhere, many in pairs carrying felled trees that they moved to bar the ways of the hard-galloping horses. There was rearing and screaming from the horses as riders spilled from saddles—and the ring and *clang* of swords hacking and being parried rose all around. Rune's own mount reared, and she sprang clear when it seemed it might go right over on its back. A moment later Arclath was beside her, down off his own horse and standing guard over her with a loop of his chains gathered in his hand.

"This way," he panted, jerking his head, and Rune ran with him, for the trees. Almost immediately, a Dragon somewhere behind them shouted, "The prisoners! The prisoners are escaping!"

Grinning foresters—the notorious outlaws known as Broadshield's Beasts, Rune supposed—ran toward them, too, swords and daggers drawn. They were everywhere, some waiting in the trees they were sprinting for . . . there was no escape, nowhere to run . . .

A grinning bearded face loomed up in front of her, telling her gleefully, "You're *mine* now, little maid!" Dirty hands reached out—

Air erupted behind the Beasts with a roar and a puff of smoke, and out of it raced bright and snarling bolts of lightning, dozens of them. One stabbed the man reaching for Rune, and he fell on his face without another word.

All around, outlaws staggered, screamed—and fell. Lightning leaped to race and crackle around an armored Dragon, fighting in the midst of three Beasts—and he shuddered, danced a few agonized and spasming steps, then crashed to the ground, smoldering.

Then, just as swiftly as they'd come, the lightning was gone, leaving nothing but the drifting smoke that had birthed it.

Off to Amarune's right, sudden vivid emerald flame blossomed around a running outlaw—and consumed him.

"Magic!" one of the Beasts roared. "Men, the *wizards* are come!"

A ragged cheer arose. Rune was astonished to see that it was coming from both the Purple Dragons *and* their foes.

"Come *on*!" Arclath hissed, pulling at her and starting to run.

Right in front of them, the world erupted in emerald flames.

Chapter Eleven

The Unseen Foe

"S-sune's . . . brazen . . . charms!" Arclath cursed, hurling himself back in a twisting leap that brought him around Amarune in a curling embrace. The blast flung them both away together, in a hurtling ball that bounced bruisingly, twice, before they skidded to a stop against the body of a fallen outlaw whose leather-clad bulk was solid but . . . soft.

Grimacing at the smell of death and blood, Rune rolled away from the dead man, clawing her way up and out of Arclath's arms in a rattle of chains.

"I've—" she panted angrily, "some strength and . . . agility of my own, you know! You don't *have* to shield me like some child!"

"Rune," the heir of House Delcastle panted, looking hurt, "you're my *lady*! I'm *sworn* to defend you! 'Tis only right! The decent thing to do!"

Their ears were ringing from the blast, ribbons of smoke drifted everywhere across the road, and fresh bursts of emerald flame *whooshed* into being, here and there, usually hurling blazing-limbed outlaws aside in doing so.

A short, burly outlaw came striding through that wrack of smoke, dead and dying men, and fleeing, frightened horses. He peered into the trees, then turned and bellowed in the loudest voice Rune had ever heard bar heralds' proclamations amplified by magic: "Hah! At *last*! Use the dread arrows! Dread arrows, all!"

By the ragged shouts of reply, those words seemed to have been a command, which could only mean—if these were the Beasts—that this short, stout, loud-voiced man must be the outlaw Broadshield himself.

With a frown, Arclath shook his chains out into a loop he could use to strangle a man, and strode toward the man. Who turned, saw him, gave the young lord an unlovely grin, and dashed away into the trees, running like a storm wind.

Rune watched open-mouthed. Gods, the man was fast!

Arclath started to sprint after the outlaw leader, but after a few strides gave up with a shrug and turned back. The spell hurling men were out onto the road, still striking down outlaws with emerald flame.

"War wizards," Arclath identified them. "*Down,* Rune!"

Amarune ignored him. A blasting spell could kill her if she was cowering on the road just as easily as if she was standing up, after all. She watched the mages come, trotting forward with wands in their hands. She could see Purple Dragon badges on the shoulders and breasts of their leather jerkins. Jerkins, yes, over breeches, with leather belts and baldrics hung thickly with rows of pouches—not a pointed hat or a robe to be seen. Yet they were wizards, all right; two had just turned and caused walls of fire to erupt on the road, immolating the barrier of felled trees.

Others fanned out among the Dragons, peering alertly here and there. "Who's in charge here? Who's the ranking officer?" one called, in the stern tones of someone used to giving commands.

Before anyone could reply, an oddly lumpy black arrow sped out of the trees and struck him in the side.

A moment later, he burst, drenching a fellow wizard beside him with glowing green wetness.

It was acid, by the way that second mage's flesh started to melt away from his bones as he screamed. Two vainly running steps later he collapsed, and his shrieks abruptly faded. His arms, flung up too late to shield his face, were down to bare bone, and abruptly fell off, revealing a toppling-from-bony shoulders skull. Rune stared at the small heap of tangled bones and sticky, slumping mess—and was suddenly and violently sick, all over the road in front of her.

Another arrow found another wizard, with the same grisly result. And another.

Then the outlaws came charging down out of the trees, bows in their hands, loosing more black arrows as they came. Rune could see the bladders bound to the arrows as Beasts ran right past her.

The outlaws ignored her and Arclath and even the armored Purple Dragons, spending all of their attention—and arrows—on the Crown wizards.

Who suddenly broke and fled back into the forest from whence they'd come. The outlaws raced after them.

"Let not a one of them live!" they heard Broadshield bellow. "Kill them all!"

The walls of fire suddenly moved to try to block the pursuing outlaws, but they merely turned and outran them, crashing out of sight amid the trees.

Arclath shook his head. "I thought I *knew* the realm," he muttered, "but this . . . this is beyond belief. *Outlaws* hunting wizards of war like game birds—or vermin—in the forest!"

"Catch those horses!" a Purple Dragon ordered other Dragons, pointing. Then he trotted over to Arclath and Amarune, his sword drawn. It was the lionar who'd earlier given the orders to "ride hard" from the first volley of outlaw arrows, and later to retreat from the barrier.

"Prisoners!" he snapped. "Come with me."

Arclath hefted his loop of chain meaningfully, but the lionar gave him a look of disgust and said, "Don't be a fool, lord. We'd all welcome the excuse to kill you—defending ourselves in the thick of your hired outlaw attack, mind—and be able to turn back rather than riding on to Irlingstar. There are dangerous outlaws in these woods!"

Arclath let go the loop and spread his hands.

"That's better," the sandy-haired officer told him. "Now mount up—we'll help, if you need it. Our way on now stands clear."

There was nothing left of the barrier but ashes and a few laggard wisps of smoke. The walls of fire still raged off to one side of the road, but there was ample room to lead the snorting, balking horses past the flames and over the hot ashes, and on.

Rune didn't disdain Arclath's help in mounting, as the few surviving Dragons handled them both with more speed than gentleness, as they hurried to get them past the battlefield. The fallen, both outlaw and soldier, and the surplus riderless, wandering horses were abandoned without a backward glance.

"We must hurry," the same Dragon, who seemed to be in command, told them curtly. "Make no unnecessary noise."

No sooner was his back turned and the horses were on the move, then Rune leaned close to Arclath. "Those arrows—what *were* they?"

"Black-painted shafts with bladders of acid attached to them. Black dragon acid," he replied grimly. "How they work, exploding inside a body like that, I'm not quite sure. How they got that much black dragon acid in the first place, and what they make the bladders from, that the acid doesn't eat through them in the space of a swift breath—now *that* I'd *dearly* love to know!"

"Silence!" the nearest Dragon snapped.

Arclath rolled his eyes and gave the surrounding Realms silence. Just as mute, Rune rode thoughtfully at his side, more than a little shaken.

The alchemist's cellar was crowded—and stank. Death tyrants rotted; it was one of the things death tyrants did. Thrust together along one wall, their eyestalks interlaced, they still took up more room than most men would find comfortable.

Yet Manshoon, currently inhabiting Immaero Sraunter's body, was certainly not like most men.

He was calmly reclining on what was left of the undead beholder that was in the worst shape of all in his slave stable, a half-collapsed mass of festering putrefaction, thoughtfully studying a lone glowing white sphere that floated in midair above him.

In its depths could be seen a fast-moving but silent scene of a battle on a forest road where gouts of green flame were erupting, Purple Dragons were dying, and outlaws were loosing arrows everywhere.

Beside him, perched gingerly on a stool and staring up at the same unfolding entertainment, was a middle-aged woman of nondescript looks who was obviously terrified and on the verge of being violently sick thanks to the reek of the death tyrants. Thus far, terror was overriding nausea.

Aside from the cowed woman herself, only Manshoon knew who this woman really was—though a great many courtiers in the nearby palace would have recognized the trembling man she'd been before Manshoon's spells had altered her. Manshoon had compelled the disgraced suspected traitor Palace Understeward Corleth Fentable to flee the palace. Now Fentable was with him in the cellar, ready to be a replacement body—someone unfamiliar in Suzail—if Manshoon needed to depart Sraunter for any reason, and in the meantime to be a "pair of hands, plus audience" assistant.

More than once, as the fighting on the distant Orondstars Road unfolded, Manshoon chuckled at what he saw. That did not make the cowering Fentable relax much.

When it was done, the much-diminished prisoner escort hastening on along the road, Manshoon waved a hand to dismiss the scene, rose, and stretched.

"No sign of Elminster," he murmured to Fentable, "so I *have* destroyed him! I have! Hmm . . . unless he sent these wizards of war. And *they* are clearly the outlaws' intended quarry, not the prisoners nor their escort. The outlaws were hoping the Crown mages would appear, were ready for them, are eager to hunt them now; their attack on the escort was purely a lure for the mages. So what makes lawless plunderswords bold enough to openly attack—to *chase*—war wizards? Or what scares or coerces them so well that they prefer facing battle spells to turning on the one that sent them?"

Somewhere else—somewhere furnished with gibbering mouthers as seating, not rotting death tyrants—two watchers beheld the same battle. They saw it in the depths of Manshoon's scrying sphere, too, because they were watching Manshoon.

Unlike the vampire's magic, theirs conveyed not just the image of the alchemist's cellar, but all the sounds from it. The taller watcher had mastered stronger scryings than Manshoon commanded more than two thousand years ago, as well as the habit of often watching what certain others were up to. Which was one of the reasons he was still around to watch anything.

"Broadshield's men initially employed ordinary stag arrows because they didn't want to waste their most valuable shafts on heavily armored Purple Dragons. Or kill the prisoners, who are the prizes they daily seek," he explained to his fellow watcher.

"Prizes . . . for ransoms?"

"Indeed. They convey their catches—all nobility of Cormyr—to upcountry hunting lodges in Sembia and there deliver them to freedom. *After* wealthy noble relatives of the prisoners yield up stiff ransom fees."

"And the poisoned arrows?"

"They saved those for the foes they know they must eliminate: the wizards of war. Every attack on prisoner escorts is made not just to gain prisoners for ransom income, but in hopes of bringing Crown wizards within reach, so Broadshield's Beasts can slay them."

"I've not seen arrows that could rend a target in an explosion before. Those blasts sprayed acid, yes, but it wasn't . . . black dragon spew, was it?"

"It was. Broadshield's 'dread arrows' burst inside the bodies they strike, as their attached acid bladders react with a certain substance smeared on the arrows. The blasts emit the flesh-melting acid, of course. They're meant to make targets die horribly—and usually succeed."

"How do these Beasts *get* black dragon acid?"

"They work with—or more properly for, though they haven't quite realized that yet—a black dragon that lairs near the isolated border region they roam in, one Alorglauvenemaus by name."

"And the 'certain substance' you've not named, that reacts with the bladders—how do you know about it?"

The taller watcher smiled. "Who do you think gives it to Broadshield? Manshoon is far from my only toy in the Forest Kingdom."

"I . . . see."

At that moment, the distant Manshoon banished the scene he'd been watching and mused aloud. Both watchers listened with interest—and one of them with amusement, too.

"So what makes lawless plunderswords bold enough to openly attack—to *chase*—war wizards?" the distant would-be emperor of Cormyr asked his cowering assistant. "Or scares or coerces them so well that they prefer facing battle spells to turning on the one that sent them?"

The two watchers exchanged smiles. Then the taller one looked at the image of Manshoon and drawled, "What, indeed?"

"You just *ran* from battle, leaving your wounded fellows and the wizards of war who came to your aid to *die*?"

Arclath's question was loud and incredulous, so all the Dragons crowded around could hear. They'd ridden hard, until the horses were exhausted and stumbling, and a halt and rest had become a forced necessity.

"We have our orders to fulfill," the ranking Purple Dragon officer—the sandy-haired lionar, who had thrice refused to give his name—snapped. "They do *not* include tarrying to fight pitched battles with brigands on ground of our foe's choosing. We are charged to deliver the two of you—*without* delay—into lawful custody in Castle Irlingstar. Rest assured we'll seek Broadshield's Beasts during our travel home. Which must be along this road, seeing as there's no other." He turned his head and ordered savagely, "Mount up!"

"But sir, the horses—"

"*Hrast* the horses! If I've had enough rest, *they've* had enough rest!"

"Oh, well then," Arclath said brightly, "I'll ride you. Because my poor mount is still weary. That'll give your poor beast a bit more rest, too!"

"Lord Delcastle," the Dragon officer said icily, "pray *belt up*. The law against 'incitement' gives me all the justification I need to gag you securely, so none of us will have to hear *one more word* out of you, if I so desire—and right now, my desire to do so is mighty strong and growing stronger, believe you me!"

"Easy," Rune murmured to Arclath, out of the side of her mouth. "There's such a thing as carrying the 'irritating idiot noble' act too far."

Arclath gave her an 'I know that well' wink and bowed deeply—and silently—to the lionar. The Dragon officer let out a sigh of exasperation that was almost a roar, turned on one spur-booted heel, and strode to his horse.

This time, Arclath was carefully assisted in mounting by no less than seven Dragons. Their handling was precise and gentle, and included gentle pats of encouragement and support. What he'd said to the lionar was obviously popular.

The ride was short. As it happened, they had halted only a dozen or so dips and bends before the gates of their destination.

"Castle Irlingstar," the lionar announced tersely and unnecessarily, as their road ascended the ridge to the stark and towering walls of a smallish keep that seemed to grow up out of the rocks rather than perch atop them. No moat, of course, nor fields, walled or otherwise—and not another building or steading or other sign of human habitation to be seen. Just the fortress, all alone in the cold wind, amid uncounted rising rocks. The road ended at its gates.

Without war horn flourish or signal, the portcullis clattered up to admit them . . . into a gloomy roofed-over forehall that smelled strongly of horses, thanks to the open stalls that lined one wall. A dozen-some fully armored Purple Dragons were waiting for them.

Two galleries overlooked the forehall, and folk lined both. Guards with ready crossbows—who looked almost eager to use them—to the right, and grim, glowering men in rather dirty fine clothing lined the larger gallery to the left, flanked by guards; prisoners, gathered to measure the new additions to their ranks.

By their leers and murmurs, they hadn't failed to notice that Rune was not only a woman, but a female who looked both younger and prettier than an old boot or a chamber pot bucket. When she looked up and gave them a wink and a smile of flirtatious anticipation, the murmurs leaped in both hope and volume.

"Dalliance later," the head of the gathered fortress guards said crisply. "For now, come with me. Lionar, I thank you for the safe delivery of these prisoners. A meal is ready for you in the lower hall. It may not be up to the usual standards, but you'll soon hear the 'why' of that. Prisoners, you are to accompany me into the presence of the lord constable of Irlingstar."

"*Delighted,*" Arclath replied heartily, as if being ushered into a meeting with a duchess he very much wanted to seduce.

"Why, it will give me the *greatest* of pleasure . . . ," one of the fortress guards murmured mockingly. Evidently earlier prisoners had adopted a manner similar to Arclath's upon their arrival.

Wisely, Arclath took the hint, saying no more during their brief journey up several flights of stairs within a watchful ring of guards who had maces and daggers ready, other than to remark once, "These chains are heavy, you know!" and later, "Do we get to see the seneschal after the lord constable? My father gave me a message for the seneschal."

"The seneschal," the guard right behind him said grimly, "is dead."

"Oh, my," Rune piped up, before Arclath could say more and get himself into real trouble. "An accident or ailment, or something darker?"

"The lord constable will tell you all you need to know," was the firm reply she got, plus the firmer order, "No more talking!"

There wasn't time to ask anything else and get a reply, even if Amarune had wanted to defy the guards. They were on their last, short stretch of gloomy passage on their way to a closed door, the few wall torches low and waveringly dim in their blackened brackets.

At their approach the door swung open, guards saluted, and a grim-looking man behind a desk eyed his two newest prisoners rather wearily.

He made a swift hand-signal, and Arclath and Rune were settled into chairs fitted with hooks for their their chains to clip into, to keep them seated. Then all but two of the guards withdrew, closing the door behind them.

"Well met," the man on the other side of the desk said dryly, stroking his mustache. "I am Lord Constable Gelnur Farland, and you will be Lord Arclath Delcastle and, ah, Goodwoman Amarune Whitewave."

"We are indeed," Arclath agreed eagerly, with a wink.

Farland eyed him coldly. "You have something in your eye, lord?"

"Ah, no, no," Arclath replied, lowering his voice into a conspiratorial croon.

"You have a nervous tic?"

"No." Arclath winked again, firmly.

"You fancy me?"

"Ah, well, *no*, as it happens."

"Then why are you winking at me?"

Arclath hesitated. "I was, ah, attempting a nonverbal signal, saer."

"I rather thought as much. Why?"

"In order to communicate with you."

"Yet your tongue seems in fine working order, your vocabulary adequate . . ."

"What is said can be overheard, saer, and we are not alone."

"Nor are any of us here in Irlingstar, ever, except when locked in cells for slumber. This is a prison, lord, not a club or a rest retreat for idlers. Anything you want to say to me can be said before these two loyal Purple Dragons, who are present to witness all that befalls between us. And the *very* thorough body search I'm afraid each of you will undergo, before you depart this room. These are long-established rules, and only the Royal Magician and the king himself can break them." Farland leaned forward across his desk and added more coldly, "You will discover we have a lot of rules, Lord Delcastle, and none of them are for breaking. Unless you yourself desire to be broken, in your attempts."

Arclath glanced at Rune, who gave him a helpless shrug. The lord constable watched this exchange, and asked politely, "Is there anything you wish to say to your fellow prisoner, Lord Delcastle?"

"Much," Arclath said happily. "She is my partner."

"In crime? Worry not, you'll be kept far apart. For her own safety, Goodwoman Whitewave will be confined far from the other prisoners, for at the present time she is Irlingstar's only female guest."

"Oh?"

"Yes. Lady Raelith succeeded in starving herself to death a tenday ago."

"Excuse me, Lord Constable," Rune said firmly, "but the king told us we would remain together in Irlingstar, Arclath and I, when he sent us here."

The man behind the desk stared at her incredulously, then threw back his head and roared with laughter. The guards standing behind the prisoners' chairs joined in.

Chapter Twelve

The Lord Constable Is Less Than Wise

Lord Constable?" Rune asked politely, when all the laughter had died down. "Just what is so amusing?"

Farland regarded her almost fondly. Grinning from ear to ear, he asked her, "You expect me to believe you?"

"I have no expectations whatsoever regarding you, saer," she replied calmly, "yet I *have* spoken the truth. Ask Lord Delcastle."

This produced a fresh explosion of laughter. It died down into Farland asking her, "D'you *really* expect me to take the word of a prisoner for anything?"

"Why not? He *is* a lord of the realm."

"As is every prisoner here except you, Goodwoman Whitewave. Yet I've somehow failed to acquire the habit of believing any of them."

Rune sighed and looked at Arclath. "What do you think the king will do to this man upon learning he refused to cooperate with us?"

"Hand him over to Vangerdahast," Arclath replied. "Or Glathra."

Farland's face changed. "Glathra?" he snapped.

"Wizard of War Glathra Barcantle. You know her?"

Farland's hand strayed toward his throat then fell back.

"Leave us," he ordered the two guards curtly.

"But lord—"

"They're both chained," Farland said testily. "If you hear furniture crashing, rush in again. In the meantime, stand well away from the door and *don't* try to overhear."

He waited stonily until the guards had gone out and closed the door behind them, then said, "Vangerdahast is dead and gone, or turned into a dragon if you believe the legends. So that much I know is no more than a false threat . . . but how did you know of my connection to G—Lady Glathra?"

"We did not," Arclath assured him. "But we were sent here after a discussion with King Foril, Royal Magician Ganrahast, and Lady Glathra."

"Oh, just the five of you?"

"No. My mother—Lady Marantine Delcastle—was also present."

"To plead for royal clemency?"

Arclath sighed. "I don't think you quite understand, Lord Constable. Rune and I are merely posing as prisoners. We're here as agents of the Crown, under orders to promptly report back to the king himself."

Farland sat back, smirking. "Of *course* you are."

"Your disbelief is obvious," Arclath said politely, "but we were given watch phrases to prove our claims. I was told to say my father gave me a message for the seneschal."

"And I was told to say: Glathra remembers," Rune added.

That name brought a glint of anger into Farland's eyes again. "I know nothing of these phrases," he said shortly. "Perhaps Seneschal Avathnar did, but he's dead—murdered. So as far as I'm concerned, you are prisoners and will be treated as such." Before either Arclath or Amarune could reply, he raised his voice. "Guards!"

The door banged open and the two guards hastened in, swords drawn.

"Put those away," the lord constable told them sourly. "These two are liars, not bloodthirsty constable-slayers. Take them to the cells assigned to them."

Arclath frowned. "So you'll not even take the sensible step of sending a message to the Royal Magician, or King Foril, or Lady Glathra to check on what we've said?"

"No," Farland said bluntly, as the guards began unhooking the prisoners' chains from their chairs. "Nor will I sit here sharing any confidences with you."

"Lord Constable," Arclath said sternly, "this is less than wise."

The man behind the desk chuckled. "D'you know how many of my prisoners—high-and-mighty nobles, every last one of them—claim to be sent here by Ganrahast or Vainrence or the king himself as undercloak inspectors, to see what we're up to? Almost all of them, that's how many! You're more subtle than most, I must say, who demand command of the castle almost before they're done saying their names! I—"

A door boomed open somewhere in the castle below, and an imperious voice gave angry orders just too distant for anyone in the lord constable's office to make out the words. Other voices disagreed, sternly, and the imperious voice spoke again, more sharply. Booted feet hurried up stairs, coming nearer.

"What *now*?" Lord Constable Farland snapped. "The next prisoners aren't due 'til the month's end! Who—"

"Pray pardon the interruption, lord," a guard puffed, shouldering his way into the room, "but there're three men at the gates who won't heed commands from any of us. They say they're war wizards sent from Immerford, though they look more like traveling tinkers to *me*, an' the one who leads them just told us all grandly he was now in command of the castle, jailers an' prisoners an' all—an' he's frozen Imgrus like a statue for drawing steel on him! Used a wand to do it! I—"

With a wordless snarl Farland was on his feet and out from behind the desk, striding hard.

He didn't reach the door before a cold voice said from the passage, "*There* you are! The *next* time I give you an order, sirrah, you will obey it or spend time as a frog! Running away is *not* the conduct I expect from—"

"And just who by the Dragon Who Rules Us All are *you*?" Farland's roar was loud enough to leave ears ringing, but the cold-voiced new arrival was unperturbed.

"Another lout of a soldier! Salute and then *belt up*, man! *I'll* give the orders here!"

"My, my," Arclath told Amarune, "this is better than a play!"

"Belt up!" Farland and the new arrival both shot at Arclath in unison, ere returning to the evidently more pleasurable activity of glaring at each other, nose to nose.

"I'm the lord constable of Irlingstar," Farland growled, "and in the name of the king—"

"In the name of the king, *you* will obey *me*," the new arrival said icily. "For *I* am Wizard of War Nostyn Vandur, leader of an *elite* investigative force of war wizards sent here by the Crown to investigate the *murder* of seneschal of Irlingstar Marthin Avathnar. Accordingly, I am now in *command* of this castle and everyone in it."

He stabbed a finger at Farland's chest. "*You* are a suspect, and as such unfit to remain in command of anything, until my investigation is complete. I—"

"Until I receive orders from the king himself relieving me," Farland snarled, "*I* am in command here in Irlingstar. *You* could be any raving fool—or an outlaw, or some charlatan mage out of Sembia hired by any of the prisoners—claiming to be a wizard of war. Continue like this, and I'll have you in chains in a cell right soonish, where you can order the walls around until you're out of breath!"

"Careful," Arclath murmured. "If he's a puissant mage, he'll be quite able to order the walls around. Ask him if he knows Glathra."

Farland shot his newest male prisoner a murderous look, then turned back to confront Vandur—only to discover that the wizard of war, or the man claiming to be a wizard of war, had stepped around him and was sitting down behind Farland's own desk.

The lord constable drew his sword.

Nostyn Vandur regarded him scornfully. "Surrender that," he ordered. "Now."

He pointed at the gleaming top of the desk, and when Farland made no move to relinquish his blade, he tapped it in a clear signal.

"Put it *down*," Vandur snapped, as one might to a mischievous puppy.

"No," Farland snarled. "Get up from that desk or I'll *carve* you."

Vandur ignored him, calling out to the passage, "Gulkanun! Longclaws! In here!"

Farland lashed out with his sword. It flashed right through the man behind the desk as if he weren't there.

"I'm protected by an ironguard, of course," Vandur said witheringly. "Seeking to slay a wizard of war who's lawfully pursuing his duties is punishable by death, man, but I'll overlook that if you apologize—here and now, and on your knees—and surrender both your weapon and your objections to my—"

"Punishable by death upon due judgment of a duly constituted trial court," Farland snarled, thrusting his blade through Vandur and holding it there while he reached for the man's throat with his free hand, "which there isn't one of within a day's ride of here. And it's only such an offense *if* you're a wizard of war."

His hand easily thrust through Vandur's two-handed attempts to strike it aside and closed around the intruder's throat.

"Even if you are, I utterly refuse to recognize your authority—and will continue to do so, until informed otherwise by someone whose authority I *do* recognize. No true war wizard would be so . . . so . . ."

Vandur did something with a ring on his finger that made Farland stagger back with a curse, fat blue sparks leaping among his spasming fingers. Farland dropped blade, which clanged off the desk to the floor. "Brusque?" he supplied helpfully. "Arrogant?"

"*Yes*, Dragon take you!" Farland snarled, wringing his hands together, his face creased in pain. "No true wizard of war would behave like this!"

"He's never met Vangerdahast," Arclath told Amarune merrily. "And obviously doesn't remember Glathra all that well, either."

Farland rounded on him. "*Will* you belt up, lord, right now, or will you—"

Words failed him, but his fists came up. Before Arclath could do more than wag a reproving finger and say, "Now, now—" Vandur rapped out, "Touch no one, insubordinate man! Or I'll discipline you here and now!"

He raised a hand into view over the edge of the desk. A hand that had a wand in it.

"You *will* listen to me, Lord Constable," he said crisply, aiming the wand right at Farland's nose, "or I'll strike you motionless until I'm done speaking and force you to hear me that way! As a senior wizard of war, I outrank *any* mere Purple Dragon *and* almost all Crown officers, barring a handful of the most high-ranking courtiers of the realm! I *will* have your obedience, and I *am* in command of this castle!"

At that moment, two men garbed like Vandur but weighed down by various bulging packs, pouches, and satchels came trotting rather breathlessly into the room.

"Sorry," one said to the man behind the desk. "We had a little trouble with the guards—"

"Later," Vandur said curtly. "Their suitable punishments can wait. Right now, it's past time to begin our investigation. This room must be in the north tower, so you, Gulkanun, get yourself *quickly* to the south tower and confirm its layout and our authority to all garrison personnel there. Longclaws, you are to find and secure all exits and entrances to the castle, just as fast as that can be done!"

The two men nodded, turned on their heels, and ran out.

Vandur rose from behind the desk, thrust his wand back into his belt, and raised a hand meaningfully toward Farland as he twisted one of several rings on it. That ring glowed as it was awakened.

"You," he ordered, "will remain here until my return. I won't be long. You might as well continue interrogating these prisoners."

He strode out, closing the door behind him. A moment later, it glowed all around its edges, a brief pulsing radiance of blue, white, and purple that faded as swiftly as it had appeared.

"A wizard lock," Arclath murmured. "I've seen many cast before."

Farland gestured savagely for silence as he headed for the door. He did not storm through it, however. He halted just before it and bent to listen intently. Arclath and Rune gave him the silence he wanted.

Whereupon, through the door, they could all clearly hear Vandur give a command, then repeat the same order in an imperious bark . . . and then start shouting.

"Seal me inside my own office," Farland hissed in grim satisfaction, "and see where it gets you, Saer Imperious."

The shouting was going on and on, rising in tone.

"The guards are defying him?" Rune asked. "Even when he waves that wand?"

"To avoid any prisoner succeeding in a bribe, there are strict standing orders," Arclath explained. "The Dragons serving here will obey only their known superiors, the lord constable, and those he personally tells them to take direction from."

Farland had turned his head to hear what the young lord was whispering. When Arclath was done, he nodded silent confirmation.

The shouting was getting farther away, too distant to make out any words. The war wizard had evidently stormed off, still venting over his shoulder at guards he'd left at their posts in his wake. Then the shouting broke off, as the distant Vandur said something startled and incredulous.

Then he screamed, a long and fearful cry that went raw and shrill—then ended abruptly.

"Stay here," Farland ordered Arclath and Amarune curtly, and he rushed to the door. It refused to open, of course, flaring into bright glows when he tried to force it.

The lord constable struggled with it, cords of muscle standing proud in his neck and wrists, then in a hoarse spitting of curses, he flung himself away and rushed across the room.

In one corner behind his desk, he clawed open a hitherto-hidden secret door and was gone.

Arclath turned to Amarune and murmured, "Now."

Obediently she bowed her head so he could comb through her hair to find the tiny chain around the base of her left ear, recover the lockpick dangling from it, and free them both from their manacles.

Click, clack, clink, ten times over, and all the iron fell away.

Arclath looked down at Rune to see if she was ready to rise—and discovered she was already past him and vaulting the desk to get to the lord constable's secret door.

The passage they found themselves in was narrow and many-branched, obviously running through the hearts of various thick stone partition walls, but Rune kept turning right, to a blind end that of course had a large, easily felt catch in it, that opened a door and plunged them out into a long, wide passage.

A guard stood tensely at his post, looking away from them down the passage. Obviously staring after where the lord constable had just gone.

"Must catch up to Farland," Arclath told the man brightly, as the Dragon's head snapped around and his halberd swung out. Rune had already ducked under it and was racing on. "Lord Constable's orders!"

The Dragon stared back at him for a moment, then nodded and pulled his halberd aside. The heir of House Delcastle ducked his head and devoted himself to running hard, to catch up to his lady and to stay with her.

The passage was longer than it looked, the torches few and dim, the black-painted cell doors many, unnumbered, and more or less identical. Arclath and Amarune were halfway down it before they saw Farland, grimly staring down at something they couldn't see.

There was a cross passage before they got to him, then another. Farland turned to watch them pelt the last little stretch up to him. His sword was drawn, but he didn't lift it to menace them.

The lord constable stood at the end of the passage. Two stairs descended from either side of the passage just before the open gate he was standing at—a stout gate door of metal bars as thick around as Arclath's wrists. Beyond that gate the passage ended at a precipitous flight of stone steps that descended down into darkness. There was a dank, rotting smell in the air.

"How did you get free?" Farland grunted, as they arrived beside him. He was out of breath, probably from rushing down that long flight of steps and then clambering back up them.

"You should believe *some* claims," Arclath replied calmly. "You've found everyone's friend, the suddenly silent war wizard?"

Farland pointed down the main flight of stairs. They were of unadorned stone, unforgivingly hard, and very steep. Fresh blood glistened on some steps.

It was a long, long way down, and they could only just make out a huddled form far down it.

"Pushed," Rune guessed grimly. "By someone he was surprised to see."

Farland nodded, face dark. "He's dead. Another murder. But by someone who was waiting for him to arrive here, or someone he was just a bit too rude to?" His upper lip lifted in a mirthless smile. "Which could be any one of our noble guests."

"Would any of your noble guests have a key to this gate?" Arclath asked.

Farland shook his head silently.

"It's almost always closed and locked, isn't it?"

Maintaining silence, the Lord Constable shifted from shaking his head to nodding it.

Which was when they all heard fast, light panting coming from one of the side stairs, coming closer. Farland's sword came up, and he strode to block the head of that stair. The climber was alone, and ascending fast. It was one of the two lesser wizards of war, his cloak clutched around him like a well-dressed matron hastening through a downpour. He came to an abrupt halt when he saw the lord constable barring his way.

After they'd stared at each other in mutual silence for a long moment, the Crown mage said urgently, "I *must* report to Saer Vandur."

Farland stepped back two paces and grimly pointed down the main stair.

The war wizard gave him a troubled look, then went to head of the stair, keeping an eye out for the lord constable rushing forward to give him a push, and cautiously peered down the long flight.

Then he backed away, blinking in astonishment.

No exclamation. No prayer. Nothing at all.

"So where were *you,*" Farland barked, loud and sudden, "when your superior was being shoved down a killing-fall flight of stairs?"

The Crown mage's face was calm, and his answer prompt. "Checking the ways in and out, as he'd ordered me to. I rushed back here to report that the kitchen door—that offers access to the midden heap—stands open and unguarded. There's no one in the kitchens."

Farland exploded in a stream of heartfelt curses.

In the midst of it, he didn't fail to notice something shifting shape—the wizard's hand, he'd thought it must be—under the clasped cloak. Viciously he slashed the edge of the cloak aside with his sword. The hands, always try for a wizard's hands, unless you've a bow and can use it well enough to send a shaft into his mouth or throat . . .

"Try magic on me, would you?" he roared, starting the backswing that would slice hand and fingers and whatever foul magic they were readying with them.

He'd been going to go right on bellowing warmer pleasantries, but stopped with a startled gasp.

The mage's revealed hand was a grey and scaly ball of tentacles, seven or more writhing, wormlike things that curled and quested in all directions.

The war wizard spun away from Farland's slicing steel—but not before everyone saw the tentacles beginning to change. Erupting and blooming into toadstool-headed growths of slimy brown . . .

With a groan of disgust, Farland snatched a mace from his belt to try to smash the monster down.

A spell came flashing out of nowhere to send it spinning from his numbed fingers.

Chapter Thirteen

Traitors Among Us

The last of the three newly arrived wizards of war stood at the head of the other side stair. The last sparkling lights of his spell winked out, one by one, as they drifted away from his raised hands.

"Even for lord constables," he told Farland, "there are penalties for killing wizards of war. Imbrult means you no menace. What you saw is the curse he lives with daily, not any sort of attack."

The lord constable regarded him for a long, measuring moment, then turned to look more closely at the wizard with the tentacles—or whatever they now were.

"A magical curse," Wizard of War Imbrult Longclaws explained quietly, holding forth his left hand. At the moment, it looked like a misshapen root dug up from a garden . . . a lump that was rapidly growing long, spiky hair. "Afflicting only my left hand. It changes continually. All manner of scaled, tentacled, or fungilike forms. Even after years, the forms it conjures still surprise me from time to time."

"A spell-cursed war wizard? I've never heard of such a thing! Why don't you have Ganrahast or one of the other senior mages rid you of it?"

"The curse holds far worse magics in check," Longclaws said patiently; he'd evidently had to give this explanation many times. "Hanging spells we know too little about to dare tampering—but we know enough about to leave them alone. Unleashed, they'd harm far more than just one Crown mage."

Farland looked from one war wizard to the other again, then said curtly, "My apologies, saer mages. We share more than one problem."

He waved down the stair. "This one is the freshest, and the most pressing. Well?"

The mage who'd spell-struck the lord constable's mace away—a tall, slab-faced man—joined Farland at the head of the stairs.

"Well met," he said wryly, nodding to the lord constable as an equal. "Duth Gulkanun," he added, tapping his own chest. Then he looked down the stair. His face went as expressionless as Imbrult's had, and stayed that way. Neither of them had loved their superior. "Vandur. Pushed, I take it?"

Farland nodded.

Gulkanun shrugged. "I'll thank whoever did this for their valuable service to Cormyr and to the two of us, *after* we imprison them and worm the 'why' of their deed out of them. Did anyone see it happen?" He looked sharply at Arclath and Amarune.

Who both shook their heads, keeping silent. It seemed safest.

"The murderer, presumably," Longclaws said dryly, pulling off his cloak and draping it over his still-shapeshifting left hand with the deft ease of long practice.

"Well, now, I'd *never* have thought of that. I *knew* I was right to call in some *brilliant* wizards of war when things started to go wrong," Farland said sarcastically.

"Lord Constable," Arclath asked soothingly, "have you anything strong to drink in your office, or some other location where we could all sit down together in relative privacy?"

"Away from my other noble guests, you mean?" Farland asked with a tight smile, closing the gate across the head of the stair and locking it with a rattle of keys. He turned back in the direction of his distant office. "Come."

As they fell into step around him, Longclaws taking the rear and Gulkanun the fore without any discussion or signal, Amarune asked, "Lord Constable, where *are* all the—ah, 'guests'? I expected they'd be gathered here to gawk and smirk."

"As per standing orders," the tall war wizard told her, "we cast fear serpents down the passages when we set about the tasks Vandur gave us."

"Fear serpents?"

"Spells that move on from where they're cast, as far as they can drift without encountering a large and unyielding obstacle—like a wall or door. They make folk move away by radiating magic that makes anything that can smell or hear feel fearful and sick. They drove the nobles out of the passages, into their cells. Fear serpents fade fast; the effects will be gone soon."

"So the murderer was immune to this spell?"

"Bore a Purple Dragon badge or the Crown ring most wizards of war wear, more likely," Gulkanun replied, "or just fought through the magic. It can be done."

"So we might be looking for a traitor among us," Arclath said softly. "The guards, I mean."

"We *always* look for traitors among us," Farland told him grimly. "Day in and day out. Sometimes we even find them."

Elminster sank back down amid the rocks, his eyes and throat stinging from the caustic reek of years upon years' worth of dragon dung.

There were no side caverns. Everything narrowed to clefts and then mere cracks in the solid rock, all running in the wrong directions to reach the surface without passing through the dragon's great cavern. She could abandon her drow body, of course, and easily drift up to the Realms Above as a trail of ashes. But, no. She'd fought in this body, reveled in its agility and freedom from ever-present pains, and did not want to relinquish it soon. She loved it. Nor did she want any part of the cruelty that would be leaving the ruined echo of Symrustar Auglamyr trapped to slowly die alone, in a body the fading Chosen was far too diminished to control.

And the dragon was awake.

Worse yet, it was a wyrm she knew. Wherefore it also knew her, albeit as a man with a different smell, and those memories—and most dragons had very good recall of the memories they chose to retain, remembrances they polished brightly and kept sharp—would make it eagerly hungry for vengeance.

Alorglauvenemaus had once, some seven centuries back . . .

But no, what mattered now wasn't long gone days and the deeds done in them. The dragon was awake, malice glittering in its eyes as it fixed its glare on the dark hole it usually backed up to void into, awaiting an intruder.

It knew something alive was lurking nearby, beyond that opening, and it had risen and recurled itself atop its great hoard, settling itself amid the clinkings and slitherings of great drifts of collapsing coins into a new position that put its head chin-down amid its heaped loot, facing the back cleft in which it had smelled and heard life moving.

Movements that had continued, albeit with great stealth and patience, after it had twice spat gouts of slaying acid down the hole.

Something was down there, something that wanted to come up. And it would come while Alorglauvenemaus yet waited, for there was *nothing* more patient than a dragon.

El could have conjured a spying eye to peer at the wyrm, perhaps even goading it into spewing more acid—but doing so would tell it what it faced, and some dragons had mastered or collected enough magic to do great harm to wizards. Moreover, she didn't need to see the dragon move into a new pose of vigilance to know what it was doing; she'd heard enough dragons, even taken a dragon's shape herself in the past, to know it was ready and waiting for her.

No, she knew better magic to employ. In some ways, dragons could be as easily goaded as dwarves lost in gold lust. Threaten their hoard, move and handle treasures they deemed theirs, and the wyrms had to fight hard to resist the rages that awakened in them.

Alorglauvenemaus would have to fight harder than some, for it had begun to settle into the sedentary, stay-at-home life of the dragon that no longer boldly fared forth to forge respect and fear, making a place for itself forcibly in the life of the part of the Realms it chose as its dominion. It made bargains with humans and other lesser beings to work for it, to be its arms and jaws and bearers of influence, while it increasingly sat and pondered and slept. Alorglauvenemaus would feel more threatened than a young dragon, yet more angry and eager for a fray than a wyrm sliding from ancient into its twilight.

El rolled over to face the unseen dark stone ceiling overhead, biting her own lip to get the trace of blood she'd need to make the magic properly powerful, spread her arms wide, and began to cast the spell.

She worked slowly and carefully, opting for calm precision and near silence rather than the swift, bold gestures that went with a shouted battle incantation.

Either would work, for one who knew the Art well enough. And Weave or no Weave, she knew her magic.

It was a very old spell, powerful but essentially simple. Some Netherese mages had called it "the Awakening," when they weren't being too fanciful in namings that sought to claim older magics as their own. *The* Awakening, stronger and less limited than other such magics. It was rarely used these days, when wizards had become walking repositories of minor magics worn on the fingers, toes, earlobes, and everywhere else, and its casting would unleash the unintended unless they stripped away and left behind all of that enchanted clutter.

They got it from us, *those arrogant archwizards,* Symrustar said tartly.

"Aren't all human archwizards arrogant?" El thought.

The answer came with a tone of amusement. *Those particular arrogant archwizards.*

Elminster sent her mind guest a silent smile. She had already removed the scepters and everything else magical she carried or wore, and left them in a cleft in the cavern below this one. She'd known the spell she would need, and the one that would be necessary after that, too.

"Rise, Alorglauvenemaus," she whispered, after the first incantation was done. "Time to dance!"

Then she rolled over and ran for the cavern wall, hard by the nearest side of the opening into the cavern. In any cave, stalactites could fall like daggers when explosions set the stone to *really* shaking.

Right on cue, the Nine Hells erupted in the dragon's lair.

It began with an ear-splitting crash, and a wild volley of crackling, ricocheting lightning bolts that blinded her and lashed on down the chute of melted, smoothed rock that descended to the Underdark. Bolts bounced and crashed and ripped the air as they went. By then, great gouts of emerald and ruby red radiance had flared, chasing the bolts, and the stones were shaking and groaning, splitting here and there and raining down dislodged fragments of themselves, large and small, in slumping roars that were lost in a greater, rising rumble that went on and on, almost drowning out the deep-throated roars of draconic rage.

In the thick of it all, Alorglauvenemaus was being tumbled this way and that, scorched and flung up against the sharp, scale-shattering ceiling by what was being unleashed beneath it. Startled and then bewildered and then enraged, it cursed loud and long in the tongue of dragons, great roars that echoed amid the heedless explosions, fury that turned inevitably to fear.

It had to get out. It had to flee while it still could.

Seared and scorched, buffeted and torn by scores of magics all clawing at it and the stone walls and each other, it scrambled and clawed its way up out of its lair. Its surging and whirling hoard pelted it with coins and shards of gems and hurtling swords as it sprang out, whirling with a great lash of its tail to glare back at where it had been, seeking its unseen foe.

The cavern was a raging chaos of erupting magics, spells that tore at each other, stabbed through each other, and shaped incongruous effects amid the tumult. The air was full of a whirling hail of tinkling, clashing coins, ricocheting in a singing, shrieking storm through which larger things hurtled and crashed.

Elminster's very old spell simply awakened all magic in a small area of effect—in this case, the heart of the hoard the dragon had been lying on—the choice magics it had gathered from a thousand tombs and magetowers and battlefields.

Light of the Seldarine! Did the Srinshee teach you this? Symrustar was truly shocked, her awe plunging El's head into tingling mind fires of excitement.

The tumult rose higher. In the cavern on the other side of a groaning wall of solid rock that had seemed thick and enduring enough a few moments ago, wands, rods, and scepters galore were spitting their discharges into a great shrieking and flashing maelstrom of Art. Explosion after explosion shattered treasures and hurled them against the cavern walls. Wards were breaking, small metal prisons failing, and more magics were escaping and flaring into life. A staff spun up into the air to spit ravening rays in all directions, seared stalactites plummeted, and glowing gems swirled through the buffeting storm like an angry swarm of bees.

Baffled and furious, Alorglauvenemaus peered vainly into the chaos, seeking a cause, *the* cause, an enemy it could fight and rend and exact proper payment in blood from, for this violation and destruction.

Magic lashed at it and burned it, crashed down upon it and clawed at its scales, battering it with such mounting pain that the dragon finally fled for good, springing out into the chill air outside. *Who* was meddling with its magic? Who?

Were there others, out here, abetting the foe within?

Surely no puny "walking meat" creature could have mounted *this*!

The dragon spread newly tattered wings and flew in a tight circle, so as to glide along the face of the peak that held its lair, peering narrowly . . .

No. No living thing was lurking, none could be seen but a few tiny, cowering birds on their usual ledges. No foe here . . .

Well, if that enemy or enemies *was* inside, and had come from below, it would come out sooner or later—and Alorglauvenemaus would be waiting for it. Or if it intended to steal, taking gold or gems back down to the depths it had come from, it would have to await the fading of all this unleashed magic to get to those treasures. And when that fading came, so too would Alorglauvenemaus, setting aside mercy and forbearance. No thieving from a mighty black dragon—not when it could seize the bones of thieves by force.

Alorglauvenemaus wheeled in the air to glide past the mouth of its lair again. Soon . . .

Manshoon smiled. Lord Crownrood, chancellor of the realm, had found the need to confer with certain sober-minded and just nobles of Cormyr as to the conduct of the leading families—and court and Crown, too—of the kingdom, in these troubled times.

The invitations had gone forth, and the time and place had been set. Andolphyn, Loroun, and Blacksilver would accept, of course.

Lurking like a shadow in their minds, Manshoon would see to that. Just as he'd seen to Crownrood's conceiving of the meeting in the first place. It would be interesting to see which of the larger fish not already in his net would rise to take his hooks, and end up caught.

Patience. Deft and stylish patience. He'd never seen the appeal of fishing before—the steaming platter of results had engaged him rather more—but now he was feeling how fun it could be. Truly slow meddling, subtle manipulations . . . he was beginning to see the long game Elminster had enjoyed so much.

Damn the Old Mage and damn Mystra, too, but a certain Manshoon was enjoying the slow and subtle. At last.

Numbed by some of the earliest lightnings but otherwise unhurt, El stretched her arms, clawed the air experimentally with her long fingers—and ducked around the edge of the cleft leading into the cavern, keeping low.

Wand blasts were still bursting against the ceiling far across it, sending increasingly large chunks of rock crashing down into the already-scattered hoard pile. Alorglauvenemaus was going to be . . . quite irate.

"Well, that makes two of us," El whispered aloud, surprised at the tremor of rising anger in her own voice. She *was* tired of constant battle . . . though there was doubtless a lot more of it ahead of her.

Bare-skinned and unhampered in the slightest, Elminster raced into the cave, his eyes fixed on a particularly large chest of sapphires that was lodged in a great heap of coins at an upthrust angle, like the prow of a ship breaking a tall wave. Its lid had broken open, revealing its gleaming contents. Rings scattered here and there among the spilled stones winked merrily as other magics raged around the cavern, as if in applause—or sympathy. Ah, she missed the Weave, that would have let her *feel* which magics lay here, what was yet slumberous and untouched, and if there was any measure of sentience among the Art in this lair at all . . .

El had to touch that chest as she spoke the last word of the incantation, then get back out of the cavern again, unscathed.

The coins were smoking hot in places, making her gasp with pain, and something that gave off a purple-green glow heaved slowly under a dune of coins as she dashed across it, a heaving that spat a great curling fireball at the ceiling—but with a whimper, El reached the chest, put her hand on its jet-and-silver side, and gasped out the one word she needed to say. And the chest took flight, rising out of the glittering hoard like a heavy, reluctant dragon taking wing, but soaring faster and faster . . .

As El scampered back to her cleft, flinging herself into a headlong dive when a fresh fury of wand bursts curdled and rent the air, the chest obeyed her will, hurtling out into the air high above Hullack Forest.

You still love to dice with death, El, Symrustar commented wryly, in a mind voice laced with a fleeting flash of emotion. Admiration? Or contempt?

El knew not, but she knew what *she* felt: anger. Anger at having to do such dancing, all the time, at the bidding of others.

Just now, a wyrm who was old and wise enough to know better.

Hah. Even before she landed in a bruising roll on hard rocks on the safer side of the cleft, El knew the ancient black dragon had succumbed to its essential nature. Outside in the mountain air, it was giving chase, diving after its errant gems with a roar. El forced the chest to turn sharply, and climb, then turn again and dive, trying to keep it out of the jaws of Alorglauvenemaus for as long as possible.

She wanted the dragon well away from its lair, because dragons could really *move* when they wanted to—and it would not go well for her if it came racing back, its retrieved chest in its jaws, and caught her in its lair or on the exposed mountainside, clambering down to greater cover and safety.

So take nothing from its hoard at all, the better not to be traced. Retrieve only what she'd brought from the riven drow citadel, and get *gone,* out onto the cliffs and down, down into the concealing forests of Cormyr!

A wise idea, Symrustar said wryly. *The dragon returns.*

The great flapping bulk of the dragon was growing larger, though it was probably still distant enough to be over the Wyvernwater.

El gave the chest a sudden twist with her mind, followed by a strong soaring, then a plunge.

The dragon whirled. Evidently it had lost its grasp on the chest. El made the distant gem container plunge again in the air. In hot pursuit, the dwindling speck of the pursuing dragon descended. Smiling, El made the chest zig and zag, soar and plunge, turning it again and again in screamingly tight curves. After all, even ancient black dragons deserve a good wingstretch . . .

Directing those aerial acrobatics all the while, she rushed through the cavern and out, then began the careful climb down the mountainside.

You should have cast a second flight spell on yourself, Symrustar mindspoke, after the second finger-bleeding slip.

"I should have done a *lot* of things these last dozen centuries," El replied, watching a jaunty parade of stones dislodged by her boots plunge down, down to jagged rocks far below. Among those waiting stone points were *treetops,* hrast it! "I've never been the sharpest blade in the armory—and have spent a lot of time being one of Faerûn's utter dullards."

Well, so she had. Perhaps she'd been succumbing to her own essential nature. Or perhaps she'd just been trying to stay alive, as more selfish, reckless, and evil beings galore lashed out at her or at folk and places she loved and was moved—or sworn—to defend. Hrast them all . . .

By the obvious scars on the rocks around and below, the dragon had repeatedly clawed away foliage and the most easily climbed spurs of rock, to make its lair as inaccessible as possible to anything that couldn't fly.

However, it was easier—if one had nerves of battle steel—to descend than come up from below. All you needed was the strength, agility—and resolve—enough to jump to the next mountainside over, in the right spot where a long ago storm or perhaps dragon battle had toppled a peak into a shower of great boulders that had tumbled down between the two heights to wedge between them, in a rugged, misshapen natural bridge.

El found what she judged to be the best spot, then leaped. After all, there *would* be time enough to work a feather fall, before she was dashed to blood-splattering pulp on those waiting rocks, much lower down . . .

She hoped.

Chapter Fourteen

A Fate Richly Earned

Elminster landed hard, skidding helplessly on loose scree, and crashed into a boulder.

The pain was wincingly intense. Drow ribs, it seemed, were no stronger than human ones.

She clung there, her teeth clenched, embracing the agony that pulsed at her every breath, until her arms and legs had stopped shaking.

Cool as winter ice, Prince of Lost Athalantar? Despite its edge, Symrustar's mockery was . . . aye, affectionate. *Of course, El. I love you, and you are all I have left, now. For my little while.*

El sent warmth to surround and soothe that forlorn mind voice, then forced herself to climb down from the boulder and work her way into the stone-choked cleft. Off the open face of the mountainside and away from a returning dragon's eyes, and not a moment too soon . . .

She lost herself in the slow, careful, and seemingly endless work of finding the next handhold and the next, deciding where to let go and fall, and where to rest and use the tiniest jet of silver fire to heal broken and bleeding fingers or restore shattered feet and ribs—and once, after an unexpected slip, most of the bones in her new body.

You're not taking very good care of it, Symrustar teased. That made the rest of the descent much easier, because El spent much of it dredging up half-forgotten curses and rude descriptions to hurl at her mind guest, in what became a mirth-filled game for them both, as the fading echo of the spirited elf he'd met so long ago in Cormanthor protested in mounting mock horror at what she was being called, and declared herself scandalized and ruined and worse . . .

And then the endless climb was almost done, with no dragon plunging out of the sky to spew acid or bite or slash with cruel claws, and Cormyr was no longer a great green carpet spread out before her, but individual trees thrusting into the sky nearby, forming a closer horizon.

El paused in a crouch on the last ledge above the ground. She was about five man-heights up from the scrub and dead trees that descended to the ditch, and the lower three of those five weren't rough mountain rock, but rather a flaring slope of loose earth and gravel, washed down the peak by many a storm and scored with countless channels carved by rushing water that had fled and was gone. She could see shadows under the closest trees, the ones that stood hard by the winding ribbon of Orondstars Road. Those shadows lay on the sometimes sun-dappled, usually gloomy forest floor of the very easternmost edge of Hullack Forest. The vast woodland that would probably be her bedchamber during the night ahead, as she slept within whatever spell-spun defenses she could mount. It would be best to get as far from the dragon's lair as she could, being as all dragons could smell or sense magic to some small, oft-unreliable degree. And she'd better start without more delay, and—

There. Right there. She could drink from that spring and then just step in under the leaves and—

Hold, what's *this?*

Out of the very spot under the trees she'd chosen, a man stumbled into view, exhausted and drenched with sweat. He clutched a dagger, blood streaming down his arm to drip from his knuckles and fingertips. He was about done in, staggering along on sheer determination. Hunter's garb, light leather but very well made, almost a uniform—

A ring on the middle finger of either hand! A war wizard!

El spun around, lowered herself until she hung from her fingertips from the ledge, and let go, twisting in the air.

She landed in a half-turn on the slope, skidded, caught a foot in unyielding stone and ended up rolling head over heels, to a muddy halt in the ditch, crushing some nettles along the way, to look up and see the war wizard—

Sobbing his last, his dagger falling from his failing hand, as three blades ran him through from as many directions.

Too late, hrast it! Too often too late!

El hissed out rising fury, fists clenching. A fourth man came running out of the forest gloom, his sword drawn back to deliver a vicious chop to the throat of the Crown mage who was already vomiting blood, dying on his feet, only held up by the swords still through his body.

Why, gods, is that so frequent a fate for those who try to work good, or stand for order? El thrust out a hand and sent them lightning, her anger making it snarl rather than just crackle down her fingertips. Her long, eye-searing bolt sprang across the ditch and the road and the second ditch beyond, flashing brightly into the gloom, where it struck the men and their swords and split to race among them, roiling and ricocheting as they shouted and convulsed, caught in its brief bright coils.

The war wizard slumped, his head lolling, scarcely touched by the lightning at all . . . already dead. His four attackers staggered and screamed and danced, their arms and legs spasming involuntarily, their hair standing on end, and their eyes and mouths wide with pain. Then something flashed forth from the war wizard's chest, bursting open the leather of his jerkin. Something bright, that spat many lightnings. A death-lightning amulet!

Elminster's bolts were gentle in comparison, already fading—but the war wizard briefly became a rigid, spinning top that stabbed bolts of lightning in all directions. El was glad of being breast-down in mud and nettles, because the men in the trees—there were six or seven of them, or even more, coming at a run to share in the slaying, not just the four he'd seen—were taking a fierce punishment.

When the amulet was spent, and the stiff body of its wearer had toppled in silence to the dead leaves and fallen boughs, only three men still stood at the edge of the forest, all of them reeling and groaning, sorely wounded. Everyone else lay sprawled and still.

El found her feet, clambered over the ditch and the road and the ditch on the other side, and ran into the trees, toward the sharp seared-boar smell of cooked men she knew she'd find.

"Who are you?" she demanded sharply of the first man she reached who was still alive.

He turned a pain-wracked face to her, roared out wordless anger and pain, and tried to slash at her with a short sword she'd not noticed until then. His unsteady swing missed entirely and sent him crashing down onto his face. She ran on.

"Who are you?" she demanded of the next man. He gave her a bewildered look; half his face had sagged as if it was melting, and the pupils of his eyes were of very different sizes.

"Who do you obey?" she snapped.

"B-b-broadshield," he choked out, and he toppled. So these were the notorious Broadshield's Beasts, outlaws who—

A shadow fell across the sky.

El raced for the nearest large tree. An arrow thrummed through the air right in front of her chin as she ran, and a second howled past just behind her. Then she was at the tree, around it, and plastered against its trunk, trying to become very still.

She could see more men coming her way now, striding through the forest with bows in their hands and murder in their hard eyes.

The foremost pair couldn't be more than a dozen strides away. They lacked bows, but bore long knives, and would reach her in a breath or so. Thick underbrush crackled as they burst out of it to close on her, raising their knives—and suddenly something large, scaly, and black plunged and snatched, with blurring speed.

It left behind a patch of sunlight that hadn't been there before, with several trees splintered and fallen and the leaves of another tumbling out of the sky, in the wake of a huge black dragon that banked along the mountainside so closely that its great batlike wings rippled at the touch of rocks racing past beneath them. As it climbed, more than branches and leaves fell from it. Something dark and wet fell, too. Something that looked like the leg of a man.

The new sunlit patch stood empty. The two Beasts who'd been hastening to kill Elminster were gone.

El kept very still, watching Alorglauvenemaus turn in the air, in a great arc that would bring it around and howling down out of the sky right . . . at her tree.

She backed hastily away to the next tree, keeping her eyes on the great black wyrm. The chest of gems was clutched in its jaws, its eyes blazed with anger, and its claws were slowly tightening *through* two wet bundles that had been men.

More of Broadshield's Beasts had almost reached the patch of sunlight, and were slowing to peer at the scar the dragon had made.

It made another, right through them.

Shrieking men fled in all directions as great claws grabbed and then tightened. Wings flapped along the mountainside again ere the dragon climbed, its shoulders surging and its wings beating—and when it was as high as the lowest clouds, it let go of all it held in its claws. El watched tiny shapes tumble amid despairing cries, and shivered despite herself. Then as faint and distant splatterings began behind her, she turned and ran through the forest, seeking thickly tangled bushes deeper in the trees.

The splintering crashes of the dragon's third and fourth visits came from well behind her, but by the time El dared to skulk warily back to the dragon's scar, Alorglauvenemaus was flying slowly above the trees examining just one body in its claws. It recognized that dead man, flung the corpse down in disgust, and flapped back to its lair.

El melted back against a tree trunk and stayed there for a good long time, watching for the dragon's return—but it didn't reappear.

There was a time when I could have saved the lone mage, defeated all these outlaws and the dragon, too, without slaying them, and . . .

Aye, there had been a time.

We all grow old, Elminster, Symrustar reminded him. *We all grow lesser. Every one of us, Chosen or commoner or rough beast. 'Tis the way of the world.*

"I . . . ," El replied aloud, roughly. "I . . . grow tired of the way of the world. And increasingly it seems the world is growing tired of me."

Are you angry? Or sad?

"Both. Sad more than angry, for now."

For now. The voice in his mind deepened, sounding for a moment more like that of long-gone Khelben speaking doom than it did wry and mocking Symrustar.

"For now," El whispered to the trees, keeping her eyes on the mountainside where the dragon would appear, if it emerged again from its lair.

Yet the breezes blew and the silences stretched, and there came no dragon.

Eventually she dared to go to the body of the fallen war wizard. That amulet wasn't something all that many of Cormyr's Crown mages walked around wearing; this must have been someone important. He either hadn't worn one of the enchanted war wizard cloaks on this little forest foray, that could teleport their wearers away from harm, or had lost it somewhere along the way.

There was no hope of healing the man, after what the amulet had done; above his waist and below his shoulders, there just wasn't much left of him. El relieved the dead fingers of their rings, swiftly checked the boots and belt for anything else of interest—two daggers and a few pouches of spell stuff, most of it spoiled—then hastened away into the forest, trying to walk more or less parallel to the winding Orondstars Road, but also to get well away from all the dead men. When dusk came stealing in, there'd be no shortage of hungry prowlers. It would be highly desirable to find a stream and walk along in it for some time, to throw off anything tracking her by scent. The rings, now . . .

As she walked, El examined them. The first, a standard war wizard ring. She slipped it onto her own hand, onto the middle finger of her left hand, just as its rightful wearer had worn it. The second one . . . could this be a commander's ring? Nay, plain but with a little "dragon snout" triangle projecting from the band, along a wearer's finger . . . 'twas that other sort. Aye, a . . . *team* ring, worn by members of perilous mission teams. Caladnei had instituted them. What luck! El slid it onto her other middle finger, and murmured the word that would make the little band identify its owner.

"Brannon Lucksar, wizard of war," the ring announced solemnly, in a hard-edged male voice.

So she'd witnessed the last exhausted, stumbling moments of the life of Brannon Lucksar—the leader of the crack war wizard team based at Immerkeep, if she remembered rightly. Lucksar may well have been the last survivor of his team, hunted down and slain by Broadshield's Beasts. Had they already killed the other war wizards?

El sighed. So much death . . . so many bad things she could do nothing about. Even when she was there in time, she managed little or nothing . . .

Lucksar's team ring revealed to her mind that it . . . seemed to have the usual powers: it could record four verbal messages, empower a sending spell, and store a little healing magic. It could also, El recalled, be readily traced by from afar by other war wizards.

Walking warily on through the forest, El listened to the ring's four messages. One was a congratulations for "Another task well-handled," from some gruff-voiced unknown older man who concluded by telling Lucksar, "Your reward will be harder tasks, a fate richly earned." Another was a breathless female whisper, "I love you; take care." A third was a terse series of instructions for finding a hidden cache in a city alley somewhere . . . and the fourth implored: "Get done with this quickly, then get yourself to Castle Irlingstar to look into the murders there before Vandur and his lads make *too* much of a mess of things."

Well, *that* much Elminster could and would do. She would go to Irlingstar—perhaps too late to stop Vandur making messes, but she'd go to Irlingstar, and there claim to be Wizard of War Brannon

Lucksar. She'd say she fell down a shaft into the Underdark, fought fell creatures there, was mortally wounded, and died in an eerie place that must have been what some arcane sages call an earth node, where the magic of Faerûn itself surged strongly. Where she somehow awakened later in this drow body, put there by a magical curse or a whimsical deity or the mindless magic of that eerie place or *something* . . . Aye. She had mental ferocity enough to mind battle any wizard of war who tried to mindspeak her—

And if you don't, I do, Symrustar piped up.

—and she'd do it. Impersonate Lucksar for a time, a normal man's lifetime if need be. This would be her first stride along the road to recruiting the wizards of war to Mystra's service, without revealing to Manshoon or anyone else that the infamous Elminster still survived.

"Ganrahast! *There* you are!"

The Royal Magician blinked, looked up from the large array of maps, floorplans, and written reports he was bent over, and smiled. "Ah, Glathra! You wanted to see me?"

If Glathra of the war wizards noticed that her superior's smile seemed a little forced and weary around the edges, she took no notice of it. She was too angry to notice much of anything that didn't bellow at her, thrust a sword or spear in her direction, or hurl a spell that sought to separate her back teeth from the rest of her.

"You're hrasted right I do!" Glathra spat angrily, firmly slamming the door closed behind her, so no guard or palace servant would stray too near, and overhear. "It's Storm Silverhand!"

"Ah! You've had your usual reports, and—?"

"I have, and our fellow wizards of war are almost unanimous in telling me that the woman seems to have wings! Or can translocate tirelessly, to whisk herself around like a god! It seems Storm Silverhand has been flitting here, there, and everywhere, all over Suzail and in naeding near every room in this palace, not to mention daily appearances in Waymoot and Espar and—and just about every last hamlet and village in all Cormyr! And they tell me she's getting past patrols and gate guards and the like with a *commander's* ring!"

Ganrahast nodded. "Those reports are correct."

"Well, *what* by the Dragon is *going on*? *Why* is she being allowed to do this?"

"It's the king's will," Ganrahast told Glathra gently. "I believe he values the loyal nobles of our land, and she *is* the Marchioness Immerdusk, however ancient the title. She has been doing vital work for the Dragon Throne. Soothing many nobles, seeking to bind them more tightly in loyalty to the Crown, in the wake of the disaster at the council."

"Oh? All the reports that have come to *my* ears speak of her visiting *commoners*," Glathra snapped. "In smithies, sundries shops, tanners—and brothels. *Not* nobles in their high houses."

"Ah, that would be her other mandate. Her obedience to the commandment of the Lady of Mysteries, the goddess all mages once held dearest, and will again."

"*What* commandment?"

"To make the Harpers once more strong and numerous."

"*What?* And you've *let* her do this? Raise an ever-present army of traitors in our midst?"

Ganrahast smiled gently. "And how exactly should we go about seeking to stop her? When we can instead watch from afar, and so learn exactly who each Harper is, what their skills are, and where they dwell?"

Glathra stared at him, chastened. "Oh. Ah. I see." Then her frown drew down again. "How do we know she's not aware of our scrying, and deceiving us?"

Ganrahast shrugged. "We know she *is* aware of our scrying. She's told me—and the king—that Harpers want a stable, just, happy Cormyr, lightly ruled by a benevolent monarch. Happily, that's precisely what King Foril wants, too. Storm doesn't mind if we know who most of the Harpers are; she sees it as a good check and balance on Those Who Harp."

Glathra frowned, shaking her head. "Yielding up such a weakness . . . I don't think I'll ever understand senior Harpers—or these self-styled Chosen of Mystra, either."

Ganrahast smiled again. "I don't think we're meant to."

The chasm was deep, its sides bare rock that was jagged in some places and smooth in others; the hardened flows of a volcano that was now nowhere to be seen.

What could be seen was an eerie purplish radiance deep down in the stony gulf, a glow that was sometimes half-bright and sometimes very dim. Great drifts and serpentine coils of shadow shifted constantly in the chasm air, undulating back and forth. A warm, sulphurous wind was blowing up out of the chasm. Those shadows were the smoke of some strange elsewhere blown upward by it, undulating endlessly as they came.

Horrid creatures came with them, long human-headed snakes with wings. There were also little ribbonlike eels that flew without wings, and spent much of their time restlessly coiling and uncoiling in the air. There were fat, wrinkled ovals with four batlike flapping wings each, that saw by means of a single oversized eye, and had cruel underslung jaws like sharks . . . and there were other things. They streamed up into Faerûn, riding the shifting smokes, in a tireless invasion that plunged almost gratefully into the dark wilderland forests above the chasm.

A sudden blue-white star flickered into being in midair above the gulf, in the heart of that flow.

The shifting shadows shrank back from it, bending away in their endless streaming . . . as it grew, faded, and coalesced into—

A long-limbed, unclad woman floating upright in the air with her long, long silver hair coiling and whipping around her like a great tangle of restless, energetic snakes. Her legs were together, but her arms were flung wide, and in her clenched hands were two things that blazed with vivid blue flames. A chalice and a sword.

Their flames howled and snarled in all directions with a quickening hunger, many of them arcing back and forth across their holder's breast as the two blue fires sought to join, visibly scorching her.

She tossed her head in pain, biting her lip and moaning from time to time, as the blue flames grew brighter and larger, their searing tongues longer.

"Elminster," the hovering woman gasped, "where are you? Be with me! Be with me now! Oh, I need your strength . . ."

She sobbed, then fought for air enough to cry, "*Elminster! Hear me!*"

That cry was loud and borne far on the rising wind from the gulf.

Yet aside from some cruel laughter from the winged snakes rushing past, there came no reply at all.

Chapter Fifteen

The Penalty For Treason Is Death

The Simbul let her head loll back on her shoulders. She was exhausted, shaking with weariness, and far from done.

And the pain was only going to get worse.

Back and forth across her the blue fire raged, faster and faster, the howls of the two balls of blue flame around her hands becoming a loud and continual roar as they built higher and higher. The dark creatures riding the shadows shrank back and mewed in fear as they scrabbled past.

The Simbul's hands were blackened yet uncharred, burned but not consumed. The tongues of blue flames were twice her height, towering blazes that stabbed at the sky—and leaned inward to touch in the air high above her. There the blue flames wrestled briefly, then blazed forth with renewed fury, forming a single raging, roiling sphere of blinding blue flame that . . .

Boiled over, collapsing down into the gulf like an extinguished geyser. Behind that flood, from the chalice and the sword in The Simbul's hands, came lances of blue, rays of eerie light that stabbed down into the roiling shadows in the depths of the chasm.

The Simbul turned in the air, tilting over until she could look down into the gulf below, moving her shaking arms to aim the rays issuing from the items she held, her body trembling with the strain. Stabbing at the rift far below.

Back and forth she moved, shifting the unfailing rays to rain down on the purple glow in the depths, seeking to obliterate it.

Slowly that radiance faded, darkening, and the shifting shadows faded with it, becoming tattered and sporadic rather than unbroken snakes.

The Simbul held her vigilance, watching and aiming intently, making certain the vivid blue fire she directed was consuming the shadows . . .

Suddenly those dark ribbons started to whirl around her, as if being sucked down a drain, the stream of monsters becoming a few struggling individuals, the shadows around them receding to reveal . . . still emptiness.

Shadows no longer shifted.

The purple glow was gone.

No wind blew up out of the chasm. It was merely a gulf of darkness and bare stones, not a rift breathing out a stream of monsters.

The Simbul floated slowly up out of the gulf, blasting the slowest of the last handful of monsters flapping toward the forests with a few fitful bursts of blue flame.

Then she flew away, slowly and wearily, hanging in the air like a dead thing.

Soon, Alassra, a soft yet mighty voice whispered out of the air all around her, the gentle words like thunder in her soul.

Soon shall come the rest you ache for. The rest you've richly earned.

The room was dark and small, but its furnishings were rich, and the lone chair was surprisingly comfortable for such an ornate monstrosity.

Sraunter the alchemist would have been nervous indeed, sitting alone in the dark, in a palatial Suzailan noble's mansion where he *knew* he did not belong. Yet the future emperor of Cormyr was quite content to lounge in the chair in Sraunter's body, booted feet up on a gilded side table, locked into the anteroom by his own hand.

He was not, strictly speaking, alone. He had the cowering remnant of Sraunter's awareness for company, crushed into a dark corner of the man's own mind, and he had several small eyeball beholderkin tucked into the bulging breast of his surcoat, in case he needed them to deliver swift messages, or warnings, or pursue anyone.

At that moment, however, he was relaxed and content, his attention several rooms away from his small, dark refuge.

In that other, brighter nearby room, a meeting was taking place. A moot he'd caused to occur with his mental meddlings. A gathering of several of his subverted nobles and as many other members of Cormyr's nobility—men he hoped to recruit to his cause without having to invade their minds directly. For each mind he forced himself upon was one more possible gap in his armor, one more way for inquisitive wizards of war to detect him. So given the patience that the removal of Elminster afforded him, it was time to see if the unwitting could be swayed to his cause by argument and their own inclination alone, rather than coercion.

It was going well. The nobles around that table, their tongues eased by wine, were busily deciding that although the ruling Obarskyrs were utterly and historically corrupt, and should eventually be deposed for the good of the realm, in the short term the greater affront to the liberty and health of the kingdom were courtiers who deceive royalty, nobility, and commoners alike, enact Crown will to their own advantages, and (as old Lord Haeldown had just put it) "oppress all."

It was agreed that regicide, however tempting to some, would bring open civil war and a long period of strife, despoiling the same fair realm they sought to free. So rather than take down King Foril—who was, after all, elderly and (as Lord Taseldon said) "like to die soon, anyhail"—they would instead seek to remove the worst of the courtiers.

Specific persons at court, the worst of the "jumped-up covert rulers of us all" (Lord Haeldown again) would be murdered in a series of "accidents." Properly done, in a careful sequence, these removals should arouse a minimum of war wizard suspicion, and serve to weaken the efficiency of Crown service and promote younger, more corruptible courtiers into the forcibly created vacancies.

"The Dragon Throne, like any other throne, stands on legs—those who obey royal commands. If we remove these legs, one by one, there will come a time when the throne *will* fall," Lord Blacksilver gloated.

"And though the penalty for fell treason is death," Lord Taseldon added, "pruning the realm of corrupt, loyal-only-to-themselves courtiers is something *very* different. Something . . . *patriotic*!"

"So who, my lords," the chancellor of the realm purred, "should be first courtier to be pruned?"

There was a little silence, broken by everyone starting to speak at once. This name was cast onto the table, and that one, with almost obscene enthusiasm . . . and when the rush of suggestions at last faltered and silence came again, one name had been mentioned far more than any other.

Rensharra Ironstave, lady clerk of the rolls. As the head of tax appraisals for Cormyr, she might be the friendliest of creatures, yet by the very nature of her office still be a thorn in the sides of all nobility and wealthy landowners. As it happened, she was *not* the friendliest of creatures. Stubborn and sharp-tongued, a shrewd woman who seemed able to sense deceit before it was wholly laid out before her, she steadfastly refused to be bribed or cozened—and seemed to take enthusiastic delight in revealing even the most minor deceptions of the nobility, making public examples of their attempts to evade taxes.

In his antechamber, Manshoon smiled. So it was to be self-interest foremost, after all. Well, it was good to know how truly *noble* the nobles of Cormyr were.

Lord Haeldown said, "I used to think our war wizards were all little Vangerdahasts—young foolhead wizards from all over the Realms he tracked down and cast mind magics on, so they became his little thralls. Mayhap they were. He certainly seemed to learn everything that befell behind closed doors all over the kingdom as fast as if he'd seen and heard it himself. Yet I doubt that outland Caladnei woman, nor this weak-nothing Ganrahast we're saddled with now, have managed the same trick. These days, our wizards of war make mistakes, often work against each other deliberately or unwittingly, and seem no more cohesive than, say, our Purple Dragons. There's no mighty mage lurking behind them who can flit from head to head as he pleases and move them all like strikers on a lanceboard. That's how Vangey survived all those assassination attempts, you know. He'd leave his body to be hewn down and leap across half the realm to land in another head, then turn around and conjure up another body for himself."

"I agree, that's what the war wizards *have* been like," Lord Taseldon agreed, "but no longer. These last few days they seem . . . different. Watchful, ready for trouble. Now there *is* a wizard linking their thoughts together—for the first time in as long as I can remember."

Lord Loroun leaned forward in interest. "Who? Surely not that nice, sensitive fool Ganrahast?"

"Hah! If he could do so, he'd have been doing it all these years, no? It's not his name they're whispering around the palace. The one they are giving tongue to, courtiers and Dragons alike, is 'Elminster.'"

Lord Haeldown waved that notion away with one wrinkled hand. "The legendary Mad Mage of Mystra? He'll be thousands of years old now—*if* he's still alive! You *really* think us all dullards enough to believe that?"

"No, I think our great-grandsires got fooled, and theirs before them. I've heard talk that Elminster has lasted down the centuries because he isn't one man, but wizard after wizard that Elminster's mind floods into and conquers. Dozens at once, so some can't help but survive, whatever befalls. That drives them all mad, of course, but what wizard isn't? Right now, I think he's inside the head of every last damned wizard of war—or soon will be."

Manshoon stiffened in his comfortable chair, his jaw dropping open. His face was suddenly hot, the mirrors all around showing him that his eyes were blazing . . .

Could this be so? Could Elminster really be commanding the minds of Cormyr's Crown mages?

The future emperor of Cormyr got up and started to pace, which in the tiny anteroom was not easy. He paced, over and over, his mind lost in furious thought.

It *could* be so! Every last damned wizard of war . . .

"Urgh!" Harbrand grunted in pain, rebounding off his saddlehorn for the fifty-four-thousandth time, and rubbing at the eye beneath his eye patch. It itched, whereas his groin had long since become one huge and tender bruise. "These saddles aren't getting any more comfy!"

Hawkspike's reply was a sullen growl. His own creaking rides were always uncomfortable, owing to his hanging as heavily in even a high-cantled saddle as a sack of potatoes. "You should've worn a bigger codpiece!"

"There *are* no bigger codpieces, friend Hawkspike! Not when one is—"

"Endowed like several competing stallions? I've heard your lines before, remember? Tell me, did they work on Old Skullgrin?"

"Hawk, Lady Dawningdown is our *client*. I'd hardly have managed to land us our commission—or escaped her mansion without my backside tasting a good lashing—if I'd been foolish enough to let my tongue run *that* freely!"

"It's run a mite too freely before," Hawkspike reminded his partner sullenly.

Harbrand sighed. "Hawk, this is getting us nowhere, and despite these sad excuses for horses—"

Their third pair of stolen mounts had been less fresh and fit than they'd gambled on, and for the last little while had been stumbling and faltering under them, clearly exhausted. However, this wild mountain country was no place to stop in. Raw rock peaks on one side, the outlaw- and monster-haunted Hullack Forest dark and close on the other . . .

"—we *are* drawing near to Irlingstar—"

"At *last*."

"—at last, indeed, and it's more than time for us to settle on a plan—however tentative—for how we're going to fulfill Lady Dawningdown's commission."

Hawkspike spat on a defenseless stone they were passing. It wasn't the one he'd aimed for, but it *was* a stone. Not that they were rare targets, along this gods-forsaken excuse for a road. "So talk."

Lady Dawningdown had hired them to free her son and heir, young Lord Jeresson Dawningdown, who was imprisoned in Irlingstar. They were to get him across the border to Bowshotgard, a hunting lodge in forested northern Sembia.

However, it had dawned on both surviving partners in Danger For Hire that they were more likely to be handed their own deaths at Bowshotgard rather than their promised payment, so they devised their own variant to Lady Dawningdown's arrangements.

They would free Jeresson, get him into Sembia, drug him to sleep and then bind and hide him. Then they'd hire a Sembian intermediary to go to Bowshotgard with the news that Hawkspike and Harbrand were betrayed by hirelings and slain, and those hirelings are now heading back to meet with Lady Dawningdown and demand a huge ransom for Jeresson. The intermediary would claim to venerate Bahamut, Lord of Justice, above all other gods, and to be shocked by the behavior of his fellow hirelings—so he fled, to reveal Jeresson's whereabouts to those at Bowshotgard, and enable them to go rescue him.

If those at Bowshotgard didn't believe the intermediary, or enspelled him to learn the truth, or slew him, Hawkspike and Harbrand would simply move on, forgetting all about the Dawningdown coins, to try their fair fortune in northeastern

Sembia and more distant locales. But, if the Dawningdown allies at Bowshotgard sallied forth to go find Jeresson, Danger For Hire could covertly plunder all they could carry off from Bowshotgard, by way of payment in lieu of their commission, and move on far wealthier.

However, all of this thinking began with the glib words "free Jeresson," and *that* was the part of it all that still needed discussion. They had the sleep drug, and plenty of waxed cord to bind a prisoner with. They even had a capture hood, to muffle and blind a captive. They had a vague idea of the layout of Castle Irlingstar, and the names of its seneschal and lord constable. And that was about *all* they had.

Harbrand gave his partner a weak, twisted smile. The sort of grin that more sheltered and civilized folk would have called a "sheepish" smile.

"Well," Harbrand began, not having the slightest inkling of what he was going to say next, "I—"

Something gray rose into view above the trees, then, and he thankfully interrupted himself to point and say, "Behold! Our destination, Castle Irlingstar!"

Hawkspike grunted wordlessly, managing to convey his deep lack of being impressed. "Looks like a—"

Whatever architectural judgment he'd been planning to deliver was lost forever in what happened next.

There was a sudden, thunderous roar that rebounded off many mountainsides, and a bright flash amid billowing smoke, as an explosion burst upward from the battlements of the prison castle.

In its wake, something huge and black and scaled flapped hastily away from the keep, roaring in startled pain.

A dragon! A black dragon, its groans deep and angry as it circled back into the mountains.

Hawkspike looked at Harbrand, and Harbrand looked back at Hawkspike. Then they both put spurs to their mounts, to hurry on toward Irlingstar.

Complaining, their exhausted horses broke into uneven gallops, plunging two bruised and unhappy riders into fresh, lurching saddle-buffetings.

The two surviving partners in Danger For Hire traded a second set of glances.

After which they both reined in their mounts, hard.

If that dragon came their way . . .

Both somehow clung to their saddles through the wild rearings, kicks, and buckings that followed.

But then they decided instead to leap off and tether the snorting, head-tossing beasts to nearby trees in frantic haste. The men got their saddlebags undone and safely rushed into cover.

Their swords and daggers had been freshly sharpened, and went through the tethers in a trice, freeing the nags to wander at will.

Into the yawning jaws of an angrily swooping dragon, for instance . . .

The two hireswords sprinted back into the trees, grabbed up the saddlebags, and ran.

They were soon panting hard—the saddlebags were hrasted *heavy*—but kept at it until their wind ran out.

Whereupon they crashed down into the dead leaves and dry needles, to lie there side by side, gasping.

They were well away from where they'd freed the horses, but a bit too far into the deep gloom of the endless forest.

They looked to where the sunlight was brightest. They'd go back to the edge of the forest, where the road was, and skulk the rest of the way to Irlingstar on foot, keeping under the trees.

Explosions, dragons . . . those extra offerings to both Tymora and Beshaba hadn't won them anything different than their usual luck.

"I *told* you," Harbrand said suddenly, "stolen things are no good as offerings. Goddesses can tell."

Hawkspike's reply was swift, pungent, and probably more of an affront to Tymora and Beshaba than any altar offering could have been.

"*I* am Lord Constable here," Farland reminded the tall, laconic, slab-faced war wizard sharply.

"So you are. I'd almost managed to forget that, despite your nigh-constant minders," Gulkanun replied. "Almost."

And he winked.

Farland was mildly astonished to find himself on the verge of smiling. This Duth Gulkanun was . . . likeable. All too vocally ironic, but far less irritating than Lord Delcastle, Master of Mockery, yonder. Hrast it, he liked this man.

"Very well," he said, turning quickly to glare at the other war wizard—the one with the curse that shapechanged his hand continually. As usual he had moved silently to stand too close. Close enough that he'd be crowding any man, not just a jailer trained to guard against such things, to keep prisoners distant, and give himself enough room to swing a mace or a sword.

This man, he did *not* like. Sly and sharp tongued, entirely untrustworthy in word and deed. A felon, Farland would have deemed him if meeting him for the first time and not knowing this Longclaws was a wizard of war. He'd fit right in with the noble guests in Irlingstar.

Aye, the man struck him as properly a prisoner, not any sort of respectable Crown officer. If they'd been alone, Farland would have reminded him sternly in an instant that the penalty for treason was death.

"Very well," he repeated, advancing on the irritating Imbrult Longclaws until the man—satisfyingly, but lord constables learned to claim and count such small satisfactions—gave ground, "we'll do it your way."

"*And* trust what answer I return with?"

Farland nodded, and he managed to quell a sigh ere he echoed, "And trust whatever answer you get."

Chapter Sixteen

A Room For The Night

Not surprisingly for a fortress built as a prison, Castle Irlingstar didn't have many outside balconies. One of its few opened off the records room, adjacent to Farland's own office.

Wizard of War Gulkanun headed out onto it now, Longclaws following him as far as the records room. There the curse-ridden wizard turned, leaned back against the desk, and drew two wands from his belt. Though he said not a word, his intent was obvious: to keep everyone at bay, back where they couldn't see what Gulkanun did. The magic of opening a small breach in the wards was a war wizard secret, and would be kept that way.

Farland glowered at Longclaws, who met his gaze with a faint smile. They both knew what Gulkanun was doing, but that didn't mean the lord constable had to like it. So many folk were trying to give him orders in his own castle that he was on the verge of losing track of them all, hrast it.

This Gulkanun—a decent sort, as far as war wizards went—needed the breach to spell speak with Glathra Barcantle back in Suzail, to report the deaths and inquire if the two new prisoners were indeed the undercover Crown agents they claimed to be.

Glathra. The lord constable's fingers went again to the pendant he wore, hidden from view beneath his ever-present gorget. It was a token from her, that she'd given him on a tender night long before matters had ended so badly between them.

"Use it if ever you need me at your side," she'd said, her eyes large and dark. Words he'd never forget.

So why was he so all-fired *glad* that some slab-faced wizard of war was talking to her now, so he didn't have to?

The Crown mages marched back into the room, far sooner than he'd expected. Farland snatched his fingers away from the hidden pendant as if it might burn them.

"Suzail now knows about the killings," Gulkanun told him, "and these two can be trusted; they are what they claim to be."

Farland inclined his head. "My thanks, saer." He turned to Amarune and Arclath. "Deepest apologies to the both of you. I hope you'll appreciate that a lord constable cannot be *too* careful."

"Of course," Arclath said graciously, as Amarune nodded.

Farland smiled and waved one hand at an apparently solid wall. He saw Lord Delcastle crook his eyebrows, and he hastily leaned forward with his keys to forestall whatever clever—and irritating—comment the noble might make, to unlock the secret door. Making a swift "stay back" Crown signal he knew the two mages would understand, he led the two prisoners—ah, *undercover agents*—through the door.

The room beyond was small, windowless, and had no other door, only ventilation holes about the size of a small man's wrist in opposing corners. Crammed into it was a cot that served both as a bed and as a seat for use with the low, plain table beside it—a table that held a decanter, two stout wooden mugs, a dome-covered earthenware platter, and a lanceboard set up for a game.

Farland lifted the dome to reveal wedges of cheese and sausages, and pointed at the decanter. "Wine." As graciously as any socially climbing Suzailan hostess, he waved the two Crown agents to seat themselves, stepping back to give them room.

"Yours for the night, Crown agents," he said gently, from the door. "We'll confer on the morrow."

Then he stepped outside, slammed the door—and locked them in.

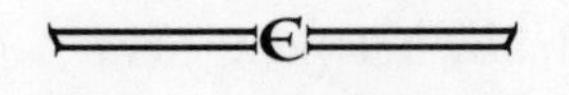

"So what," Elminster murmured aloud, "would Brannon Lucksar do?"

Use the secret war wizard way in, Symrustar suggested dryly, inside her head. *If the chapbooks and tavern tales can be believed, there always is one.*

El sighed, nodded, and started along the castle wall, trailing his fingertips along the dark, rough stones and watching his rings closely. If they glowed, that just might mean a secret entrance.

If not . . .

Hammer on the prison doors and try to seduce the guards who show up. That *should get you arrested.*

"Everyone should carry a Chosen in their head," El murmured aloud. "They're *so* helpful."

In the back of his mind, Symrustar made a very rude sound.

Arclath charged the door, furious, but he might as well have been hammering on and clawing at solid stone.

Pulling and tugging and shoving the immobile door vainly, he called the lord constable some choice things ere he gave up, panting, and spun back to Amarune.

"I'm sorry, Rune," he sighed. "I was such a *fool*! I should have seen that coming, should've—"

Amarune's fingers tapped across his lips, to still his speech. She gave him a crooked smile and held up one of her boots. She must have slipped it off while he was attacking the door.

He watched her press with her finger and thumb at the front corners of its heel, where the heel curved in before flaring out again to underlie the rest of the foot—and pull gently, straight back.

The heel slid off the boot, revealing itself to be the hilt of a short dagger. "Careful," she breathed, holding it up. "This is *razor* sharp."

"Where did you—?"

"Storm. She got it from a Harper in Suzail for me." Rune set the dagger on the table and shook the boot, her hand cupped to catch whatever fell out of the revealed cavity in the foresole that the dagger blade had been sheathed in.

Out dropped something small, wrapped in silk. She did something deft with her fingers and thumb that splayed the silk bundle open, and Arclath found himself looking at an array of lockpicks.

"I'm the Silent Shadow, remember?" Rune whispered with a smirk.

Slowly, Arclath smiled back.

His lady glided close and embraced him. The better to murmur disbelievingly into his ear, "Are those two *truly* wizards of war? Have *you* ever heard of a war wizard who has to live with a magical curse?"

Arclath shook his head. "No, and—"

He promptly forgot whatever else he was going to say as the floor surged under their feet, as if trying to rise to meet them. The table, decanter, and all sprang into the air, and the whole room rocked and swayed to the tune of a deafening, growing thunder.

Dust fell in a sudden, heavy cloud, and as Arclath spun Amarune around and rushed her to the nearest wall, trying to shield her, pebbles pelted them, and larger stones could be heard crashing down here and there.

The stones around them groaned alarmingly . . . but as that ominous sound deepened, the thunder faded, as did the shuddering and swaying.

Long moments later, only the dust still moved, swirling chokingly, setting them both to coughing. As they hacked and shook, everything else quieted.

Then light abruptly flooded in. The door that had been locked was snatched open again, and a frowning Gulkanun was reaching through it to clutch at Arclath's arm.

He hauled the young lord back out of the cell—Rune right behind him, hopping as she reassembled her boot and got it back on—and into Farland's office.

Where the dust was thinner, though some cracks had made jagged paths down the walls that certainly hadn't been there before—and

Longclaws was restraining the lord constable, one hand clutching the man's gorget and the other holding a wand warningly in Farland's face.

"Come," Gulkanun commanded grimly, turning his head to extend that order to his fellow mage and the lord constable, as well as Rune and Arclath. "For now, we're keeping together."

Longclaws released Farland and waved him toward the door. The lord constable burst through it at a grim run, the rest of them right at his heels.

Two murders, and now an explosion they were rushing off to investigate—

"Ah, *adventure*!" Arclath exclaimed delightedly.

Beside him, Rune rolled her eyes.

Unexpectedly, Gulkanun started to chuckle.

The mood among the duty detail of war wizards on the battlements of the naval base at the eastern end of Marsember was sour . . . and getting worse. A full-throated storm was rushing ashore, right over them, nigh-drowning Marsember for the ninth time that tenday. The rain had worked its way up from pelting to lashing down, then to hammering the flagstones and cobbles hard enough to bounce back up and wet chins from below. Now, as usual, it had begun to slant like the murderous down-thrust lances of aerial cavalry, driving stingingly into even the most carefully cowled face.

The Crown mages huddled in their weathercloaks, their hoods up and shoulders hunched, already drenched and getting colder. Rain-warding spells were useless up on the battlements, thanks to the old, powerful, and many-layered wards that protected the towers against hostile magics. They tried to squint through the deluge—with even less success than they managed to ignore the wet creeping into their boots and running down their necks inside their weathercloaks.

"Tluining weather," one wizard muttered. The one beside him nodded in miserable silence. They were all eyeing, with more than a little suspicion—or trying to, in the storm, and didn't the smugglers and slavers *love* these sorts of storms?—a ship running into the public trading harbor. It was bucking the wild waves down there, amid all the rocking, rising, and falling moored ships, and—

It was time. Every last one of them was intent on his work. Diligent fools.

Manshoon said the last word of the incantation, and his spell took him from dry but overcast Suzail to the naval battlements of storm-lashed Marsember in an instant.

He appeared right behind the line of war wizards. *Just* as he'd planned. He allowed himself the moment necessary to form a wide smile of satisfaction before he spread his hands and cast his next spell.

It dashed all the wizards of war against each other, bruising and breaking limbs and leaving some dazed or nigh-senseless, before thrusting them up into the sky in a tight, feebly struggling tangle. They hanged there in midair, stabbed at by the lightnings of the passing storm, while he cast his next spell with unhurried precision.

It struck them like a falling castle wall, and flung them high and far through the storm clouds, trailing a few ragged shouts, to rain down out in the open sea beyond the breakwaters, broken and dead.

Manshoon looked to the right, then to the left. Heads were turning far along the battlements, at the corner towers where Purple Dragon sentinels stood, in the only posts in all Cormyr where they were allowed to eschew armor and to stand without spears at the ready.

Some of those sentinels were starting to run in his direction, and to shout. What he'd done to the Crown mages had been seen.

Manshoon smiled almost fondly at the running men. "This thinning of the war wizards," he murmured, "is going to be as easy as it is enjoyable."

And as the fastest of the running soldiers came close enough to see the face of their future emperor, he gave them a broad smile of greeting—and vanished, leaving only bare, rain-swept flagstones for them to hack and stab at.

Dust was everywhere, though the rumbling and shaking had stopped. Farland was coughing hard but sprinting as if he didn't need to breathe or rest, along grim stone passages and down gloomy stairs and along more passages and up yet more stairs. Panting, Arclath, Amarune, and the two war wizards kept right on his heels.

Everywhere they ran, they heard shouting. Frightened, aggrieved prisoners bellowing through the gratings in their cell doors. Demanding to be let out, or crying for aid, or shrieking and sobbing that they were hurt, by all the gods, and needed "Succor, *now*!"

"Anyone who can plead eloquently isn't hurt *that* badly," Longclaws commented as they rushed past entreaty after entreaty—and into a din of fresh ones, ahead.

As they hurried on through the dust-shrouded fortress, it seemed most of the noble prisoners of Irlingstar were more frightened than hurt. A few were wandering dazedly, blinking through masks of thick dust, freed by the blast as walls had cracked, and the wards around their cells had faded.

The fear serpent spells that had been prowling the corridors were gone entirely, and as Farland and the others hastened, increasingly they saw prisoners who were *almost* free. Cell doors yawned wide or had fallen, but the men they were meant to confine were trembling in midair, caught in stubbornly persisting wards that kept them on the verge of being held in place; they could struggle forward *very* slowly, if they strained and fought with all their strength.

Farland kept going. Past the steep stair where dead Vandur still lay, awaiting a proper investigation before burial—and providing meals for the rats until the blast had sent them scurrying, no doubt. Past the boarded-up shaft that had served as a "food up, chamber pots down" elevator until too many prisoners had been wedged in it head-down by cruel fellow inmates and left to die. All the way to the series of heavy doors that guarded the approach to the south tower.

The first set of doors was locked, but the lord constable of course had the keys, and barely slowed on his way through the doors. The second pair of doors was cracked but still standing, the locks twisted but holding. Farland's stout kick served where his keys no longer could.

The third set of doors sagged half-open, locks and latches broken and the spandrels above shattered and sagging. There was daylight beyond them where the fourth pair of doors should have been, that opened into the south tower.

Lord Constable Farland skidded to an awkward halt just beyond the third doors and gaped, too shocked to spew obscenities.

The south tower was . . . missing.

Instead of stone rooms and ramparts ahead, they were treated to a cool breeze and a splendid view of the Thunder Peaks marching away south, on their left, with the last winding bend of Orondstars Road just below and the great dark green carpet of Hullack Forest flooding away south and west for as far as they could see.

Farland moaned, as if he were about to be sick.

Amarune frowned at the cold, then calmly pulled her jerkin up to her chin to hold it there, so she could unwind the cord she'd wound around herself, under her breasts.

Gulkanun gave her a grin and took one end of it. Longclaws and Arclath assisted, her beloved gesturing to her to spin around. She obeyed, swiftly yielding into their hands a neat coil of black cord she'd long ago prepared for climbing by tying knots in it at intervals.

The lord constable had been trying gingerly to peer down over the jagged edge where his fortress now so abruptly ended, scrambling hastily back whenever stones sagged or fell away under his boots.

The moment Gulkanun tapped him with one end of Rune's cord, he looked up, nodded, seized it, tied it around himself in a crude sling, and was over the edge almost before they could brace themselves to take his weight.

Rune snatched up a scrap of broken-off wall bracket to guard against the paying-out cord being sawn at by the raw edge of broken stone Farland had vanished over, but she'd barely crawled to where she could thrust it under the moving cord before it stopped moving and the lord constable called hoarsely, "Pull me up. I've seen enough."

"So," Gulkanun asked a few puffing moments later, as they helped Farland to his feet, "what's 'enough'?"

The lord constable shook his head, seeking words. He'd gone so pale that old scars and pimples stood out on his face like startlingly dark festival face painting.

"More than the tower's gone," he said grimly. "The whole south face . . . blasted away, every floor laid open. I could see the passages like a column of holes, all the way down. For now, that is. Everything's sagging."

As he spoke, they heard a long, slow clattering crash from somewhere below the edge. It was the sound of stones falling away from Irlingstar like a lazy rain, as the shattered blocks beneath them crumbled and slumped.

Farland winced as if someone were smashing a precious treasure. "There'll be more of that. I don't think anything's safe, as far back as the central well."

"The stairs where Vandur fell?" Arclath guessed.

Farland nodded wearily. He looked close to tears.

"Mind!" Longclaws said sharply, darting out to clutch at the lord constable and drag him back. A deep, yawning groan had begun in the stone around and beneath them.

As they all hurried back past where the fourth pair of doors should have been, the stones off to their right started to lean.

As they stared, that slow lean became an inexorable topple . . . and an entire pillarlike buttress of the castle wall collapsed. It broke up as it fell so its descent became a roaring cataract of tumbling stone that shattered several trees and carried them away in an instant—exposing two men who'd been hiding behind them.

Two heavily armed men in motley leather armor adorned with gorgets and codpieces and other mismatched pieces of metal armor here and there, among all the pouches and baldrics and dagger hilts.

The five agents and officers of the Crown stared down at them.

"I am the lord constable of Castle Irlingstar," Farland growled. "*Who* are *you?*"

The two strangers looked back up at him, taking heed that the hands of the two men flanking him were rising as if to work spells—and that one of those hands looked like a bouquet of flowers whose leaves were rapidly growing into curling, questing tentacles.

"Uh, Harbrand," one of the men—the one who wore an eye patch—blurted out, before jerking a thumb at his companion. "*He's* Hawkspike."

They both added rather guilty grins to these names.

"Ah . . . any chance of a room for the night?" Harbrand asked. "There's a *dragon* flying around out here!"

The doors of the well-hidden chamber deep in the haunted wing of the royal palace of Suzail were firmly spell-locked. Some conferences required privacy even from royalty.

"Glathra, just get used to the fact that some things are going to be kept secret even from *you*. Until the time is right for you to know."

Glathra glared back at the spiderlike Royal Magician Vangerdahast, and spat, "But I *should* have known *all* about this! It's vital to my work!"

"It's no more than a distraction from your work until we know it functions, and safely, so it can be relied upon," Lord Warder Vainrence husked, from where he sat slumped in a chair. He was still weak and pale, but recovered enough from the spell trap that had almost slain him in the palace cellars to rise from bed at last. "If we can use it for a time before word of it spreads, we'll gain that much more by it. And word will spread fast, mark you; in the first reports brought to me since I've been up and about, some nobles have already begun to talk of war wizards as recently seeming very 'watchful.' So until you truly needed to know . . ."

Glathra's eyes blazed, but she turned from glowering at him to give her glare to the current Royal Magician of Cormyr.

Ganrahast merely nodded and told her, "Correct. Hence my orders to that effect."

Wizard of War Glathra Barcantle slammed both fists down on the table in exasperation, then whirled to face the silent, silver-haired woman sitting beside her, and wagged a pointing finger almost in Storm Silverhand's face. "Yet *she* knew—and she's not even Crown-sworn, or of Cormyr!"

"She knew because she did most of the work of perfecting it," Vangerdahast growled, advancing across the table like a crawling spider. Glathra shrank back in revulsion, hating herself for her fear and disgust and finding fresh fury in his unlovely grin. He *knew* how she felt about him and was coming at her deliberately!

"Just as I knew about it because I did the rest of the work," the spiderlike thing added, ere turning abruptly and crawling away.

"And as it happens, Lady Storm *is* Crown-sworn—and is of Cormyr," Ganrahast said quietly.

"Not to *our* king! Nor is she a citizen dwelling within our borders, who pays taxes to the Crown! She presumes a lot, on a title bestowed centuries ago!"

"As to that," Vainrence said with sudden heat, "we wizards of war *all* presume a lot. It's what we do. Now *have done*, Glathra. I'm not sure how much longer I can stay awake, and this is important."

Glathra looked away from him, and at Storm Silverhand. Keeping silent, Storm gave her a friendly smile, but Glathra pointedly turned her head away.

And found herself looking at Royal Magician Ganrahast, who shook his head sadly as he drew a coffer from his belt, opened it, and began to set forth its contents, in a gleaming row down the center of the table.

Rings, all identical. Plain bands except for the little dragonsnout point each one bore. War wizard team rings.

"The new mindlink magic works through these," he murmured.

"A *mindlink* that *works?*" Glathra was unable to keep all incredulity out of her voice.

Ganrahast blinked. "Well, ah . . . no one's gone mad just yet."

Chapter Seventeen

I Am Your Gentle Reminder

"Until now, we've not issued many of these," Vainrence added, "but this last tenday, we've been getting them to all wizards of war we can reach." He pushed one ring out of the row, toward Glathra. "This one's yours. The rest are linked to others already being worn by several of our fellow Crown mages."

Glathra eyed it suspiciously. "Are any of you wearing them?"

Vainrence raised his hand to show that he was.

"Anyone else?" She glared at the man-headed spider. "*You?*"

"Of course." The spider rolled over like a toppled child's toy, to display a bright ring snugged right up to the root of one of its nether legs. "I crafted them, after all."

Glathra frowned. "I thought you said—"

"I don't work much magic at all, these days," Storm told her calmly. "However, I witnessed a *lot* of Elminster's spellcraftings, down the years, and remember them all, very clearly."

"So—"

Storm interrupted Glathra smoothly, "So while you take the time to decide if you dare put your ring on, dear, suppose we get to discussing the reason why everyone else at this table is so eager to start using this light, communications-only, *non-coercive* mindlink."

"I've only your word for that," Glathra snarled. "For all I—"

"*Enough*," Royal Magician Ganrahast told her, his voice just short of a roar. "Lady Storm has the right of it. What matters is not our new magic, but the reasons we need it: far too many nobles plotting treason, and our growing need to respond *swiftly* to foil attacks on any Obarskyr—and on our fellow courtiers, several of who have been killed or wounded since the council."

"Not just courtiers, but our fellow wizards of war," Vainrence said heavily.

"*What?*" Glathra was too astonished to keep her voice low.

"In the last few days, war wizards across the kingdom, outside Suzail, have fallen silent—presumably slain. More than a score already."

Glathra fell back in her seat aghast.

"You're being told *now*," Ganrahast said sternly, before she could voice the protest he knew would be forthcoming. "Though we lack a revealed and declared enemy, it seems Cormyr is at war. With itself, perhaps—yet I very much fear that longtime foes and neighbors are part of this, or soon will be. We cannot afford traitors within. We must smite treason where we see it, not waiting for investigations and trials."

Storm shook her head. "No, Royal Magician," she said quietly. "Once you ride that horse, tyranny has begun, and you are no longer defending anything worth fighting for."

"Too late, Lady Storm," Vangerdahast grunted, his spider legs taking him a little way down the table to face her. "I took to riding like that long ago, just to keep something called 'Cormyr' standing. As the one who tutored us both said: 'the time comes when all airs and graces are torn away or must be cast aside, and ye must do what ye must do.' That time has come."

Storm locked gazes with him. "That time came, and has gone. The time for trust and holding to laws and principles has returned. For those who can."

Glathra swallowed her instinctive retort, drew in a deep breath, then asked Storm gently, almost humbly, "Forgive me, lady, but who are you to tell us, the law keepers of Cormyr, to keep to laws?"

"I am your gentle reminder," Storm replied, "before the commoners outside these walls tell you the same thing far more fiercely. If they rise, their telling will spill blood in this palace, and the Dragon Throne may well not survive."

Glathra went pale, but hissed, "Is that a threat?"

Storm shook her head in sad denial. "A prediction, from one who's seen such risings too often before. As Elminster once told me . . . if you cannot be a shining example," she murmured, "be a dire warning."

One of the line of team rings on the table suddenly burst, its fragments pinging and singing around the room. One shard sliced open Glathra's cheek as it hurtled past. She managed to stifle a shriek and settled for clutching at where the blood welled forth.

"Another good man gone," Ganrahast said grimly, looking down at the scorch mark on the table where the ring had been.

Vainrence shook his head. "Good *woman*. That was Laeylra, in Waymoot."

Glathra stared at him. "Lael? She and I served together at—at—" She burst into tears.

Storm reached out a long arm and gathered the wizard of war to her breast, to cradle her while she wept. Vainrence muttered a curse and looked at Ganrahast.

"No," Vangerdahast snarled, before the Royal Magician could say anything, "You bide *here*, to muster and give orders, and refrain from rushing off and playing the dead hero. Right now, you are of far more worth to the realm as a live coward."

The spiderlike remnant of one of Cormyr's most powerful mages turned again to give Storm a look, over Glathra's shaking head and shoulders, and added, "Kindly *don't* remind me of the circumstances in which Elminster told us those helpful words. I've remembered them, all by myself."

Storm gave him the merest ghost of a smile.

The lord constable's office, Amarune thought sourly, was beginning to feel all too familiar.

She and Arclath and a grim Farland and the two war wizards were crowded into it, neglected stomachs growling, to confer. At last. They had spent some tense moments locking people behind various doors, after checking that those doors—and the walls around them—were in a fit enough state to confine anyone. The two rogues hight Hawkspike and Harbrand had been hustled into the castle and locked into a suite of rooms meant for visiting priests or Crown healers, the nobles who'd dared to wander the halls had been firmly locked into various cells, and it was time to start deciding what had caused the explosion. Or how to go about uncovering that cause.

Was it "the" murderer, slaying other intended victims in a great explosion? No less than seventeen minor nobles were now missing, and at least some of them had to be dead given the blood and severed hands, feet, and other chunks of blood-drenched bodies strewn in the great heap of rubble due south of where the castle now ended.

Or was it the murderer getting killed himself—or herself, or *themselves,* hrast it—when something exploded before it was supposed to?

Or did the blast have nothing at all to do with the murders?

These two suspicious new arrivals, now, Hawkspike and Harbrand—thorough rogues if ever any of the five Crown-loyals had seen one—did they have anything to do with either of the two slayings, or the explosion? Or did the dragon they said they'd seen? Both of them insisted it flew away into the mountains right after the blast, a tale that was altogether too convenient—yet was echoed by a few of Irlingstar's imprisoned nobles, who'd been given no chance to confer with Hawkspike and Harbrand.

"A black dragon *is* rumored to lair somewhere nearby in the Thunder Peaks," Farland said glumly, as if admitting a personal crime, "and has been sighted many times over the years. Not by me, but by many I'd trust. It's never been known to approach Irlingstar or raid out past the Hullack into settled Cormyr proper—so far as I know, at least."

Gulkanun nodded. "We'll tackle the dragon later—if it attacks us, or after we hunt it down, if that becomes necessary. Right now, we have a shattered prison and a lot of deaths, two of which couldn't be the dragon unless it can shrink down greatly in size and breach the wards, or send spells through the wards . . . and I personally doubt any dragon can do either without leaving the wards destroyed in its wake."

Everyone but Amarune nodded. She followed the Crown mage's reasoning, but knew too little about warding magics to agree with anything.

"Exactly how many nobles are incarcerated here?" Gulkanun asked the lord constable, "and who are they?"

Farland looked doubtfully at Arclath and Amarune, and the taller war wizard snapped, "*Aside* from these two, whom I judge you can speak freely in the presence of."

The lord constable regarded Gulkanun stonily. "I rather think that is *my* judgment to make."

"Sworn officer of the Crown," came the mildly voiced reply, "I feel moved to remind you that all of us have sworn oaths of service, and are here because we're serving the Dragon Throne right now. Setting aside rank, I ask you to consider which of us commands spells that can turn others of us into frogs, or garden statues . . . or chamber pots."

Arclath grinned. "Spoken almost like Vangerdahast," he said approvingly.

Farland ignored him. "Is that a threat?" he snapped at Gulkanun.

"And if it is?"

After a moment of tense silence, Farland turned his head to favor each person in the room with his coldest glower, then said heavily, "The time has more than come for the full truth from all of us." He turned to Arclath and Amarune. "Suppose you forget all about keeping secrets, and tell us precisely who sent you here and why."

"We promised someone rather higher in rank than you that we'd keep *his* secrets," Arclath replied coolly, "and we'll continue—"

"You promised the king," Gulkanun interrupted flatly, "in the presence of the Royal Magician, Lady Glathra, and your mother. There was also someone else present, whose identity wasn't shared with me."

"Storm Silverhand," Amarune supplied. "The Marchioness Immerdusk. Tell them everything, Arclath."

"Everything?" he asked reluctantly.

"*Everything*," she said firmly.

"Well . . ." Arclath gave his beloved a doubtful look, then said in a rush, "You know our real names already, and that we're not really prisoners, and who sent us. We've come to Irlingstar to find someone within these walls who hails from Sembia, who's trying to take over the castle or free its noble inmates and spirit them away into Sembia, to work treason against Cormyr from there."

Farland gave him a disgusted look. "Oh, come now! There's no—"

"Perhaps, lord constable, the 'someone' is you," Arclath said firmly. "Please understand that I haven't one shred of evidence to that effect, but your attitude of disbelieving dismissal is *not* shared by the king—and what better way to frustrate an investigation than to sneer and deride and refrain from cooperating?"

"How do you know the traitor inside Irlingstar is Sembian?" Longclaws asked quickly, waving Farland to silence. Surprisingly, the lord constable bit back whatever he'd been drawing breath and leaning forward to say, and sat back with a silent frown.

"I've no reason at all to believe King Foril Obarskyr would lie to us," Arclath replied. "Why would he? Well then, he told us that wizards of war had overheard a passing spell sending, a verbal message they believe reached its intended ears without any attached suspicion of their hearing it. It was a man's voice, saying this: 'We'll wait at the usual place, because it's clearly our side of the border. If any Dragons come for us there, the griffonbacks'll be waiting, and they'll taste the new hurl bombs.' "

"And how would you interpret that message, lord constable?" Gulkanun asked quietly.

Farland stirred. "That whoever's waiting for escaped prisoners from Irlingstar has alerted the Sembian border patrols—the ones that ride griffons, in the sky—to be ready for Cormyreans pursuing them."

Gulkanun nodded. "I hear it the same way." Beside him, Longclaws nodded.

"So now," Amarune spoke up, "*you* tell *me*, lord constable, why we should trust *you*, when it's feared prisoners might so readily escape Irlingstar. And"—she turned to give Longclaws a hard and direct stare—"*you* convince me that you're a war wizard, yet have some sort of magical curse or affliction. I've never heard of a Crown mage going uncured of such a thing yet continuing to serve, so *are* you a wizard of war, truly?"

Farland started to speak, but Longclaws flung up a blue and floppy-fingered hand that was busily turning into several clusters of scaled, greenish black talons, to silence him.

"We're here to investigate the lord constable *and* everyone else in Irlingstar, just as you are. As for *this*—"

With his unchanging hand, the war wizard gestured at his talons, just as they collapsed into flopping, writhing, rose pink tentacles, then started to shift into a tight cluster of what looked like questing, dribbling boar snouts.

"—I suffered this years ago, when fighting outlaw raiders on the Moonsea Ride beyond Tilverton. We routed them, ere a black-dragon-riding wizard appeared and served us the same way. He gave me this, and half a year later caravans brought us the tale that the legendary Manshoon the Deathless, Black Cloak Lord of the Zhentarim, riding a great black wyrm, had 'humbled an army of Cormyr bent on conquering the Dales.'" Longclaws gave Rune and Arclath a mirthless grin. "So if I ever encounter this Manshoon . . ."

"*If* you ever encounter Manshoon," a sharp-edged, lilting, melodious new voice interrupted, as yet another secret door swung open, "you'll probably last for as many moments as he bothers to toy with you. I'd seek nobler aims, if you want your life to hold fulfillment and satisfaction."

Everyone turned to stare at the new arrival.

It was a curvaceous, darkly beautiful female drow.

She smiled at them as she held up her hands, wriggling long and slender fingers to draw attention to the rings adorning her two longest fingers: a war wizard ring, and a wizard of war team ring.

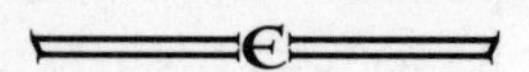

"'Tis roast stag tonight, lord," the equerry said eagerly.

"Of *course* it is," the commander of High Horn replied testily. "It would be something I love, on a Darlhoun debriefing night! Well, try to save *some* for me!"

Thrusting his helm and riding gauntlets into the equerry's hand, Lord Sunter strode inside, past the wonderful smell rolling out of the banquet hall—his stomach promptly rumbled its own longing hunting call—to the stairs. It was a long climb to the top of the main keep tower.

Not for Umbarl Darlhoun, of course. Hrasting war wizards could just *float* up, couldn't they?

So Darlhoun would be there waiting for him, of course. Sitting behind Sunter's own desk as if it were his own, smiling that smug smile and dusting his hands together—and patting yet another stack of parchments as tall as a war helm. He'd not depart until every last one had been thoroughly discussed, even if the stars came and went and a new morning was well under way.

And the man was so hrasted *cheerful*, so genuinely nice and sympathetic and diligent and . . . and . . .

Sunter wanted to wring his neck, and hated himself for feeling that way. His stomach rumbled again.

"Tluin," he whispered under his breath, "I need a *drink*."

When at last he reached his own rooms, almost at the top of the tower, and unlocked the door, he discovered he really did need a drink.

Happy Wizard of War Umbarl Darlhoun would never be cheerful to anyone again.

Someone had dismembered him all over Sunter's desk, thoughtfully taking the head and the meeting's stack of parchments away with them, and arranging the limbs and torso to neatly hold in the blood, and frame a message written in Darlhoun's intestines: "A gift from your future emperor."

"Make that a dozen drinks," Sunter said aloud. "After I'm done throwing up."

The last fading monsters clawed vainly at the darkening twilight sky as the flickering, fading purple radiance reclaimed them.

Blue flames snarled around the purple glow, constricting it, hemming it in. Purple flames flared, and as swiftly died away, leaving the glow smaller and fainter.

The Simbul fed what was left of the rift more and more blue flames, bearing down despite her trembling weariness.

"Go," she gasped, tossing her head back and setting her long silver tresses to renewed writhing. "Begone forever."

The rift winked one last flash of sickly purple, almost impudent in its timing, and died.

Leaving The Simbul reeling in exhaustion.

"How long now, Mother Mystra?" she gasped wearily.

Not much longer, Cherished One. You have taken care of the worst of them.

"And El and Manshoon? How many have *they* done?"

"Not one, yet. Manshoon . . . disappointed me."

"But not surprised you," The Simbul interpreted. "He tried to slay El the moment I departed, didn't he?"

Not quite. I believe it was about six moments after you departed.

The one-time Witch-Queen of All Aglarond snorted, sputtered, tittered like a young lass for a moment—then threw back her head and roared.

In mere moments, the thunderous laughter of a goddess echoed hers.

"Who," Wizard of War Duth Gulkanun snapped, his most powerful wand aimed and ready in his hand, "are you?"

"Gulk, Gulk, I know our paths rarely crossed, and oh-so-*cordial* Nostyn liked me very little, but don't you remember Brannon Lucksar?"

Gulkanun blinked. "I do, and I distinctly remember Brannon Lucksar as a good-natured man I liked and admired. A *man*, not a she-drow!"

"So I was," the lithe, dark-skinned . . . *person* . . . across the room replied with what Gulkanun—busily swallowing, his throat suddenly dry—could only term a jaunty, *sultry* smile. Gods Above, no one had told him that the evil, slay-on-sight dark elves were so . . . hrasted *beautiful*. She was . . . very far from being a man. Whew.

"Until the curse," the she-drow added sadly. "Longclaws here knows all about curses."

The war wizard she'd just named already had two wands trained on her. His face tightened as he shook them warningly, his flaring anger clear. One wand dipped and wavered alarmingly as the hand holding it started to change again.

For his part, Farland slowly drew his sword. Arclath stepped in front of Rune to shield her. She promptly used that shielding to covertly draw one of her daggers and hold it ready to throw.

"How did you get up here?" Farland growled at the dark elf. Who gave him a smile, and slowly lifted one long, shapely leg.

"Used this. And my other one. We call it 'walking,' back in Immerford."

She stroked her raised leg thoughtfully—a long and languid move that made Longclaws growl aloud, deep in his throat, before he could stop himself—and added in a teasing purr, "Lothan always told me you and Avathnar rode the halls of Irlingstar on the backs of crawling prisoners. I never believed him, of course, but now . . ."

"I meant," Farland said deliberately, his sword out and hefted meaningfully in his hand, "that you almost certainly had to swiftly *murder* several of my guards to reach the passage you just came in here through."

The drow waved a dismissive hand. "I've slain no one in Irlingstar. A few simple spells served to temporarily—and *harmlessly*—immobilize several guards, so I could join this little council."

"*Die*, lying drow," Gulkanun said coldly, and he let fly with his wand.

Beside him, both of the wands Longclaws aimed flashed into life, too.

"Idiots!" Arclath shouted. "You'll kill us . . . all . . ."

His angry shout faded away. Nothing at all had happened. The magic of the wands, that *no one* could possibly outrun, had flashed across the room and—

Vanished. Doing nothing, it seemed.

The drow was very much intact. More than that, she was leaning against the wall, still smiling, and examining her fingernails, the very picture of unconcerned nonchalance. The air around her crackled and tiny motes of light winked into momentary being, from time to time, the unmistakable aftermath of a powerful unleashing of magic, but . . .

"Lying, murderous drow!" Farland barked, striding forward. In an instant, his sword acquired scores—hundreds—of winking motes of light that clinged to the blade. He shouted in pain and let it fall, his sword arm jerking around in wild spasms.

Cursing, he grabbed his errant limb and staggered back, falling against the wall. "How long have you been hiding in the castle?" He spat as he slid to the floor. "You've been slaying everyone, haven't you?"

The drow shook her lovely head. "No, Lord—"

That was as far as she got, before an explosion rocked Irlingstar again.

Chapter Eighteen

When I Tire Of It

The blast seemed to begin somewhere distant, but rolled right at the lord constable's office like a racing, raging dragon, its roaring and shaking growing louder and nearer with frightening speed.

That rising tumult almost drowned out the screams and shouts erupting from noble prisoners all over the castle as fresh dust fell and curled, more pebbles and stones rained down, and new cracks raced across walls that groaned anew.

The doors of the lord constable's office—*all* of them, including three secret doors known only to him—burst open as the force of the blast reached the north tower. They banged wildly as an unseen titan's hand seemed to snatch up the room and shake it, hurling the furniture and the room's six occupants off walls, floor, and ceiling . . . and then, very suddenly, everything fell silent and still. Except for the ever-present drifting dust.

Only the drow stood unscathed, the dust shunning a sphere of clear air that surrounded her.

"Magic, obviously—probably fueled by the hrasted wand firings," Farland snarled from the floor as he glared at her, too dazed to keep from thinking aloud. He and the other Crown loyals were still wincing, rubbing bruises, and picking themselves up when some dust-covered men staggered along the passage and in through the main door of the office.

These new arrivals were prisoners, by what could be seen of their dust-caked finery—mainly, that it wasn't any sort of Purple Dragon armor or uniform. A few were clutching Purple Dragon *swords* in their hands, which meant some guards were down, probably dead . . .

Farland hefted his own weapon and strode forward, less than surprised to see that Lord Arclath Delcastle had acquired a blade from somewhere and was at his side.

"Down steel," Farland ordered the coughing, stumbling nobles. "In the name of the king—"

The foremost noble spat at Farland's boots. "*That* for the king!" He sneered, sketching an elaborate duelist's flourish in the air with his stolen sword. "Now *you* down steel, sirrah, or I'll carve that sword out of your hand—and go right on carving up the rest of you! I'll have you know I took sword schooling with the famous Narlebauh! And had lessons with Helnan, too!"

A second noble sliced the air in an even more elaborate flourish. "Ah, Helnan, what an amusing little cockerel. Cut off their noses first, *I* say," he drawled. "A man looks rather comical, without a nose . . ."

Of *course* these prisoners would be well-trained swordsmen. Farland sighed, drew himself up, and prepared to die fighting.

"Defend and disarm," the drow murmured, "aren't those your standing orders, lord constable?"

"*Belt up,*" Farland ordered savagely, not looking away from the leisurely advancing nobles for an instant. For their part, those recently escaped prisoners stopped and stared at the shapely dark elf, drawing back before swords could be crossed.

The drow languidly, almost wantonly strolled forward, a dark and eerie radiance flickering up and down her shapely limbs, a stranger glow flooding from her beckoning eyes.

The sword-wielding nobles gaped at her in earnest, going pale and backing into the rest of the escaped nobles right behind them.

"A drow! *Run!*"

"Invasion from the Underdark! They'll butcher us all! Cormyr is doomed!"

Suddenly the nobles all turned and fled, running hard through the swirling dust, crashing into doorframes and each other, cursing and shouting.

Farland sprang after them, barking, "Back to your cells, gentlesirs! For your own safety, back to your—"

The rout lasted for two passages and a guard post, ere it reached the large ready chamber where two halls joined the main passage. There, amid the fading dust, some noble prisoners rallied to defy the lord constable, waving weapons they could only have wrested from more than a dozen guards—who must now be stunned, sorely wounded, or dead. Swords sketched salutes, slid through elaborate duelists' exercises, and flourished with all the deftness of court champions.

Farland came to an abrupt halt, watching all the displays of swordsmanship, and wondered just how long he could last against—what, fourteen?—expert swordsmen.

Then he saw Lord Delcastle glide over to stand at his shoulder, his sword ready—and the dancer, or thief, or whatever she was; the Whitewave woman, appear beside his other shoulder, a fearless little smile on her face and several daggers between her fingers, ready for throwing . . .

"Well, well," said one of the nobles, giving them a choice sneer. "Three of you, against all of us? What'll that be—a few more moments of sport? Show us how well you can beg and scream! Leave the woman alive for, heh, the *usual* purposes . . ."

He strolled forward, slicing the air wildly with his sword like a butcher seeking to sharpen two blades against each other, the grinning line of armed nobles moving with him—when a horrible scream rang out from right behind them.

The nobles whirled around, snarling curses, afraid that guards had arrived in a stealthy attack to sword them down from behind—

But they saw only one fellow escaped inmate down on the flagstones, all alone with no one around him. They all knew him—couldn't help but know him. It was Lord Quensyn Rhangobrar, one of the most arrogant and bullying prisoners ever to swagger around Castle Irlingstar. He lay on the floor clutching vainly at his own throat, blood spurting from between his fingers. He kicked feebly at the floor, writhing in his own blood, choking and gurgling.

And there was no one at all around him, no one nearby.

Rhangobrar gave a last, agonized gurgle—it rattled in his throat horribly—and slumped dead, twisted on his back with one knee up. His hands fell away, and they could all see the raw, gaping ruin under his jaw.

His throat was largely gone, torn or cut out.

Lord Quensyn Rhangobrar had just been murdered. By a person, beast, or force unknown, more or less in front of their eyes.

Thessarelle's Platter was one of the most upscale dining establishments in Suzail, but had long since been deemed "*so* four summers ago" by the nobility. Its very unfashionability had long since left it quiet and desperate for trade. Therefore, it was eminently suitable for those seeking a superior experience without having to drop overmuch coin. Wherefore these nights, Thessarelle's—to call it "the Platter" was considered distinctly uncouth—was a favorite haunt of high-ranking courtiers, outlanders visiting Suzail, and Cormyrean wealthy folk who lacked titles and harbored no ambitions to soar socially. On this particular early evening, two patrons of the establishment were dining alone at adjacent tables.

One always ate alone, by choice—the quiet, bespectacled Rensharra Ironstave, Lady Clerk of the Rolls. The head of tax appraisals for all of Cormyr, she had few friends, and had to be seen to be free of such encumbrances as Cormyrean dining partners who might be thought by watching eyes to be attempting to bribe her, work deals with her, or to get her drunk and then seek to poison her. She did not mind being given a table in a bad location, close to the kitchens and facing all of the traffic of arriving and departing diners.

The other bad table was customarily given, by Thessarelle's gliding, murmuring, impeccably mannered staff, to the most boorish outlander or party of outlanders to darken their doors, in an attempt to keep them as distant as possible from other diners, regular clientele in particular.

On that night, a certain Mirt the Moneylender easily won the title of "Most Boorish Outlander" without even trying for it. So it was that he came to be seated, with three bottles emptied before him after only one platter of fried hocks-and-tongues, and well before the arrival of his ordered "best side of boar," at the table beside the one Goodwoman Ironstave was smoothly conducted to.

"*Well,* now," he said jovially, giving her a wide and welcoming smile. "Well *met,* beauteous lady! Which goddess are you, I wonder, stealing down to enchant mere mortals this fair even?"

Rensharra had been brought up to be polite, even if most of her daily work of dealing with deceitful nobles and wealthy merchants forced her to all too often be sharply and bluntly candid, so she turned away to hide the heartfelt roll of her eyes from him. He was, after all, an *outlander*—and by his accent, from the Sword Coast or somewhere equally westward and barbaric—and probably knew no better.

"You flatter me, saer," she announced in a flat, no-nonsense voice.

"How can I do anything else, when yer beauty is like a sharp sword, piercing my heart—or somewhere rather lower?" His wink was large, exaggerated, and accompanied by genuine amusement. Gods, there was a proverbial fallen-star twinkle in his eye! Rensharra snorted. He was so . . . charmingly *crude.*

"Your vision, saer," she told him tartly, "must be faulty. It leads your judgment astray."

"Oh, but that's *wonderful,*" he gasped, in the manner of a swooning princess in a badly acted play. "To be led astray by such a splendid woman, so swiftly! Tymora smiles upon me, surely—as, I see, do you. Could it be that yer own innate love for waywardness . . . dare I say yer *hunger* for straying . . . matches my own? Ah, but I'm too bold by half! Let me claw desperately at what is left of my manners, and offer you my name—Mirt, Lord of Waterdeep—and my purse, to furnish you with whatever you desire to drink and to eat, here in this superior dining establishment, this night! *Pray* accept my offer, by way of making amends for my coarse, forward, *low* outland ways! We are direct in Waterdeep, we charge at what we desire, we seek to board and conquer swiftly, but I daresay that's less'n acceptable hereabouts . . ."

"Mirt," Rensharra Ironstave said crisply. "I've heard that name around the palace. You . . . sat upon the head of a certain wizard of war recently, I believe."

"I did, and—"

She raised one hand and her voice with it, firmly interrupting whatever sly lewdness he was uttering. "I'd like to hear all about it. Over a bottle of whatever wine you recommend, *if* your offer to get me drunk on your coin is real, and not mere lust-hungry-lad babbling?"

Mirt recoiled. "Lady, lady, do not think for a moment that my offers are anything less than real! I stand by my utterances, I do, and—"

"Lord Mirt, you less than surprise me," the lady clerk of the rolls informed him, and she turned to tell the server who'd just glided up to her table, "I'll have whatever the gentlesir here feels moved to feed me."

The server's half-lidded, bored eyes opened wide, and he cast a swift glance at Mirt, who dispensed another of his exaggerated winks, leaving the server to struggle to control his customary mask of facial impassivity. He blurted out, "*Very* good, Goodwoman Ironstave," spun around, and rushed away.

"I do believe you've *scared* the man," Rensharra said reprovingly, discovering that she was genuinely enjoying herself—and her company—for the first time in, well, *years* . . .

"I, lady?" Mirt protested in mock horror. "I said nothing to him, nothing at all!"

"*You*, lord, don't need to!" Rensharra replied, lifting her hand to him in the court manner.

A moment later, her always-cold fingers were clasped in a warm, hairy, yet gentle paw that did not tug at her, but conveyed her fingertips to lips ringed with a long, sweeping mustache that . . . tickled.

She giggled helplessly, whereupon Mirt released her, proffered his fourth bottle—the only one that wasn't already empty—and inquired, "Will you begin getting drunk, lady? Just for me?"

Rensharra burst into a guffaw. The man was *outrageous*! Like a playful boar, or a gruff old minstrel lampooning a flamboyant noble a-wooing—and, by all the gods, she loved these coarse flirtations. She was, after all, in Thessarelle's, where the staff knew her rank and position; one scream from her could have this man hustled away in a trice, so she was quite safe. Moreover, she'd spent too many lonely, melancholy evenings here toying with food that was superb, yet . . . wasted, somehow, when one dined alone. Bah! Let this be a night of adventure, where she would give as good as she got.

"I believe I will, Lord of Waterdeep," she announced. "*Providing* you answer me truly, gallant Mirt. Is it *true*, what they say about men of Waterdeep?"

"Which saying, lady?"

"The one about driving hard until the tide turns?"

Mirt coughed briefly, startled—by such a query from so demure a source—into taking some wine up his nose. Recovering, he grinned.

"*Yes*, lady. It is. I believe in candor, between friends."

Rensharra looked at him over the rim of the just-filled tallglass he'd handed her. It had been clean, because he'd been drinking directly from the bottles.

"I accept you as my friend of the table, Lord Mirt, and quite likely my friend, period. Were you hoping for something . . . closer?"

"You *do* believe in candor, lass! Well, now, I do believe I *am*. Do yer hopes run along similar trails?"

"If you drink me under the table," Goodwoman Ironstave told her tablecloth demurely, "you may have me under the table." She set down her glass and looked up. "Or more sensibly, being as this *is* Thessarelle's, under another table, elsewhere, of your choosing. Or, perhaps, wherever else we may both devise. *After* we eat and drink sufficiently for you to prove that saying true, of course."

"Of course," Mirt agreed, sketching a deep bow. Being as he was still seated, his dipping gesture merely planted his nose in the platter in front of him.

He straightened up, dripping, wearing an expression of long-suffering martyrdom, and snorted most marvelously like a boar backing away from a trough. Rensharra burst out laughing again as he reached for what little was left in his fourth bottle.

Only to hurl it hard and accurately past Rensharra's shoulder, into something that squealed in wet and wordless pain.

"*Down*, lass!" he roared. "Under yer table, and keep going!"

The lady clerk of the rolls ducked in her chair, but turned to look at what was behind her as she slid out of it—so she was in time to see the elegantly dressed man with not much left of his face but blood and bottle shards collapsing back against the drapery-bedecked wall. His hand—which held a knife in it—fell away from a rope it had failed to slice.

The rope led up—she was under the table, but still peering—to a pulley lost in the shadows of the lofty ceiling, from which dangled a wicker basket about the size of a coffin.

Something flashed, out of an upper gallery, right at that rope.

Mirt gave a growl and came up out of his seat in a lumbering rush that sent his table over on top of Rensharra's table, toppling it.

The heavy, metallic *crash* that slammed into those improvised shields a moment later splintered one tabletop before the basket spewed its deadly contents all over the vicinity: scores of cleavers, carving knives, cooking spits, and skewers, accompanied by broken glass and a glistening sea of lamp oil. Followed by racing flames, as the lit lamp that had been balanced atop it all met that flowing oil.

Rensharra was too startled to scream, but she managed a strangled *peep* as Mirt snatched her out from under the tables, tore the flaming half of her gown right off her and flung it into the growing conflagration. He took the instant necessary to comment, "*Nice!*" . . . then spun and towed her across the room.

"But—but—" she gasped, seeing other diners gawking, "this isn't the way out!"

"Nay," Mirt growled, bounding up the stairs and dragging her along like a child's toy, "but *'tis* the way to the gallery!"

Halfway up that stair, they met a man hurrying down. A man armed with a murderous snarl and a knife. He slashed at Mirt, who flung up his arm to take the blow—and sprang upward to turn that fending movement into a hard punch just above the man's knee.

The man hopped, howling in pain, and Mirt's slashed and bleeding arm crashed home, landing a hard punch in the man's crotch. The knife clanged somewhere down the stair, the man shrieked and collapsed, and Mirt let go of Rensharra long enough to take the man by the throat and one knee, turn, and *heave*.

This was not a man meant to fly. Instead, he plunged and struck the knife-studded, blazing basket and tables with a crash even louder and heavier than the one that had ended the deadly basket's fall. He struck, spasmed once, then lay still, his arms and legs dangling, his body impaled and starting to drip. Rensharra winced.

Mirt turned and offered her his arm. It was bleeding copiously, but she took it as if nothing were amiss. Mirt grandly led her back down the stair to where servers and a cook and Thessarelle herself were scurrying. Diners were fleeing or craning to see, buckets of potato water from the kitchens were being flung onto the flames, and the man sprawled in the heart of that fire, with several knives through him, looked very dead.

"I *do* hope," Mirt said politely to Thessarelle, as that pillar of hauteur started to scream and sob, "you won't be charging for the floor show."

Pressing a small but bulging purse into the nearest hand of the dumbfounded proprietress, he led Rensharra toward the kitchens.

"The entrance is—"

"*Never* use a front entrance after a slaying's gone awry," Mirt growled. "That basket was meant for you, lass. Someone with coin enough to hire others . . . you haven't angered any nobles lately, have you?"

Rensharra managed a weak smile as he hustled her through kitchens where pots neglected too long were starting to steam, and sauces to scorch, out into an alleyway.

"I—I'm the head tax collector of the kingdom," she told him, as they hastened through its noisome gloom together, Mirt peering this way and that. "I anger nobles daily. And when I tire of it, I irk them some more."

"*Good* lass," he replied fondly. "You look much better with half yer gown gone, by the way."

"My reputation—"

"Lass, lass, if yer head tax collector, yer reputation can only be *helped* by a little bouncing bared flesh! Yer precious reputation only has one way to go!"

They turned a corner at the end of the alley, out into a lamplit street, and Mirt added, "*That's* a little better! The farther we get—"

A Watch patrol came out of the next alley, and promptly rushed to surround them, unhooding lanterns.

"*What's* this, then?" the patrol leader barked.

Mirt grinned, bowed, and indicated his bedraggled partner. "As you can see, lads," he crowed, "the lady likes it *rough*!"

Her face flaming, Rensharra struggled to manage a wink and a smile, then struck a pose she hoped was, well, provocative.

Silence stretched . . . then ended abruptly. On all sides, upstanding members of the Watch hooted, chuckled, or roared approval.

"Lucky *bastard*," one added, clapping Mirt on the shoulder, as the patrol started to move on.

"Wait," another said suddenly, turning back and shining his lantern full on Rensharra's face. "Aren't you—?"

"Yes," she purred, taking a step toward him. "I am."

The Watchman's face split in a delighted grin, he gave her a salute, then bellowed, "Onwaaard!" and hurried after his fellows.

"You see?" Mirt said affably. "Yer reputation—"

Rensharra Ironstave found herself trembling, on the verge of tears, suddenly cold and afraid, as weary as if she'd worked a long day, and ravenously hungry.

"Mirt," she said firmly, "take me home. Your home."

"Of course, lass," he rumbled, patting her arm. His hand left bloody marks on her sleeve—her only surviving sleeve. "I've a warm bed. And cold chicken."

Chapter Nineteen

Bloodshed Inevitably Erupts

The prisoners of Irlingstar, nobles all, had been gleeful about the first two deaths, but the explosions and the killing of Lord Quensyn Rhangobrar had, it seemed, abruptly changed their collective mood.

"*Do* something, constable!"

"Aye! *Our* hides are at risk, now! 'Tis your duty, no less!"

The shouts were loud, angry, and fearful, the demands that Farland do something many and shrill.

"Kill this drow here, for a start!"

That indicated dark elf gave the furious and tentatively advancing noblemen a wry smile, and murmured the last words of a spell.

And the very air around them flickered, *flowed,* and . . . every last noble facing the lord constable and the five standing with him staggered, sagged—and crumpled to the floor, unconscious.

In the silence that followed, Wizard of War Imbrult Longclaws spun around to fix the she-drow with a suspicious glare, his wand ready in his hand. "The wards are . . . *gone,* in this room at least," he challenged her. "How did you *do* that?"

"Magic," the dark elf told him serenely.

Gulkanun moved to face her, his wands in hands and taking care to keep well away from Longclaws. The drow had slipped aside when they'd come out into the room, to keep her back to a wall so she couldn't be attacked from two sides. She was watching him realize this, and smiling. Gulkanun's frown of suspicion grew darker.

"Duth Gulkanun," she said to him, "I don't like being in this body any more than you like having a drow telling you she—he—is a wizard of war. Yet if I'm going to have to constantly guard against you and Longclaws waiting for a good chance to blast me, I'll not be able to obey my orders—the commands that come from Lord Lothan Durncaskyn, but that my oath to the Crown tells me I must regard as if they came from King Foril himself—with any speed or effectiveness. So what can I do to convince you I'm Brannon Lucksar? Do you want to hear watchwords? Some of the little secrets only we wizards of war know? Royal Magician Ganrahast's favorite color?"

Longclaws snorted. "As if we'd know that."

Gulkanun shot him a quelling glare, then turned and asked the drow challengingly, "What does Lord Durncaskyn most mourn the loss of?"

"Publicly? Knees that serve him well. Privately? Esmra Winterwood, who kept a gowns and lace shop in Immerford, and died of heartstop two winters back. He hoped they'd be wed, and was busily wooing her when she fell ill."

Gulkanun and Longclaws looked at each other and shrugged. The drow was right about the knees, and probably about the woman, too. There'd been rumors . . .

Longclaws lifted his chin and fired his own query. "Just how did you come to meet Manshoon?"

"The first time? On a still-secret Crown task that took me to Westgate, years back. He ruled it as Orbakh, you know."

"We *do* know," Gulkanun said coldly.

The drow merely smiled. "My second time was in the Stonelands, after a spell duel I saw from afar while investigating something else, that brought a dragon down dead out of the sky. I was fortunate to escape with my life, that time."

"Investigating *what*, exactly?"

"Let's just say it had to do with shades seen trading in a . . . locale strategic to Cormyr. You'll appreciate that certain orders prevent me from being more specific. I saw Manshoon again last winter, in an alley in Suzail, when he let his guard slip for a moment. He's acquired a habit of talking aloud to himself. By now we've learned to watch for him, and heed reports of his being seen. After he visits a place, bloodshed inevitably erupts."

"You're not telling us all of your dealings with Manshoon," Gulkanun said accusingly.

"No," the drow said calmly, "I'm not."

"How long are these nobles going to sleep?" Farland broke in. "I'm more than a little suspicious of this dark elf, myself, but it seems to me that a little reluctant trust is in order about now."

"Well said, lord constable," Arclath agreed quickly. "Crown mages, I'm no wizard of war nor palace insider, but I've sat around tables recently with Ganrahast and Vainrence and Glathra—more recently than any of you, I'll wager—and it seems to me this, ah, lady is either Lucksar or knows enough of things only he would know that you'll not catch him—her—out as a false Lucksar. I say trust her for now, and let her get investigating."

"Investigating is *our* task," Gulkanun said flatly.

"Mine, too," the drow told him. "If you'd prefer we walk shoulder to shoulder in this, never parting, I've no objection—so long as you don't use that agreement to restrict where I go and with whom I speak."

Gulkanun and Longclaws traded glances again, then slowly nodded to each other, and sheathed their wands.

"Investigate," Gulkanun told the drow. "We'll stay with you, much of the time, and hear what you hear, see what you see, and heed what you do."

The dark elf sketched a bow with liquid grace, then turned to the lord constable and said briskly, "In the interests of uncovering who's blowing towers up and murdering folk in Irlingstar, I'm going to ask you many questions. Please take no offense; I seek information, not to insinuate anything." She spun to regard the two war wizards and Arclath and Amarune and added, "By all means interrupt with queries of your own, as they occur to you. I am by no means 'in charge' here." She turned smoothly back to Farland. "What do the wards of Irlingstar normally allow in the way of magic?"

The lord constable winced. "Beyond that they block transloca-tion, sendings, and mind-to-mind contact in and out of the castle, I don't know all that much about them. They hurl back most destruc-tive magics cast from outside, and prevent quite a few from working at all inside Irlingstar, but as to the details . . . those were known to the Crown mages stationed here."

He cleared his throat. "You may have heard that some of my predecessors betrayed their office—took bribes from prisoners, and the like. That may have had much to do with how little I was told about the wards. I've heard that both seneschals and lord constables in the past have known much more than I do, and I've seen—briefly, not to peruse and learn details—some written records of what the wards do. Avathnar had them sent back to Suzail soon after taking office. He told me they were just weapons against us if they ever fell into the wrong hands."

The drow nodded. "So before any of these recent killings and explosions, just how many folk were in Irlingstar? Everyone, not just incarcerated noble guests."

Farland frowned. "Two and twenty guards, who report to me. Me. Sixteen castle staff—masons, smiths, hostlers, and the like—who reported to Seneschal Avathnar. Avathnar. Eight who worked in the kitchens—all women from Immerford, some old, some young. And two message riders—Crown messengers in training—stationed here. Not counting the lord and lass, here"—he nodded at Arclath and Amarune—"we had twoscore-and-six prisoners. The castle can hold four times that, with every guest in his own cell. Er, could, that is, before the . . . south tower went down, and all."

"Name me the most dangerous of those prisoners. Not the most annoying—I'm sure they all compete for that ranking—but those you judge truly perilous."

Farland frowned. "Now that Rhangobrar's dead—he was a real instigator and manipulator, who could stir many of them into any mischief he wanted, and usually avoid direct involvement himself—I'd say Cygland Morauntar, Bleys Indimber, and Raldrick Ammaeth. Young lords, all. The first two are heirs of their houses, and Ammaeth's a second son who twice tried to arrange the killing of his older brother before he was brought here. Convicted murderers, all three; no morals whatsoever, no inhibitions. We've others who can be ruthless, cruel, and even savage in their bloodletting . . . but those three . . ."

"No compunctions at all?"

"None. They *understand* rules and customs and etiquette well enough, as constraints on others they can make use of—but not as anything that should bind them. Most of my efforts have been to keep their holds over others as weak as possible, and prevent any of them from getting together."

"So those three we chain to the walls of separate locked cells, far from each other and the rest," the dark elf suggested, "and the others we round up and temporarily confine in one place, disarmed of anything sharp or magical, and give them as much wine as they want to down."

Gulkanun raised an eyebrow. "While we—?"

"While we search every other nook and cranny of this fortress for intruders."

Farland coughed. "There are two persons in a cell, right now. They were outside the walls after the south tower fell. Asked for shelter from a dragon, gave their names as Harbrand and Hawkspike, and say they're Crown-licensed investigators-for-hire. 'Danger for Hire,' they call themselves. Never seen two such clumsy law-sly rogues in my life."

Lucksar smiled. "Take me to them, before we do any of the rest. I should be able to get them to tell us more than they've shared with you thus far."

Gulkanun looked stern. "By enspelling them?"

"That wasn't my intention, no."

Arclath turned to the lord constable. "Let's be about it. I'd welcome some answers—before the next blast."

Farland winced, nodded, waved for everyone to follow him, and strode off down the passage.

"Well, *someone* connected to the palace is organizing treason among the nobles—and I'm getting more and more suspicious of Chancellor Crownrood."

"We're all suspicious of this courtier and that noble, Rymel. D'you have any evidence? Something that can be waved in his face, not 'you were seen with Lord Stumblebones, and the next day Stumblebones got drunk and yelled that the Dragon Throne should be hurled down' stuff. If *that* were all it took to get traitors into cells, half the court and all the nobles of the realm would be in the dungeons, right now!"

"No," Rymel said heavily, "I don't have anything I can openly challenge Crownrood with. Yet. But I think I know how—*urrAAAghh!*"

"Rymel? Rymel?"

The younger war wizard's voice was high and shrill with fear. Vranstable had heard a man sob like that once before, after being stabbed. It had been the last sound that man had ever made.

So he got his wand out and ready before he peered cautiously around the corner.

"Rymel?"

Another wand—Rymel's wand—was thrust into Vranstable's mouth, choking him.

His own dying sob sounded even worse.

Manshoon shook his head as the second body slumped. "Killing these fools isn't exactly difficult," he murmured aloud. He wiped the wand clean on his second victim's robes and retrieved the other wand from Vranstable's hand. "Why, I'm doing Cormyr a favor, weeding out such weaklings."

Elminster smiled. Aye, she knew these two.

"Well met, Drounan Harbrand. Or do you prefer 'Doombringer'?"

The man she'd greeted gaped at her, then shut his mouth hastily without saying anything.

The drow hadn't waited for a reply; she had already strolled over to the other man. "And you, Andarphisk Hawkspike—how are you keeping? Or should I call you 'Fists'?"

The five Crown folk standing behind the dark elf watched the two men in black go pale.

"H-how do you know us?" Harbrand asked, finding his voice. "We've never met."

The drow walked back to him, advancing until they were face to face, and gave him a knowing smile. "Oh? I know all about you, Drounan. Shall I share it with everyone? Even the things you might not want Fists here to learn?"

Harbrand swallowed. Hawkspike had turned to glare at him, but the drow stepped between them, and advanced leisurely on the scarred brawler.

"And you, Fists," she purred, "are you ready for your partner to hear about . . . Sulblade?"

Hawkspike fell back, gaping at her. Behind the smiling dark elf, Harbrand was frowning. "What *about* Sulblade?"

Hawkspike shook his head frantically. "Don't believe her, Droun! Whatever she says, don't believe her!"

Oh, El, you are evil, Symrustar purred merrily, inside Elminster's head.

The commander of High Horn quelled a sigh and gave the visiting wizard of war a sour look.

"No, nothing since Darlhoun's murder," he said shortly. "We're not missing any more Crown mages. If you'd like to search for one, I hear Rorskryn Mreldrake's still missing. Or have you found him yet?"

It was the war wizard's turn to sigh. "Lord Sunter," he said patiently, "I'm aware you hold little love for wizards. Yet there's no need for anger on your part. We *are* on the same side, you know. We revere and guard the Dragon Throne, too."

Erevon Sunter ran a hand down the old sword scar that gave his chin its twisted look, and he nodded abruptly. "I know. I'm just . . . unsettled. Fed up. Half the nobles in the land talking treason, darker rumors every day, monsters we've not seen in sixty summers suddenly everywhere, pouncing on my patrols . . ."

He looked up, fixed the war wizard with tired eyes, and growled, "Why don't you tell me the truth, for once? What has brought you here, to stand and ask me your coy questions? *Tell* me. Something's happened, that much is plain. Well, what?"

The Crown mage was young. He hesitated, then took a step closer and said in a swift, quiet voice, as if he suspected there were spies hiding in every corner of the commander's office, despite it being at the top of the main keep tower, "Lord, wild magic has been seen in the skies by night, in many upland corners of the realm, these last few nights. Blue flames, great wild conflagrations in the skies, sometimes with a lone, flying human outlined at their heart."

Lord Sunter studied him. "And you don't know what to make of it, you mages, and you're scared," he said slowly. "Well, now you have company in that." He got up, went to his suit of armor on its rack in the corner, lifted the visor of his war helm, and took out a decanter.

"Flagons yonder," he said briefly. "Sit down, drink up, and we'll talk. *I* want to hear the truth about these rumors of Vangerdahast coming back from the grave as some sort of spider thing." He chuckled as he sat down again, and unstoppered the decanter to pour. "Probably pure fool-tongue wildness, being as they're talking about that old goat *Elminster* striding around the royal palace, too, but . . ."

As he saw the expression on the young wizard's face, his words faltered. "Oh, tluin. Hrast and tluin and all gods *damn*."

"That about covers it, yes," the war wizard whispered, holding out both flagons to be filled.

Arclath, Rune, Farland, and the two war wizards watched with interest. With a few drawled words Lucksar had terrified the rogues.

Rune could read their faces like two glaringly headlined broadsheets. The two men in black were suddenly facing a beautiful, menacing female drow they'd never seen before, who obviously knew all about them and could tell it to war wizards and a lord constable, in a cell full of chains and manacles in the heart of a Cormyrean prison they were already locked into . . .

"If—if you promise to swear by Lolth to say nothing at all about our pasts," Harbrand stammered, "we'll . . . we'll answer any questions about why we're here."

"I swear by the deadly kiss of Lolth," the drow replied. "Talk."

"I—we—uh—"

"You came here to get inside Irlingstar, didn't you?" the lord constable asked sternly. They nodded, and he asked, "To do what?"

"Fulfill our commission."

"We *gathered* you were hired by someone," Gulkanun said sarcastically. "To do what?"

"Get someone safely out of Irlingstar, then out of the realm."

"Into Sembia. Who?"

"Uh, ah . . ."

"Look at the shorter one!" Rune snapped suddenly.

An odd expression had appeared on Hawkspike's face. It had gone from anger, in place of its customary surliness, to apprehensive, to queasily uncomfortable. They watched that discomfort grow, and be joined by astonishment.

"What's happening?" Farland barked. "Is someone using magic on you?"

Hawkspike suddenly tore open his codpiece, snatched out something small and metallic—that was starting to glow—and flung it as hard as he could, high over everyone's shoulders, through the doorway and out of the room.

They heard it clatter on the flagstones and slide.

"What *was* that?" Farland roared, rushing to pinion Hawkspike's arms. "Sirrah, if you've—"

From the passage outside there came a sudden roar. A roar that burst back into the room like a hurtling dragon, filling it with force and fire.

Royal Magician Ganrahast suddenly clutched his head, shrieked, and crashed down face-first onto the table, thudding against its polished top senseless and staring, blood streaming from his eyes and nose.

"Here we go again," Glathra snapped, rushing to his aid. Vangey had already scuttled along the table to the stricken Royal Magician. Vainrence and Storm crowded around Ganrahast, too.

"Don't touch him!" Glathra warned the silver-haired Harper, but she was ignored. Storm stared at her own finger, used that stare to make blood well up out of it somehow, and thrust that bloodied finger up Ganrahast's bleeding nose.

After a moment, she reported calmly, "He was working with the mindlink. Something struck at him through it."

"Well, lady?" Vangerdahast demanded gruffly, dancing impatiently on his spider legs. "Can you heal him?"

"I'm healing him right now," Storm replied, "but Vainrence, if you can fetch in some *real* healers—priests, Wizard of War Sanneth . . ."

Without a word the lord warder bowed his head and hurried out.

"What are you doing to him, exactly?" Glathra asked, sounding more apprehensive than suspicious.

"Holding his mind. Like something frozen in ice, I'm keeping it as it is right now, so it can't get any worse. Shielding the rest of it against the damage."

"I didn't know you could . . ." Glathra let her words trail off, not knowing what to say next.

Storm gave her a gentle smile. "We should get to know each other better, Lady Glathra. If you knew more about me, you might just begin to trust me."

"Might," Glathra echoed, managing a wan smile.

"Then," Storm added dryly, "we could even start to work on liking each other."

Glathra winced. "I deserved that," she whispered. Vangerdahast walked away down the table, carefully not looking in her direction or saying a word. Storm merely smiled.

Then many priests and war wizards were crowding into the room, Vainrence with them.

"Sanneth," Storm said as firmly as any king, "cast your spell—you know the one—and link to me. Holy ones, please heal this man, as *gently* as your prayers can. Sanneth and I will guide what the gods give you."

She was obeyed without query or hesitation, but it seemed a long, tensely silent time before Ganrahast groaned, his arms jerking around for a few moments. Then he tried to sit up, closing his staring eyes so he could start blinking wildly.

"Ganrahast?" Glathra asked. "Royal Magician?"

One of the priests wiped away the blood. Ganrahast sniffled, shook his head, groaned again, then gasped, "Y-yes, it's me. I'm . . . back."

He looked at Storm, and Sannath beside her, and added fervently, "Thank you."

Both the Harper and the war wizard merely nodded gravely. Without a word Sannath stood up and quietly ushered the priests out of the room.

"Well?" Vangerdahast rasped the moment Vainrence had closed the door on them. "What by all Nine of the Hells happened?"

Ganrahast smiled wanly. "I, ah, felt the scrutiny or at least the reaching out to me of a team ring. Its wearer was seeking me. I in turn reached out to the mind wearing it—a mind I don't think I know, which suggests that the ring wasn't being worn by anyone who's supposed to have one. Yet I can't be certain of that; I didn't have long enough to, to . . ."

"Taste that mind, and identify it," Storm murmured helpfully, earning herself a surprised look from Glathra.

"Taste, yes. What I did manage to feel was that the mind of the ring wearer was of tremendous power. It sensed me, sought to block me—and then, everything seemed to . . . explode."

"Whereabouts was that mind?" Vangey asked sharply.

"In the northeast of the realm, somewhere remote," Ganrahast murmured slowly, grimacing as his attempt to remember brought on throbbing mental pain.

"Irlingstar," Glathra said grimly. "Of *course*."

Sraunter's cellar was again aglow with Manshoon's scrying spheres. The incipient emperor of Cormyr sat at his ease in their midst, intent on only one sphere. In its depths, he was watching a black dragon he'd spotted flying among the Thunder Peaks while seeking isolated war wizards at work in the eastern borders of the realm. If he could destroy them, he would awaken fears of a Sembian incursion, so as to draw more wizards out for easy slaying.

There was something intriguing about this ancient black wyrm. It wasn't one he'd ever ridden or conversed with, to be sure—but it seemed *familiar*, somehow . . .

In his sphere, the dragon was swooping closer to the prison keep, Castle Irlingstar—and an explosion promptly erupted from an upper room of the castle, blowing out windows amid gouts of flame and tumbling stone dust.

Manshoon blinked in startlement, and from its hasty back-flapping, followed by angry circling rather than fearful flight, the dragon seemed startled too.

It glided *very* close to the castle walls, passing the keep and peering in . . . then, though Manshoon saw no attack upon it, nor any reaction at all from inside Irlingstar, it flapped away in frantic haste, as if pursued by its bane, fleeing into the mountains.

Something powerful must be in there, to cause explosion after explosion. Something *unusual* and powerful, if it could frighten an experienced and powerful dragon . . .

Manshoon waited to see if more of the castle would blow up, in case the dragon had fled an explosion it could see was imminent.

Yet time passed, and no second blast occurred.

So, now . . . a fresh problem. How to scry past or through the castle wards, to see inside Irlingstar . . .

Chapter Twenty

Watching The Wildness Unfold

"*Faster*, hrast you! Faster!" Harbrand snarled.

Hawkspike was panting too hard to answer.

They pelted down the narrow stone stair, crashed bruisingly off the walls of what was *hopefully* the last landing, stumbled and almost fell down the last flight of steps, and nearly ran onto the points of the spears two guards were holding—guards who stood in front of a very solid-looking metal door.

"Hold!" one of the guards snapped. "Prisoners are *not* to be—"

"We're *not* prisoners!" Harbrand roared—as Hawkspike grabbed both spears and fell to the floor, swinging himself forward and kicking at the guards' ankles.

They fell atop him, cursing and struggling. Harbrand promptly clubbed the backs of both their necks with his fists, then tore one guard's belt dagger from its sheath and battered their heads energetically with its pommel, smiting them both senseless.

Hawkspike struggled to get out from under the senseless guards and trampled the sagging Dragons in his haste to follow Harbrand. Harbrand had snatched the rings of keys from the belts of both guards and was feverishly trying every key that looked remotely likely to be right in the three locks that secured the door—head-high, ankle-low, and in the middle.

A few gasping moments later, the door banged open and Danger For Hire burst back out into the waiting wilderness and then sprinted for the welcome cover of the trees. They were a good long way into the leaf-littered gloom before Harbrand found breath enough to rather grimly suggest to his colleague that Hawkspike forthwith provide some explanations. "*What* just almost killed us? And what by the Dragon Unseen did you *throw*, anyhail? Since *when* did we own any Gondar *bombs?*"

Hawkspike went right on crashing and struggling through the forest, making no reply but violently and repeatedly shaking his head, in negation or denial.

Harbrand caught up to him and shoulder-slammed him, snarling, "*Not* deeper in! Do you want to get eaten by wolves—or worse? Back to the verges, where we can follow the road and not get lost!"

Hawkspike's shakes became a nod or two. That lasted until he tripped on a leaf-covered root and fell headlong.

Harbrand hauled his dazed partner upright with a snarl of anger, and they both stood there panting for breath, Hawkspike's face a mask of mud, twigs, and leaves.

When he had enough breath back to manage a deep sigh, the Doombringer plucked several ugly forest mushrooms off Hawkspike's face, and demanded wearily, "*Tell* me, Hawk. Where'd you get the flashbang? And just when were you going to get around to telling me about it? How many *other* secrets are you keeping from me? Just what is all this about Sarl?"

Sarl Sulblade had been one of their partners in Danger For Hire, before his sudden, violent, and until now mystifying death. The drow somehow knew that Hawkspike had killed him. Harbrand needed no words from his partner to get that far, and Sulblade had been a right nasty bastard, but it would be nice to know . . .

Hawkspike was back to fervently shaking his head.

Harbrand sighed again. "Forget all that, Hawk. Forget what I just asked. Just tell me: what happened back there in the castle, just now?"

His much-scarred partner wiped away mud, saw a handy fallen tree, and thankfully sat down on its huge trunk. A snake, disturbed by the arrival of his behind, promptly slithered away. Hawkspike watched it go, then said slowly, "That was my fair-fortune charm. Bought it from a caravan master in Suzail, who said it was real magic, came from a temple of Tymora, and would bring luck. Just a little everbright-treated silver image of the goddess, smiling, that's all. I've had it for years. Make the girls kiss it, when they find it . . . the few girls I get."

"That caravan master tricked you into carrying a bomb?"

Hawkspike shrugged. "I know not, Har. It's been riding with me for three years, now, winter and summer, day and night. I've dropped it, fallen on it . . . it's baked in the sun, gotten wet, nigh-froze with my breeches on the cold stone floors of winter nights . . . just a good-luck charm."

"Until?"

"Until just then, back in those rooms where the dark elf bitch was letting on she knew all about us. All of a sudden, I felt fingers—*solid* fingers, cold but solid, where no fingers should be able to reach. *Fingers,* Har! Fumbling with the thing, turning it around. Which is when I remember, Har—the only *seams* on the charm are around her little backside and chest. Which means they can be pressed in. And I get scared, real scared. So, to be rid of it, I flung it away—as far away as I could get it. You know the rest."

Hawkspike was panting out of fear, sweat glistening on his unlovely face, his eyes large and haunted. "Those fingers . . ."

"Never mind them. You got rid of them, didn't you?"

Hawkspike nodded. "Went with the thing. Don't think the blast killed anyone, do you?"

Harbrand shook his head. "Too small, too distant. Flung us all down the rooms—good thing the walls weren't closer, or we'd have been smashed like flung eggs. Stunned everyone good and proper, 'cept maybe the drow and Lord Constable Mightyroar."

"And us," his scarred partner grunted, heaving himself back up off the green, moldy tree trunk. "I'm thinking we were shielded from the worst of it by everyone else's bodies."

"Ah, but our luck continues to be simply *glorious,*" Harbrand replied bitterly, taking him by the shoulder to hasten him on through the verges of the Hullack, away from Irlingstar.

"A bright new morning," Vangerdahast rasped in Glathra's ear.

She winced. The mere thought of a man-headed, oversized spider riding on her shoulder gave her—no, *enough,* she was *not* going to think about it again. She was going to get over this, going to—

"Relax, lass. I'm not going to bite you," what was left of the most infamous Royal Magician in all of the kingdom's history that most living Cormyreans knew said rather gruffly, shifting on her shoulder. "Not on our first dalliance, anyhail."

Glathra stiffened. "Lord Vangerdahast," she said warningly, "I . . ."

"You what? You've realized your blusterings don't frighten me, and you're not sure of my powers, so you don't know what to threaten to do? Is that it?"

"You tluining old bastard," she whispered feelingly. "You—you—"

"Ah, the young," the spiderlike thing on her shoulder said almost merrily, "*such* eloquence they command. Call me 'Vangey,' lass; it trips off the tongue swiftly, so you can get to the swearing faster."

"You sound just like Elminster," she muttered. "Will I start to sound like that in a century or two, I wonder?"

"You're highly unlikely to live that long, lass, given your temper and inability to hold your tongue. You *might* learn to curb both those things, but I see no sign of that."

Glathra sighed and retreated from battle into silence. It was bad enough she had to stand and watch Storm Silverhand ride out of the palace on one of the best horses in the stables—one of King Foril's *personal* mounts, hrast it!—to travel the realm soothing angry nobles and contacting potential Harpers. It was worse that Ganrahast and Vainrence had both ordered her to serve as Lord Vangerdahast's steed and viewing platform; she suspected they'd done it so that she was forced to accept his presence, and he could keep her from doing anything to thwart Storm or warn fellow war wizards of her impending arrival in their particular corner of the kingdom. She settled for telling Vangerdahast—*Vangey?* That made him sound like a toy, or a pet!—grimly, "We must get a look into Irlingstar—or at what's left of it, if that blast was as powerful as I fear it was."

They could trace Arclath magically, and had, but that merely confirmed he was in or near Irlingstar, yielding them nothing about his condition or circumstances at the castle. Moreover, there were no safe or "familiar" teleport destinations, to anyone currently in the palace, near Irlingstar. Given its proximity to the Hullack and the Thunder Peaks, and the generally shaky reliability of teleportations thereabouts since the Spellplague . . . portals might be faster and more reliable than a series of translocation jumps, or teleporting to Immerkeep and faring overland from there. The closest reliably functioning portal linking the palace with anywhere near Irlingstar had its near terminus in an always-guarded room in Vangerdahast's tower, a short stroll east of where she stood. Its far end was inside Castle Crag, three hard days of riding on good, fast horses west of Immerford.

"Hmmph," Glathra commented, as Vangerdahast raised one of his spider legs to wave to the departing Storm. She did not join in; his farewell could do for the both of them. "Given how wildly busy the Thunderstone-based wizards of war are just now, it'll be faster to farcall the three Crown mages in Hultail, and send two of them on horseback up along Orondstars Road and *around* most of Hullack Forest to Irlingstar."

"Indeed," Vangerdahast surprised her by agreeing. "So why, most decisive leader of war wizards, didn't you farcall them the moment after Ganrahast told us about the blast?"

"I suppose," Glathra replied icily, "my mind was elsewhere."

She hastened back into the palace, not caring if he fell off her shoulder or not, to farspeak Hultail and issue crisp orders that two of the duty wizards of war stationed there were to depart for Castle

Irlingstar in all haste and report back what they found immediately—including the fates of all inmates, Lord Delcastle and his fellow prisoner Amarune Whitewave, in particular.

The Hultail war wizards scrambled to obey.

Well, that was *one* thing that had gone the way it was supposed to, this day. Would that there might be more before sunset . . .

Manshoon smiled. Problems, always problems. People, he could take great delight in slaughtering fittingly. When the problems didn't involve people, some devious thinking was always involved . . . and over the years, he'd grown to enjoy such scheming. So, now . . .

Irlingstar wasn't that old a prison. Oh, a keep had crowned that ridge for a fair while, but hadn't it been some robber baron's hold, way back when? Then the fortress of a border baron of Cormyr, as the reach of the realm widened . . . well, whether he remembered a-right or not, the wards in place had to be new; no older than the reign of the current king. Which meant they would be relatively puny magics he might be able not just to breach, but to destroy.

Yet was the time right for such a bold display of power? It would rouse the wizards of war in earnest, and if Foril wasn't too gone in his dotage, he just might be able to portray it as the kingdom under magical invasion, wherefore all loyal Cormyreans must rally to king and banner, or Cormyr itself might well be swept away . . .

No, that sort of tumult and armed alertness would make his own work far harder, and a lot less fun. So, no great hurling down of the wards.

Which left him facing the same challenge: with the wards up, how was he to spy into Irlingstar? If there was to be no breach, then slyness must suffice . . . corruption . . . just which Crown mages were nearby, that he might coerce or cozen? For wizards of war could pass through the wards magically, if they bore the right tokens—rings, usually—or else be admitted into the castle if they showed up at its gates and convinced the guards to admit them. If a future emperor of Cormyr happened to be riding the mind of such a supplicant at the gates, that patient and clever mindrider could see inside the prison fortress that way, without any need to attract unwanted notice by forcing a way through its wards or bringing them down at all.

Now, there should be war wizards stationed at Immerford, Hultail, and Thunderstone . . . they accompanied border patrols, didn't they? Yes, especially since Sembia had begun using griffon riders. So he'd best start looking for handy wizards of war . . .

Manshoon's smile widened. These matters were really so simple.

The lady clerk of the rolls leaned across the table and snared the thick and hairy wrist of her dining partner before it could lift and drain a flaring flagon that was as large as her head.

"Lord Mirt," she said gently, "there's something I must say to you."

Mirt fixed her with a fond smile and rumbled, "Hmmmm?"

"Last night, you were kind gallantry itself to me. *After* playing the swashbuckling hero and saving my life—and I'll never forget that. You took me home and fed me, then bundled me into bed and told me old nursery tales until I fell asleep. I've never before had a breakfast of half warm broth and half warmed wine, but—just the once, and because of the delightful company—it, too, was splendid. I . . . I've never before been treated so kindly by any man, in all my life. And you . . . spurred no charge against me."

"Well, lass, if you'd been Waterdhavian born and bred, I'd've assumed the spice of danger would have had you roused for a good romp, but . . . every lady is different, and deserves the treatment she needs. I want a lady to *lead* the romp, not be deceived or forced into anything."

"Good," Rensharra Ironstave said firmly, "because tonight, I think I'd like that romp. Will you come home with me?"

A twinkle appeared in Mirt's eye. "Well, now," he rumbled. "*Well, now . . .*"

Aye, 'tis me. Kindly gasp or otherwise react not. *The two war wizards are watching.*

Rune smiled wryly before she could stop herself, but kept her eyes closed and said nothing.

Except in her mind, where she didn't try to hide—couldn't have hidden—her delight at learning the beautiful dark elf bending over her was really Elminster.

You found a body, I see, Rune thought.

I did. Like it? 'Tis wonderful, *to be inhabiting someone young and supple again, without all the aches and pains.*

What happened to her? Did you . . ., Rune thought.

Nay, lass, I did nothing but come along after a nasty worm from elsewhere had devoured her mind, and claim the empty body left behind. I watched the war wizard I'm pretending to be die, though. I need ye and thy gallant Arclath here to keep my secret about this, though. Or matters may very swiftly get very *messy.*

That much, I can see well for myself, Old Mage. El, it's good to have you here with us.

Ye may not think so, soon. Trouble has a way of skulking after me like a hungry beast.

That, I also know, Rune thought. *Yet I'm starting to expect it—and to enjoy watching the wildness unfold.*

"This one seems fine," El said aloud then, and Amarune felt new hands on her wrist, then neck, then forehead.

"She's awake, or nearly so," Gulkanun agreed, his voice coming from just above her. "I'd rather let her surface on her own than slap or shout at her, though."

"Her companion is rousing," El—no, Lucksar, she must think of him only as Lucksar now, or she'd make a slip—added.

Indeed. I'd appreciate no slips for the next tenday or so. Longer, if ye can manage it.

So it was that Rune came awake nodding and chuckling.

Across the room, a rather scorched-looking Imbrult Longclaws gave her a stare. "Never seen *that* sort of awakening after a battle blast," he commented.

Farland winced. "Better'n my *knee*."

"You still have both your legs—and you can even walk," Longclaws replied. "Beyond my bruises and a little burned hair, everyone seems fine. After an explosion like that? The gods must love us!"

"Really?" Farland grunted, getting up, putting weight on his bandaged leg, and wincing again. "They've a hrasted funny way of showing it."

"*I* thought trying it in such an open, popular, fashionable place like Thessarelle's was a bad idea from the start," old Lord Haeldown grunted.

Lord Loroun shrugged. "And so you wagered against success and made some coin. Stop complaining! I *lost* a fair purse."

"Pah! That's not the point, youngblood! If you have to count your coins, you shouldn't be wagering at all. Keeping score in wealth is all too *common* a practice in the first place. I meant that intending to do something and then not elegantly carrying it out at our first attempt bespeaks clumsiness on our part, and tells the rest of Cormyr—*titled* Cormyr, anyhail, and that's the Cormyr that matters—that our reach is neither strong nor sure."

Lord Loroun flushed and said coldly, "I seldom need lectures on how to be noble from older men. I seldom listen to them twice. After the first one, I draw my sword and duel—removing anyone's need to listen to that particular source of advice ever again. Be warned, lord."

"Ah, the young are so *subtle*, too," Haeldown told his tallglass, raising it to the light to enjoy the play of color in the wine. "And patient. Straight to the threat, without any wit beforehand. Perhaps it's because you can muster none, hmm?"

"I've no need to listen to this—" Loroun retorted angrily, planting both hands on the table as if to rise, but Lord Taseldon slid a long and elegantly tailored arm across Loroun's chest with a sigh.

"Loroun, this elder lord dug a pit before you, and you leaped right into it. Learn, master your temper and stretch your patience, and learn some more. It's how youngbloods last long enough to become sly old dogs like Haeldown, here. Now let's get back to discussing the failure of our initial attempt to murder the lady clerk of the rolls, and more importantly, how things will be different *this* time."

"Tonight," Loroun snapped, "you didn't even try for a slaying at a dining lounge! I want it to be *public*, dramatic, so all Suzail sees and talks about it! How does it strike fear in anyone, if we poison her alone in her bed, and the palace can pass it off as fever?"

"He took her to Razreldron's," Taseldon replied, "and with all those private booths—"

"Huh," Lord Haeldown grunted, "*and* all those lowcoats Purple Dragon officers, who just *love* to run their swords through people!"

"—quite so, lord; and with all those lowcoats officers, we've little chance of success. However, later, when they seek a bed to dally in . . ."

Loroun smiled slowly. It was a fox's satisfied smile.

Lord Haeldown frowned. "Sword them while they're rutting? Seems unsporting to me! Still, there are worse ways to go . . ."

He held out his tallglass, Taseldon and Loroun *clinked* theirs against it, and they all chortled together.

Chapter Twenty-One

The Sweetest Sight

"I never thought the sweetest sight I'd see this tenday would be a *drow* handing me a goblet of my own wine," the lord constable of Irlingstar grunted. "Yet I thank you."

The way his eyes roved up and down the shapely dark elf bending over him made it clear he was regarding drow in a whole new way.

"Inside this," she replied in dry tones, "I'm Brannon Lucksar, wizard of war, remember?"

"Oh, er. Ah. Of course," Farland grunted, flushing.

They were all back in his office. New guards were in place on the door the two hireswords had fled through, and none of the doubled guard detail had keys to the locked and closed door they were standing watch over.

Aside from bruises—Farland's knee was so stiff he lurched along rather than strode—and a slight, recurring ringing in Arclath's and Gulkanun's ears, they seemed to have recovered from the explosion unscathed. Gulkanun and Longclaws even seemed to be starting to trust the dark elf.

"I . . . I'm sorry we were so stern with you," Longclaws said to her. "I . . . well, I still find it hard not to be alarmed when I find myself staring at a drow."

Lucksar shrugged and smiled. "*I* feel somewhat alarmed when I see the hands assisting me turn into tentacles, or"—she gestured at his hands—"vinelike sucking things. Yet I step past that and move on, for the Dragon Throne."

"Indeed," Gulkanun said politely. "You seem . . . preoccupied."

"I am," the dark elf replied, taking care not to look directly at Arclath and Amarune. She'd mind-touched both while reviving them, so they knew she was Elminster. They'd been rather quiet since then; best not to make it harder for them by looking their way or talking to them overmuch. It would be all too easy for an "El" to pass their lips, and all war wizards would have been warned about Elminster skulking around the kingdom, by now . . .

"Well?"

El shook her head. "Turning over all I've seen and heard since arriving in my head, to see if anything occurs to me." She looked at Farland. "You're sure those two who escaped hadn't managed to get into the castle before the blast, when you discovered them?"

Farland frowned then shook his head. "They couldn't have. No. Absolutely not. Nor did they strike me as the sort of killers who'd pounce and then get clear so swiftly. Twice."

Gulkanun nodded. "I judge them as you do. Not skilled enough."

El nodded. Good, he'd successfully turned aside Gulkanun's query. He *was* preoccupied, but not by anything to do with uncovering murderers or hurlers-of-bombs. Yet. Rather, he was trying to think of a good place to remove and hide the team ring he was wearing, in case Vangerdahast or Ganrahast or anyone else could trace him—or launch hostile magic, like the mind-touch from afar he'd felt, just before the blast had flung it away from him—through it. He had to remove it without Gulkanun or Longclaws or anyone else noticing, and stash it somewhere it wouldn't be found but that he could readily retrieve it from . . .

Hmm . . . Every jakes in Irlingstar was thoroughly inspected before and after each use to prevent them being used as ways of transferring items from prisoner to prisoner. There was very little extraneous furniture—Hells, very little furniture at *all*—to offer places of concealment for anything . . .

"*I'm* tired, if none of the rest of you are," Farland announced. "We need a battle plan. The six of us against everyone else in Irlingstar."

Arclath nodded. "Until we know who's been killing and causing the blasts—and they may not be the same persons—we have to treat the guards, the prisoners, and the passages and stairs where some unknown intruder might be lurking, all as foes."

"Exactly," Farland agreed. "So how do we get through the night ahead of us, and wind up alive come morn?"

"Work on the wards," Lucksar suggested. "Use them to make new walls, and doors that can't be forced. After we securely confine all the remaining prisoners in separate rooms for the night, we work a ward around all of them, wrapping them in one big box. Then we work on the wards to securely seal all exterior doors. Then confine all the guards and staff except the six of us together in a cluster of rooms that include the kitchens but are away from all doors—so any kitchen back doors must be excluded—and ward them into their own box. And *then* we barricade ourselves separately in rooms we can lock from within, and get some sleep. All save for Wizard of War Gulkanun and myself; we'll stand watch."

"Over each other," Gulkanun said wryly.

Farland nodded wearily. "I like the sound of that. The rest of you?"

He saw nothing but nods. "Good. Let's do it," he said, draining his goblet and heaving himself to his feet with a grunt of pain. "I'm not getting any younger."

"Or prettier," Lord Delcastle muttered, but Farland had been expecting some such comment, and managed a grin. Before the inevitable yawn.

Rensharra, it appeared, had a private passion for sky blue silk and gilt. Lots of gilt. Carved, curlicued ornamentations everywhere, all heavily gilded.

Mirt tried hard to keep his eyebrows from climbing to the top of his scalp and staying there.

The rest of her small tallhouse was tastefully luxurious, a long, narrow haven simply and sparsely furnished in creams, rich crimsons, and new but deep-stained, polished wood. The bedchamber, however, was dominated by a tentlike bed in Old Tashlutan style, with streams of blue silk descending from a central crown to its corners, and from there flaring in pinned-down pleats to the floor. Gilded flourishes were everywhere: the sheets, the pillows, even the hrasted carved, upswept corners were gold . . .

"So, Lord of Waterdeep," the owner of the grandiose tent teased, eyeing Mirt from its far side. "Care to . . . catch me?"

"Well, now," Mirt growled, "if it comes to pouncing, are you a kitten—or a tigress?"

"Come and see," Rensharra purred.

With a roar Mirt lurched around one end of the bed—only to receive her gown in the face as his intended prey tossed it at him in the wake of her cartwheel away, across the bed.

She came up smiling. "I find it warm in here—do you?" Her eyes pointedly raked him from head to flopping old seaboots, ere she kicked off her own fashionable anklestar boots and fled from the room.

Mirt pursued her, obediently unhooking his jerkin as he went.

The attic door stood open, its glowstone unhooded to light the way, so he followed.

The light proved to be coming from the far end of the attic, where a clattering noise announced that Rensharra Ironstave was the owner of a box hoist, and had just ridden it down out of sight, probably into her cellar.

Mirt grinned and started working the winch. All good fun, this . . .

He was wheezing in earnest by the time the box appeared up out of the depths—containing her underslip, of course—and he was able to step into it and thankfully let go of the crank.

His plunge down the shaft was as noisy as it was swift, so it wasn't until it ended with a dull, meaty thud that he noticed something was amiss.

Of course, the black-gloved arms sprawled out from under the box, and the thin ribbon of blood sliding out to join them, were the sorts of sights he'd seen all too often before.

He could tell at a glance that the arms were far too brawny to belong to Rensharra, so he spared them no more attention than to snatch up the needle-pointed dagger they'd let go of—covered in sticky orange-green Calishite poison, of course. In his experience, hired slayers sent to silence targets of lower rank than nobility and rulership seldom traveled alone.

The only light coming into the cellar spilled down an ascending stair at the far end of what looked to be the typical labyrinth of apple baskets, crocks of preserves, and shelves of oddments, so Mirt headed toward it.

He was halfway there when Rensharra screamed, and something made of crockery shattered loudly. Mirt went up the stairs like a bellowing bull, trying to sound frightening enough that anyone who'd cornered the lady clerk of the rolls would be distracted from making an actual kill by the volume and apparent formidability of an impending attack.

What he saw in the room above—her dining hall, by the looks of it—was Rensharra at the top of an ornamental pillar, clad only in net leggings, a clout, and a decorative black lace belt, kicking frantically at the hands of a masked and gloved man in black leathers who was half up atop her sideboard, trying to catch hold of her ankles to haul her back down. She'd just pulled off her dethma and was flailing him across the face with it, its metal-tipped breast cups clanging with every blow, as high and shrill as metal windchimes.

A second man in black leathers lay sprawled motionless on his back across the dining table, his jaw gaping and the shards of what must recently have been a large crockery flower flute scattered around his head—water, flowers, and all.

Mirt laughed aloud at what he saw, shouted, "Never fear, lass! I'll save you!" and charged down the room, snatching up a chair as he went.

The man trying to snare Rensharra turned and dropped to the floor, clawing out and hurling a belt knife at his large and loud new foe.

Mirt batted it aside with the chair and threw his own newfound knife. It struck the man's neck, stuck there for a moment, then continued on its way to quiver in the wall above the sideboard.

The man cursed, sounding more frightened than furious, and grabbed another knife from his belt.

Mirt threw the chair.

The man howled in pain as the hurtling furniture smashed some of his fingers, drove his arm back around behind him, and sent his second knife clanging and clattering into a corner. Then the chair hit the sideboard and rebounded off it, one leg askew, to strike the man from behind. It slid onward a little way with the somewhat dazed man draped atop it—but when it stopped, its rider tried to turn to face Mirt and haul out a short sword.

He'd half-managed it, starting to sway and shout something desperate that came out strangely slurred—so the knife bore *strong* Calishite poison—when Mirt reached him. And planted a firm, hairy fist in his face.

A nose shattered, blood spurted, and the owner of both went down, toppling to the floor like one of those proverbial felled trees.

As Rensharra screamed again, Mirt was already looking up at her to give her his best reassuring grin, so he saw where she was looking and knew instantly that the source of her fresh fear was back down the room behind him. He ducked, grabbed the chair he'd just thrown, and threw it again, back down the room.

Peering after it, he watched a furious man in the latest expensive and stylish lords' evening garb dance aside with a flourish of his rapier and snarl, "I'm *not* losing *this* wager! How many hired sword swingers does it take to butcher one silly bitch of a palace scribe, anyhail?"

"More than you brought," Mirt informed him, lurching to meet the noble and plucking up chairs as he went.

The noble sneered at the first one, was staggering after the second, and was swordless, dazed, and bleeding from a scalp graze after the third and last chair. It happened to be the last seat on Mirt's side of the long dining table, so the Lord of Waterdeep planted one boot in an available crotch—taking care to angle up and under, so as not to break any toes on the inevitable armored codpiece—and as the stricken noble doubled over, put his best roundhouse right into the man's throat.

The noble went down with a dying sob as Mirt grinned in ruthless satisfaction. Aye, it's hard to go on breathing through a shattered and flattened throat. Their master's fall left four armed retainers he'd brought along still to deal with—but one look at their master jerking and strangling on the floor had them whirling around to flee headlong.

Mirt decided to snatch up the noble's rapier and pursue them, to at least ventilate a few backsides. If witnesses telling tales to the Watch could be whittled down to one man, or several wounded men, the Watch might have fewer lies to wade through—or mistakenly swallow.

So it was that he returned to Rensharra drenched in blood, none of it his own, to find her barricaded in her bedchamber. The rest of her garments seemed to have vanished.

"My hero!" she gasped over the tangled barrier of furniture, her eyes alight. "No one ever fought to the death for me before!"

She tossed aside the splintered chair leg she'd been ready to club the wrong intruder with, and started flinging aside elements of barricade with furious energy and a fine disregard for dated styles of furniture, to welcome her right intruder.

"You deserve a reward," she panted, when she'd cleared enough for her to drag Mirt into the room. "Come and claim it."

A moment later, she demonstrated those words had been a command, not mere suggestion or entreaty, by taking hold of his blood-soaked belt and hauling, hard.

They fell into the waiting tent together.

"He's shaking," the drow murmured warningly to Gulkanun, nodding her head at Longclaws as the spell-cursed war wizard staggered wearily into his room and slammed its door.

"Means he's exhausted," Gulkanun said tersely. "He did most of my ward work, knowing I had to last the night awake standing watch. With you."

The dark elf nodded. Longclaws had been the last of their colleagues to retire to a room. All of her suggested alterations of the wards were done, and everyone was beyond tired. She and Gulkanun regarded each other, neither of them smiling. Silence fell. In it, the curvaceous dark elf strolled slowly toward Gulkanun.

"I would prefer you kept your distance," he muttered.

"*You* still don't trust me," she murmured accusingly, still advancing.

"*Back*," he ordered her sharply.

Not slowing her same leisurely pace, she came right up to him, and reached out with one slender, long-fingered hand. Those fingers were reaching for . . . his wrist—of the hand he was using to grasp the butt of a still-sheathed wand.

Out from behind Gulkanun's back, snake-swift, came his other hand, with a long needle in it, to jab that dusky drow hand.

"I *suspected* you'd try something, drow!" he said grimly. "I'll—"

Her arms were closing around him, needle-transfixed hand and all, as he snarled and snatched out that wand, to feed her—

Nothing at all, as he stiffened and went silent. Frozen and helpless.

Elminster had flowed through feebly and vainly clawing dark elf fingers into Gulkanun—and overwhelmed the war wizard's mind.

It took Manshoon some time to find any wizards at all in Hultail. Farmers taking slowly creaking carts to market could be seen everywhere, filling the muddy streets, but were well outnumbered by unhappily bawling rothé, goats, lambs, and oxen penned outside the fleshers' and butcher's yard. There was even activity at the wagon sheds, where a Moonsea-run wagon needed a new wheel and rails yestereve at the latest.

Yet there was no sign of the modest keep he'd expected to find. It wasn't until he caught sight of a small tile-roofed stone cottage half-hidden under some sprawling old trees at the back of the moat-and-palisade-surrounded Watch yard that he saw what he was looking for—a line of wizards' robes hung out on a washline.

Real dusk was drawing down, and a lamp was lit in that cottage, but only one man emerged to take in that washing before dewfall. A lone, unconcerned man, who waved cheerfully at the various members of the Watch who were—with their armor off, down to their breeches and shoulder braces—dumping out kitchen wash water into a pit ere returning to their barracks. So the duty war wizards in Hultail were sadly depleted in numbers, it seemed. Three down to one, without anyone seeming alarmed in the slightest. Which meant they were on duty nearby or out on a mission.

Manshoon fetched himself another decanter from what he'd been able to salvage from Dardulkyn's cellar, sat back at his ease, and farscried around Hultail anew. Finding a continued distinct lack of wizards.

So, as real darkness came down, he peered along the Wyvernwater banks and up and down the Thunderflow, seeking blazing torches or activity. And still found nothing. The roads, then, the one to Thunderstone first.

There! Winking, bobbing lights . . . lanterns on lancepoles, held by mounted Purple Dragons. Armed and equipped for rough country, and riding in a ring around, yes, two wizards of war. Crown mages making speed through the night in wild country, which meant great urgency. They were heading for Thunderstone—and almost certainly, beyond Thunderstone, Castle Irlingstar. Well, now . . .

Yes, *well* now, indeed. Manshoon allowed himself a gleefully ruthless smile.

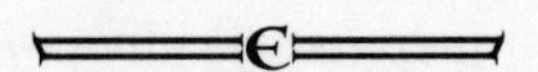

"So, my lords?" Young Lord Raegl Halgohar was handsome and charming and seldom had to pay to fill his bed. His dalliances of the early evening had been with two sisters from Suzail who'd clawed scratches he was quite proud of all down his back, before he'd left them to the hungry mercies of his groom and his page. He himself had proceeded to this gathering of noble wagerers with just his bodyguards—who were happily gossiping with the bullyblades of fellow wagering nobles in the outermost chamber, over the very best spiced eel fest bites. "Your faithful spell hurlers were yawning like bored cats on my way in, so I *know* you've been spell-watching the fun. How went the slaying of Rensharra Ironstave?"

Someone cursed feelingly, by way of reply.

"It did *not* go," Lord Haeldown explained rather smugly. "As in, she did not die. Again."

"Thanks to our fat and aging champion of a Lord of Waterdeep?"

"Indeed," Lord Loroun said shortly. "That old rogue is costing me a fortune."

"Whose?"

They all laughed politely at the old joke. It was an open secret among the Suzailan nobility that Loroun had moved from slavery and buying and selling city buildings into targeted moneylending that involved slaying his debtors and seizing all he could of their holdings before kin or other creditors arrived.

Lord Taseldon and Lord Haeldown wore satisfied smiles.

"Ah," Halgohar interpreted, sitting down across from them. "You wagered against, again?"

"We did," Taseldon confirmed, pushing a decanter and a tallglass across the table. "Join us in a drink to our continued success?"

"Gladly." Halgohar looked down the table. "Loroun, where are you *finding* all these incompetent assassins? Accomplished killers can't be in *that* short supply."

"After all the attempted settling of scores between rival lords gathered here in Suzail for the council, you'd be surprised," came the dark reply. "So many bodies were dumped in the harbor a few nights back that they blocked two main sewer grates. The Dragons were so gleeful when they started recognizing faces that they hushed it all up."

"Hmm," Halgohar commented, as a darker thought struck him. "I wonder how often that sort of hushing happens?"

Loroun's smile held no mirth at all. "You'd be surprised."

Chapter Twenty-Two

I Am The Ambush

Ah, ye used carrion crawler brain fluid. Good. The paralysis will soon pass, leaving this body as usable as before.

The voice inside Gulkanun's head felt human, and male, and . . . old. Ancient and mighty, a mind of depth and power, accomplished in both worldly experience and in the Art. A mind that had seen much, done much, shaped magic for centuries . . .

You knew King Berost? Berost the Bold? You're that *old?* Gulkanun thought.

I am. My name is Elminster. Aye, that *Elminster. Best known these days as the Sage of Shadowdale. Widely rumored to be a madwits old mage who deludes himself into claiming to have been a Chosen of Mystra. I am mad, and old, and a mage—and that claim is true.*

I . . . I . . . Gulkanun thought.

Be neither awed nor alarmed, Duth Gulkanun. Ye serve a worthy cause, and command respectable Art, and greater than that, good morals. Kindness, fairness, diligence; ye'd be surprised to know how truly rare these are, and ye have them all. Which is why I need ye—and Longclaws, and all the other worthy wizards of war of Cormyr, from Royal Magician Ganrahast to the rawest novices.

Need me? Need us? Gulkanun thought.

Aye. A door seemed to slowly swing wide in Gulkanun's mind, spilling out bright glory . . . glory that rolled forward to embrace Duth Gulkanun, sweeping him along in a bright, rising flood that shared the goddess Mystra's commandment to recruit the wizards of war to work for a better future for Cormyr and all the Realms, a commandment laced with Elminster's own excitement.

Gulkanun found himself ecstatic, moved by a greater joy than he'd ever felt before, a gleeful plunge into glorious certainty. He could believe this invader in his mind, trust this powerful intellect touching him, because he could *see* that it was all true. There truly *was* a goddess of magic come back from oblivion, a good and true and wonderful Mystra, and she had indeed commanded Elminster, her once and again servant, to find blueflame and seal rifts to guard the Realms, to recruit the wizards of war and bring new glory to Cormyr, and . . .

I have never been able to so clearly know *I'm being given truth, before. It is . . . wonderful, beyond all wonder I've ever felt before. This is* trust. Gulkanun thought.

It is. Now, will ye stop being suspicious of this beautiful dark elf? She was a fell and evil servant of Lolth before, though young and of little accomplishment, but she has no mind but mine, now. We should waste no more time, but work together henceforth.

Yes, oh yes! Starting how? What should we do right now? I— Gulkanun thought.

Rough hands were suddenly clawing at Gulkanun, pulling him away from the drow he dimly realized he'd been embracing like a lover.

He turned, mind a-tumble with Elminster and the glory he'd brought shining in it, to look into the angrily frowning face of Imbrult Longclaws.

Who'd silently opened his door and charged forth to haul his friend Gulkanun out of a dark and fell embrace, one hand outflung to shove the drow back and away with a fine disregard for feminine anatomy. "I *thought* she'd seduce you, the first farruking moment she got the cha . . ."

Imbrult's rush of words faded into awed silence as the glory—and Elminster—flooded into his mind, too.

Under the lash of Vandur's tongue and arrogance, he and Gulkanun had begun as fellow sufferers and silent allies, but become fast friends. They'd worked together for four long years, and liked and respected each other more than anyone else in either's life. They were . . . El was showing them their gratitude and friendship for each other, how they truly felt. Their joined minds reeled. Duth's thoughts and memories plunged into Imbrult's, and vice versa, in a happy maelstrom of mingling and discovery.

Their faces were wet with tears, their arms were around each other, and they were making excited, inarticulate noises they only dimly noticed as the thoughts flashed back and forth among the two of them and Elminster. Around them and through them and cradling them, the great and glory-filled mind of Elminster . . .

We must do this! Oh, Cormyr! To banish hunger and want and treachery forever, and . . ., Imbrult thought.

Abruptly, their excited sharing was rudely interrupted again. This time it was Farland breaking the link. Gulkanun and Longclaws staggered, half-dazed.

The lord constable had torn the dark elf back and away from the two men, and held her with a dagger to her throat.

"I've *heard* all the tales about drow," he growled, "and didn't quite believe they were the seductresses some have said, but I guess . . ."

"It's not what you think," Gulkanun snapped.

Farland's sneer was savage. "I guess not, hey, Saer Hurlspells?"

Then his face changed and he stiffened, trying to scream and failing. *Something* was flooding into his mind . . .

It was time to go adventuring again.

Oh, not in an overbold way that would alert the wizards of war and the entire court to his presence and ambitions. Not something even a nearby Harper would notice, unless one was actually standing by the roadside when he intercepted those two Crown mages who'd ridden out from Hultail.

No, this time he could revert to the way he'd fought in the early days, when the Zhentarim were a bright new idea and rising power, rather than rulers of anywhere or anyone. And he could do it with an assist from his own later days—and Chancsozbur's tomb. It had been *years* since he'd even thought of that reckless fool. A man so steeped in his own overconfident stupidity as to think he could get away with swindling Manshoon. Breaking all his joints and leaving him with two worms to slide up his nose and devour him slowly from within had been a fitting fate for the dolt, but his service to Manshoon hadn't ended there. Oh, no.

Lord Chess had been sent to seize Chancsozbur's holdings and sell them off before his kin could arrive to claim them, and to use the coin to construct the elaborate tomb—a modest stone mausoleum on a wooded hillside near Masoner's Bridge. The fool's bones still lay in a great stone block of a coffin, its lid adorned with Chancsozbur's effigy—and the floor concealing a stone-block-locked turntable that could be used to swivel the coffin aside and reveal a stair down to a lower chamber.

The men Chess had brought with him had made short bladework of Chancsozbur's arriving kin, leaving no one to command the keys to the mausoleum save the Brotherhood. So for decades the Zhentarim had used the upper room as a smuggling way den, while in the room below their First Lord Manshoon had carefully stored several of his clones to await future needs. His other selves were all gone now, of course, awakened after deaths or taken elsewhere to more secure hideholds.

Yet all of that had left Manshoon knowing the tomb very well. Which made it a safe teleport destination. From there, he could readily translocate from landmark to landmark he could see ahead in the desired direction, to intercept those two war wizards. So the tomb awaited, only a teleport casting away . . .

Ah, but wait. Chores first. Banishing the scrying spheres, Manshoon cast the spell that hid most of Sraunter's cellar—death tyrants and all—behind a false, conjured stone wall. Someone might blunder down here, a thief or busy-nosed Crown inspector or Watchman; everyone was suspicious of alchemists, after all. So let them find Sraunter's noisome cesspit and the usual refuse of old broken furniture and the like, not a waiting row of undead beholders.

If an intruder broke his spell and saw what was behind it . . . well, they were on their own. He'd left his tyrants awake and under commandment to slay and pursue all life. If someone did unleash them, they'd probably still be hard at it when he got back. There was a lot of life in Suzail.

Gelnur Farland was drowning in shame and disgust and anguish.

Mind-raped by a dark elf whose throat was *right there* under his blade, that he should have killed before she . . .

What was this, by Crown and—?

The mind flooding into his was male, and human, and old, dark with the weight of many, many memories. A wizard's mind, a—oh, no, *no,* was this a war wizard trying a mind-ream? Were they both going to be driven mad? Was it starting already? Was—

The intruding mind was as powerful as a looming castle, if he'd been a small toy cottage. An overwhelming dark and warm flood, it raced through his thoughts, his own memories, looking hard for something. Seeking . . . any evidence of disloyalty to the Crown, or that Gelnur Farland had anything to do with the murders in Irlingstar. And finding none, and smiling inside Gelnur's head with such a flood of pleasure that Farland moaned aloud.

Who *was* this, by . . .

An old bearded mage walking alone, long of Shadowdale. Old Mage, Old Sage, he of all the tales about the Doombringer of Mystra, the man who'd been a maid and a . . .

He could see more and more of the intruder's mind, and was being shown ever more of it, memories splendid and terrible, devils and dragons in the sky and the City of Song and terrible battlefields beyond counting . . .

Elminster am I. Aye, ye know me. I am the one of thy grandsire's tales, and one of the stories told in the taverns about the Chosen of Mystra.

"By the fabled kisses of Alusair!" the lord constable gasped aloud.

Oh, a fitting oath, for they were sweet, they were indeed . . .

Whimsically, Elminster shared two vivid memories, thrusting the scenes into Farland's mind like two turning, winking gems, one after the other.

The first . . . a fireside, by night, in the open forested wilds of northern Cormyr, among many laughing men in armor, making camp and hobbling mounts—splendid horses. Then walking among these merry noblemen in their bright armor to a tall woman who was unstrapping and tossing aside her own gleaming, firelit plates of armor, plate of the finest make, curved and molded to fit her sleek body . . . bared in the firelight. She turned to him with a bright smile and embraced him to take a kiss, not grant it . . . Alusair, young and warrior strong and proud, the spirited, wanton, wild princess . . .

The fireside faded, and in the darkness beyond it the second gem rushed up and swallowed Farland, plunging him into the dark stillness of an empty, cobwebbed, echoing high hall: the royal palace of Suzail, in the infamous haunted wing. And out of the gloom came a gliding shadow with the gleam of spectral armor and the same tumbling fall of hair and the same face, but older and etched by sadness and loss and fury after driving fury. It stole up swiftly, in a rush that embraced to take a kiss, but at the last moment hesitated to plead wordlessly for it . . . and cried what were but ghost shadows of tears when a kiss was granted. Followed by lips that hungered and brought icy searing pain as they stole the warmth of life from Elminster as he kissed her, Alusair the life-stealing ghost.

There ye go. Now ye know what ye swear by: Alusair's fabled kisses, indeed.

Farland cursed then, shaken—and the oaths he used were far fouler and more colorful than the splendor he'd been shown.

He flung away his dagger and started to weep.

The tomb was far colder than he remembered.

Especially on this chill sort of morning. Ground mists were rising and streaming knee deep through the trees as Manshoon strolled out of the tomb and went looking for a distant spot in the right direction, to teleport to across the Wyvernwater, and from there east and north, from high place to high place. The Crown mages might have been foolish enough to ride all night, but more likely they'd made camp beside the road, slept just long enough to rest the horses, and would be journeying again about now.

Manshoon stretched and smiled. Choosing a high and distant field, he cast a teleport to take himself there. Then again, from Nuth Tammarsaer's high east pasture to Rauntaun's Tor. Thence to the ridge behind Lockspike Fang. Standing atop it, on wind-scoured rock in a chill breeze with a startled eagle taking wing from its favorite lookout perch away from him, he could look down on Orondstars Road.

There. Twelve Purple Dragons riding in a ring around two mounted men not in armor: his war wizards. His prey.

He chose the next bend in the road, so he could be standing nonchalantly waiting for them.

His captors were back, and terror was like a cold white arm coiled through him, chill fingers tight around his heart.

Mreldrake swallowed, then swallowed again. His throat was as dry as old bones, and he was trembling violently. He knew that they knew just how frightened of them he was . . . and he no longer cared.

At least they were smiling.

"We are pleased with your continued successes in the use of your new magic," one said.

"You've become quite adept at murder," another added approvingly, like a tutor praising a young child.

As he stared at them, standing facing him in the room they'd made his prison, almost close enough to touch, Mreldrake found himself suddenly longing to be back in the royal palace of Suzail. Even being under Manshoon's hand had been better than this . . .

He was quailing inwardly just as much as he was quaking outwardly. They could slay him at will. How then could he, dared he, try to delicately inform them he'd made himself essential to working the magic he'd developed, and therefore—he hoped—unexpendable?

They were smiling at him now, almost fondly. Yet in their eyes, he could see it, yes, there was a glint of glee . . .

"Your attempts to save your own hide by working yourself into your new spell have amused us greatly. Be aware that we've no intention of killing you." *Not yet*, the tone of the captor's voice added.

Well of course not yet. Not when what he knew would be so useful in enabling them to swiftly and quietly conquer Cormyr.

They came around the corner, riding easily in the brightening morning.

Manshoon stood wide-footed, his arms folded across his chest, smiling faintly.

"Power is mine, and I *am* power incarnate," he murmured to himself as he watched the Purple Dragons frown, rein in, and bark a halt.

One man, alone in the wild borderlands, by his pose so insolently sure of himself, either meant an archmage or the visible decoy for a hundred hidden outlaws waiting in ambush.

"*I* am the ambush," he announced politely. "All by myself. For I am an archmage, the mightiest you'll ever meet in your lives. Which—with one exception—will be ending now."

Nonchalantly he released the spell he'd cast and held ready while waiting for them to ride into view.

Twelve Purple Dragons and their mounts were suddenly shrieking, tumbling carrion, their cries dying abruptly as his whirlcone tightened around them and its unseen blades of force started dismembering them in midair. Bloody limbs bounced into the ditch behind them, where the road curved back toward civilization.

"Ah, civilization," Manshoon murmured, watching the two wizards survive unscathed thanks to their wards. Spent in saving them, of course, leaving them defenseless against his next spell. "We *are* far from it these days, aren't we?"

Their first frantic magics flared and burst against his shield as he calmly and unhurriedly cast another spell. When it was done, one of the war wizards stood scorched and dazed on the road, his robes aflame and his horse gone. Only the untouched Crown mage managed a second spell against Manshoon's shield, taking it down. By then, the future emperor of Cormyr had unhurriedly worked another magic—and the scorched wizard of war had become two booted legs surrounded by ashes, standing in the middle of Orondstars Road.

The surviving war wizard cast his strongest battle spell, rocking the road around Manshoon, whose conjured mantle absorbed the death sent so desperately to claim him. Its job done, the mantle sighed into nothingness, leaving him unguarded. By then, of course, he'd hurled a mind doom at the lone surviving Crown mage, and was inside the hapless fool's head.

He shattered and conquered his mind in less time than it took his victim to sigh.

So this was enthusiastic young Wizard of War Jarlin Flamtarge. Well, well. Manshoon burned out his new minion's war wizard ring until it had no powers left, and could no longer be traced from afar. Hultail was a remote post, neither important nor busy; Flamtarge hadn't possessed a team ring.

"Have a good journey," Manshoon said politely to the horse, gentling its mind with one of the spells he was proudest of, one of the few restorative ones he'd ever mastered.

Then he teleported back to Sraunter's cellar in Suzail, but left his awareness mentally riding Wizard of War Jarlin Flamtarge. His newest mind pet, now riding on alone along Orondstars Road, bound for Castle Irlingstar.

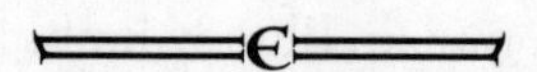

The Simbul plunged down out of a midnight sky feet first, her silver hair billowing behind her.

Rushing up at her was a desolate, ruined keep, standing in a rugged vale deep in rocky wilderlands, a lonely riven fang.

It was not unguarded; malgodemons and nabassu in great numbers flapped up from those crumbling dark parapets to challenge her.

She plummeted, surrounded by a sphere of glowing blue radiance that faded into sudden visibility, a whirling open-work sphere outlined by the tightly curving orbits of many flying objects—no two alike, but all blazing with blueflame.

The dark flying guardians came at her from all sides in a vicious storm, but she smote them from the sky with spells hurled forth from her ever-swifter-whirling cage of blueflame, a cage that seared and melted to sighing tatters every demon that blundered into it, keeping them from reaching her. The cage fell with her, to touch and melt through the keep's stone walls as if they were but air and shadows.

The cage descended still, drifting down, down through the heart of the ancient and riven fortress into an eerily glowing well in its depths. Yet another rift in the Realms, through which more demons were appearing, boiling forth in an endless fell stream.

The Simbul clawed at the air around her to pull the cage in tight, and make of it the rift-rending dagger she would need.

"As El would say," she murmured aloud, "here we go again."

Dagger and all, she slid into purple-white agony.

Chapter Twenty-Three

Giggling And Guffawing

Demons clawed at her, tearing at her hair and the smooth flesh of her shoulders. She heeded it not, lost in the icy fire of the rift as she fought it . . . quenched it . . . destroyed it.

Leaving herself empty and weary, the blueflame items dulled and circling her slowly.

Claws raked her again, more and more of them, as emboldened demons flooded in at her from all sides, erupting out of the dark recesses of the ruined fortress, trying to pounce on her, to drag her down, to rend her . . .

Ducking and turning, slapping and entangling and tugging with her long silver tresses, The Simbul fought to keep from being overborne and buried under murderous demon bodies. Battling to stay on her feet, she blasted her assailants with spell after spell.

And they died. Talons and grotesque barbed limbs and many-fanged jaws rained down on her in a grisly downpour of black and burning ichor as her magic made demon flesh boil and demon bodies burst.

The wounds they gave her stung like fire and wept not just her blood, but licking flames of silver fire.

She lashed them with that leaking fire, striping it across snarling faces and sting-studded tails and cruel clutching claws alike. And where silver fire touched demon hide, that darksome meat melted, collapsing into wisps of stinking smoke with astonishing speed, burning demons to nothingness as readily as the blueflame items had. And still they came.

She spent her spells, one by one, taking down a small army but facing an endless, ever-growing one. Spending precious silver fire to bend a spell for opening wards into a spray of disintegration, and a magic for sending messages afar into a flesh-dicing whirlblade storm . . . her arsenal was almost spent.

"El," she cried aloud, as more and more demons fought through the sagging, slowing web of blueflame objects, now drifting darkly and trailing only the faintest blue glows, to claw at her, "where are you? I need you!"

Despair came quickly as shrill demonic laughter was the only reply, her attackers gathering thick and deep now, crowding each other in their hunger for her destruction.

"*Elminster*!" she screamed. "Oh my love, *hear me*!"

"I *really* don't think any true Cormyrean needs lessons in how the realm should be governed from some sly outlander Harper who can make her hair silver," Lord Breeklar said coldly. "I've heard quite enough of your prattle. Begone." He turned. "Guards, throw this woman out. No need to be gentle."

"If you *don't* mind, Auldus," Lord Hamnlaer snapped, "*I'll* command my own guards, in my own house. I want to hear more about these new rights. If Foril's willing to trade some of his powers over us all for new laws every citizen must follow, let's be hearing the details." Behind him, his guards, who'd hastened forward at Breeklar's call, hesitated and peered around at the faces of all the seated nobles.

"Lord Breeklar," Storm said calmly, "Lord Hamnlaer is right. Trying to silence a messenger whenever you don't like the *sound* of a message, without hearing what the message truly is, is to leave yourself forever unprepared for everything life hurls at you. That's merely a fast trail to many bruises and a swifter grave than necessary." She raised her glass. "And for your information, Lord Breeklar, I *am* the Marchioness of Immerdusk. Every whit as noble, and as 'true Cormyrean,' as you are, and of older lineage. The Breeklars, as I recall, came from Westgate less than four generations ago . . ."

"Do you *dare* insult me?"

"Do you *dare* try to act insulted?" Storm replied, in perfect mimicry of Breeklar's fury. Then she fell into chuckles, shaking her head. "Apologies, my lords," she told the table at large, "but I just can't play the haughty overblown noble as well as Breeklar, here. I grew past that stage long, long ago."

"Oh," Breeklar said nastily, "this'll be your 'I'm centuries upon centuries old and knew Baerauble and King Duar and the Immortal Purple Dragon personally, and I know what's right for you' pose. Which is either a pack of lies, or you're some sort of foul demon or swindling elf who can put on human shape long enough to cozen us! Well, I'll not fall for such—"

He paled and grabbed for the ornate half-basket hilt of his sword, because Storm had stood up abruptly, upsetting her goblet of wine across the table. Nobles all around it tensed and reached for handy weapons, and Lord Hamnlaer's household guards started forward again.

The Lady Immerdusk seemed oblivious to them all. She was seeing things far away, her face going pale and sad, and—though her parted lips didn't move at all—she was murmuring something soft and small, that issued from her throat with the shrill high ring of a distant scream: "*Elminster*! Oh my love, *hear me*!"

That great, dark, warm and magnificent mind was suddenly gone from Gelnur Farland's. Leaving him overwhelmed and . . . desolate.

He was on his hands and knees, sobbing like a little lass, himself again but . . . abandoned, all those rich memories and loves and delights all gone, taken from him all at once.

In a whirling trice the sweet memories had ended in a greater rising rage than he'd ever felt before, a rage not his own that had begun with a distant scream: "*Elminster*! Oh my love, *hear me!*"

Demons overwhelmed her, tore at her, driving sharp talons deep into her, trying to tear her limb from limb by sheer strength.

They were starting to manage it, too. Tendons and sinews began to fail, tresses were torn out by the roots, and agony kindled all over, dragging a scream out past her clenched teeth. She was going to die here, going to fail Mystra . . .

Oh, no, Alassra. You fail me not. Call the blueflame to you. Will it to you.

Mystra! The goddess had heard her!

Hope surged in her like fresh cooling fire. The Simbul obeyed, or tried to, struggling to gather her will in the raw red heart of deepening agony. Demon talons had shifted from her limbs to the softer, easier target of her belly and torn into it. They were pulling at the edges of that wound, seeking to tear her wide open and rip her apart. Her legs and hips were drenched in her own warm blood, and her torso was one great gaping wound . . .

Mind that not. Call the blueflame.

The Simbul called, and felt the floating objects that held blueflame start to respond, curving in closer to her.

Demon bodies were in the way, clawing and crowding and surging. This was hopeless . . .

Hope, my darling daughter, is a lantern we all need, and we must never yield it up. Not even for me. Take firm hold of your hope, and keep calling the flame to you. Beautiful blueflame . . .

The blueflame converged on her, the items that bore it searing holes through the demons as they came. Demons shrieked and roared as they died or were maimed, many of them falling away.

Yet more snarlingly crowded in. Haures and rutterkin, glabrezu and nameless wormlike clutching things . . . no matter how much they clawed at incoming blueflame or swung weapons or worked magic at it, they could do nothing to stop or slow or strike aside the called blueflame—for touching it brought disintegration, and magic only made it blaze more brightly.

Into your wound. Draw the blueflame into you.

The Simbul did as Mystra commanded, and the silver fire roiling within her and leaking from her wounds snarled in hungry coils around the blueflame, merged with it . . . and consumed it.

Quite suddenly, she was full of white-hot, raging power. Might that boiled up her limbs, that moaned in crackling restlessness through her hair . . . that was hurled out of her as she cried out in pain.

Power shot from her eyes in beams and gouted from her nose and mouth, stabbing in all directions in a blinding-bright flood that devoured demons and the walls beyond them alike.

Dark fragments of walls toppled ponderously away from The Simbul, down into crashing ruin, crushing more demons. Others fled in all directions, shrieking.

Screaming loudly enough to drown them all out, in pain and exultation and sheer fury, The Simbul soared up out of the keep, shedding the ashes of broken demons in her wake, a leaping comet that soared high into the night sky.

"Tluin," Hawkspike gasped, trying to roll over. Plaguespew, but he was stiff!

"Hawk?" Harbrand yawned. "You awake?"

"*No*," Hawkspike snarled firmly, though he very much was. Not that he wanted to be. He ached all over, cold and sharp stones jabbed him with every movement, he was hungry—his stomach growled, on cue—and, yes, he needed to relieve himself. Achingly.

Overhead was dark, rough stone. They were in some cave or other they'd found. Yes, he remembered now . . . a big one. They'd spilled some flash oil on a branch and made a torch that'd burned long enough to search it thoroughly. One vast room, a natural cavern that came furnished in old bones and refuse . . . but nothing recent, and no beast smell, so it wasn't a lair for anything at the moment. They were somewhere high in the mountain foothills near Irlingmount. And, of course, come morning, they were stiff and sore, and decidedly not well rested after an uncomfortable night spent huddled on unforgivingly hard, sharp rocks.

"Tluin tluin *tluin*," Hawkspike told the world, wincing as he rolled into a kneeling position and more unyielding stone promptly bruised his knees. He heaved himself upright to stumble unsteadily over to where he could lean against the cavern wall. His mouth tasted like he'd been licking a beast cage.

Harbrand, of course, was already up. Hrast him.

And stretching on the far side of the cavern, like a tavern dancer readying herself for something acrobatic. Grinning, too.

Gods above, the bastard was going to be *cheerful*.

"I," Hawkspike's partner announced, breaking off stretching with a series of kicks and flexings of his arms like some sort of drunken wrestler, "need to ease the old bladder. And get a drink. We heard a stream, last night, didn't we?"

"Unnh," Hawkspike agreed, pointing to where he vaguely thought the flowing water might be. They had heard water tinkling—a small but flash-flowing run—somewhere off *that* way.

Of course, to pee or drink, they'd have to go out into that bright slice of the world waiting yonder, beyond the entrance . . .

He picked his way carefully along the wall, not trusting his balance yet. Oh, but his bones were cold . . . The only good thing was, Har wasn't moving much faster. Which meant he'd be saved from hearing quite a few mocking comments, at least until—

Something blotted out the morning light. Hawkspike looked up—and froze. Clear across the cave, Harbrand had done the same thing, becoming a gaping, pale-faced trembling statue.

The cavemouth was a descending gash as long as a grandly sprawling cottage. Completely filling it was a black snout that thrust a long way into the cave. A snout that was attached to the scaled, curving-horned head of . . . a black dragon.

"*Naed*," Hawkspike gasped, and he eased his own bladder right there and then, favorite codpiece and all.

Wise and cruel draconic eyes slid across from Harbrand's similar distress to watch him.

"Well met," the dragon said, parting his jaws—those *fangs*!—in a slow, soft smile. "I am Alorglauvenemaus, and I find myself in need of some replacement Beasts."

"Oh?" Harbrand managed to quaver, from across the cave. "W-what *sort* of beasts?"

About then, Hawkspike decided that losing control of his bladder was an ineffective tactic. So he chose another: falling over in a dead faint.

"That's a good idea!" Harbrand said brightly—and he fainted, too.

A moment later, the cavern rocked to a deafening roar. Alorglauvenemaus was guffawing.

"Such . . . glory," The Simbul mumbled, watching dawn creep across the mountains. Enough of the power was gone from her that she was herself again, in control once more. Hanging high in the air, she healed herself, flexing and stretching in gasping ease. All pain gone, she was stronger, more vigorous, and more *alive* than she had ever been. "Thank you, Lady Mother. What now?"

Now you must go and hunt more blueflame, of course. Many more rifts await.

The Simbul groaned, then managed a grin. "Well, *that* one was . . . intense fun. And I'm getting good at this; must be all the practice."

Must be, Mystra agreed, and they found themselves laughing together again.

The lord constable of Irlingstar struggled to his feet, dimly aware that Elminster—the sleekly menacing drow he'd had in his arms, his knife at her throat—had run headlong from him, down a passage and away.

The dark elf hadn't been Lucksar at all. Lucksar was dead, and no more help was coming . . .

Someone was shouting, several someones; prisoners, noble voices he knew, angry and afraid.

"Are we *all* going to be killed while you do nothing?"

"The war wizards are murdering us, one by one, while you just stand there and laugh!"

"Killers! So much for your vaunted justice!"

"What?" Farland muttered wearily, still reluctant to leave all those memories behind, to forget the warmth of that mighty mind wrapped around his . . . what had brought this shouting on? Had there been another killing?

There had. The guards had just found Lord Arlond Hiloar lying dead in his own cell doorway. Ah, yes, perfumed Arlond, fair-haired and delicate, icily arrogant to everyone but more often withdrawn, always fondling and stroking a little spiral-seashell-shaped ivory snuffbox he carried with him. Not long before he'd been found dead, he'd been seen standing in that doorway, watching and listening as louder prisoners, in their own doorways up and down the same passage, had demanded to be let out. All of them had been kept to their rooms by the invisible walls of the new wards; Elminster's "secure boxes."

Hiloar was alone in his cell rather than sharing it, and aside from the wards, it had no other way out except through solid stone walls. All of which still stood undisturbed—like the wards. At some time during all the bandinage, he'd simply slumped, unnoticed by his fellow prisoners until his fall. Slumped because his throat had been slashed open, the cut so deep that it had gone almost right through his neck. The blood was . . . copious.

The nobles in the nearest rooms were the most frightened. One was shouting—no, two, now, make that three as another took it up—that the castle must be haunted, and it was Farland's "Crown duty" to get them all "out of here" to somewhere safer. The always-half-flooded dungeon cell in Immerkeep, the manacle pits in Wheloon, the dank mold-infested prison cellars in Marsember—anywhere!

Farland sighed, considered some choice curses but flung them aside unuttered, and decided he'd just about reached the same conclusion these scared nobles were so unpleasantly voicing. Though by any sober measure, he commanded less than a sixth of the manpower he'd need to keep any sort of control over such highnosed and well-connected prisoners, once they departed Irlingstar. Not to mention that taking such a bold step without permission from above would mean his neck and worse. He needed clear orders confirming any such move, and a good tell-truths talk with senior courtiers and war wizards—Lord Warder Vainrence, for one—before he let one noble outside the castle.

"Gulkanun? Longclaws?" he growled, going to them so they could hear him through all the shouting. "If we're to move anyone, I need you to try to magically contact the lord warder . . . and failing him, Ganrahast himself."

Both Crown mages nodded.

"Of course," Gulkanun replied, "but we'll be needing someone to stand guard over us while we work. Forcing a contact through the wards won't be easy."

"Guarding? We'll take care of that," Arclath announced calmly. At his shoulder, Amarune nodded—and flourished a knife she should not have had. Farland lifted an eyebrow.

Then he shook his head wryly, told them all, "Of course," and he started pointing, to arrange Delcastle, his lass, and himself around the two mages in an outward-facing armed ring.

The two war wizards had barely begun casting when *another* scream rang out, from some castle chamber nearby. A high and despairing cry that soared above the angry shouting from the cells, stilling them—before it was cut off suddenly, to end in horrible wet, choking gurgles.

El had to get away from everyone, to where her will could be gathered not just to hurl Art, but to listen for a response from somewhere distant, and to try to feel where that somewhere was. Just as fast as she could.

Halfway down a steep stone stair, well away from any cell or guard, she stopped, sat down against a cold stone wall, closed her eyes, and tried to fight down her panting. So she could reach out . . .

Alassra, I'm here! Where are ye?

Her silent call rolled out into echoing distances, rolled . . . rolled . . . El strained to listen and to feel, seeking any response.

Nothing.

She tried again. *Alassra, beloved, 'tis me, Elminster. Ye called, and I'm here. Where* are *ye? How can I help ye?*

Rolling out . . . away . . . away . . .

Nothing.

Nothing but a sudden burst of searing white fire, like a slap across her mind, a roaring bright inferno too distant and painful to locate—

Before it was gone, leaving her with silent nothing again.

Again she called, straining, snatching out one of the drow daggers she'd taken from that shattered Underdark citadel, the one that had prickled with a faint enchantment. She bent her will fiercely upon it, trying to drain its magic to bolster her calling . . .

After what seemed a long time, the black glass dagger sighed into gritty dust in her palm, and El called again, loud and strong. To no avail.

She hadn't the Art to reach her Alassra. Or she was too late. Always too busy, always too far away . . .

"No," she sobbed aloud, suddenly furious.

She stood up and slammed one shapely drow fist against the wall beside her. There was a flash like awakened fire, a deep-throated *boom,* and the wall cracked, tiny shards clattering down the steps below her.

Arrrgh! Magic when she didn't need it, but it failed here when sheeeee*ARRGH!*

"Elminster!"

That shout from back down the passage above was frantic, and came from the lungs of a young man and a young woman. Voices he knew: Arclath and Amarune. Eyes of Mystra, but why did *someone* always need *her?*

"Haven't I served long enough?" she spat down the deserted stairwell. "Why me? Why *always* me?"

She whirled around and raced back up the stair, her eyes blazing, the rage that had been building in her for years—centuries—rising almost to choke her.

Ye've called, and Elminster is coming. Ready thyself, Realms.

Chapter Twenty-Four

Something Stern And Clear

"I am no cheap swindler, lackey! *I* am Lady Jalassra Dawningdown!"

Eyes flashing and wattles quivering—or so it seemed to Rensharra, given the pendulous display of scented and powdered dewlap across the desk—the outraged noblewoman shot to her feet, her bejeweled earrings dangling, and snarled, "You'll *die* waiting for me to pay these outrageous demands!"

The highborn Lady Dawningdown spat copiously on the tax documents Rensharra Ironstave had prepared and just finished politely explaining with largely gentle observations noting that however noble one happened to be, one could not escape paying annual cobble-and-lantern taxes on every additional city property one purchased. The bill was high because modest fees on sixty-one Suzailan homes, shops, and stables, when combined, did mount up, but of course could be paid out of the rents those properties brought to their owner, namely Lady Jalassra Dawningdown.

Then she stormed out of the office of the lady clerk of the rolls, viciously decapitating a defenseless plant and its vase with her gold-handled cane on her way.

Rensharra sank back into her chair with a sigh, passing a weary hand over her face. Nobles! Were they *all* going to be like this, forevermore?

Spitting fury and defiance seemed to be the favored tactic for them all this season. Ignore the bills, turn away tax collectors, or set dogs or more exotic pets on them, and when the bill was upped for late payment—a *season* late—storm into the palace offices. To claim penury in just-bought fine garments *and* in a staged or real towering fury.

Rensharra set about tidying Lady Dawningdown's thick file to clear the desk for the *next* one.

Nobles disputing their taxes always demanded to speak to the chief responsible official—herself—and always smashed things, bellowed or venomously hissed threats, and stormed out again when they were done. To await the next and even higher bill, so they could repeat the same so-polite, cultured performance. However, noble bellowers always paid up before the Crown started confiscating property in lieu of payment, she'd noticed.

The lady clerk of the rolls drew in a deep breath and allowed herself to relax. Perhaps the day would get better, after this.

Perhaps.

"Well, well," an unpleasant voice drawled from the landing above. "What have we here? Why, a dark elf, I do believe, one of those evil and dangerous creatures, yet *so* beautiful! Such a tempting evil! It's almost our duty to slay it, yes?"

"So it is! *After* we taste its beauty, mind, for beauty is its own reward and a life spent cultivating beauty is the life a noble deserves!" another oily voice agreed.

Stolen guards' knives were flourished, as the noble smiles above them widened.

"Come up to play, little drow beauty," the first escaped prisoner beckoned mockingly. "Why, Gustravus, she seems almost *eager*!"

Eyes blazing but saying not a word, Elminster raced up the stair. When the hands reached for her, she didn't slow in the slightest.

The prisoners barely had time to scream.

"Relrund! Torz! I've work for you!"

Lady Dawningdown bit off those words like she wanted to gnaw something. Her two eldest bullyblades exchanged glances, keeping their faces carefully expressionless. Someone was soon going to die.

"Take the two younglings with you, go straight to the office of Rensharra Ironstave—the lady clerk of the rolls, they call her, as if she was *remotely* worthy of carrying a title, even an empty one—and beat her to death. Make it last and see that she suffers, but keep her fairly quiet or you'll have half the guards in the palace down on your necks. Just so you'll show no mercy, be aware that she's the kingdom's chief *tax* collector."

Fixing them with a glare that left no doubt at all in their minds that she was neither drunk nor fooling, their employer settled herself into her usual seat in the back corner of her coach and slammed the door so fiercely that things rattled all over the conveyance.

Relrund and Torzil bowed in her direction with careful precision—she'd be watching, of that they had no doubt at all—did off their swords and put them in the front seat of the coach, collected their two fellow bullyblades and had them do the same, and strode into the Palace.

They were still wearing their daggers, both visible and hidden, and the short iron bars they carried inside their left boots. And though they said not a word aloud to each other, they were thinking the exact same thoughts as they strode.

A tax collector. This was going to be fun.

"Stay," Farland ordered Amarune and Arclath curtly, as the horrid gurgling faded. "I'll go and see."

The young couple nodded obedience.

"So," the lord constable muttered under his breath as he hurried along the passage, his drawn sword in hand, peering at prisoners in their doorways and heeding their fingers pointing him onward, "behold the brave and stalwart lord constable of Irlingstar, arriving for the latest viewing of a victim of the unseen slayer."

This time, the throat-slit noble sprawled in his blood in his cell doorway was Bleys Indimber. Well, no loss, he, and—

Something slid into Farland's wrist, a sudden kiss like fire and ice. He jerked away as blood spurted.

Naed! The very *air* was slicing at his sword wrist!

He swung his sword at his invisible attacker, or at least where his attacker must be standing—but slashed only empty air.

Farland cut at the air wildly in all directions to try to keep his unseen foe at bay. His eyes told him there was nothing there, that his sword was cleaving emptiness, but . . . was that something *solid*, just for a moment, brushing against his arm?

Farland spun and grabbed, lunging with his free arm and trying to grasp whatever it was, the unseen solidity that—

"Eeeearrgh!"

It stung like fire this time, as more blood spurted and some of his fingers flew off! An invisible blade had cut them—but there was nothing for him to grab.

His own sword had just chopped and backswung and hacked and there was *farruking nothing there.*

Farland spun around and fled back down the passage as fast as he could sprint. Wizards . . . he needed the wizards, or he was a dead man! The prisoners called taunts or encouragement or shrank back in fear as he pelted past them, running for his life.

A few running strides later, the unseen blade bit into his sword hand, hard, above his half-sliced wrist. He roared in pain, stumbling with the sheer burning fire of it, but he didn't slow. He didn't dare slow. His sword clanged on the flagstones behind him. Most of his hand, he knew, was still clutching it.

He had to keep running, had to . . .

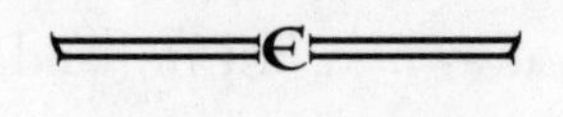

Rensharra looked up. "Can I help you? This is the office of the Clerk of the Rolls, not . . ."

The four men wore rather ruthless smiles. They had quietly and carefully closed her office door in their wake, and strolled toward her.

"Are you Rensharra Ironstave?" the foremost, oldest-looking man asked her. "Who just now spoke with Lady Jalassra Dawningdown?"

No. Oh, no. Rensharra put her foot on the pedal that would ring the alarm gong, stood up and stamped on the pedal again, then slid around behind her chair.

"What are *your* names, gentlesirs?" she snapped sternly. "Are you behind on your taxes?"

The nearest man gave her an unlovely sneer and said over his shoulder, "She's the one. If we cut out her tongue, it should quiet her a bit."

Then he flung his cloak. Its edges were weighted to make it swirl fashionably—which would help it encircle her head and shoulders.

"I *like* what I see," said one of the younger three. "Can we play with her a bit? After we separate her from her tongue?"

Rensharra snatched up her chair in desperate haste, intercepting the cloak. Then she ducked aside as its wielder came around one side of her desk, slashing at her wildly.

His knife got caught in the cloak, of course, and Rensharra dragged the chair free and brained him with it. Which left her exposed to a hard punch from the man coming around the other side of her desk.

"*Help*!" she screamed as she staggered back to the wall with her head ringing and one eye watering, the chair up in front of her like a shield. "Ruffians! Murderers! *Help*!"

The third and fourth men, their grins wide and delighted, came right *over* the desk.

"That's Farland," Arclath snapped, listening hard.

"He's running this way," Rune agreed tensely, peering down the passage.

Then they saw him. The lord constable was running full-tilt toward them, his eyes wide. He was streaming blood—gods, his sword hand was gone!

"Gulkanun! Longclaws! Stop your spells!" Arclath barked, as firmly as any Crown oversword or battlemaster. "Now!"

Farland was cursing, or trying to through his frantic gasping. He was close, and getting closer fast, his eyes wide with pain and fear.

"Stay back! Guard yourselves! I'm under attack!" he panted. "Invisible bl*aae*—"

The air beside Farland's head thickened into a knifelike edge, and they saw the merest shadowy suggestion of two dark eyes and a scowling, sweating brow above them, a malevolent, determined presence . . .

As that edge whipped in and around, and Farland's throat burst open in a shower of gore.

"Elminster!" Arclath and Amarune shouted together, in desperate unison—but the sinister presence beside the lord constable was gone in the next instant. Farland stumbled, sagged while still running, and crashed untidily to the flagstones.

He slid to a bloody stop at their feet, his legs still moving feebly, his life-blood spurting in all directions.

It was a solid chair, of olden style, with a high back and long, thick legs—which was all that kept the knives from her face. For a breath or two, until one of them ducked down and stabbed at her legs.

"*Help*! A rescue!" Rensharra screamed, as loudly as she could. The man she'd hit with the chair was rubbing his head and giving her dark looks, and the other three were close around her, crowding in against the chair. In a moment they'd grab her arms from both sides, and it would all be over—

Behind them, her office door opened.

Her underclerk's astonished face appeared, his mouth dropped open in astonishment—and that was all she saw of him, as one hairy hand appeared from behind him and shoved his head down and out of the way. Its owner trampled him with a roar of obscenities and hurled a dagger that *thunked* solidly home into the shoulder of the gloating attacker on Rensharra's left.

Who stopped grinning to shriek and reel away from her along the wall, cursing and groaning.

"Mirt!" she sobbed. "*Save* me!"

Before the words were out of her mouth, a second dagger hit the man right in front of her in the back of the neck. He spat blood at her, his eyes wide and staring . . . and he started to slump, dragging her chair with him.

The third man backhanded Rensharra hard, tumbling her onto the floor atop the second man and the chair. Her eyes blurred with tears and a sudden burbling in her ears. Then he ignored her in favor of facing the new and bellowing threat who'd just felled two of his fellows.

The man she'd first hit with the chair also turned, bent to tug something from his boot—and straightened up again with a short iron bar in one hand and a long, wicked looking dagger in the other. "Just who the tluin are *you?*" he growled, stalking back around the desk.

"Mirt, Lord of Waterdeep," came the reply, "and your death!"

The man with the iron bar burst out laughing, and waved his two fellow bullyblades forward. The one who'd taken Mirt's dagger in his shoulder was moaning in pain and cursing, but he got on his feet and headed menacingly toward Mirt.

Rensharra got up, picked up her chair, and swung it hard.

The man with the iron bar never saw it coming. The chair slammed into the back of his head, splintering one of its legs, and he went down, toppling on his face with a crash.

The nearest bullyblade looked back over his shoulder, startled by the sounds. Rensharra threw her chair, as high and hard as she could.

It hit the floor right in front of him, bounced, and crashed down onto his foot.

He howled and hopped in pain—right onto Mirt's blade. Who used it like a handle to swing the gutted man around into the last one, slamming them both against the wall.

Then the stout and wheezing Lord of Waterdeep snatched up the fallen iron bar and brained both bullyblades several times, just to make sure. When they lay still in their spreading blood, he turned back to the man Rensharra had felled and battered the back of his skull, thoroughly.

"Are you all right, lass?" he panted, straightening up from his bloody work. "Did they—?"

"Hit me a time or two, that's all," the lady clerk of the rolls replied, her voice quavering just once. "But they were going to cut out my tongue, and then—and then—"

Her voice soared into tears, and she rushed into his arms.

"Have some fun," Mirt grimly finished her sentence for her, holding her tight. "Pity we'll need a priest, now, to make what's left of *them* talk. I'm taking you out of here, the moment I've collected my steel. And this iron bar—handy, this."

So it was that Lady Dawningdown was very soon thereafter brusquely evicted from her own coach, where it stood in the palace foreyard waiting for her bullyblades to return with word that Rensharra Ironstave had been satisfactorily dealt with.

She took one look at the face of the old fat man hauling her forth from her back corner as if she weighed nothing at all, and another look at Rensharra Ironstave's stern face, and then looked away. Without a word, she took herself off across the palace yard as fast as her cane could help her scurry.

A moment later, her coachmaster and both coachjacks all came hurtling down face-first onto the cobbles, bouncing in the dust and cursing and clutching bleeding and broken noses—and her finest day coach was rumbling away as fast as the fat old man could whip its horses, out onto the Promenade with a rising rumble.

"Stop, thief!" she dared to call, then, shaking her cane at the dwindling conveyance. Not that anyone heeded, of course. The palace doorjacks merely gave her shrugs when she informed them what had befallen, so she crisply told them all something stern and clear, and started walking.

By the time she reached the eastgate, to complain to the Purple Dragons on gate guard duty and demand fast riders be sent after the stolen coach, she thought better of demanding anything of them at all. The coach had almost run over those guards as it raced out of the city, and they were still muttering about arrogant nobles and telling each other they'd recognized the Dawningdown arms on the doors, oh, aye, to be sure . . .

Muttering some choice curses of her own, Lady Dawningdown marched over to the nearest rental coach, to hire passage home across half of Suzail.

Prudence, even for expendable mindslaves of the future emperor of Cormyr, was occasionally desirable.

So it was that for the last leg of his journey, Wizard of War Jarlin Flamtarge had let his horse go and departed Orondstars Road for the concealment of the trees bordering it.

Now, however, the walls of Irlingstar loomed above him. He stepped down into the road for the last few trudging strides uphill to the nearest gate, where he swung the great clacking knocker, identified himself to the guards, and was admitted.

The lord constable, it seemed, was busy in an upper passage. He told the anxious guard he'd find his own way there, and set off up a stair. At its head was a long passage running the length of the fortress, or so it seemed. There was also another stair, leading higher, but for the moment, Flamtarge ignored it in favor of strolling down the long passage.

The first cell doorway had a bored-looking noble standing in it. Who spat at the passing war wizard the moment Flamtarge was close enough.

With a sneer, the Crown mage hurled a blasting spell into the noble's face. It flared into harmless brilliance as it was intercepted by an unseen ward that stretched across the doorway. The noble decided it was his turn to sneer.

Well, well. This would not do at all. Manshoon cast a spell Flamtarge did not know, burning a hole in the ward for just long enough to immolate the sneering noble.

As smoldering bones collapsed in a heap of swirling ashes, he gave them a jaunty sneer, and proceeded on down the passage.

Former Wizard of War Rorskryn Mreldrake tried to appear calm. He was sitting alone in his locked and spell-sealed prison, but of course his captors were watching everything he did, and listening, too.

Their requirements had been clear. So it was that despite the successful string of Irlingstar deaths, Mreldrake was making minor adjustments to perfect a means of magically wielding his conjured, wraithlike shearing edge of force from afar. This blade could bypass wards by being willed to manifest within them, but his captors wanted it to be able to shear through wards, or at least pass through them without delay or impairment.

Yet despite their carping, their dozens of tiny criticisms, what they'd ordered had been accomplished. The lord constable of Irlingstar was dead.

So it was with satisfaction, albeit weary satisfaction, that Rorskryn Mreldrake took a break from dealing death in Irlingstar and making future slayings more elegant to stretch his cramping fingers and sip some tea.

He was no traitor. What he'd done was for the good of Cormyr—and so, both just and right. Many courtiers and nobles wouldn't see it that way, of course, but they were the villains, not he. Ah, this tea was . . . comforting. Yes.

Only their families might decry his judgment that the imprisoned nobles of Irlingstar were utterly expendable. Why, he'd heard even timid backroom palace scribes describe them as wastrels and troublemakers that Cormyr—and everywhere else—would be better off without. So there was nothing at all wrong or villainous about using them as the subjects of his . . . experiments.

The explosions had been unfortunate, but such things happen when one is experimenting. They were no more than the unforeseen results of trying to shape his cutting edge of force into handlike shapes, to try to wield magic items from afar. Every such attempt had been disastrous. Contact between his edge and enchanted items always made the magic items explode. And the backlashes always left him unconscious and mentally reeling for quite some time thereafter.

Even the most stubborn of his captors seemed to have seen enough of such disasters. He'd unwillingly and unintentionally proven that it wouldn't work—his edge couldn't be used to work other magics from a distance. However, just using the forceblade to slice throats worked quite well. So, let the throats to be sliced henceforth belong to foes who mattered.

Such as Manshoon, and the one called Elminster, too . . .

Chapter Twenty-Five

Echoes In The Weave

"I . . . I did not know dragons took such an interest in the doings of humans," Harbrand said feebly. "Aren't we just, uh, *food*, to you?"

"Belt *up*, idiot," Hawkspike suggested, beside him.

The dragon chuckled again, with a deep thunder that shook the cavern—and their back teeth.

"I did not begin life as a black dragon," it told them. "I call myself Alorglauvenemaus now, but in truth I'm a man—a wizard, transformed by my own Art. Once, I was feared within the Brotherhood and unknown outside it."

"The Brotherhood? The Zhentarim?" Harbrand asked.

"Yes. I am Hesperdan of the Zhentarim. I took dragon shape nigh a century back to keep watch over the mage Vangerdahast, the self-styled guardian of Cormyr. He had been the kingdom's Royal Magician and its court wizard and its true ruler, all at once—and when he deemed the time right, he retired from it all to take dragon shape. I was suspicious of him then, and I am suspicious of him now."

"Oh?" Harbrand asked, starting to become genuinely interested. He'd begun talking just to try to buy a few more breaths of life, but . . .

"Oh, indeed. Despite being lesser in Art, he'd quietly become the most dangerous tyrant mage of us all, his reach even greater than Manshoon's thanks to the wizards of war he commanded. I believed curbing his schemes was the most important life work any mage could concern himself with. I still believe that."

"And so?"

"And so, along came the Spellplague and changed everything. The gods laugh at us all."

"So how did it change you? Are you trapped in dragon shape?"

"No, but the blue fire did me ill. It afflicted me with long periods of being Alorglauvenemaus—by which I mean, long periods of not remembering I was Hesperdan at all."

Harbrand and Hawkspike looked at each other. Neither of them had to say a word to tell each other what they'd both realized instantly. If the dragon—or Hesperdan, or whoever he really was—had told them this, it meant he had no intention of their surviving long enough to pass this information on to anyone.

Some days, Immerkeep felt like a prison stuffed with mad inmates, all intent on making him join their ranks.

Yes, King's Lord Lothan Durncaskyn *was* in a bad temper, he admitted to himself—and it was getting worse.

Immerfolk were a testy lot at the best of times, given their ever-lengthening list of just grievances, and now he wasn't merely saddled with Harklur and Mrauksoun and Faerrad—he had Lord Tornkresk to deal with.

King Foril was a worthy monarch, kinder and wiser than most and less cruel than many, but the trouble with men like that was that they admired the decisive and capable. Which meant they sometimes ennobled the wrong capable men. Tornkresk had been a lord for what, nine years? Ten? And already, in the guise of "being loyal to what Cormyr *should* be," he and his band of well-armed hireswords were busy here, there, and everywhere around Immerford, goading folk into angry attacks on Crown servants, inspectors, and even Purple Dragon patrols.

So here the king's lord was, with no war wizards left to contact Suzail or Arabel for him, and a desperate need for swift help. He needed reinforcements to blunt Tornkresk's goad, but not just Purple Dragons ready to swing their swords and become Tornkresk's handy targets. He needed enough war wizards to enspell everyone into the ground, and some smooth-tongued courtiers with placating coins to toss—and he needed all of them *right now*!

A door banged in the outer office, and there were voices. Raised voices. One was his duty bodyguard, denying passage. The other was gruff, wheezing, and accepting no such refusal.

Durncaskyn slapped a hand to his dagger, murmured the word that awakened its ironguard enchantment to protect him from hurled knives and crossbow bolts and the like, and went to his office door. Who wanted to harangue the ever-helpful king's lord *now*?

He opened the door a crack, his foot behind it to keep it that way, and peered out. He was in time to see a fat old man whose seaboots flapped and flopped at every step hurling the duty bodyguard bodily out the office door, then turning to steady an exhausted looking, disheveled woman. And lead her right to Durncaskyn's door.

Well, time to be decisive and capable. Durncaskyn flung the door wide and stood in it. "Yes?"

"Yer Foril's local lord, here?" the old man growled, looking Durncaskyn up and down, but not slowing his determined lurch forward.

"I am." Durncaskyn stood his ground. "Who are you?"

"Mirt, Lord of Waterdeep. This is Rensharra Ironstave, Lady Clerk of the Rolls. *Yes*, the highest-ranking tax collector in the realm. She needs the most secure guarded shelter you can provide. Right now."

Durncaskyn blinked. "What?"

He gave the woman a look, but she was out on her feet, reeling, her gaze directed at the floor. Mirt swung her to one side so she'd not be caught between them as he advanced—and kept on tramping straight forward. "You'd be Durncaskyn?"

"I—" They collided, chest to chest, and Mirt kept right on striding.

Exasperated, Durncaskyn shoved him. "Get back! And get out of here! I'm—"

"Terribly busy just now, saving the realm? That I can well believe, but right now I need you to see that protecting this fair lady is the most important—"

"No. Did you not hear me? *No.*"

Durncaskyn thought of himself as a solid man, still strong despite far too many hours spent sitting behind desks or standing around talking and listening. So he was a little astonished to be taken by a fistful of doublet, hoisted off his feet, and rushed backward into his own office.

The lurching and shuffling old man even dragged the woman in with them, as he snarled into Durncaskyn's face, "I've been getting the *distinct* impression since my arrival in this fair kingdom that its local lords are a pompous, lazy, useless lot. Prove me wrong. *Please* prove me wrong."

"I don't take kindly to being bullied in my own office," Durncaskyn snarled back, "and *I* decide what constitutes—"

"Being an utter slubberdegullion? Well, decide faster!"

"Why? Why the great rush?"

"If I have to lock you in yer own dungeon and start emptying yer coffers to hire bullyblades enough to keep this fair lady—the king's head tax collector, let me remind you—safe, it's going to take me some *time* to let everyone hereabouts know I'm the new king's lord. That's why the rush, loyal Lothan."

"And if I agree to protect her?"

"Then where are yer guards? She stands in peril *right now*—and in need of a bed and a garderobe, not to mention a light hot meal and a little good wine. And see if you can resist the temptation to lock her in any sort of cell, too—it might keep me from removing yer *head* and locking it away, instead! I ask again: where are yer guards? The likes of that bumbling idiot I tossed aside out there couldn't keep away a lad with a slingshot!"

"As to that," Durncaskyn replied dryly, bringing up both hands to try to wrench himself free of Mirt's hairy fist, "they're right behind you."

Purple Dragons crowded into the outer office, their swords drawn. The angry bodyguard Mirt had thrown out of that room was with them, pointing at the fat old intruder and spitting a stream of curses and commands.

Mirt looked profoundly unimpressed. "Them? They look like a mob of untrained dolts, to me. Where're their scouts? The man with the ready crossbow and some sleep syrup on his loaded quarrel? The *backup* bowman, for when the first one misses? Hey?"

"Hey," Durncaskyn agreed wearily. "At ease!" he barked over Mirt's shoulder at the Dragons. "Wait out in the passage, all of you!"

They eyed him doubtfully.

"*All* of you!" Durncaskyn roared with sudden fire. "And close the door after you go out!"

He added a glare, and kept it on them until they'd all reluctantly retreated and shut the door. By then, he was unsurprised to find the lady slumped in his own desk chair, and Mirt rummaging in his cabinets for decent wine to give her.

"Bottom drawer," Durncaskyn told him. "The swill on display is for visiting complainants—such as yourself."

That earned him a grin from Mirt. Durncaskyn fetched one of the chairs kept for visitors, drew it up to the wrong side of his own desk, sat down, and said, "You seem a forceful man, but decisive enough, possibly even capable. Perhaps we can make a deal."

"As one snarling bull to another?"

"Indeed. I will wholeheartedly extend to this good lady the dubious shelter of Immerkeep if you, Lord of Waterdeep, will go to Suzail for me, without delay. To fetch the help *I* so desperately need."

A decanter of Durncaskyn's best wine thunked down on the desk between them. "Explain," Mirt suggested, filling glasses.

The king's lord obliged.

Wherefore, a short time later, after kissing Rensharra thoroughly and accepting a second decanter for road thirst, Mirt of Waterdeep strode right back out of Immerkeep, patted the neck of one of the fresh horses that had been hitched to his stolen coach, and began a wild race back to Suzail.

Decisive and capable men did those sorts of things.

Clouds were everywhere, but they were the white, wispy, spun-silk sort, betokening no rain or lightning. The *Sword of the Clouds* was gliding along under half-sail.

No grand skyship of the Five Companies, she, but an ancient Halruaan treasure only recently salvaged from dust-shrouded, motionlessly floating neglect in a ruin by the adventurers who crewed her. And kept busy shuttling envoys, vital messages, and precious treaties to and fro above southerly realms—when they weren't mooring briefly to various high towers and turrets to conduct daring night robberies and kidnappings, that is.

Yet Vaeren Dragonskorn had never called himself a pirate. "Pirate" was such an *uncouth* word. "Adventurer of the skies," now that was an attractive phrase. Aye, adventurers of the skies are we, aboard the *Sword* . . .

A skyship much heavier than it had been when this particular voyage had begun, thanks to the treasures of the rival wizards Algaubrel and Sarlarthont, crowded into the shallow hold. Strongchests upon strongchests full of coins and gems and metal-bound grimoires, statuettes and many curious metal items that gave off weird magical glows, and things that were better undisturbed until off-loaded in a mountaintop hidehold. Thinking of which . . .

Dragonskorn turned and nodded to the helmsman, who could see the needle-sharp tops of the Rauntrils ahead just as well as he could. Such peaks were perils as well as landmarks, and—

There was a sudden commotion behind him. The helmsman gaped. Dragonskorn spun around—and started gaping too.

The woman standing on the deck amid his startled crew was tall and queenly, despite being barefoot and either lightly or entirely unclad. He couldn't be sure which, through all her hair. It was *silver*, by the Wildwanderer, and almost as long as she was—and it was curling around her like a colony of angry snakes or hungry maggots or—or—

"Who is your captain?"

Her question brought no helpful replies, but that was hardly surprising. The crew happened to be all male and the *Sword*'s recent schedule had kept them long from the company of women, so their swords were out and the air rang with their responses, the politest of which was, "Who by the waiting, wanton charms of Sharess are *you?*"

"I am best known as The Simbul. Which one of you captains this ship?"

Before she could receive any useful reply, she caught sight of Dragonskorn, and said, "Ah! It would you!"

She strode toward him. Valkur and Baervan, she *was* bare skinned!

"Saer," she said politely, "I have no quarrel with you or your crew, but I *must* have the blueflame in your hold."

"Blueflame?"

"Some of the enchanted things you carry glow with an intense blue flame that looks like fire but is not hot, and ignites nothing. I require it of you."

"You do." Dragonskorn looked her up and down. "And you expect me to just yield them up?"

The Simbul sighed. "No," she told him, her face grave, "I expect you to resist me. I'd rather you continued to live, instead, but . . . I know too much of humans, down the centuries, to expect your polite assistance. Yet I'd be grateful—delighted, even—if you'd surprise me."

Dragonskorn smiled—and then sneered. "Oh, I'll surprise you, all right. *Take her, men*! Yet remember: as your captain, I get her first!"

As the crew of the *Sword* roared in glee and converged on the lone woman in a rush, The Simbul regarded Dragonskorn sadly and shook her head.

Then she lifted one empty hand and gave them fire.

"Magic! She has magic!" one crewman shouted warningly as a ring of flames blazed up out of nowhere, and the closest running men to the silver-haired woman all crashed to the deck like discarded dolls. Cooked and sizzling discarded dolls.

"Well of *course* she has magic," someone else snarled. "She appeared on our deck out of farruking *thin air*, didn't she?" That same someone else hurled a hand axe, hard and accurately, right at the woman's head.

The Simbul watched it come, her face calm, and made no move to duck or leap aside. By the time it flashed up close to her, the air was full of hurtling knives and cutlasses, converging on her like the men who'd hurled them. She stood motionless, and let them all rush right through her, the axe first, to bite into or clang off whoever was directly beyond her. Cries and curses rent the air.

Then there rose another roar, this one of fury—and the surviving burly crew of the *Sword* charged at the woman from all sides, their arms out to grapple and throttle.

In a swirl of silver hair that hooked ankles, slapped blindingly across faces, and curled tightly around necks, The Simbul moved at last, ducking and rushing and diving like a Calishite dancer.

Metal weapons flashed through her as if she were but an illusion, though her hair and feet and fists were solid enough, as she tugged one man off-balance to sprawl onto the upthrusting sword of another, then leaned unconcernedly forward into the vicious slash of a third man to jab at his eyes with two rigid fingers. Screams and grunts started to drown out the curses.

Yet the sky sailors were neither cowards nor weaklings. When at last they buried her under their combined brawn, punching and kicking, she soared up off the deck in a struggling ball of arms and legs and entwining silver hair—and let out another flash of magic that left everyone stunned and senseless, to fall like so much limp dead meat and crash onto the deck. Or rather, to fall onto the heads of their fellows, as unseen magic deflected each falling man subtly this way or that, to strike a man standing below.

A breath or two later, the deck was strewn with groaning or silent sprawled men, with barely a handful still on their feet. The Simbul descended to the littered deckboards and resumed her stroll toward Dragonskorn. "I only want the blueflame in your hold," she reminded him calmly. "Not to take lives or harm your crew."

Shaken, Dragonskorn drew the long, curving saber at his belt. He knew it was magical, having torn it from the dying hand of a wizard's bodyguard who'd fired fatal lightnings from its tip at some of his crew, and having used it since to drink in bolts of lightnings in the storms the *Sword* sailed through. Aiming it at her, he fed her lightning.

It snarled into her, crackling through her hair and along her arms and legs, and he saw pain on her face. Snarling, he sent more lightning into her.

The Simbul kept coming at him, walking more slowly.

"Die, hrast you!" he shouted. "*Die!*"

Her teeth were clenched in a silent snarl, agony creasing her beauty, but still she came, trudging right into the flashing, snapping maw of what his blade could lash out.

And then, with a snap and a spitting of sparks, his lightnings died. Leaving her an arm's length away, smiling.

"Thank you for that," she murmured. "I feel *much* stronger now."

"Do you, witch?" he shouted, infuriated, and he flung his sword down, to clang on the deck at their feet. "*Do you?*"

He sprang at her, clapping both hands around her throat. And squeezing, tightening his two-handed grip with all the straining strength he could muster, until his face was red and his arms quivered . . . and she sagged, her eyes large and pleading. Doomed.

Vaeren Dragonskorn threw back his head and laughed in triumph. He was still laughing when her fingers closed around his elbows, broke them effortlessly, then slid down to his wrists and served them the same way.

His grip broken, he whimpered in agony—and she swung him up into the air and hurled him high and far.

Overboard, far beyond the *Sword*'s rail, to scream his way down and out of sight amid the clouds below.

As The Simbul walked the rest of the way to the covered companionway that led below, no one disputed her passage, or dared to come anywhere near her.

Elminster ran like a storm wind, racing along the passage with her hair streaming behind her and her eyes afire.

There! There were the two war wizards, Rune and Arclath beyond them, peering her way, calling her name.

And there, beyond them on the floor, sprawled in a dark and spreading pool of blood, was Lord Constable Farland, whose mind she'd so recently shared.

A mind now fading and . . . gone.

She had come too late. Once more.

"Noooooo!" El screamed, a raw shriek of anguish that soared into fresh rage.

Why could she never save the good ones?

Why?

There were, as it happened, only two blueflame items in the crowded hold. There were plenty of glows from other magics, flaring gold and copper and all the hues of the gems of Art as she reached out with the gentlest of seeking spells . . . but only the two sources of blueflame. A rod of office like a miniature Tymoran temple scepter, flared at both ends, and a crescentiform pectoral of beaten metal that looked like an oversized, too-low gorget.

"Mystra," she murmured, "what powers have these? And which ghosts are bound within them?"

I know not, until you awaken them. I am . . . much less than I was.

"I had guessed as much," The Simbul said quietly. "How much do you remember?"

Much and . . . not much. Memories mingled with memories, some my own, some from all of you Chosen and others loyal to me, those who survive and those who are . . . gone.

"Can you sense us now, as we move around the Realms, striving on your behalf? Steal into our minds, and see what we're doing?"

Of course. You few. My daughters and my longest lover.

"Lover? Elminster?"

Elminster.

"Wasn't that the Mystra before you?" The Simbul dared to ask.

Echoes in the Weave, my daughter, echoes in the Weave . . . we see and feel so much that happened before us, in the Weave; it becomes part of us, the memories of the Mystra who birthed you becoming part of me, so I become that Mystra . . .

"I . . . see."

Then you see more keenly than I do, most of the time. I was mighty, once.

The Simbul could think of no reply. She was too busy, all of a sudden, shivering.

Chapter Twenty-Six

Fear The Unseen

"El," Rune said anxiously, her eyes wide with fear, "we saw him slain! It was . . . a man, I think, half-seen, behind—"

"Let me," El snapped, kissing her, flooding into her mind, seeing it all in an instant.

". . . in . . . ," the dark elf finished her sentence in a murmur, already done. She let go of Amarune almost roughly, still afire with anger, and told them all, "We've a far better chance of fighting this slayer if we link our minds and stay linked, to share each other's eyes."

"We?" Gulkanun asked.

"All of us. Arclath, Amarune, you, Longclaws—and me. Linked, we'll walk together, ready-armed, and approach prisoner after prisoner. We mind-touch each one and so eliminate them from suspicion, until we find the murderer."

"Who *must* be in the castle," Longclaws agreed. "That sort of sustained attack can't be worked through the wards."

Elminster and Gulkanun nodded in grim agreement. It was Gulkanun who reached out then, to take the dark elf's hand.

The linkage began as a disorienting, alarming experience. It was one thing to be cradled in the dark, wise power of Elminster's mind, and quite another to share it with four other curious, fearful, and uncertain awarenesses, colliding and getting memories tangled together . . .

El, Amarune asked in a trembling mind—voice, *will we go mad?*

Fear not. I'm been mad for centuries. It's not that bad.

Centuries?

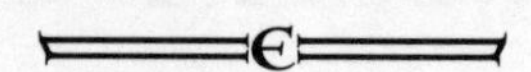

Mreldrake sipped more tea.

It was time to see and hear the results of the farscrying spell he'd left working while he'd made the latest adjustments to his slaying magic. Would Farland's death leave them all despairing? Fleeing into the woods or swording each other or letting the prisoners go free? Well, of course, if he didn't look, he wouldn't know. He called up the spell.

"Elminster!" two voices promptly shrieked together.

Mreldrake spat out some curse or other, aghast . . . and discovered he'd spilled the dregs of his tea all over himself.

Were they using a spell? No, they couldn't be; it was the clever young noble and his doxy, who almost certainly hadn't any talent for the Art between them, beyond being able to unleash magical trinkets they bought. They were shouting, no more and no less. Which meant Elminster must be someone inside Irlingstar, someone *nearby* in the castle.

So Elminster must be in disguise, being as a certain imprisoned Mreldrake had already farscried every living person in Irlingstar, *twice*—including the two human skeletons walled up and forgotten in the foundations of the north tower—and not found Elminster.

It *had* to be one of the war wizards!

Rorskryn Mreldrake waited impatiently until the farscrying that the spell had preserved showed him the two war wizards—standing together, staring down in horror at what he'd done to Farland. Two of them, one with a hand that kept changing into different things—tentacles, polyps, strange nameless growths. A miscast shapechange spell . . . or, no, one being held always at the ready, for instant use against a foe!

The other Crown mage wasn't powerful enough to hope to cast a shapechange magic that was more than illusory, or that would last longer than the time the casting took. So this "Longclaws" *had* to be Elminster.

Mreldrake stood up, carefully cast the spell that was now his crowning achievement, reached out into distant Irlingstar—and diced Imbrult Longclaws into so many ribbons of bleeding meat.

Wizard of War Jarlin Flamtarge was unaccustomed to skulking, but he was young and agile and possessed a good sense of balance.

So with Manshoon riding his callow mind and guiding him with the guile and wisdom of many dark years, he had moved through the castle largely unseen—and the few who had seen him had been swiftly silenced. Heh. *Fear* the unseen . . .

All the shouting had come from *this* direction, so . . .

He stole from room to room, until he was close enough to see and hear murmuring voices.

"Linked, we'll walk together, ready-armed, and approach prisoner after prisoner. We mind-touch each one, and so eliminate them from suspicion, until we find the murderer."

"Who *must* be in the castle. That sort of sustained attack can't be worked through the wards."

Jarlin peered cautiously out the door of his room, whose former noble occupant now lay dead and out of sight.

There they were, nodding and holding hands, swaying and saying incoherent things; establishing their linkage. And releasing each other, to turn and walk in his direction in smooth unison, truly united.

Then came a dark swirling and much blood, as the shorter of the two war wizards collapsed in a welter of gore.

The other Crown mage erupted into a ringing shout of anger and grief, the noble and his dancer whirled to cry to the drow, "*Do* something!"

So Elminster was here—and the drow was Elminster!

"Hide in the woman, of *course,* Old Foe . . . ," Manshoon said aloud, in Sraunter's cellar. Then he bore down hard, making Jarlin an utter automaton for the moment. *Your hands be mine, all of you mine to move . . .*

He forced Jarlin *through* the crackling, searing ward, into a charge at the shapely dark elf. Yes, pounce on Elminster and deliver a paralyzing touch spell, rather than trying to blast him from the cell with a battle spell.

If this dark elf was a body Elminster had possessed, he could trap the Sage of Shadowdale in it, and hold the drow captive for torture and interrogation because there were things it could not do, that the unfettered Elminster could.

Pounce, my pawn!

Jarlin rushed, crashing through Gulkanun and then Arclath Delcastle, then leaping to grapple with the drow—

Darkening air, as sharp as a razor, sliced down murderously at the lithely ducking drow—and cut Jarlin Flamtarge in two.

"No!" His mind slapped with the wildly flaring agony of his dying pawn, Manshoon seethed, clutching his head and snarling in wordless rage. Who *was* this unseen slayer?

Head ringing, he *forced* himself to straighten, then he bent all his strength to concentrating his will.

He was the mightiest of mages, the emperor-to-be, not any of these puny magelings hurling nastiness around a prison castle! Not even Elminster had power enough to stand up to him! He would do what no other could manage, these days. He would reach back into that dead mind and force Flamtarge's severed torso to work a spell. Just one.

It would come unexpectedly from a dead man, and buy him the time he needed to frustrate this slayer, to keep him from killing Elminster before he, Manshoon, could capture Elminster and peel open his mind and force every sneering secret from him at last.

Steeling himself, the future emperor of Cormyr cast a spell, wrapped it around his will, and flung his awareness at distant Irlingstar.

The air glowed suddenly, the unseen blade of air audibly striking something unseen and magical.

"You're using the wards as a shield!" Arclath gasped.

Elminster nodded grimly. There was another ringing shriek, as the air on the other side of the drow's head flashed into brief radiance.

"'Tis a man behind it," El announced calmly. "One man, far from here . . ." Her face eased. "Gone. Didn't want to be seen longer, and recognized. Which means it's someone who thinks they *will* be recognized, by one or more of us."

"M-manshoon?" Rune asked.

The drow shook her head. "No. *His* mind, I'd know in an instant."

"Naed," Gulkanun gasped, behind them. "Oh, naed!"

Hearing the horror in his voice, they whirled around—in time to see the severed torso of the young stranger writhe and spasm and shove at the flagstones to sway unsteadily upright.

Dark, wet blood was still pumping out of it, and its hands glistened with gore, hands that moved in sudden, deft gestures as the torso swayed.

Arclath cursed and drew back his blade to chop down those hands and ruin whatever magic was being worked, but Elminster flung out a swift and strong arm to catch and hold the young noble's sword arm.

"Someone afar is working through this dead man, to cast a spell I know. Let him work it. It will keep the unseen slayer out of this passage for some time."

"What if he goes on to cast something that fries *us*?"

"Then I'll let you chop him apart, bloodthirsty young Delcastle."

"Won't Arclath be in danger, if he tries that?" Rune asked quickly.

The dark elf gave her a grim smile. "Of course."

Manshoon groaned. He'd done it, but his *head* . . .

Later. Give in to the pain later.

Right now, he had to earn his superiority one more time, and beat everyone.

He already knew the best "tracer" among the war wizards: Ondrath Everwood, a quiet and timid youngling who spent most of his days in a nondescript upper floor office of an unassuming building in Suzail—one of the Crown's "hidden houses" in the city—farscrying for Crown and court, to order.

Ondrath Everwood didn't get out enough, to breathe fresh air and see the sun. So it was high time someone paid him a social call.

The empty coach was bumping and rattling enough to jar anyone's back teeth loose, but Mirt was in no mood to slow down. Boots hooked under the safety rail, reins wound around one arm and the driving whip in his other hand, he was making good time, by the gods, and—

Naed, farruk, and hrast it, a road patrol!

On the road ahead, the Purple Dragons were already hauling at their reins, getting themselves and their horses out of the way—but they were also flinging up their arms and bellowing sternly at him to halt.

Mirt roared right back at them, giving them the password Durncaskyn had furnished him with, and not slowing in the slightest. He repeated it thrice, just to make sure—but as the bouncing, swaying coach plunged through them without incident and managed the next turn, the wheels on its left side squealing in protest, Mirt looked back over his right shoulder and saw that *yes*, by Beshaba, they were following him!

And unless they'd mistreated their horses, Purple Dragons could certainly ride faster than he could lash these already straining nags to drag a coach along, even if it was empty—er, except for one over-padded Lord of Waterdeep . . .

They were spurring their mounts, all right. Hrast them.

Well, wondergods, what the *Hells* good was a password, if—oh, *tluin*!

Across the road right ahead, as he came around a tight bend, were a dozen or so riders, all in a clump, riding together. Liveried men-at-arms, a banner, overdressed highnose in the center of it all . . . a noble, with a retinue. Filling the road, and not giving way.

Mirt stood up and bellowed curses at them, waving his whip around and around above his head and making it clear he wasn't going to swerve or slow.

Now they were yielding way, the dolts, but—

No! The lordling was pointing at the coach, and yelling in anger. Now he was shouting orders, and hrast it if they weren't obeying like trained cavalry, swiftly forming a curve . . .

If Mirt veered so as not to plow into them, their configuration would squeeze him by narrowing the clear road ahead, forcing him at a gentle angle off the road into an overturning crash in the ditch . . . or to a stop, to face their blades and disputations.

With a sigh, Mirt hauled hard on the reins, and started making the whistlings and chirrupings that all horses in Cormyr seemed to know meant, "Stop. Now."

Dust flew, the coach groaned and bounced and landed with a crash and bounced again, reins flew amid rearings and loud, complaining neighings . . . and the snorting, blowing horses finally brought the shuddering conveyance to a halt. With the traveling lord and his armsmen ranged alongside it and in front of it, just as the farruking highnose had intended.

"Get out of the road!" Mirt roared at him. "I'm on urgent Crown business!"

"In Lady Dawningdown's coach?" the noble shouted back. "I very much doubt it, *thief*!"

He spurred his horse forward, to come up right beside Mirt. "Get down from there, or I'll have my men drag you down!"

"Get out of the way!" Mirt snarled, "or the king'll have yer guts for his next garderobe seat!"

Those words seemed to ignite the noble to screaming fury. He erupted in an inarticulate series of shrieks, that soon became a gabble of, "I care *naught* for the king!" and "How dare you speak thus, to your better!" and "I'll have your tongue out by the roots for such rudeness, sirrah!" and other things Mirt didn't wait to hear.

Right out of patience, he unhooked the unlit but full coachlamp from its bracket beside him, and emptied it down into the noble's shouting and oh-so-handy face, wishing he had flint and steel handy, or a ready flame.

To the accompaniment of highborn retching and choking sounds, he tried to get the coach moving again, but several armsmen had firm hold of the beasts' bridles and the harness, so with an exasperated growl Mirt swung himself down over the front of the coach, lurched along the trail and then into the saddles of his poor horses—and launched himself from standing on the foremost saddle right into the armsman holding that lead horse.

The crash was satisfactorily bone jarring, and the armsman he'd landed on swayed in his own saddle, dazed and winded. The armsman's horse reared.

Then everyone was shouting, and horses were plunging and rearing everywhere. Those fools of Purple Dragons had ridden headlong into the stopped coach and the noble's men. In the heart of all the tumult and shouting, Mirt kept hold of the neck of the armsman's horse, kicked the man out of the saddle, fell back heavily into that vacated seat—and managed his loudest shout of the day, right into the horse's ear.

It reared again, bucked in the air, and came down running hard, on along the open road to Suzail, thank all the gods, with Mirt clinging grimly to the saddle.

As the horse gathered speed in a lengthening gallop, he crouched low and murmured encouragement to it. Looking back, he could see some of the noble's armsmen and a few Purple Dragons belatedly beginning to pursue him.

Well, guts and garters, this just got better and better . . .

It was almost *too* easy.

Half a dozen eyeball beholderkin, unleashed to drift around young Ondrath Everwood, snared his attention long enough for him to curse, snatch out a wand to deal with them—and mumble a few frantic unheard words into the cloth Manshoon had slipped over his face from behind, before he went limp.

The cloth was soaked with tincture of thardflower; the nigh-instant senselessness it brought on wouldn't last long, but then, Manshoon didn't need it to.

He calmly teleported them both back to Sraunter's cellar, where he bound the young war wizard into a chair. The alchemist didn't have much call for cord, but the eyestalks of his death tyrants, and the long tentacles he'd augmented some of them with, would suffice. Besides, the fearsome decaying creatures looming silently above his captive would probably have a salutary effect on Everwood's powers of agreement. As in: to anything, hastily.

Those augmentations were going to be very useful in the near future, when he needed loyal courtiers around him. Not this rabble of double-dealing, self-interested slyjaws and malingerers that currently afflicted the palace. Yes, augmentations. Spending all that time farscrying those deluded cultists in the sewers of Waterdeep had been wearying indeed—but in the end, time not *entirely* wasted.

Manshoon amused himself by magically purloining a grand meal from the tables and kitchens of a club on the Promenade, complete with wine, while he waited for the young man to revive.

Ondrath Everwood was going to trace the Unseen Slayer.

And then enter Manshoon's service, either willingly—or as Manshoon's new host body. It was time for Sraunter to once more become Sraunter. The soon-to-be emperor of Cormyr was becoming more than a little tired of dispensing little vials of lust dust to Suzailans hungry for a night's conquest, or wrinkled wives desperate to reclaim the affectionate attentions of their husbands.

A desolate Duth Gulkanun was on his knees in the spreading blood. The heap of sliced and diced meat in front of him was scarcely recognizable as his friend and colleague—but he'd *watched* Longclaws being murdered, right . . . hrast it . . . *here*. There in the gore, close enough to touch, some sucker-tentacle-things moved, one last time, turning . . . back into human fingers.

"No," he muttered, his lips trembling. "*No*, Imbrult. No."

Rune put a comforting hand on his shoulder. As if that had been a signal he'd been waiting for, the kneeling wizard burst into tears.

"El," Arclath murmured, as they stood over him, "what do we do now?"

The dark elf's eyes glittered with anger. She pointed at the two halves of the dead man who'd come rushing out at them. "*That* was a war wizard. See the ring, the robes? Which means there was at least one person—him—hiding in Irlingstar. Our Unseen Slayer might be another. It's high time to *really* search this place, from top to bottom, accounting for everyone."

"And then?"

"And then we'll go into every last mind, until we find the killer."

"You shall be avenged," Gulkanun told the remains of his friend fiercely. He got up slowly, and turned to Elminster. "You were talking of a search?"

"Aye," the drow told him. "Let it begin."

"Let it begin," Gulkanun echoed grimly, and they set off to scour out Irlingstar.

It had been easy, after all.

Ondrath Everwood was busily and painstakingly farscrying Irlingstar. Which meant it was time to take care of a certain loose end by the name of Malver Tulbard.

Manshoon went to his scrying spheres. The duties of Wizard of War Malver Tulbard included random inspections of certain Suzailan shops—including that of the alchemist Sraunter. Foiling him was easy enough, but an incipient emperor was apt to be very busy for the next little while, and it would be unfortunate if the man came blundering in and found Everwood, or discovered the death tyrants. So it was time to take care of thorough, diligent Malver Tulbard. Permanently.

He'd long since discovered Tulbard's weakness: buttered snails. Buttered snails served in spiced wine, to be specific. As prepared by either Gocklin's or The Bright Sammaer, rival exclusive upstairs dining clubs along the Promenade. So if Tulbard wasn't out prying into someone else's business, he was likely to be at either Gocklin's, or . . .

There. Gocklin's. The scrying image showed Tulbard clearly, alone at a back corner table, belching politely behind his hand as he applied himself to a second heaped platter of steaming hot snails.

Manshoon teleported himself there, to a bare stretch of elegantly tiled floor beside an unoccupied table at the far side of the back alcove the haughty club staff had relegated the war wizard to—and fed Tulbard a generously fatal amount of stabbing lightning. It crackled all around the war wizard, clawing at a suddenly visible shielding around the astonished man . . . that collapsed to the floor but drank the last winking sparks of the lightning as it did so.

Manshoon struck again, using the swiftest and most unobtrusive spell he had ready. A forcedagger, that struck invisibly wherever he pointed his finger. If Tulbard wasn't wearing any protection over his heart . . .

Ah, but Tulbard was. A molded, silk-sheathed throat- and chest-plate. Evidently other upstanding citizens had been annoyed by Tulbard's diligence in the past. Or the man feared the entire world was out to get him.

Manshoon settled for slicing the war wizard's fingers to ribbons, and ruining the spell the man was desperately trying to cast.

Snails finally forgotten, the man surged to his feet, so Manshoon obligingly hamstrung him.

Tulbard crashed onto the table, then to his knees, trying to sob out something. Probably a spell.

"Just *die*, annoyingly persistent Crown mage," Manshoon murmured, advancing out of his corner.

It was perhaps a dozen strides to where Tulbard struggled on the tiles, but before the future emperor of Cormyr had taken two of them, a noble who'd been dining at a table not far away had lifted his fingers from his fingerbowl, dried them, taken a scepter from his belt—and walked across the room to shield the stricken war wizard.

Manshoon now faced a stern-looking lord who was going gray and running to fat. Lord . . . Tauntshaw, wasn't it? One of the wealthy city lords, an investor and landowner. Who was aiming that scepter as if he knew how to use it.

With a sigh of disgust, Manshoon sent a spell at him that should have him shrieking in fear, wetting himself, and fleeing headlong through the club. A noisier frill than most archmages sought, when indulging in murder, but—

Hrast it if the meddling lord wasn't protected by a shielding spell, too! Was *everyone* in Suzail a dabbler in the Art, or did they all just have spare coins enough to buy small arsenals of magics they fancied they might just need someday?

Lord Tauntshaw's scepter spat howling death at Manshoon.

Who sneered, as his many-layered shieldings easily foiled it, and kept walking. He'd have that scepter, and leave two victims rather than one . . .

Men hastened nearer from all over the club, and Manshoon saw wands in the hands of several house wizards, and nobles brandishing all manner of toys.

No. Another time. Sraunter's cellar beckoned.

The unknown mage who'd been stalking toward Lord Tauntshaw—and the moaning, weeping wizard of war on the floor behind him—vanished in mid-step.

A house wizard cast a swift spell. It made a soft white radiance blossom where the man had been, a glow that roved around hastily, then faded away.

"He's gone," its caster announced. "Not lurking and invisible. Nor will he or anyone else soon be able to teleport back into where I just searched."

Many crowded around the wounded man, and around Lord Tauntshaw, offering congratulations. Lord Phaelam gave Tauntshaw a friendly pat on the arm. "Deadly little toy you have there. Well done. I didn't think you even *liked* war wizards."

"I don't," Lord Tauntshaw said shortly. "Yet I like even less attacks upon the institutions of our kingdom. To attack a wizard of war is to assault Cormyr—and if we don't defend our fair realm, it will fall, and we shall have nothing."

He turned back to his own table, and the dressed roast that would be cold by now, and added over his shoulder, "Fittingly, for we shall *deserve* nothing."

Chapter Twenty-Seven

Until You Can Rest Forever

"Unnh," Mirt told the whirling-past world, wincing as his thighs started to *really* ache. "I'm getting too old for this. Hrast that interfering noble! I want that coach back!"

The world offered no reply.

'Twas being just as helpful as it usually was. Underneath him, his borrowed horse merely tossed its head and relieved itself one more time, not slowing in the slightest.

Not that he wanted it to. Mirt turned for another cautious look back. Aye, they were still right behind him, still hot for his blood.

He'd ridden far and fast, and that had to be Halfhap ahead, just over the rise.

Ah, so it was—but, hrast and damn, there was a mounted Purple Dragon patrol, outbound from Halfhap, on the road beyond the rise.

They moved to stop him, of course. Mirt bellowed at them and waved wildly at them to move aside, but his spent horse was slowing and shying already, he wasn't going to manage it—

"Curse you!" he shouted at the Dragon officers who closed in to intercept him. "Don't you let folk *use* the roads you build?"

"Hold!" they both commanded sternly, rather than answering him.

Mirt looked back over his shoulder. The pursuit was thundering right along, and he could see Purple Dragons among them. *Naed.*

"I'm holding," he growled at the patrol blade who'd just taken hold of his horse's bridle, "but I need you to *listen.*"

The thunder of hooves behind him grew, and some of the riders were shouting to the patrol, to catch and hold this "dangerous thief, this noble slayer!"

Noble slayer? Oh, aye, the *coach* . . .

Mirt shouted Durncaskyn's message into the faces of the frowning Dragons who were surrounding him.

Some of them at least were listening. He could tell that from their faces—in the last few moments before his pursuers, riding hard, crashed right into the midst of the patrol.

Horses reared, kicked, screamed, and bucked, men fell off everywhere, other men cursed or shouted orders, someone blew a war horn, someone else drew his sword and started hacking, a dozen Purple Dragon blades sang out of their scabbards, and—

"Bugger *this*," Mirt growled to himself, somersaulting forward out of his saddle into the ditch. If he could roll and manage not to break anything, come up and relieve one of these stoneheads of his horse, and get past . . .

The spell that struck him made everything seem to hush, so it was in an eerie peace that Mirt noticed that everything—shouting men pointing at him, rearing horses, swords being swung—was happening slowly. Very slowly.

Then his gaze was caught and held by the dark, level eyes of a man riding with the Halfhap patrol, who had to be a war wizard. The young, severe-looking man who'd enspelled him.

"Listen to me," Mirt tried to call to him. "I need you to . . . to . . ."

The silent, slowing world went away, except for those severe and disapproving eyes. The mouth beneath them wasn't smiling, not at all . . .

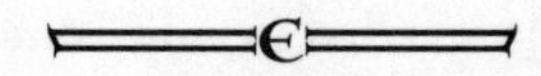

"You have a visitor, saer," the Purple Dragon murmured, unlocking Mirt's manacles. "He's been searched thoroughly, but beware—some of these nobles have poison hidden away in right sly places."

"Nobles?" Mirt asked, with a frown. He remembered many stern questions, stern and then dumbfounded Purple Dragon faces ringing him as they heard his answers, and Halfhap abruptly erupting in a flood of shouting, hurrying men. It seemed Durncaskyn would be getting the help he needed, at full gallop.

Then he'd been chained to the wall in a cell for "later questioning," his tales of the king and Lady Glathra and Rensharra seeming to strain credulity more than a bit too much.

When the spell that made the world seem faint and far away wore off, he intended to get himself out, somehow. He'd been chained with his wrists well away from his belt, so the little lockpicks there and in his boots might as well have been back in Waterdeep . . . but unless they were going to spoon-feed him, they'd have to unshackle him *some*time.

The cell door opened again, and the same Purple Dragon looked in and then turned and announced expressionlessly over his shoulder, "I'll be down the passage, beyond where I can hear anything less than a shout. With your four bodyguards, lord." He turned his head again and gave Mirt a distinct but stonefaced wink.

Ah, *nobles*. Specifically, his visitor was the one who'd deprived him of his coach on the road. Striding into the cell looking spitting angry, too.

"Coach thief!" Mirt roared at him.

The noble's eyes bulged, he went from red to dark crimson, and cords stood out in his neck. All in the instant before he whirled around and caught hold of the departing guard's elbow. "Introduce me to the prisoner," he snapped.

The Dragon looked startled. "Uh, ah . . . lord, this man calls himself Mirt, Lord of Waterdeep. Mirt, this is Lord Austrus Flambrant, uh, head of House Flambrant of, ah, Cormyr." He fled.

"Horse thief," Lord Flambrant snarled, not even waiting for the cell door to close, "what have you done with Lady Dawningdown?"

"Put her out of her coach for urgent Crown business," Mirt snapped. "Why did you poke yer long nose into things and try to stop me, anyhail?"

"What? How *dare* you—"

The last of Lord Flambrant's temper fled, and he went for Mirt, raining a flurry of blows into the paunch and hastily raised forearms of the prisoner who promptly sat back down on the bench. Launching a kick up between Flambrant's legs that parted noble from codpiece and sent the lord's head into a swift and hard greeting with the low stone ceiling, Mirt deftly brought his knee up as the stricken noble descended. It managed a satisfactorily solid meeting with His Lordship's chin—and if Flambrant hadn't been senseless before, he certainly was now.

Collecting Flambrant's purse for travel expenses and his dagger for troubles ahead, Mirt clapped the unconscious, blood-drooling noble into the manacles and strode out and down the passage.

Only four bodyguards? Huh. He could be on a horse fast enough to catch up with the relief force, and get back to Immerford as soon as they did. If this was the competence of Cormyr's nobles and soldiery, he trusted no one but himself with guarding Rensharra.

"This is . . . exhausting work," Gulkanun said grimly. "Even when you're doing it all."

The drow gave him a nod that was both angry and weary, as they headed for the next cell.

Elminster, Gulkanun, Arclath, and Amarune had searched Irlingstar from dungeon to battlements. Unless someone was buried alive in the great collapsed heap of rubble where the south tower had been, no one was hiding anywhere inside the castle who wasn't already accounted for. Then the mind-touching had begun. The kitchen staff first, then the castle staff, then all of the guards. No murderous slayer.

Which left only the noble prisoners. Who had been resecured in separate cells, warded away from each other by invisible walls of magic that brought silence, so the painstaking mind-touching could continue without interruption or delay. The nobles were willful, unpleasant men, even when they weren't confined and angry—and now they were also deeply afraid. They resisted the touch of a drow furiously, even a shapely female drow who purred flirtatiously at them as she approached . . . and El had found it necessary to take a few bruises from some of them before she could get into their minds and render them docile.

She was uncovering a lot of unsavory things—including not a few murders—but finding no unseen slayer. Seven men hadn't been the murderer they sought, so far, and she wasn't sure how many more hostile minds she could wade through, before—

She and Gulkanun parted the wards, to deal with the eighth noble. Who lay sprawled face down on the floor in a spreading pool of fresh blood.

"Oh, naed," El breathed. "To the next one! Hurry!"

They were too late. The tenth and eleventh lordlings, too, were dead.

"At this rate, Foril won't be needing this prison any longer," Elminster snapped. "'Tis time to try something else."

"What *sort* of something else?" Arclath asked. For safety, he and Rune were staying with El and Gulkanun as they worked.

El frowned. "A spell I dimly recall, intended for another purpose entirely, that *might* locate and highlight the killer's magic as it manifests, but before anyone else gets slain."

"If you're fast and lucky," Rune murmured.

El shrugged. "*That* goes for almost everything in my life. Weapons, everyone."

She enspelled the blades they were carrying. "These should all now serve to parry the air blade we saw at work. Gulkanun, be ready to shield me; I'll cast the tracing spell now."

The war wizard nodded grimly, flexed his fingers, and stepped back to the wall, to watch Elminster narrowly from there. El backed to the wall beside her to begin casting. Arclath and Amarune stood back to back on El's far side, trying to peer at everyone intently.

As El gestured and started to speak her incantation, the air in front of her promptly thickened into a blade—but struck at Gulkanun first. The war wizard shouted, his ready spell flashing into a bright parry.

Arclath ducked around Elminster in a lunge, the tip of his sword encountering that thickness of the air, just for an instant, but otherwise slicing or spitting nothing at all.

Then something icy slid into his shoulder, and Rune cried his name and started hacking desperately at the empty air there.

Arclath spun around and thrust out, parrying the unseen edge for another fleeting moment. Then they were hard at it, panting and whirling, desperately fighting something they could barely see—until a soft and golden glow rushed from Elminster's hands, making the forceblade darting through the air shine forth clearly. They saw something else in the spreading golden radiance, too: the blade's wielder, behind it, a ghostly figure that was clear enough for them all to identify him.

"Mreldrake!" Elminster and Arclath snarled in unison.

Everwood had been watching what was unfolding in Irlingstar for some time. Manshoon had long since joined him, to stand behind his chair and observe. Matters were growing . . . interesting.

The shapely drow spread her hands, the golden glow flooded forth, and—

"Mreldrake!" Manshoon snapped. "And Elminster must be either the drow or the war wizard! Time to take care of them all at once!"

He snatched out one of his eyeball beholderkin, cast a mind-scrambling spell on it that when triggered should stun everyone who got too near it, and teleported the little flying sphere to the corpse of Jarlin Flamtarge.

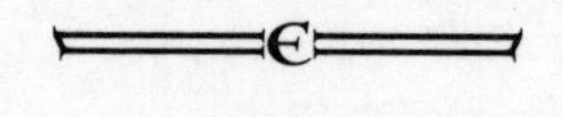

Duth Gulkanun blinked. A tiny beholder, small enough to fit in the palm of his hand! It had just *appeared* in the air, right there—

Without thinking, he used his shielding spell to try to thrust it back into the slicing edge of the Slayer's forceblade.

An unfamiliar, disembodied voice murmured something, and a tiny whirling glow erupted from the flying beholder.

Elminster knew that voice.

So, now . . . before whatever magic Manshoon was trying to visit on them could erupt, let's just send it elsewhere—along the magical link binding this forceblade to Mreldrake, for instance!

Smiling grimly, he spent a little silver fire to do just that.

Oooh, Symrustar applauded. *Nasty.*

The sealed doors of Mreldrake's room were flung open. His three captors burst in, not troubling to hide from him that they were shades in their frantic haste.

They were just in time to be caught, along with Mreldrake, in the spell lashing out from the tiny beholder.

The mindscrambling made Mreldrake and the closest Netherese shriek helplessly, as pain stabbed through their heads.

For everyone in that room, the world *stretched* impossibly, and started to swirl . . .

As he was swept away into madness, the slowest, farthest-back shade managed to snap out a ready spell.

The eyeball beholderkin was small, and close, so it had no chance to escape.

It burst, sending a harmful backlash to the one who'd sent the mindscrambling.

The backlash howled into the cellar, into Manshoon—and his head exploded.

Or rather, Sraunter's body was beheaded. The alchemist was already standing behind the war wizard, his hand on Everwood's shoulder, so Manshoon simply left one expendable pawn for another.

He flooded into the dazed, brains-bespattered Crown mage's mind and seared it to nothing.

Everwood trembled and spasmed for what seemed forever, but was in truth no more than a few fleeting instants.

Then he grew still again—burnt out, a vessel for the future emperor of Cormyr.

Who made Everwood smile more cruelly than the young war wizard had ever smiled in his life.

This new body was young and strong, and fairly competent in Art. In less time than it took Manshoon to swallow his own anger—or Sraunter's headless body to topple to the floor, forgotten—Manshoon gathered all the magic he could bring to hand, that he could link together with a spell already in his mind.

And he hurled it all at the three shades in Mreldrake's room.

The shades clawed at each other, their mad shouts slurred, as they staggered helplessly and nigh mindlessly around Mreldrake's prison.

Hostile magic suddenly erupted into the room, lashing them with emerald flame that snarled and rebounded off the walls—and was gone again, just as suddenly, as its fury overwhelmed the tenuous linkage between the room and its distant source.

Mreldrake and the shades gasped in agony, but their pain passed as swiftly as it had come.

Whatever the flame attack had been, it had failed—and shattered the mindscrambling afflicting them in doing so.

Wincing and groaning, the shades hurried out of the room and spell-sealed it again, to cast shielding spells on themselves as fast as they could.

They paid no attention to their unconscious captive, left behind sprawled on the floor.

Above Mreldrake's unconscious body, his spell collapsed.

And in distant Irlingstar, his forceblade silently faded away.

"We've got to get out of here! *All* of us!"

If the kitchen staff or the guards of Irlingstar were unwilling to take orders from a dark elf—even a beautiful female one—they didn't show it. Elminster rushed up and down the passages, parting the wards to let prisoners out of their cells. She was ordering the abandonment of Castle Irlingstar immediately, regardless of what Ganrahast or anyone else might say or think later. No one argued.

A few of the freed prisoners promptly attacked her—or Gulkanun, or Rune and Arclath—and there were several brief, nasty tussles, but every one of them ended with the nobles defeated. Nor were hostilities renewed; the promise of getting out of "this death-trap," backed up by the fear of being left behind, alone and warded into a cell without food or water to face the unseen slayer, convinced everyone.

In a surprisingly short time, they were gathered at the main gates, and then spilling out of the castle together—cooks, guards, prisoners, staff, and all. Only to come to a dismayed halt.

Something blocked Orondstars Road. Something large, dark, and scaly.

The black dragon Alorglauvenemaus was waiting for them, and it was smiling. Its first spew of acid melted the frontrunners into wounded, dying agony.

One of them was Elminster.

Panting in pain, her legs gone at the knees and her pelvis and belly slowly melting, El propped herself on one elbow and fought to make her failing body cast protective magic.

Now, El. Now I repay you, by giving you my last. I loved you. Farewell, old rogue—and conquer!

Symrustar's mind-voice was warm and weeping. Before El could even think of a protest, the last of her washed through his mind, clearing it of pain, of weary worrying, of everything except what had to be done. A shielding, thus . . .

Amid all the shouting, scattering, fleeing folk of Irlingstar, she was almost done, gasping and shuddering out the last words of the spell, when the dragon noticed her.

Alorglauvenemaus turned its head toward the nearest trees of Hullack Forest, hard by the road, and commanded, "*Now.*"

Two crossbows cracked, and two heavy war quarrels sped out of the treegloom. One took the struggling drow through the shoulder, and the other tore out her throat on its way past.

Even before Rune could gasp, Harbrand and Hawkspike stepped out of concealment to peer at the results of their archery. Each of them trailed the bow they'd just fired, and cradling a second, loaded crossbow.

Seeing that the drow was down, they stepped back into the forest. Whereupon Amarune ducked her head down and sprinted for Elminster, Arclath right behind her.

She was halfway there when a crossbow quarrel crashed into her shoulder, plucked her off her running feet, and left her down and sobbing in the road.

Arclath flung himself atop her, to shield her. Gulkanun fell to the ground right behind him.

"Can you heal her?" Arclath asked the war wizard pleadingly.

Gulkanun shook his head and snapped, "Stay with her. I'll go to Elminster. If anyone knows how to twist this or that handy arcane spell into healing, she will. Er, *he* will."

"Yes, but—"

"I'm doing this," Gulkanun said flatly. "Even if it means the end of me, that . . . matters not. Nothing matters, since my Longclaws was taken from me."

He rolled over and up, leaping to his feet and running, changing direction sharply once, twice, and—a crossbow quarrel slammed into him as he reached Elminster.

Snarling in pain, he fell onto what was left of the dying drow. Silver fire flared, the quivering shaft of the quarrel melted away—and Elminster flooded into Gulkanun's mind.

The wizard rolled over, dragging the dissolving drow torso over as a shield, and worked a swift spell. Then he stood up to face the dragon.

"Oh, *that* was boldly done," Alorglauvenemaus said mockingly, and he spewed a great cloud of acid right at Gulkanun.

Another rift closed, and of course more monsters slain. At last.

The Simbul stared at deep gashes in her left shoulder as she drifted away from her latest battlefield, exhausted and reeling. The blueflame items in her hands flickered dully, almost spent.

"I am *becoming* blueflame," she mumbled. "Mystra, it hurts, and the madness is coming back . . . I can feel it . . ."

Not long now, loyal daughter, came Mystra's firm reply. *Not long until you can rest forever.*

The cloud of acid struck something unseen in front of Elminster, and boiled away. Good. The shielding he'd just cast was broad and high, and protected Arclath, Rune, and most of the Irlingstar folk still on the road.

The nobles who'd ducked down into the ditches were not so fortunate. Even before El stepped back to heal Amarune with a burst of silver fire, many acid-melted Cormyrean lordlings screamed, gurgled, and died.

Gulkanun had retreated to the back of his mind, no longer despairing. El sent him a reassuring rush of warmth and gratitude, then turned and worked the mightiest battle spell he could swiftly hurl.

Before it could take wing, the great black dragon was struck. By his shielding spell first, its edge of force thinned like Mreldrake's blade. It sliced deeply, almost severing one great wing, even as Elminster's whirling spheres of flame slammed into the rest of Alorglauvenemaus.

Writhing on the road, its lashing tail and wings churning up dust, the scorched dragon screamed in pain.

The sound was almost deafening, and in its growing agony the dragon rolled over and over, like a wounded man down in a fight and trying to get clear, its tail and intact wing flailing the road and ditches alike.

Elminster raised his arms—Gulkanun's arms—to hurl another spell at the dragon.

And the air above Alorglauvenemaus winked, four bright stars appearing out of nowhere, stars that flashed and then were gone—leaving behind four rotting, mold-covered beholders of monstrous size.

Hanging menacingly in midair, their eyestalks and tentacles writhing, they stared down at the wizard standing in the road.

Chapter Twenty-Eight

Win Yourself A Happier Ending

"*Manshoon*," El muttered angrily, and he worked a spell that should maim at least four death tyrants before they could spread apart to fly at him from all sides.

He was halfway through that magic when another two crossbow quarrels came humming out of the trees.

He swayed aside and one missed—but the other crashed into him, spoiled the spell, and hurled him down on his back on the road, winded and in pain.

He could taste blood, and in the sky above the beholders were floating menacingly forward.

Behind them, the dragon was fleeing, lurching along the road like a gigantic wounded dog in an anxious hurry to be elsewhere, its tongue hanging out as it panted.

"Enough of this," El snarled, fighting the pain. "Rune, Arclath—clasp your hands firmly around some part of me. And let any noble who wants to do the same."

Arclath Delcastle was neither dull nor slow-witted. "Where are you taking us?"

"The royal gardens in Suzail," El gasped.

"I dem—*requested* this audience," Lady Dawningdown said sharply, "because I now have rather more than the usual number of complaints. Your Majesty will appreciate—"

King Foril Obarskyr, who walked at her side as they wended their way along some of the shadier paths of the royal gardens, nodded politely. He'd become very good at politely appreciating nobles' bitter complaints, long before his first meeting with Lady Jalassra Dawningdown—and that meeting had been happier decades ago.

Lady Glathra and the lord warder walked a pace behind them, and several watchful veteran highknights were farther ahead.

"—that a lady of breeding and station, such as myself, who has reached the golden age I now enjoy, no longer takes pleasure in the jolting of a saddle, and prefers to travel in the *relative* comfort of a coach! I hope you'll agree that any Cormyrean who can afford such a conveyance should have the perfect right to—"

The highknights shouted as they were bowled over by the sudden appearance, amid a bright blue flash of magic, of more than a dozen ragged bodies, tumbling out of nowhere atop them.

The lord warder cast a swift shielding, and Lady Glathra dragged out her two most puissant wands and yelled for the rearguard of highknights and war wizards to get themselves over here, *right now*.

"The king is under attack!" someone bellowed from across the gardens, and knights and Purple Dragons started converging from everywhere, swords out and running hard.

The sudden scramble and fray would have ended in real bloodshed if strong forcecages and shielding spells hadn't come into being around the new arrivals.

As it was, hurrying highknights unceremoniously bowled Lady Dawningdown over. Whereupon some ill-smelling and disheveled young lordlings, in haste to loudly complain to the king about the murderers he was letting loose into his prisons to just dispose of anyone he desired dead, trampled the toppled lady face first into a freshly manured flower bed. Whereupon Lady Dawningdown discovered she had just acquired something to *really* complain about.

When it all got sorted out, the complaining prisoners were hustled away by most of the Purple Dragons. Many of the wizards of war and highknights, with Lord Warder Vainrence, conducted King Foril to safety elsewhere.

Leaving Lady Glathra to glean some detailed sense of what had happened at Irlingstar, so as to deliver a proper report to the king.

"Consider yourself under arrest," she began, giving Gulkanun a glare and keeping both of her wands leveled at him. "We will decide on the future of your career in service to the Crown later. For now, I require—"

"Oh, for the sake of the Dragon *Throne*!" Amarune snarled in utter exasperation, plunging into a somersault that became an extended double-leg kick at the back of the war wizard's head.

Glathra went down like a felled sapling.

Leaving Arclath, Amarune, and Elminster all gazing wearily at each other.

"My place," Arclath suggested. "I want a feast, a bed, and most of all a *bath*."

They all fervently agreed—even Gulkanun, inside the mind he was sharing with Elminster.

In a corner of the royal gardens, Lord Wenderwood reached a decision and abruptly stood up.

He'd been sitting on a bench under a sculpted felsul tree, patiently awaiting his turn to talk to the king on that day's garden stroll.

The guard who'd been escorting Lord Wenderwood had gone running to old Foril the moment the war wizard bitch had shouted for help, and hadn't yet returned. The guard was starting to, though, trudging back to inform his noble charge that royal audiences were unexpectedly over for the day.

So much Lord Wenderwood, with his monocle or without, could already see for himself. In truth, there was nothing at all wrong with his eyesight, and he'd readily recognized Lord Delcastle, a number of other young lords who'd recently been shut up in Irlingstar—and the flash of a translocation spell.

His master would very much want to hear about this. Accordingly, Lord Wenderwood turned his back on the approaching guard, who was still two intervening flower beds away.

It was the work of but a moment to unleash the eyeball beholderkin from inside the breast of the best Wenderwood formal jerkin, to send it back to Lord Manshoon.

This Everwood had a young, quick, *useful* mind. He should have done this *months* ago!

Manshoon stretched his new body's arms and legs, looked down at them approvingly, and nodded. Yes, this would do *very* well.

Now, back to the scrying spheres. That backlash shouldn't have done much—

One of his eyeball beholderkin swooped down the cellar stairs like a bird, hung there in front of his face, and hissed at him. Manshoon touched it with a finger. And smiled.

"Well done, Wenderwood!" he said aloud, clapping his hands in delight and reaching out to the mind of that noble.

"So, off to Delcastle Manor the conquering heroes stroll, hey?" He stroked his chin thoughtfully, as an evil smile spread slowly across his face.

"Yes," he murmured aloud. "Magic seems to fail again and again, so let us try older, more brutal methods."

He went to gather what he'd need to work a spell to reach out to all of his subverted nobles at once. Well, all who were still in Suzail.

He needed them to hurry to Delcastle Manor at once. With their freshest poison and favorite weapons.

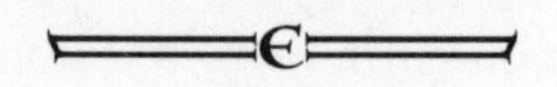

"Lord Durncaskyn?"

The voice was polite, and cultured, and unfamiliar.

Durncaskyn looked up from his desk.

A well-dressed man with the sort of slender walking stick only nobles and the wealthiest Sembian merchants used was standing at the door to his office, an expensive leather scroll case in his hand.

"Yes?"

"King's Lord Lothan Durncaskyn?"

"*Yes*," Durncaskyn repeated. "The king can only afford one local lord here in Immerford, let me assure you. And who might you be?"

The man strode to Durncaskyn's desk, uncapped one end of the scroll case, and with a deft flick of his wrist spun a document out of it, flipped it up in to the air with a practiced flourish to unfurl it, and thrust it at Durncaskyn.

"I am known professionally as Rantoril, and I'm here to honor this agreement."

Durncaskyn took the parchment, but kept his eyes on its deliverer—as the man smoothly drew something long and slender and steely out of the case, and drew it back to launch a stabbing lunge.

Durncaskyn was already hurling himself and his chair over backward, so he missed seeing whatever it was that felled Rantoril, but he heard the meaty *smack* of its strike. And the heavy thud of the assassin hitting the floor.

He rolled to his feet, snatching out his belt dagger, and . . . found himself ringed by booted feet.

He looked up.

The tall and slender woman smiling down at him had hair as silver as polished ceremonial court plate armor—hair that hung down to her knees. She was dressed like a forester, in leathers and high boots, and wore a long sword at her hip that looked like it had come from the royal armory.

"Storm Silverhand," she introduced herself gently, reaching out a hand to help him up.

Durncaskyn took it, and he was astonished at her strength. The owners of the other boots proved to be youngish men and women who were also clad as foresters, but had normal hair. One or two of them might even have been Immerfolk. Some of them were lifting Rantoril's limp body and bearing it away.

"Who . . . what . . . ?"

"I'm the Marchioness Immerdusk, traveling the realm in the name of the king. These good people are Harpers—as am I—and your recent visitor was a Sembian who's never been known as Rantoril before. He'll sleep for a day or two. He was hired by Lord Leskringh."

"*Leskringh?* That old—"

"—hind end of a rothé, as you were going to say, has been taken into custody and will be tried by his peers within a tenday, with Rantoril giving evidence. I'm afraid one of your clerks was badly wounded; I'll be leaving a Harper in his place to guard you."

She clasped Durncaskyn's arm affably, steered a goblet of his own wine into his hand, then strode for the door.

Durncaskyn blinked. "But . . . where are you going?"

"To greet the relief force Mirt is bringing you, before one of them strikes down the wrong person and plunges all this end of Cormyr into civil war," she replied sweetly, without slowing.

"No," Arclath breathed. "Gods, no."

A moment ago, their trudge to the gates of Delcastle Manor had been a matter of weariness. Until they'd seen the gates standing open, askew, bodies sprawled beyond them.

Arclath had rushed forward, Rune racing to stay at his side and Elminster right behind.

Arclath's home looked like a battlefield.

There were pools of blood, buzzing with flies, inside the gates and up the drive, with forever-silent Delcastle retainers and splendidly dressed men—Great Gods, prominent noblemen of Cormyr!—lying dead everywhere.

They'd been much hacked, their lifeless staring eyes almost hidden beneath swarming flies. The fighting had been with swords and daggers, and it had been brutal.

The doors of the mansion itself yawned open, with dead men heaped on the steps. Arclath rushed inside, calling his mother's name, with El and Rune right behind him. They found more dead Delcastle servants, and more dead nobles.

Aside from the flies, there was a terrible silence. No moaning wounded, no defiant men with blades . . . just the dead.

Arclath made for his mother's bedchamber.

Lady Marantine Delcastle was sitting propped up against the end of her palatial bed, her legs pinned under three dead nobles. More slaughtered lords made a thick and bloody carpet all the way to the door.

She was covered with blood, her head slumped onto her shoulder. A slender sword, crimson and black with darkening gore, had fallen from her hand, but she still clutched a dagger, ready on her breast.

Her fine gown was slashed to ribbons, one shoulder carved open to the bone. Many blades had pierced her.

"Mother!" Arclath wept, clawing dead men aside to uncover her, reaching to cradle her.

At his touch, she stiffened and whimpered. El cast a swift spell to heal, and another to banish pain.

Arclath's look was beseeching. "Can you save her?"

El shook his head, slowly and grimly. "Too many poisons warring in her—every last one of these lords must have tainted their blades. Only the poisons struggling in her veins has kept her alive this long, but . . . no. 'Twould need a god, Arclath, and I've never been one of those."

He reached out to cup Marantine's cheek, to lift her head upright. "Yet the pain is gone from her now. That much I *can* do."

Arclath embraced his mother fiercely, his arms trembling, and kissed her.

She opened her eyes and managed a twisted smile up at him through his tears.

"Be happy with your dancer, my son," she gasped, blood welling out of her mouth with every word. "Live long, and win yourself a happier ending than I have . . ."

Then she slumped, her eyes fixed on his, going dark and endlessly staring.

Lord Delcastle collapsed in racking sobs. Amarune cradled his shoulders, holding him close.

Elminster watched them for a moment, then reached out and gently stroked Marantine Delcastle's eyelids down over her staring eyes. One wouldn't stay down, retreating to give her a grotesque wink.

"This is *enough*, and more than enough," the Sage of Shadowdale snarled suddenly, standing bolt upright. He spun away and stalked across the heaped dead, reaching out with his mind as he went.

He was three rooms away before he found a noble, buried under three others, who wasn't quite dead yet.

The mind was going dark, sliding inexorably into extinction, but there was still a glimmer . . .

Elminster plunged savagely into that dying mind, to read whys and whos and . . .

"*Manshoon*! Of *course*!"

He stalked through the house and out into the Delcastle gardens.

Looking up into the sky, with the bloodstained sward of the manor grounds stretching out on all sides, he threw back his head and furiously called Manshoon to battle.

He did not have to wait long.

Rising into the sky above bustling Suzail came six, seven . . . nine spherical hulks the size of small coaches, gaping-mawed flying spheres that looked dead and rotting, covered with snowy and sickly green furred molds—yet moving, their dangling eye-stalks lifting and writhing as folk shouted and ran, on the streets below.

As one, they drifted purposefully toward Delcastle Manor.

The only man standing in the Delcastle gardens watched them come, his lip curling. Manshoon had sent his beholders rather than coming in person. Of course.

Elminster raised his hands, murmured a spell that smote undead with silver fire—and blasted them down.

In an instant, every last death tyrant burst into drifting dust, like so many puffs of smoke.

More came, rising up into the sky in slow menace. War horns sounded from the palace and the royal court, horn calls that were answered from the city gates and the harbor tower.

El waited until all the menacing eye tyrants were close enough to reach with one casting, then served them the same way he had the first wave.

Four out of this dozen did not fall into dust, but kept coming. So Manshoon did command some living beholders, after all . . .

El lashed them with a net of lightnings that would feed on magic sent against it, and watched the beholders shoot forth rays and beams that only strengthened the crackling bolts that seared them. One fell from the sky, another burst like a raw egg, and the last two burned as they came, spinning and shrieking in their ongoing agonies.

El greeted them with a spell of many fireballs, blasts of flame he tried to send inside their many-fanged mouths. His aim was true, and flaming gobbets of beholder hurtled across the city sky.

Men in robes appeared by the gates and past the fountain at the far end of the Delcastle gardens: war wizards, with wands in their hands, intent on Elminster.

He ignored them, reaching forth with his mind, trying to reach Manshoon. Who had to be nearby, who was probably lurking somewhere just yonder, beneath where the beholders had risen.

El had his silver fire, but there was no Weave everywhere around him that he could call on or wrap himself in or ride elsewhere on an instant's whim. There was just him, and the dwindling spells he had ready, against a foe obviously prepared for the day.

"Saer!" a stern voice called, from the gardens behind him. "Surrender! Have done! This unlawful mage duel—"

Elminster ignored the rest. If these converging war wizards were that foolish, if they could not see the peril to their city and their kingdom—or were already subverted by Manshoon—Suzail might well be doomed. He needed their aid, not their attempts to arrest or oppose him. Another beholder came, a much smaller one, and it was trailing something that looked like a tiny cloud . . .

The first volley of wand blasts clawed at the mantle spell El had cast around himself, and reduced it to shimmering, snarling fury.

He translocated himself to the fountain, felled one of the war wizards there with a sharp chop to the back of the neck, snatched the wand from the fool's failing hand, and subsumed its power to invigorate and steady his failing mantle.

All around him, shouting Crown mages hurled spells and fired wands and—

He was elsewhere again, at the gates this time, punching another wizard of war and seizing another wand.

It exploded in El's grasp, the flash almost blinding and deafening him, even as his mantle drank it and kept his hand from destruction. Then he was caught in a barrage of twenty wand blasts, thirty . . .

In searing agony he took himself back to where he'd first been standing, arriving in a stagger, his mantle gone and his contingency melting spell after spell out of his mind to meet and counter what the Crown mages were hurling at him. Some of them were showing battle cunning, firing their wands even before he reappeared, anticipating where he'd . . .

The beholder, utterly unscathed, ignored by the war wizards in their eagerness to smite a lone man within easy reach, was close now, descending as it neared the Delcastle walls.

And here he was, magic giving out, beset by these young *fools*.

"Ganrahast," he snarled, "don't you *train* your wizards any more? Can't they *see*? And *think*?"

Spells flashed down from the sky, fireballs that hurled war wizards into the air, burned and broken, and lightning bolts that stabbed across the garden, spearing Crown mage after Crown mage.

They were coming from the air *behind* the lone beholder . . . Blood of Bane, Manshoon had devised eyeball beholderkin that could unleash spells! A *swarm* of them!

A spell winked forth from one, then another, lashing down . . .

Well, at least some war wizards had finally discovered wits enough to look up and see where the slayings that sought them were coming from. They fired their wands into the sky, casting spells at the beholder, too, in a quickening inferno above El's head that rent the sky like storm thunder.

That beholder exploded.

Wild lightning stabbed down, blazing beholderkin were flung in all directions like embers from an erupting volcano, the gardens rocked as its trees blazed up into one great bonfire, and . . . sudden silence fell.

The sky was empty, fires burned everywhere in the gardens as charred tree trunks spat sparks, and . . . bodies were everywhere.

More war wizards arrived, stalking warily forward in a slowly tightening ring around one man.

Who was on his knees, just two spells left in his weary mind and his body shrieking with silent pain. His skin crackled like brittle parchment paper and fell away as he tried to rise, the seared flesh beneath stinking like roast boar.

So this was how it was all going to end, after all these centuries. Blasted apart by young fools lashing out at the wrong target.

Fitting, somehow.

"Mystra," he whispered. "Alassra. I loved you both."

They were moving in for the kill, somber and wary, wands aimed and fists thrust forth with awakened rings aglow on their knuckles.

"*Now*," someone commanded sternly—and the barrage began.

"Idiots," El spat, as darkness claimed him.

Chapter Twenty-Nine

Doing What Needs To Be Done

The wizards of war fired carefully, concentrating on the mouth and hands of the man on his knees, trying to make sure there'd be no sudden flurry of spells coming back at them.

"No closer," one warned his fellows. "Contingencies. Blast him from right where you're standing."

They lashed the dying man with spell after spell. Magics that raged and snarled, but seemed suddenly not to be touching their target. Instead, they were rising up around him, in a bright and climbing spiral that licked the sky like a great tongue of flame. *Blue* flame.

A flame that suddenly sank down into a fury of raging fire, fiery tongues of eye-searing-bright silver and of that same rich blue, that became . . . a tall and furious woman aglow with raging blueflame and silver fire.

"Fools! Ungrateful wretches!" she howled, her silver hair suddenly stabbing out in all directions around her. "Have your miscast magic *back*!" Deadly spells howled out from her in all directions across the gardens, hurling war wizards out over the walls and against the manor and its gates with shattering, splattering force. When none were left standing, she spun around, fell to her knees, and embraced her Elminster.

"My love," she gasped, between kisses, "have me again, now—and forever!"

When their lips met, there wasn't much left of the man in her arms except the seared and blackened head she was holding, and a mangled wisp of shoulders and torso beneath.

Silver fire flowed into him, poured into him as Alassra Silverhand's tears fell like rain and her body darkened, and she spent all she had into healing and restoring and sharing. Her own body started to melt away, her legs becoming his, her arms dissolving as his grew . . .

Farewell, my love. Her last mindspeech echoed in every head for blocks around, reducing bewildered Suzailans to helpless tears, melting them with its tenderness. They wept, but knew not why.

Her long fingers went last, melting away from his jaw with a sigh, errant silver hairs drifting away.

The Simbul was gone. Forever.

Leaving a restored, whole man, dazed and tottering as he found his feet. He was tall and hawk-nosed, and his eyes were blue but glowed with silver—and blazed with rage.

He was alive and whole because his love had sacrificed herself to save her Elminster, pouring all her life-force into restoring him. He felt young again, strong. The Art was alive and dancing within him, with more silver fire roiling around than he could comfortably hold for long.

Ah, so *this* was what had been driving his Alassra mad: all the seething, roiling silver fire inside her. Oh, it hurt; it was burning him, fighting to burst out of him. Well, he'd indulge it, and soon!

Folk rushed toward him. El turned to give them death, but found they were Arclath and Amarune, their bone white faces wet with tears, their mouths working.

"El? El, is it you?" Rune managed to sob, reaching for him. Just as Alassra had so often reached for him . . .

She rushed into his arms, clung to him tightly, and cried his name. El looked bleakly over her shoulder at Arclath, who was standing uncertainly nearby, staring back at him. Looking scared.

Well, so he should, this young noble. He knew what he was looking at. He saw an archwizard who wanted to deal death to *so* many.

"What good is it all?" Elminster rasped at Lord Delcastle, almost pleadingly, his own tears coming, coursing from despairing holes of eyes. "To have all this power, to work all these centuries serving a bright cause, helping folk—if I cannot save the ones I love? Tell me it has all been worth it! *Tell me!*"

Arclath swallowed, on the trembling edge of tears. No one should ever look so . . . desolate. Nothing should ever happen that was bad enough to make a mighty wizard's face look like this. "I—"

"*Tell me,*" Elminster howled, "so I can tell you that you *lie*, and lash out at you! Smiting you down just as unfairly as this world has so often treated me! Mystra *spit*, I have been through this *so many times*! You'd think I'd be used to this by now, this loss, this treachery, the—the bedamned unfairness of it all!"

With two angry strides done in less time than it took Arclath to even think of reaching for his sword, the Sage of Shadowdale had spun Rune out of his arms with infinite gentleness, stepped past the heir of House Delcastle and gripped Arclath's arms with the crushing force of two owlbear talons, the better to turn him until they faced each other. He roared into Arclath's paling face, "Yet I *never* get used to it, lad! Under this armor of drawling cynicism and world-weary jesting, I cry the very same way I cried when the magelords swept down on my village and left me kinless and alone in Athalantar! Again and again I lose those I love—places I love, entire *families* I love, whole *kingdoms* I hold dear! Well, I'm sick of it—sick, d'ye hear?"

He flung Arclath aside like a child's doll and stalked across the corpse-littered Delcastle lawns, snarling, to stop at the edge of a flower bed, fling up his arms, and roar, "*Enough*! By the silver fire within me, by the Art I love and wield, by all the faces of those lost and fallen that I grieve, I go now to war! In their name let me rage, in their memory shatter and despoil and hurl down! 'Tis time to hurl castles into the air, and snatch soaring dragons down from it! *Eorulagath*!"

That last word crashed around Suzail like a clap of thunder, rolling from spire to balcony and rooftop, splitting windowpanes, as half-deafened citizens winced and staggered.

Before the echoes of that word of power started to fade, lightning split the sky, raging around Elminster like an impatient blue-white cloak of flames. Up the crackling lightning swept, bearing the tall thin wizard his own height above the scorched turf, and more—and then he was gone, in a blinding flash of light, borne elsewhere in an instant.

On hands and knees in the rubble, clinging to stones with numbed fingers as the backlash made every hair on his body crackle and stand on end, Arclath Delcastle winced, feeling his teeth rattle.

Wherever the Sage of Shadowdale had taken himself, Arclath hoped it was far, far away. He did not want to be as close to Elminster, just now, as, say, on the same continent.

For centuries Elminster had kept his grief, and much of his temper, tightly leashed. No longer. Oh, by Mystra, *no longer*.

He was trembling to let it loose now, to indulge his rage at last . . .

"At *last*!" he bellowed atop the Old Skull in Shadowdale, seeing folk running from the inn below to gape up at him, gouts of silver fire escaping his mouth with every word. "Let scores be settled!"

He stood suddenly in a cellar, where a self-styled incipient emperor was hastily scrambling up from a seat among glowing scrying spheres.

An unlovely woman who had until recently been an understeward in the palace stood in front of Elminster, reaching for a wand and snarling a curse.

With a grim smile, El took hold of the deadly end of the wand—and let Fentable trigger it.

Nothing happened at its tip, but as Manshoon gaped in astonishment, and the intruder in his cellar held back the startled would-be emperor's spells without even looking up, the full fury of the wand's magic washed back out through the hand that held it.

Corleth Fentable was ashes and charred bones, well on their plummeting way to the floor, in an instant.

Former Wizard of War Rorskryn Mreldrake was brewing a fresh pot of tea and wondering if his captors would ever let him set foot outside his far-too-familiar room again, before they killed him—when one wall of his prison abruptly vanished. In silence, and without any mess or disturbance at all. It was simply . . . gone, to reveal a street outside lined with many buildings, and a gentle breeze, and—

A man stepping out of that empty air, at least one floor above the street, to give him a smile that held no warmth at all.

"I think your greatest spell had best die with you," Elminster told him.

It was the last thing Mreldrake ever saw or heard.

El calmly swung the kettle off the hearth and poured it into the teapot, ignoring the man-high wisp of swirling ashes beside him.

The spell that should have blasted him, the hearth, and most of that side of the room to dust and tumbling stones appeared to do nothing to him at all.

Nor did the two spells hurled after it.

In their room-rocking wake, El looked up from the pot at the hurlers of those magics, the three shades who'd kept Mreldrake captive in this room. He dispensed another smile that held neither mirth nor fondness. "Tea?" he asked, as mildly as any kindly hearthside hostess.

He did not give them a chance to reply.

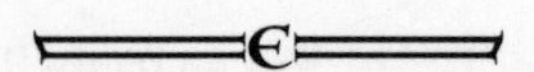

The flames, or tendrils, or whatever they were appeared out of nowhere to snatch Harbrand and Hawkspike out of the corner of the cavern where they glumly waited to die.

The next thing they knew, they were both sitting on the floor of their landlady's office, stark naked, and she was rising from her desk to stare down at them, open-mouthed in astonishment.

Harbrand and Hawkspike stared back up at her, suddenly and uncomfortably reminded of how much coin they owed her.

"Madam," a tall wizard said politely from behind them, just before he vanished, "I give you: Danger For Hire."

Alorglauvenemaus rolled over with a grunt of pain. The only healing spell he could cast while in this great body helped but little. It was going to take a *long* time, and castings beyond his counting yet, before . . .

He hadn't troubled to even *try* to think what magic those two poltroons had managed to awaken, to snatch themselves away from him. There would be time enough later to learn what it had been. Learn leisurely, as he tore them apart at the joints *so* slowly, and learned so much more . . .

"Hesperdan," said a quiet voice from behind him, "it is over."

"Elminster!" the wyrm growled, twisting its head as it flung itself over again, so it could get the Old Mage with acid before—

The man who'd once been his ally, who mind-melded with him in the days before his treachery, was smiling an almost affectionate smile.

He went right on smiling as the great wall of silver flame rushing out of him broke over Hesperdan and took everything away in an instant, plunging him into bubbling silver oblivion . . .

"Ruin him," Lord Breeklar sneered. "Buy up all his debts before nightfall and rouse him from his bed at sword point to demand payment. Then let him stew until morning. I want him out of his house before highsun tomorrow. Offer to hire his wife and daughters as bedmates in one of my brothels."

His steward bowed and hastened out, leaving the noble to sit back in his chair and smile. His gaze fell upon the decanters left ready on the tray, and he idly selected one as he looked at the next sheaf of parchments.

So many debtors yet to punish, so many business partners still to swindle. Ah, work, work, work . . .

How he enjoyed it all. Why—

"Breeklar, ye're far from the worst of Suzail's lords, but gleefully destructive to those who come within thy reach and notice. Not to mention needlessly rude to marchionesses."

The voice that shouldn't have been there was coming from close behind Breeklar's right ear. He spun around, his fist rising with its poison-fang ring at the ready.

"Who *are* you, and how dare—?"

There was no one there.

One of his decanters clinked. The lord whirled back, furious—and lost his nose as heavy cut crystal crashed across his face.

The man who'd swung it and calmly replaced it on the tray, albeit spattered with Breeklar's blood, also held all of the papers from Breeklar's desk.

"I should really read all of these, to learn who ye should be repaying, but I have a *lot* of nobles to deal with, and ye really aren't worth the trouble. Die, worthless parasite."

Lost in his pain and bewildered rage, Lord Breeklar didn't even have time to protest as coins burst out of his coffers and chests, all over the room, to rush into his mouth and nostrils, pouring down his throat, choking him.

His office held a lot of contracts, bonds of indebtedness, and copies of the threatening missives he'd sent. By the time his steward and underclerks came running, the bonfire was impressive.

Almost good enough to serve the helplessly wide-jawed, purple faced dead man slumped in his chair as a fitting pyre.

In a deep, corpse-strewn Underdark cavern, weary drow warriors raised a ragged cheer as reinforcements arrived. Just in time to deal with a fresh flood of nightmarish creatures out of the widening rift.

Scaled, undulating bodies surged, tentacles lashing out with terrifying speed. Drow were plucked into the air and crushed, or their necks broken, almost before they could scream. Then they were flung down among their fellows with bone-shattering force—and the long, dark, powerful tentacles reached for fresh victims.

More and more monsters crowded through the rift, almost too quickly to get past those busily slaughtering the drow with such ease. The sickly purple-white glow was deepening, flooding out into the passages around like a deadly gas, roiling and billowing.

Drow blew war horns in desperation, priestesses worked spells to alert their distant city, and those who could fell back. The peril was deepening, the rift large enough to split the cavern clear across, now, and the beasts coming through it too numerous to hold back. The battle was lost.

From one of the passages a silent thunder rose, a roaring in every mind, a teeth-chattering call that held hunger and malice and rising fear.

Fear that made it break into an audible, endless whispering scream long before its source burst into view, encircled and lashed by a moving cage of blue flames that forced it along the passage, burned into it repeatedly as it squalled and shrieked and rushed into the cavern.

It was the glaragh, much grown but seared and blackened and shuddering in agony, its tail lashing helplessly under the goad of the merciless web of blue flames. Straight at the rift it raced, or was herded, trumpeting wild pain even as it devoured and mindslew everything in its path. Deadly tentacles flailed in vain ere they were sucked in or crushed under that vast, racing bulk, and small hills of rotting, long-dead drow corpses vanished as the glaragh plowed through them without slowing in the slightest.

Then purple flames blazed up to meet the blue, too bright and furious for the handful of surviving drow to watch—and the thunderous scream of pain ended abruptly.

The glaragh was gone, driven back to wherever it had come from, and the rift it had come through was dying in its wake in an ear-shredding high singing of devouring blue flames.

Blinded and deafened, drow fell to their knees or staggered blindly until they struck stone and slid down it, to roll around clutching their heads. Above their moans, the conflagration in the cavern slowly faded, and all light and tumult with it, leaving behind only darkness.

And the strewn dead, to show that there had once been something here to fight for—or against.

A lone blue flame burned in midair, moving slightly, almost as if it were peering this way and that to make sure the task was done.

Then, almost impudently, it winked out.

Manshoon frantically raced around the cellar, snatching up a wand here and an orb there. He *couldn't* be without that, or those, or the—

The glows of his scrying spheres all winked out at once.

A moment later, all the magics bundled in his arms went off together, destroying his forearms and much of his face in a single roaring instant.

He staggered back blindly, wracked in agony, fighting to see anything through his helpless tears.

"Ye couldn't resist," Elminster said disgustedly from nearby. "Ye've never been able to resist."

Manshoon managed a curse. Something stole through his body. A tingling, a magic that . . . that left his limbs frozen, unable to obey him.

He could still think and speak, but . . .

"Thy undeath gives me an easy hold over thee," El told him grimly. "So I can begin to avenge just a few of those ye've slain, the lives ye've blighted."

"Oh?" Manshoon spat defiantly. "So who made *you* the righter of wrongs?"

"Mystra. Yet I don't right all wrongs. Even after a thousand years, I haven't *time*. So I do what is needful about some, a little of what I can regarding others, and forgive the rest."

"Forgive?" Manshoon managed a sneer. "As priests do?"

"As all of us do, or should. If ye can't forgive a wrong, ye become its prisoner—or rather, shackled to thy own hatred, thy own thirst for revenge. I've grown weary of imprisonment, so I do a lot of forgiving."

"So why not forgive me?"

"I should. Ye're crowing-to-thyself crazed, after all, and less able to withstand it than I am—and too much of a deluded fool to see how a hidden one is manipulating thee."

"*What?*"

"Nay, I'm not going to tell thee. Let that be the little worm that gnaws at ye, as you perish. Let *that* be my revenge."

"Revenge!" Manshoon spat, trying to see the potions he'd hidden among Sraunter's useless concoctions and dyes and acids, on the shelves yonder, through eyes that wouldn't stop streaming. "What would *you* know of revenge, meddler? You've always had a goddess—and your fellow Mystra slaves—to guide you and guard you and do it all for you."

"Aye," El agreed gently. "And one of them was you."

"Pah! I *pretended* to serve, to get the magic I wanted!"

"Ye think she didn't know that? Just what d'ye think a goddess is, anyhail?"

"A larger shark, a larger wolf, among all the rest of us. You're a fool if you think otherwise."

"Can ye *really* see only wolves, Manshoon?"

"There are only wolves—and sheep. And when the sheep are gone, it's a wolf-eat-wolf world out there."

"Is it? Well then, we should be doing something to change that, shouldn't we?"

"Change! Everything changes, Old Fool—but nothing truly changes. Just the names and faces of those on the thrones, until they're hurled down by the *next* names and faces!"

"Ye can change thyself, Manshoon. Ye can be better. We can *all* be better." Elminster turned away, then added over his shoulder, "Some of us try that, from time to time, in our lives. Most of us don't bother."

Manshoon bared his teeth in a wordless snarl of defiance, and raced across the room to the shelf. *That* bottle, and that one, all he had to do was smash them, drink splinters and all, and—

He was half an instant away from the shelf when it vanished in a racing flood of silver fire, a flood he crashed into a moment later, rebounding off the sagging, softening remnant of what had been a solid cellar wall, and—

Staggering until he fell, his very limbs melting, caught in a ravaging he couldn't escape, couldn't fight, couldn't withstand . . .

"I did not come here to taunt with ye and let ye escape, Manshoon. I came here to destroy thee."

Manshoon heard that, but no longer had lips or tongue or mouth to reply. He was going . . . he was joining the silver roaring . . . he was torn away into it . . .

Chapter Thirty

Last Things

"You have a visitor, lord," the heavily armed Harper at the door murmured, as gently as any palace doorjack.

King's Lord Lothan Durncaskyn looked up from his desk without even bothering to sigh. He was in a far better mood than usual, with things *finally* getting done around Immerford, its folk happy, the—

The man who strode into the room was clad like a forester. Or rather, the rare sort of forester who liked to wear a long sword at his hip. His face seemed familiar, somehow . . .

He gave Durncaskyn a nod and a rather sour grin.

The king's lord stared back at him, frowning. "*Sunter?* Is that you? What brings you here?"

The man nodded again, and without waiting for an invitation he plucked up a chair, sat down on it, and put his boots up on Durncaskyn's desk. "It is, Loth. And to answer you, a long and dusty ride brought me here; got anything to drink?"

"But . . . well, of course—here, the last of Braeven's Best—but why aren't you at High Horn? Keeping the realm safe against orcs and invading armies, and worse?"

Lord Sunter raised his eyebrows as he accepted a flagon. "Guard our borders? When we have all too many of our own nobles riding to war right in the heart of Cormyr—and the likes of *Elminster* on the loose?"

Durncaskyn shrugged. "I've heard the rumors, too, but . . ."

His voice trailed off as he caught sight of something on the wall and started to stare at it. His mouth dropped open.

Sunter turned his head to see what was so gripping and did the same thing. Before snarling out a curse, draining his flagon, and slamming it down on the desk with the words, "That's it. I quit. It's farming for me, from now on. Somewhere on sleepy back lanes, far from any of our borders. Got any sheltered sisters I can marry?"

Durncaskyn was still staring at the wall too hard to think of a reply.

That particular wall of his office sported the usual fine map of Cormyr. An official one, issued by the palace; both men had seen dozens of copies of it before. However, neither was used to seeing such a map silently burst into flames, all by itself.

Flames that were a vivid, dancing blue.

What had been Manshoon slumped, like logs crumbling in a fire, then melted and was gone. Hard-eyed, Elminster watched his old foe whirl away into silver flame that blossomed and grew.

He clawed at it with his own fire, raking as much as he could of it into himself, wresting Mystra's power from one unworthy. One who would see other days beyond this one.

Even before an eerie wisp swirled out of that fire and raced up out of the cellar and away, El knew why destroying Manshoon was beyond him. The vampire who as a man with many bodies had ruled Westgate, and Zhentil Keep before that, and founded and led the cruel Zhentarim, had carried Mystra's silver fire in himself for too long. It would take a god—perhaps two of them, acting together—to destroy Manshoon utterly and forever. Unless, like his Alassra had, Manshoon sacrificed himself willingly.

Hah. As if *that* would ever happen.

El let the silver fire roar straight up, consuming the building above him, making the shop of Sraunter the alchemist a neat pit between the neighboring buildings, a gap in a row of dingy teeth. And then he brought it down again, taking the fire that was forever back inside him—his own, and Alassra's, and what he'd torn out of Manshoon.

It was too much.

He'd known it would be. Yet he dared not let more leak out. Not when the likes of Manshoon were lurking, to take it and empower themselves and work worse mischief. So he drew it in, fought to hold it, and the *real* agony began.

Up from the ravaged cellar he soared, a silver comet seeking the sky, up and over the great green sward of Jester's Green, heading north.

"*Arrrrrgh*!" he shouted into the wind of his own racing flight. Oh, he'd known it would hurt, but *this* . . .

He was diving, racing down out of the sky, startled riders on the road scrambling for the ditch. There were carts and wagons rushing up to meet him that *couldn't* move—he veered into the trees, fighting to slow himself. It would be a poor gift to the Forest Kingdom to burn a great scar through the King's Forest, or to shatter trees from here to Mouth O' Gargoyles . . .

Snarling, El fought for control. Enough, at least, to be able to jet out silver fire with some precision and slow himself, so as to drop down gently.

He managed it. Somehow he won that fight and landed gently on rotting deadfall wood and leaves without any flames at all . . . and found himself lurching dazedly through the fallen-tree-littered floor of the vast wood.

And stumbling over the first such rotting obstacle and falling on his face. Aye, fittingly greet the glorious conquering hero . . .

El got up again, though he didn't remember doing so. *Too much fire* . . . it was leaking out of him at every staggering step.

"Too *much*," he groaned aloud. "Oh, Mystra, the *pain*!"

He fell against a tree, silver fire splashing out of him to race up and down its trunk, charring it in an instant.

"Mystra," he gasped. "That's it! Mystra will know how to help me . . ."

He staggered a few steps, leaking silver fire in a smoking rain as he went, then sprang back into the air on a jet of silver fire, to fly on through the King's Forest. Seeking a certain waiting cave.

Gasping in pain, breathing out silver fire and leaking it from fingers and knees to scorch everything he touched, Elminster landed in a whirlwind of crisped and crackling leaves, staggered a few steps, fell to his knees, and stayed there.

Just here . . . aye . . . he crawled into muddy, stone-studded darkness that still smelled faintly of bear. Through the tapestries of tree roots, over the bear's moldy old gnaw bones, and down into the stony cavern at last.

Where those great, keen silver-blue eyes of fire hung in midair, awaiting him.

"Goddess," El gasped, still on his knees, "I . . . I . . ."

You blaze with my fire, most faithful of men. Will you freely yield much of it to me?

"Oh, Mystra, *yes*," he groaned, reaching for her.

For an instant he thought two shafts of blue radiance lanced out of those eyes to drink silver fire from him. Then he felt arms grasping him with cruel and hungry strength, pulling him up and into a womanly embrace.

Silver fire caressed him, more silver fire poured out of him, his body seemed to *become* flame, flames that flickered and shrank and roiled as the goddess he'd served so long, the faint vestige of the Mystra he'd never stopped loving, hungrily clawed silver fire out of him, in a roaring flood that went on and blessedly on . . .

He was nothing, he was everything, he was soaring, leaving all pain behind . . .

He was standing in a cavern that was a cavern no more.

The rough and solid stone roof, the earth above it, and tall forest giants of trees above that were all torn away and hurled high into the sky or seared to nothingness in mere moments, leaving him standing in a new clearing, the empty sky above.

The air was full of blue light and the awed wordless song of a thousand unseen voices . . . and towering above El, shaped tall out of the blue glow, was the Lady of Art he'd first met so many centuries ago.

"I have returned," Mystra whispered, soft words that were full of awe and exultation . . . and a thunder of power that shook Elminster and the ground beneath him and the rustling, creaking, swaying trees of the King's Forest for miles around.

A star of silver brightness kindled in the blue glow beside Elminster, and faded into Storm Silverhand, every last strand of her silver hair on end and standing proud from her, as if she were some sort of strange peacock. She looked astonished and delighted—and in one bound they were in each other's arms, both of them leaping to meet each other. The blue glow took gentle hold of them in midair, and floated them into each other's arms.

Rather dazedly, they hugged and kissed, then leaned back in each other's arms to laugh together, then look each other up and down, as if not quite believing they were whole, and here.

Elminster found his tongue first. "Well, I'm back," he said hoarsely. "I'm Elminster again. I think."

"If you've started thinking again," Storm jested, "the Realms are in trouble indeed."

"Indeed," El replied dryly, and he kissed her again, hungrily this time, his arms tightening around her as if he intended never to let go.

They hugged each other tightly, and wept together happily, as overhead the silver-blue and glowing sky filled with Mystra's song.

"No, no, *no*, you dolt! While you're striking that grand pose, what d'you think yer foe'll be doing, eh? Standing back to admire?"

Mirt lurched forward, right through the ringing blades of the Harpers he was training, the ironguard magics that protected them all letting blades slice them without harm, as if they weren't there at all.

"You cover yerself like *this*, see? If you don't, what you'll see instead'll be a blade plunging right through yer heart. Or throat. Or whatever other part of you yer foe feels like gutting."

It was the bright and breezy afternoon of the ninth day after Mystra's Return. Beyond Mirt, on the shadier side of the glade, Amarune and Arclath were tutoring other pairs of Harpers in the finer points of real-world bladework.

Storm and Elminster sat on a mossy bank, leaning back against the massive bough of a shadowtop split in some long ago tempest, that had decided to grow horizontally along the ground rather than up into the sky. They were also leaning into each other, shoulders together. At peace.

Storm was harping gently as she watched the swordplay, and there was a gentle smile on her face.

"I feel happier than I have in a long time," she murmured. "What with Mystra restored, and Manshoon no more."

"*A* Manshoon is not what he was," El corrected her. "He survives, after a fashion, and there are more of him. Like many a wealthy merchant who trades in a large handful of lands, he has many Manshoons."

Storm winced at the pun and lifted a hand from her harp strings to wave at the Harpers in the glade. "This is next, for me. And for you?"

"There remains," Elminster said gravely, "the matter of Larloch."

"I would have given much," Lord Ambershields murmured, "to have seen this Storm Silverhand—Marchioness Immerdusk, indeed! What dusty old scroll did Foril pull *that* title out of, I wonder?—strolling to meet the king wearing nothing but her hair and a smile."

"I'm sure *you* would, old ram," Lady Harvendur replied tartly. "*I*, on the other hand, would have given rather more to see Vangerdahast schooling Glathra Barcantle. They say that Ganrahast and Vainrence asked to be tutored alongside her, just to quell the worst of the battles. Much good it did them. That's how that fire got started in the haunted wing, you know!"

"Heh. I didn't know, but must confess I'm not surprised in the slightest. There's been more confounded *tumult* around here since we first started hearing all these rumors about Elminster the Deathless. Why, they say he's built an altar to Mystra in the haunted wing, and is making every last wizard of war in all the kingdom kneel at it and pray to her *every night*! Whatever next?"

"Good government?" Lady Harvendur joked.

Lord Ambershields rolled his eyes. "Huh! *Now* you're dreaming aloud! We'll have dread Larloch out of the depths of time to chair a Council of Dragons, before we see *that*!"

The lass had an eye, to be sure. When she was finished bending builders to her will, they would have a home that was both beautiful and practical.

Mirt stood on the threshold of the western front door, waiting for his partner of the evening to adjust her gown *just* so, daub scent here and there, and all the rest of it. Looking out over the cobbled and garden-planted forecourt, he smiled happily. Aye, all in all, the mansion he and Rensharra shared was delightful.

So was having, at long last, a lass who understood his needs, just as he understood hers. Free to both take anyone as a partner for an evening or three, or even a tenday, but contentedly returning to each other's arms, again and again.

"I believe I'm ready, Lord of Waterdeep," a husky voice murmured from behind him, a moment before a strong and shapely arm slipped through his.

Mirt turned his head to give Glathra Barcantle a fond smile. "Ah, but you look beautiful, wench. Let's stroll out and dine."

"Wench?" Her tone held warning. "Is that a Waterdhavian endearment?"

"It was back when *I* flourished, girl," Mirt told her gruffly. "Oh, what now? Is 'girl' somehow demeaning now, too? Gods, lass, the way yer dressed, yer sure telling the watching world yer a girl!"

"*Your* girl, this evening," Glathra agreed happily, as they strolled out into the forecourt.

Only to see Rensharra Ironstave, in an even more magnificent gown that left one shoulder crested and the other bare, departing the eastern front door on the arm of her gallant for the evening. King's Lord Lothan Durncaskyn looked decidedly dapper in tailored black, with one of the fashionable new tailcloaks swirling at his every stride.

Mirt went right to Rensharra, and they let go of their respective partners for long enough to embrace, kiss, and wish each other a delightful evening.

"Don't forget the way home, now," Mirt warned. "I've slaked a haunch in wine, for us to share at dawn."

Rensharra smiled, then purred, "And I've a surprise for us to share, too."

Mirt growled suggestively, wiggling his eyebrows.

She chuckled. "No, not *that*, but let me assure you that it's not a new tax assessment, either."

Mirt bowed deeply. "Until dawn, then."

She bowed right back, almost spilling out of her low-cut gown in the process. "Until dawn."

They all went on their ways smiling, thinking of that bright dawn ahead.

HERE ENDS THE THIRD BOOK OF *THE SAGE OF SHADOWDALE*